Sacred Trust

A vicarious, high voltage adventure
to stop a private powerline.

Wayne D. King

DEDICATION

For Alice and Zachary who every day make life a joy; and for my mother and father, Roger and Roberta King, who took a risk fighting to clean up the Pemigewasset River, at grave threat to life and limb, and gave us all a gift for the ages.

ACKNOWLEDGMENTS

This story is a work of fiction. With the exception of historically accurate individuals, like Presidential candidates, any resemblance between the main characters of this book and real or other fictional characters is purely coincidental.

To avoid tipping my hand on any of the other characters and incidents in this book I have provided a much more complete detailing of the accuracy of certain stories and historical characters in an afterword at the end of this book.

No book is the work of one individual alone. I am grateful to Alice my girlfriend, my wife and the love of my life, who is my biggest cheerleader even when I have lost my confidence. My friends Darryl Thompson and Charlie Feuer who have been loyal and true friends for many years helped me proof and improve the story.

Stephen Farrell and Michael Hutchings, who in large part were the reason for any success I had in politics and have remained true friends through thick and thin since then both helped read, proof and improve the story.

Charles Walbridge and Arthur Bradbury helped me by passing along the book to others who might be able to help with the process of publishing. Both Charlie and Arthur are friends with whom my long friendship began when they were my counselors at camp.

Thanks also to my dear friend Osita Aniemeka who allowed me to use his name for a character in the book and who is one of the great heroes of Africa working every day to carve out a brighter future for his (and my) beloved Nigeria.

Finally, thanks to Mike Marland for his talents in crafting the cover of Sacred Trust and to my friend Sean La Roque-Doherty, (Esq.) who provided me with legal advice to prevent me from having Eric Clapton knocking on my door, demanding royalties - though he can knock on my door for any other reason anytime.

Trust

Trust noun

1 a: assured reliance on the character, ability, strength, or truth of someone or something

1 b: one in which confidence is placed

2a: dependence on something future or contingent: hope

2b: reliance on future payment for property (as merchandise) delivered: credit

3a: a property interest held by one person for the benefit of another

3b: a combination of firms or corporations formed by a legal (Though not necessarily lawful) agreement, *especially*: one that reduces or threatens to reduce competition.

~ Webster's Dictionary

3c: A group of people who join together to achieve an objective, ideal or end result. (Though not necessarily lawfully).

~ Edward Abbey's Dictionary - if he had written one

"Treat the earth well: it was not given to you by your parents, it was loaned to you by your children. We do not inherit the Earth from our Ancestors, we borrow it from our Children."

Ancient Indian Proverb

Prologue

Cindy Fallon looked at her smartphone sitting face up on the passenger seat as she drove through the night heading home on the desolate roadways of New Hampshire's Great North Woods. She was running late. Her boyfriend was planning to meet her at her parent's house. It would not be good for him to arrive before her. He was not a particular favorite of her father and giving them quality time alone was not an idea that Cindy felt would lead to anything good. If she kept moving she would be late but might be able to intercept Jamie before his orbit intersected with that of her father. Safety, and the law, dictated that she should pull over to make a call or send a text. That would be the safest approach but if she were unable to reach Jamie it would virtually assure that he and her father would cross paths, and, quite possibly, swords.

She reached for the phone. Picked it up, paused, then put it back down. She was coming up on the Balsams Grand Resort, which meant that there was likely to be traffic that made calling or texting more perilous. Once past the resort, the next few miles would be through spruce fir forest with very little traffic likely. Texting, or calling, while driving then should not be a problem.

She passed by the hotel then picked up the phone and began to type in a message to her boyfriend, then she decided she had better call . . .ironically, "just to be safe".

She only took her eyes off the road for a moment but when her eyes returned back to the road she was well into the opposite lane and headed right for her was a huge semi towing a car carrier and blaring its air horn.

Cindy yanked the wheel and the car fishtailed back across her lane and onto the soft shoulder of the rural road.

Again she turned the wheel; this time trying to steer herself away from a close encounter with the dark forest without steering herself directly into the path of the Semi.

Where the hell did this truck come from? The thought passed through her head as she attempted to thread the needle that she had, herself, created. She was on a long straightaway. She should have seen the truck when she picked up the phone just moments before. Yet here it was bearing down on her . . . lights flashing and horn piercing the night.

Herbert Johanssen, who was attempting to run dark on the last mile before the resort, to avoid calling attention to the felonious activities taking place in the back lot of the hotel, was forced to reveal himself to avoid squashing the little car before him like a bug on his windshield. Michelle would never forgive him if he sacrificed some hapless driver in the very first official action of The Trust.

The two vehicles missed one another by no more than six inches in the final moments of the near-encounter.

Cindy looked up into Herbert's panicked eyes as they passed, not even making an effort to hide the phone that was still tight to her ear.

Then she looked in her rear view mirror and the truck was gone.

"Shit! Shit! Shit!!!!!" Inside the cab of the truck Herbert slammed the driver's wheel with each utterance as he shut the lights back off, leaving Cindy Fallon wondering if she had imagined the whole thing as darkness enveloped the straightaway behind her, and the lights, that should have been reflected in her rear view mirror, vanished like a mirage.

Herbert navigated the last few yards and pulled into the parking area. Daniel Roy and Sasha Brandt were lined up waiting for him to arrive. He leapt from the truck before it had even come to a full stop.

"We've been made!" He hollered, "Get the cars onto the carrier as fast as you can. We have to get the hell out of here!

Part 1   The Trust

Chapter 1 Stonebridge

Charlie Stonebridge hadn't been in the Thirteen Mile Woods area of New Hampshire going on ten years now and the memories flooded over him as he drove his old Land Rover up Route 16.

He drove the Rover as much for the necessity of space to accommodate his six foot six frame as for its ability to navigate the muddy roads and fields that were the daily sojourn of an experienced wildwater paddler. He could fit three boats on the roof; need be, with the paddles lashed beside them.

Now-a-days, Stonebridge bought his boats retail, but there was a day when the only way one could find a covered boat - especially for a towering hulk - was to build it yourself. He had made his own boats - and a pretty good portion of his living - by building boats that the early generation of whitewater enthusiasts would use to pioneer both the sport and the territory.

On this trip he had brought only one boat because he was going to be leaving the Rover while he paddled and fitting extra boats into the rig was tight and an invitation to thieves.

He passed Unity Street in Berlin, the route to Success Pond Road and the Mahoosuc Mountain Range, and wondered if he would have time for a quick hike into "the Notch". On his left he noticed Tea Bird's Cafe - recommended to him by a friend - but he was on a mission at the moment and not inclined to stop for lunch no matter how good the food was. He headed north out of the city.

"Burr - lin " he rehearsed in his head as he drove on, not Berlin as they said in Germany, or outside of New Hampshire. Who could blame them he thought. Folks up here may be willing to stick with the name but they weren't going to pronounce it the same. Germany may be an ally now, but memories run deep and a lot of "Burrlin'" boys gave their lives on the beaches of Europe and the road to Berlin, Germany, and those memories linger on. There had to be a distinction.

"West My-lin", he continued his line of thought, keeping a careful eye out for moose that were usually thicker than black flies right about now. It was dusk along the area of Rte 16 that some locals called Moose Alley, especially the ones associated with the Chamber of Commerce who were always looking for another angle to draw folks north of the Notches.

Actually there was an ongoing war of words among the Chambers of Commerce in Berlin, Groveton and - from time to time Bartlett and North Conway - over the claim to the name. A visitor to the White Mountains and The Great North Woods areas of New Hampshire could very easily become confused and disoriented if he or she happened to travel through all three areas in one day and stop somewhere to shoot the breeze with locals. In Colebrook, Moose Alley was a short stretch of Route 3 just before West Stewartstown and the Canadian border where the salt-licks of the roadside sphagnum bogs offered plenty of browse early in the spring and the runoff from road salt spread the previous winter made for some delectable dining, well seasoned, for the big critters. Then there was another stretch if you stayed on Route 3 and kept to the Northeast through Pittsburg and past the Connecticut Lakes, headwaters of the Connecticut River that formed the boundary between New Hampshire and Vermont from top to bottom. Truth be told this one - the Pittsburg Moose Alley - was probably the one with the most legitimate claim to the title by virtue of both the density of the Moose population and the naming rights associated with longevity.

But Stonebridge wasn't headed for Pittsburg, though he always wanted to take a trip up there to see some of the spots associated with the Republic of Indian Stream.

Indian Stream. Most folks, even New Hampshire natives, were unaware that in 1832 a small independent nation was established, borne of the border disputes between the French Canadians and the US Government over this fertile valley on the border of the US and Canada.

Seems that the treaty of Paris had included some ambiguous language describing the territory in and around Indian Stream and this created a whole raft of problems for the folks in the area, not the least of which was those blood sucking tax collectors from both countries demanding payments, followed closely by a sheriff enforcing tax collectors' orders.

It didn't take very long before the three hundred or so hardy residents of the area decided they wanted nothing to do with either the US Government or the Governments controlling Canada. They formed their own Constitutional Republic. Neither the British nor the Americans - of course - recognized the validity of the Republic but that did not stop the people of Indian Stream. They created their own constitution and they set about charting their own course.

The Indian Streamers were a hardscrabble bunch, didn't have the funds to build a jailhouse in their little Republic so they took a huge potash kettle, turned it over upside down in the middle of town, and whenever they had need for a jail they just lifted it up and put the scofflaw under it then dropped it back down. After one or two sweltering days and cold nights it put the fear of God in almost anyone who was otherwise inclined to infringe on the rights of his fellow man. "Yessir," Stonebridge thought, " frontier justice, served up in a kettle."

He rounded the bend coming out of Milan and for the first time got the full panorama of the dark and verdant boreal forest with the Androscoggin River flowing lugubriously along through it. How many times had he seen it before? Yet it still reached deep into his psyche, stirring up old memories of mist covered mornings on the river, the growing thunder of the Pontook rapids in the days before they dammed it up and turned one of the most wild and beautiful stretches of river and rapids into a twice daily amusement ride, fully dependent upon when the ideal time for power generation happened to be.

He thought back on the days before the dam and on the tepid efforts to stop it. No one chained themselves to a gate or locked arms across the road to prevent the trucks from bringing in the turbines. And now here it was, not especially magnificent as an engineering feat, certainly not any Hoover Dam or Grand Coulee, but a burr on the ass of a great river just the same; and where once a Kayak could run the course of the mighty river anytime day or night, now you were lucky to get a decent release once a day and you had to time everything around it just to run this stretch. It was still fun, sure. But they had strangled the wildness out of her.

And he had just watched it happen. . .

John Prine blared out as he drove on singing: "That's the Way that the World Goes Round." and Stonebridge sang along with the song as it played.

Regrets were strange things. The women you lost, the friendships you failed to nurture when only a little effort would have made the difference; the fights you walked away from - good fights, fighting for justice, for wilderness, for peace, all because it would have been a little inconvenient at the time.

Yes, regrets were, indeed, strange things.

Regrets, seasoned with age were the things that denied you the peace of slumber - - that deep sleep that nourishes your soul, not the restive, disquieting sleep of the disappointed and the damned.

He'd driven up here, all the way from "Yeehaw" West Virginia, looking to recapture something from his youth; Some superpower that had been sapped by everyday life; by backyard barbecues and old spice commercials; by 9-5 work and 5-9 boredom. He had it once. They still told legends about him along the paths he had trod.

But he wasn't a legend in his own mind.

He was a heaping, steaming, pile of regrets.

He was approaching the intersection of 16 and 26 in Errol and feeling a bit tired. He turned the wheels and brought the Rover to a stop in a gravel pull-off and closed his eyes for just a moment.

• - • - •

Dusk on the Saco River; Mauve fading to pink against the black backdrop of the mountain silhouettes; The blue-green line of the Saco a winding swoosh through the blackness of the valley floor.

Four townies, local thugs, stood on the bridge calling down to the canoe shelters that were scattered across a large sandbar. The canoes were turned over providing a shelter for equipment and one solid anchor for the painter lines used to hold the tarps that formed the shelters. Paddles were strategically placed as poles to maximize the space under the tarp. All told there were eight shelters set up across the sandbar, a patchwork of bright colors, muted by the evening, with flashlights coming on and off like fireflies moving under and around the tarps.

The boys from the camp were already half asleep in their tents, exhausted from a day of paddling and portaging and now trying desperately to forget the hunger in their stomachs after one-by-one they had quietly buried the meal that the counselor had cooked. It was a sticky mess of rice, raisins, and some kind of mystery fish; three things that just did not belong together in the same dish, no less in your stomach. But if they had complained they would have been given a second helping and made to eat it; and then, to top it off, they would have been given dish duty. As a result, each boy surreptitiously slipped off to a spot where they would not be seen and buried the evidence.

Even Stonebridge, the second in command of this intrepid group of 12 year-olds, was hiding in his shelter trying to avoid the cook-cum-lead-counselor. He had joined in the vast conspiracy when he came upon a boy burying his dinner and promised not to tell as long as he would dispose of Stonebridge's as well.

"Come on girls, we have somethin' to show you! Called the boys on the bridge above, thinking they had stumbled upon a girls camp and salivating over the idea that they might be able to find some action here in a town where any girl their own age - who actually knew them - would have nothing to do with the braggarts.

"We can come down there, just as easy," called one of them. "Maybe we'll just come on down and show ya."

The full moon had just risen over the horizon and cast a pale yellow light down on the shelters. Causing the chatter from the locals to increase hoping to rouse the unsuspecting lovelies from their sleeping bags.

But Stonebridge had heard enough.

"You boys stay here", he said, reaching for his double bitted axe (his trademark in those days). The boys obeyed his orders but couldn't resist the temptation to peer out to watch. Stonebridge stepped from the shelter and the boys watched in awe as he raised himself up to his full six feet six inches, stark naked and holding his double bitted axe high above his head. In his best fake falsetto he called "come on down boys, we'd just love to play with ya'll!"

• - • - •

Stonebridge awoke and smiled at the memory of how fast those local hoods had retreated - as he turned the land rover back onto the road.

It was like a scene out of a Yosemite Sam cartoon, where you hear the ping and zip and see nothing but the dust of the retreat. He chuckled and half consciously uttered "Tarrrrnation!" as he turned east at the junction and headed toward Lake Umbagog. In moments he had wheeled across the bridge over the Androscoggin River and put the town of Errol - all 20 houses on the main street - in his rear view mirror, heading for Moll's Rock.

Chapter 2 Brandt and Roy

A blood-curdling scream rose up from the base of the Cascade, loud enough to flush a pair of rotund spruce grouse from their low perch nearby, their flapping wings reverberating through the woods. In reality, the scream was more a joyous celebration than a response to pain – though the temperature of the water cascading down Mahoosuc Arm delivered its fair share of pain as well; exhilarating pain, as in shocking, numbing, brain freezing, cold-ass pain. Daniel Roy reached for the ball of horsetail he had gathered along the trail coming in, a luffa substitute that was very effective at removing the mud covering his calves from the boggy sections of trail skirting Speck Pond.

He could have stayed at the shelter at Spec Pond but he was trying to avoid the thru-hikers, people hiking the Appalachian Trail from Maine to Georgia. It wasn't that he hated through-hikers . . . those peak bagging, know it all mothers; speed freaks who had no appreciation for the journey, because they were obsessed with schedules, food drops, mail stops, and the obstacles between themselves and their next camping spot . . . well maybe it was.

But he rationalized it by making the excuse that he just didn't want to be drawn into a fight over hiking the AT as they called it. They didn't even have time to call it the Appalachian Trail; "The AT" was their nom de plume. They were obsessed with doing everything as fast as humanly possible, though they would spend the rest of their lives torturing everyone they ever met with their tales of the trip. Dragging out every story until it consumed more time than the actual leg of the journey.

Besides, staying at the Speck Pond Shelter couldn't compare with a quiet campsite far enough from the trail that he would not run into any humans at all and he could just lay out his poncho and sleeping bag as long as the sky remained cloudless and the horsetail cirrus of an approaching front did not portend a coming storm.

He was just beginning to take on the grunge from the trail when she burst out of the trees at a dead run - a huge white wolf-like dog at her side. Pretty impressive as the steepness of the surrounding woods meant that she had to have descended through the birch forest at full speed, like a slalom skier weaving through the course at breakneck speed bent on a medal caliber run. Her raven hair tied in pigtails bent at angles attesting to the fact that she was halfway between launching herself upward high enough that she had time to assess the ground beneath her to land safely and launch again covering almost as much vertically as horizontally with each movement.

Her momentum carried her into the clearing at the base of Mahoosuc Cascade just as she looked up and saw his naked body glistening from the water as the droplets bursting with each contact of his skin created a glow in the late day sunlight. "Jesus" she exhaled, though it came out more like Jeeeessssis, bursting out of her lungs like an 18-wheeler loosing its air brakes.

Trying to gather her wits and her breath at the same time she bent over, hands on her knees. "I expected a dead hiker from the sound of your scream." I figured someone had wandered too close to the edge of the cascade and gone over."

Daniel didn't bother trying to cover his nakedness. After all he had endured the bracing temperature to get clean and he wasn't about to get out until he was finished washing his body, even with a stunningly beautiful woman staring at him. He finished up and for good measure tossed his towel over his shoulder instead of wrapping it around him as he walked from under the falls; a mischievous look on his face and a twinkle in his eyes as he brought the towel up to his head to dry his hair. "What were you figuring to do if you were right?" he asked. "Is mouth to mouth still an option? I mean . . . I can role-play if that works for you."

Anger flashed in her eyes, "why you arrogant son of a bitch", they said.

"You God damned through hikers go blindly through the most beautiful mile of the Appalachian Trail with no appreciation for it, bitching and moaning about how hard it is and how long it takes you to make a mile, and then you think that everyone you meet is going to kneel down before you and worship the ground you walk on. You . . ."

"Whoa there lady," Daniel broke in, "first, I just finished coming down off The Arm, I haven't even hit The Notch yet, and for your information I plan to spend the entire day tomorrow reveling in the glory of the experience. I packed in some orange juice to make snow cones with the snow that lies hidden deep in the caves along the trail, my camera and tripod to document the experience; and a saw, chisel and wrench just in case I'm inspired to rework the trail sign to send the through-hikers down to Success Pond Road. They will be fighting off the mosquitoes and moose along Success Pond Road for half a day before they realize that Mahoosuc Notch was the other way. That will really put a crimp in their plans and they'll be complaining for the next two hundred miles about the time they lost in the Notch."

"I'm thinking that if I do that on both ends of the Notch I'll have the whole place to myself or at least limit it to those who know the area or can read a map. Have you hiked it before?"

The fire in her eyes had dimmed some. He clearly was not a peak-bagger as they said in the parlance. The reference came from a book she had read from her father's prized books shelf: <u>Zen and the Art of Motorcycle Maintenance</u>. The author had devoted pages to outlining the difference between the hiker who cherished the experience of the hike and the one obsessed with reaching the summit as fast as humanly possible adding it to his or her list of statistics, never bothering to chew on a sour spray of Wood Sorrel to quench his thirst or pause, watch and listen to a White Throated Sparrow's lonely call as it rode the sweet Balsam breeze.

The obsessive hiker was the "Peak-Bagger" and while the phenomenon occurred everywhere, nowhere was it quite so transparent as it was here in the Mahoosucs, a range of Appalachian mountains running from Gorham, New Hampshire to Grafton Notch in Maine just over the border. The Mahoosucs were the last great, unrestricted mountains in New Hampshire. There were bigger mountains, like the Presidential Range and the Carter's just to the south; and, there were mountains where limited bureaucratic restrictions allowed one to experience the old-style freedom of hiking without selling your soul to the government with use permits and fire permits and where camping restrictions created virtual cities of overnight campers at some locations. But the Mahoosucs provided high country ridge hiking, even an alpine bog or two, and relative freedom from the prying eyes of Uncle Sam's trek police.

Though it is on the Appalachian Trail - few enough hikers trekked this way that the range has few of the restrictions that other more prominent mountain ranges have. In the Mahoosucs, one could still camp on the summit of a peak and fall asleep to the music and dance of the spheres.

And then there is The Notch.

A one mile stretch along a relatively flat valley between two mountains, known as a col. Rarely more than a few hundred yards across at any one spot, Mahoosuc Notch is a geological wonder borne of the last ice age some 11,000 years ago. From the valley at the base of the Notch huge granite and diorite cliffs rise on either side, denying the sunlight from providing warmth on even a summer day except for a few precious hours; dropping their ice cleaved bones into the notch over the millennia to form a boulder and moss strewn landscape with caves that hold their icy snow from the previous winter's snowfall well into August - creating a natural air conditioner effect even on the hottest summer day.

Hiking through Mahoosuc Notch is a slow process best done with a partner with whom you can collaborate to negotiate the challenges of boulders with passages that require one to remove a backpack and pass it through first before squeezing through or passing the backpack down from a vantage point that provides a fine view of the challenges ahead but a drop that would severely injure a hiker who fell with pack still on his back.

For the adventurous spirit all of this makes Mahoosuc Notch the most thrilling and memorable mile of the Appalachian Trail. But to the peak bagger, who measures the experience by the speed with which he completes the mile, it is the "longest mile" the section of trail that thru-hikers dread on their approach and curse at their back.

To Daniel Roy it was, therefore, an experience that took the measure of a man.

Or a woman . . .

Apparently, Sasha Brandt shared that view as well, because a smile crept over her face as Daniel was winding up his naked rant and she reached out her hand to introduce herself.

"Hi, I'm Sasha Brandt."

It seemed an odd gesture under the circumstances.

Chapter 3   Linda Levy

Cambridge, Massachusetts

Your Honor?
Counselor . . .

Linda Levy paced nervously outside the courtroom in the Brooke Courthouse building. Boston was a great city but it was beginning to feel just a bit too close right now. She was thinking about jumping into her vintage mustang with her North Face dome tent and sleeping bag, along with her climbing ropes, and heading for Rattlesnake Mountain in Rumney, New Hampshire. There was nothing in the world more exhilarating than dangling 250 feet off the ground trying to bust a move on a new route. She may be pushing 50 but she could still play with the best of them.

When she was young her father would take her to the Shawangunks in New York. In those days the "Gunks" as they were called, were the premier climbing mecca in the Northeast. The Shawangunk Ridge is a backbone that extends across three counties in New York, mostly in the Catskill Mountains. Officially it is the long easternmost edge of the Appalachian Mountain chain running from Maine to Georgia. Her father had always warned her that pronouncing the name right was the difference between being treated like you belonged and treated like an alien in these parts, accordingly, she had learned to swish her way through the word as it was intended - barely noticing the "H" and both "A's" so it came out more akin to Swan-gunk".
Understanding the importance of the correct pronunciation of Shawangunk came in handy in New Hampshire too, where a raft of Indian names usually allowed the locals to distinguish other locals from Massholes and other flatlanders. The Kancamagus Highway was the premier test in the North Country. Locals had been pronouncing it Kank - ah - mog - us for a few hundred years but the aliens seemed to be drawn toward calling it Kank-ah-may-gus which was a dead giveaway.

In fairness, the "Kank" as everyone fondly called it, was almost as confusing for the locals. Over the course of the past fifty years the Department of Transportation had spelled the name of the road at least three different ways on road signs. In point-of-fact, there was probably no "proper" way to spell or pronounce the word. After all, the first hundred times the word was recorded in writing - at least by a white guy - it had probably been by some half-literate explorer or trapper or settler who couldn't write much more than his name anyway. What was correct, what was truly right, could only have been recorded by a red hand and all of the ones in this area were without written language.

In the Shawangunk days, Rattlesnake was only a glint in the eyes of a few hardy pioneers of the sport including a fellow named George Wendall who was an old army buddy of her dad. Wendall had been trying to get her dad to make the trip to New Hampshire but with Linda in tow he always felt safer climbing where there was plenty of protection and support.

As a peace officer, Dad was big on protection and precaution. He had retired at fifty and he continued to climb for another few years until he took a bad fall on a particularly challenging pitch in Yosemite. By the time dad had hung up his pitons - about the time the rest of the climbing world switched to chocks, cams and bolted protection - The sport had diverged into Traditional or "Trad" climbing and Sport Climbing and Rattlesnake was just beginning to come into its own as a sport climbing mecca. Its proximity to Boston made it more appealing from a logistical point of view and in short order Linda had come to love New Hampshire. Well, the North Country of New Hampshire at least, with striking mountains and lakes and folks that were cut from a kind of libertarian cloth, whether they were conservative or progressive. She couldn't get enough, in fact, and what she had quickly learned was that no matter where you came from in New Hampshire you drew your "New Hampshire identity" from the White Mountains. Rugged, individualistic, and tolerant of differences . . . a willingness to let a person live the life they chose as long as it did not impinge on the rights of others. It was kind of a corollary of the old saying that the "rights of my fist end at the edge of your jaw line."

With Massachusetts just to the south and Vermont to the West providing ideological contrast, New Hampshire, for many years, had a reputation as a bastion of conservatism, but there was more to this place than met the eye. Sure, there were a couple of nutty old cranks like William and Nackey Loeb who owned the only Statewide newspaper and Meldrim Thomson a governor who had suggested arming the national guard with nuclear weapons and who used a half mast flag to protest everything from foreign policy to the speakers that the University students brought to campus; The latter, fearing that they would infect folks with new ideas. Yet, it was also the first state in the nation to expand rights for gays and lesbians and for years it was on the forefront of the battle for transparency in government with its "Right to Know" law requiring almost all government meetings to be open to the public and to publish their proceedings and actions.

The more time she spent in New Hampshire the more convinced she was that it might just be her "spot on the porch" . . . In the long run anyway.

Straight out of college Linda chose to follow her father into police work. As a degreed candidate she could easily have slid into an administrative job in the Boston "Cop Shop" but she wanted to know the feel of the streets so she chose the more traditional route of attending the academy and bearing the brunt of a force that still put their rookies through a frat-like hazing.

Women were especially subject to that hazing, though over the years that had changed, mostly. At the same time she joined the force she also enrolled in Law School to get her JD.

There were no trust funds in the Levy house so she had accepted her father's financial help for her undergraduate degree but she knew that getting a law degree was on her. She shopped for the best deal she could find and ended up in a continuing education law program at Boston College where most classes were held during the day which meant that her "Cop Shop" hours were the hours classically referred to as the graveyard shift, midnight to seven am. It was - at times - grueling when there was a required class that only met at 8am with no time for even a catnap; but somehow Linda persevered on what turned out to be the five-year plan.

She finished Law School just as she was starting to feel like a member of the squad and spent a tortured six months secretly applying for law positions while at the same time working in the Boston Police department. Finally, she accepted a job with a prestigious Boston firm where she was to do double duty, corporate law, real estate, mergers and acquisitions and - when needed - criminal law. Her Boston PD background provided the advantages of both knowing the players and knowing the game.

After another five years, try as she might, she could just not seem to get comfortable in her lawyer suit. She found herself still preferring the cop bars to the button down ones, and - while she loved the snappy repartee of certain colleagues - she'd rather hear the banter of lifelong cops who mixed cynicism with the salt of the streets and just the right dose of healthy skepticism to create an idiom that was as comfortable as an old favorite wool sweater was to her. Thus, at almost 40, she went back to full time policing . . . back to the streets.

In truth, she'd never been happier and more comfortable in her own skin than she was now, back on the force. Though there was a personal price. Each step that she took to get where she was today required a period of intense focus to excel. Proving herself on the force initially and establishing herself at the firm, all of the late hours, hurried meals, meetings and homework left very little time for a social life, much less a relationship. As a result, Linda's longest term male relationship (aside from her father) was Maximilian a fourteen something Maine Coon cat who was big, bad and independent as hell. Half his left ear was gone, no doubt from an alley fight in the days before some animal control officer had netted him when the neighbors started complaining that "Max" was interfering with their right to enjoy their new fancy condominium.

On the day she brought him home from the shelter Max bit her . . . Not an auspicious start to their relationship. Rather than trying to force things, she just put out some food and water, kept the windows and doors closed and settled in for the long haul - content to wait him out. It was - as it turned out - a whole lot easier than developing a relationship with a man. Max was aloof for the first few weeks, but around week five, as Linda was sitting on the couch watching Syracuse play against Duke in the final four showdown and nibbling at a bowl of popcorn, Max casually walked across the ridge of the couch and dropped down and nestled himself into a soft afghan draped over her lap. Before long he was purring away and Linda was stroking his head and scratching behind his ear-and-a-half and he clearly decided that this was better than that wonderfully dirty old alley.

Maximillian and Linda formed a bond but Max was not particularly helpful when it came to her social life. He had a nasty habit of planting himself in a chair in the bathroom when Linda had male company and when some unsuspecting male tromped into the bathroom in the middle of the night, scratching his balls and yawning, Max would give him a quick and painful swat on his bare ass, assuring that he would be fully awake as he scampered back to bed. If Max waited until the visitor was on his way BACK to bed the results could be even worse. In the name of safety, Linda made it a point to warn him.

Male relationships were just not her strong suit. She got along great with her colleagues on the force and her professional relationships were fine, with one notable exception - judges - and especially young male judges. No matter what their ages judges treated her in a condescending and arrogant way, but the young ones seemed to be the worst. They were already condescending enough with cops as it was, but there must be something in the water in the Boston area because young and old, and everything in between, judges didn't give women cops a bit of credit for having a brain.

The door to courtroom three swung open as the bailiff wielded an unusually large ring of jangling keys, pulled the key out of the lock and stood back to let the crowd of people flow into the courtroom. Most of his opening and closing these days were done with his security badge but his authority around this place was vested in his key ring that jangled like a soulful prison ballad every time he moved. For some reason it conferred an authority on him that no key card could hope to create.

"Oy ye, Oy Ye! Oy Ye! Draw near!" Came the baritone voice of the male Bailiff calling the court to order as the judge swept into the room. Linda noted that he was a new one. Fresh out of Law school by his looks and she guessed that his balls were pinstriped under that robe by the way he carried himself. Not a hair was out of place and he had that always-wet look.

She wasn't sure how they achieved that these days. When she was little her uncle Harry used Brylcreem but she did not recall seeing ads for Brylcreem in years.

Harry was on the force too and she was pretty sure that he was not actually her uncle but had never bothered to ask. That would raise the matter of her mother who had gone out for gas one evening when Linda was three and never came home. She was not the victim of foul play - in fact Linda had a pipeline to regular information about her mother from her favorite aunt - her mother's sister - who had recently recounted her mother's six moves back and forth between upstate New York to Southern California in the last year.

The room continued to stand in deference to the judge who was wetting his bed when most of them were already adults, until the Bailiff told them to be seated.

Linda was here to testify on a drug and weapons arrest. Just last month as she was browsing Facebook she came upon a selfie taken by one James Feniwick Harrison. Harrison had taken a shot of himself standing in front of a car trunk filled with handguns and drugs ranging from weed to heroin and oxy. Harrison lived in Boston and his mobile delivery business took him all over the greater Boston area.

Harrison was too cute by half because in his selfie he had covered half of the license plate for each of the three selfies. He was sure that no one could identify him, except that he had made the mistake of covering one side of the plate in one photo and the other side in the second photo, thus allowing the full reconstruction of the license plate and a no-brainer on probable cause. It was a classic in the Darwin awards category.

The bust was clean and simple but Harrison had lawyered up and today his lawyer was attempting to quash the search of his vehicle. Today's hearing on the motion to quash should have been a very simple matter. Should have been.

"Commonwealth of Massachusetts vs. Harrison" the bailiff called out.

The Judge recognized the defense attorney to introduce his motion.

"Your honor, we move to quash the search of Mr. Harrison's car. The officers had no probable cause to search the vehicle and without the search there is no violation of the law."

Jim Evers, the assistant district attorney, a tall affable fellow with a Boston accent, more from the North End than the patrician Beacon Hill crowd, rose to address the motion.

"Your honor, we would like to call officer Linda Levy to testify on this matter. It was officer Levy who initiated this search and she can speak to the issue of cause."

Linda was sworn in and seated herself in the witness chair.

Evers went straight to the matter at hand.

"Officer Levy, you were the lead officer in the investigation that ended with the arrest of Mr. Harrison. Do you have any doubts that you had probable cause to make the arrest?

Levy responded, " The suspect made the mistake of covering one side of his license plate in one selfie and the other side in a second selfie, thus allowing us to do a full reconstruction of his plate. This was probably the cleanest arrest I have ever made. You'd have to be brain dead to think otherwise."

The Judge sneered a bit and said "I'll be the judge of that and I do not see this as cut and dry as you appear to, officer."

He was clearly itching for a fight.

"The existing law as well as the case history clearly gave us cause to conduct a search and given what we saw in the selfies the likelihood that he was going to have more drugs in the trunk once we opened it gave Judge Colleen McGee a clear path to issuing a warrant for the search.

The judge continued, "Judge McGee . . . Officer, do you consider yourself an expert on search and seizure?"

Levy:" Well, yes your honor. None of us would be much in this business if we weren't experts in assessing probable cause.

Judge (getting wound up now): So you know the law better than anyone in the courtroom?

Levy: Linda paused and then responded, "Well, yes, it appears so. "

Judge: "More than the Court, officer?"

Evers was beginning to doubt his choice of Levy as the witness on this motion.

Levy: Not wanting to answer this question but also not willing to back down from this young upstart. "Regretfully, yes."

Judge: "How dare you insult the Court!"

Levy: "The record will reflect that I simply and honestly answered the Court's question."

Judge: "You are close to contempt. I suggest if you want to be an attorney, you attend law school, and if you can pass the bar, spend the next few decades studying the framework of the law and the Constitution."

Levy: "Thank you for the advice, but I have already done that."

Judge: "Where? On graveyard patrol (chuckling)?"

Levy: "No, I was forced to work graveyards so I could attend classes during the day."

Judge: "Classes? Community college classes?"

Levy: "No, law school classes."

Judge: "Stop this nonsense. If you are an attorney, I am the Duke of Earl."

Levy: "Should I address you as such for the rest of this proceeding?"

Judge: "I've had enough (smirking). If you can't produce a bar card in ten seconds, I will hold you in contempt. "

Levy, reaching into her pocket: "Bailiff, please pass this to the Duke, ahhh, my apologies, the Judge."

Judge: (Examining the bar card) "The motion to suppress is denied. Officer, you are excused. I guess you're the one I've heard about."

Levy: "May I be permanently excused from this courtroom?"

Judge: (despondent). "Call the next case."

Within fifteen minutes Linda Levy was headed north on I93, top down, the Boston skyline in her rear view mirror and the White Mountains on her mental radar. Max was perched on the ledge of the back seat, wind blowing through his fur, looking content and ready for an adventure.

Chapter 4 Hank Algren

Henry James Hieronymus Algren pushed back from his Mac where he was working on a flyer for the latest in a long line of right wing Republican candidates for State and Federal Office.

It was time to feed the deer.

Henry, or "Hank" as he was better known had three great loves, Politics - the conservative kind, served up steaming hot with lots of red meat; his deer; and fishing.

Hank was tall, over 6 foot three inches, lean with the kind of shape one gets from years of hard work, not hanging out at the gym; and a slight limp he'd earned when he found himself caught between two big bucks fighting over the rights to service a group of does. He would probably have been able to get rid of the limp if he had not been testy about physical therapy. Hank didn't take to anything called "therapy"; he figured it was for pantywaists and pussies and his daddy didn't raise no pussy; so he went right from the hospital to the pasture and skipped the therapy, trading his stride for his pride and never looking back.

He'd grown up on this farm in Bristol, New Hampshire, a farm that used to boast one of the largest milking cowherds in the state. His was the 6th generation of Algrens on the farm but his grandfather had jumped at the chance to sell off the herd during the whole herd buyout program of 1985. For a while it looked like the farm was just going to close up - maybe even fall into the hands of the developers who had identified nearby Plymouth State College as a "comer" - but Hank was a resourceful fellow and he convinced his grandfather to let him buy a small herd of European Red Deer, an ungulate in the Elk family, and before long they had a thriving herd offering everything from breed stock, meat, sausages, pemmican, to smoked meat and jerky.

While local beef farmers were getting fifty cents a pound on the hoof for beef critters, Hank was selling his red deer to Whole Foods (those commie symps) and Trader Joe's (better, but still lefties) - among others - for $30 a pound. Hank thought this was pretty great, even if he did have to dance with the "berets and Che's crowd" But when he landed an Asian distributor who had sources for selling powdered antler to Japanese men who couldn't "get it up" he thought he'd died and gone to heaven. He'd keep the lefties all in Brie for the next 50 years if they continued to bring him customers like this.

With all this business, he had thought about giving up his small business as the local Apple repair center but decided to hold onto it just for the perks of first release software and discounted hardware.

The other thing about being a Deer farm was that they had also become something of a celebrity resource within the community. Where back in the dairy days no one seemed to pay much attention to them, now people talked about them as if they had some magical power. They were "that awesome deer farm" and cars driving by the farm now seemed to be noticeably less crazy as neighbors slowed down hoping to catch a glimpse of the deer in the pasture.

Raising deer wasn't easy by any means, these were, after all, some big and fast critters, and despite his take no prisoners brand of politics and his truly conservative outlook on life, Hank was a soft-touch when it came to these beautiful animals and found it difficult when it came time to butcher them. He compromised by contracting a friend who handled the bulk of the slaughtering and cutting and he picked out a few of the big bucks - especially two he named Mirabeau and Robespierre - that he kept as pets. He rarely "harvested" the females because they were the brood stock of the farm and the rest remained nameless, never having more than a number attached to their ears, preventing him from getting too attached.

Hank donned his Red Sox cap and stuffed his feet into a tall pair of rubber boots he had owned since Ronald Reagan was President, and ambled out the door. As he made his way he grabbed a five-gallon pail and scooped a few quarts of grain into the bucket. The deer were manageable but they were still essentially wild - with the notable exception of Mirabeau and Robespierre who actually followed along behind him and poked him with their noses to get one of the apple slices that he kept in his coat pocket. But the rest of them were still shy, even with Hank, but a bucket of grain shaken in just the right way could entice even the shyest deer.

Normally, Hank fed the deer with hay from one of those big white hay pillows you see these days, but tonight he would use traditional baled hay and he'd need to put out a few extra bales of hay for the deer because he was going to spend the weekend fishing on Lake Umbagog in the northern part of the state.

He'd been going up to the area known as The Thirteen Mile Woods since he was eight years old when his uncle would take him and his kid brother up to a hunting camp in the Town of Errol. It was really just a little shack off a dirt road with gravity fed water and an outhouse, but it was always an adventure, an adventure that had turned Hank into an ardent conservationist. He never used the word 'environmentalist' because even though it was pretty much the same thing he didn't want to be lumped in with Democrats and RINOs (Republicans in Name Only) who ate weeds and seeds and never saw a business that they didn't want to regulate to death.

Hank loved the woods and the lakes and rivers. He was as excited as anyone else by the return of nesting pairs of Bald Eagles to the Umbagog area and - just by imagining it - he could almost feel the thrill that went up his spine every time he saw an Osprey tuck its wings in and dive for the water to come up with a trout or largemouth bass that had made the mistake of surfacing at the wrong moment. It was a magnificent sight. The Osprey - nearly bone white from a distance - rode the air like a bolt of lightning, flashing down from the sky. It dove straight into the water; along the way achieving speeds of nearly sixty miles an hour as it hurtled from the sky . . . and it rarely came up short. The sight of the raptor taking back to the sky with a huge fish flailing in its talons was a thing of wonder.

It was the birds, more specifically the big birds of prey - the raptors - that had first turned him against the proposal to bring high-tension power lines down from the mega-dams of Quebec in Canada. They had only just gotten a new foothold in the region and already man was creating an existential threat to them. But since the day he first put that "No Granite Skyway" bumper strip on his old truck he had learned more and more about this proposed project by Polaris Electric, and the more he learned the more he had become convinced that it was a threat to a way of life that he was already seriously worried about disappearing.

It was a bit disconcerting nonetheless.

A lot of assumptions that he had built his life on were called into question.

Well, he'd have some time to think about it over the next few days. Thinking-time was one thing that was in abundant supply on a solo trip to Umbagog.

Chapter 5 Herbert & Michelle

Michelle Kane pulled her Prius into the gravel drive of Herbert Johannsen on a quiet road in Groton, New Hampshire. Johanssen had called her to tell her he was thinking of selling his house and asked her to drop by to give him an idea of its value. Just as she pulled in she saw Herbert from the corner of her eye. He was leaping from the ground, grabbing a length of thick rope that hung down from a cross beam placed at the top of two telephone poles that were purchased from the electric company when they were running the power into the property.

The rope was about 35 feet long and she watched as the nearly 65-year-old Johanssen ascended it, using only his hands, his feet dangling. One hand over the other he pulled himself to the top, paused and then lowered himself back down.

Johanssen was six feet four with the body of a much younger athlete, a twinkle in his eye and a pronounced slur in his speech that got worse as the day went on or he got tired for one reason or another. At forty-five, more than twenty years before, Johanssen was an officer in the Coast Guard, specializing in the cleanup of environmental spills. This specialty - and a stunning 140 IQ - as well as a gregarious and warm personality, two traits that usually do not blend, made him a valuable asset to the Coast Guard at home and abroad where he went frequently to hold seminars and to provide expert witness testimony. All of this provided him with just enough cover for his other "occupation" as an undercover military intelligence operative. Accordingly, one could argue, he was either on a brilliant and promising career track or on a sure pathway to an abbreviated life, when he became the first official case of Lyme disease in the United States.

It wasn't called Lyme disease then of course, it was simply a completely puzzling set of symptoms that put Herbert Johanssen into a coma lasting over a month from which he emerged forty-five days later testing out at an IQ of 75, barely able to walk and with a 'peach inspediment' or a speech impediment depending on who was describing it to whom.

When his doctors told him that his condition was permanent and that he would never recover from the toll taken on his body by Lyme disease, It took the Coast Guard less time to muster Johanssen out of the Guard than it took for him to come out of his coma. Within two months of his unceremonious ouster Herbert had bought a small log cabin in the Town of Groton New Hampshire.

He knew he had to move.

He knew he lived in Groton, Connecticut.

But he wasn't thinking too fast on his feet just yet and while he was determined to prove the docs wrong, he wanted to give himself all the "advantage of the ground" as they say in the military, so he just asked the real estate agent who was listing his house in Groton, Connecticut to find him a place that was secluded and rural in a town called Groton that was not in Connecticut.

That town turned out to be Groton, New Hampshire. His agent, a sweet young newbie was, to be understated, thrilled to have two sales generated from one lead, until she found out that Groton, New Hampshire had a population of 80 and was, generally, the kind of place where someone had to die in order to generate a real estate listing.

As it happened, Herbert bought the home of a sweet old gentleman farmer, named Herron, who had recently passed. When he was told it came with a dog named Taffy and four Nubian Goats he tried to object but his speech impediment turned the word "awful" into "Awesome!" and in two shakes of a lamb's tail (or more accurately a Nubian Goat's stub) Herbert had a new - somewhat furry - family and a two bedroom log cabin, without electricity. Luckily, it didn't take long before he was in love with all of his new roomies and despite the fact that the goats girdled every tree in the front yard and every fruit tree he tried planting, he was at home - and if happy were not an appropriate descriptor for someone in his circumstances, he was, at least, sanguine about his domestic picture and ready to fight his way back to health.

The first things he did after establishing himself in Groton, and having power brought into the cabin, was to build an obstacle course in his backyard, akin to the courses he had trained on back in "spook camp"; to plant a garden to nourish his body; and, to procure a library card at the Rumney library to nourish his mind. Groton, too, had a small library but it was only open one day a week and Herbert felt that he needed to have better access to literature than would be afforded by a library with 150 works on its shelves. Finally, despite the fact that he had a PhD in nuclear physics, he enrolled in some Continuing Ed classes at nearby Plymouth State College. After a few months, he switched into a schedule of night-only classes because he found that walking the streets of Plymouth during the day was highly problematic for him. His unsteady gait, the slur in his speech and some other impulsive behavior brought on by the Lyme disease (the physicians initially thought that his brain damage had created a form of Turret's - which turned out to be a misdiagnosis . . . the BASTARDS!) Nonetheless, it all marked him as the town drunk or something akin to that. Even the police were treating him as if he were under suspicion, despite continued intervention by Michelle on behalf of her new friend.

She waited a few seconds after Herbert had descended the rope to round the corner but she couldn't help but remark on what she'd just seen.

"That was amazing! You went up that rope like a freakin' navy seal."

"Well, that's what I was, sort of . . . only tougher." He replied. "Those guys are pussys." He said, his face somewhere between a spittle-coated sneer and an irreverent smile. "You never hear about the guys I was with."

Kane and Johanssen laughed when they both finished the line . . . "Because I'd have to kill you!" Ok it was silly, stupid, trite, and predictable but it was a sign of their mutual affection and that was just fine with them both at the moment.

Kane had given Johanssen his first job after the move to New Hampshire. She loved his spirit from the moment she met him, the way he called New Hampshire "New Hamster" and then pretended that his speech impediment was the culprit. Always sporting his sly "Arabian" grin. Johanssen wasn't Arabian but he was dark and handsome in the way a mysterious Arabian character from an old movie would have been. She could certainly imagine him undercover on the streets of Damascus or Abu Dhabi or Tunis, and the knife scar she could see, highlighted now, from his exertion on the rope, just above his belt line, made her imaginings even more vivid.

So Michelle Kane, barely able to cover her own Realtor dues, brought Herbert on board at Kane Realty with just a few ground rules to avoid having customers think their real estate agent was drunk at nine am in the morning. Herbert didn't sell a lot of Real Estate, but he used his job to begin to invest in properties himself and by the time he had moved on he had amassed a nice little portfolio of properties, creating sales where otherwise there were few and he and Michelle had agreed to an arrangement where he kept his license hanging at her office and worked independently buying and selling with Kane handling all of the administrative work.

During that time his gait, and his speech both improved markedly, to the point where his own infirmities were no more or less of a challenge than the hidden idiosyncrasies and demons that the vast majority of us struggle with in an effort to achieve some semblance of normalcy in our lives. And Herbert Johannsen, born in the metropolis of New York, seasoned in the salt filled air of the Groton Coast Guard base, and honed in the back alleys of Cairo . . . became a country boy.

"What happened Herbert?" Michelle asked. "I thought this was your spot on the porch. One day you are showing your Nubians at the state fair and the next you are talking about moving? What's that about?"

"Granite Skyway", that's what it's about," he said sadly. Alluding to a proposal by the Polaris Electric company to bring power down to the New York City area over a high tension highway running from the Canadian hydro-plants owned by Hydro-Quebec right down through some of the most beautiful parts of New Hampshire. "Those 150 foot towers will come right through my land here. I am getting out before those bastards turn my little piece of heaven into a humming, buzzing, steel ranch, raising electrons to line the pockets of fat cats on Wall Street."

He paused a moment and said "it's a story almost worthy of a Frank Zappa song - and he did his best - though poor - Zappa imitation as he half-spoke and half-sang 'I'm movin' to New Hamster, gonna buy a little farm . . . raise me some electrons . . . keep me and the missus warm.' " As he said it, he reached across Michelle's field of view and grabbed an old mop head hanging from a nail on the barn wall and plopped it on his head completing the Zappa tribute.

Michelle laughed and then became serious.

"But, you're not on the preferred route," she said. "They probably won't even come this way."

"Besides, the project hasn't been approved yet. We can still stop it and I'm doing my best to make sure it doesn't happen at all."

"I know Michelle. Believe me I hope you are successful but take it from me, They will come this way because all those fancy folks who are CEOs and COOs of nameless companies along Rte 28 have their second homes over in the other valley. The first concession will be to move the route over here where the powerless dwell and that will cut off the money supply to the opposition. Like a damn lion slicing off an old cow from the herd; the herd cares, but not enough to look back. All those folks who are feeding the opposition with their money now will fade away the minute that they announce the move."

"I'm getting out while I can." I don't want to leave but I am too old to fight both Lyme disease and Polaris Electric."

A quiet settled between the two and it was clear that both were wondering what the future held, for their lives and, yes, for their relationship, because even though there were two decades between them and a world of other differences, Michelle and Herbert had - as much out of convenience as anything else - settled into a relationship of sorts over the years since they were cast together by old man Herron's farm and a passel of Nubians.

"And what about me?" Michelle asked quietly, almost in a whisper.

"Awww Michelle! " he half whispered

" I'm an old man. I fell apart twenty years ago and I'm still trying to crawl back out - but by the time I do that, I'll find out that the only thing on the other side is the long dark of night. The big sleep." He said quietly.

"You need to move on and I'm just holding you up."

"You bastard," she whispered, as the tears welled in her eyes.

"Look," Herbert said, "this is not the time to talk about this, we need some quiet time, without distraction. I've put the canoe on the truck this morning; let's take old Taffy over to Linda's where he can rest his bones on a nice warm neighbor's rug for a few days. Then we'll grab the fishing poles and head up to Moll's Rock. It's early fall and it will be beautiful and still on Lake Umbagog . . . Just you, the bald eagles, and me. We can share our catch with them and share our hearts . . . figure all this out." he said softly.

"She leaned her head on his shoulder and softly punched the front of his chest as she did. "You sonofabitch, how is it that you can be both an insensitive lout and a sweetheart at the same time?"

Johannsen smiled slyly. "Trade secret, Darlin'. It's in the DNA of the 'Black Norwegians'. The reason you never heard about them, only the Black Irish. Them Irish fellas can't keep a secret to save their lives."

"Now we Black Norwegians, that's a horse of a different color. We've been slipping around in the background for ten thousand years and no-one's the wiser. Makes us great spooks. But truth be told, there's not a lot of call for spooks in Norway, too many peace-loving folks - those namby-pambies. My people had to come over here to find some action."

Herbert continued, "We'll take a nice leisurely drive up north to Colebrook, grab a couple of steaks and some wine, maybe we can even catch a glimpse of the Mooseman, then we'll pop on over to Errol and paddle from the back side of the lake over to Moll's Rock. "

"It sounds wonderful," Michelle said in a hushed tone, "sign me up . . . Bastard!

Chapter 6   Thomas

Herbert and Michelle wheeled their shopping cart through the doors of the IGA in Colebrook, New Hampshire. The cart, loaded with groceries for their fishing trip, looked like it was on the last leg of a recycling marathon, having survived as it passed from one chain to the next on down the line until it reached its final stop here in Colebrook. Herbert was passing through the doors when the latest issue of the *Colebrook News and Views* caught his eye. Herbert grabbed the paper, stuffed it into one of the bags and continued on toward the jeep.

They had just gotten into the Jeep when "he" appeared, coming around the bend in the road, leading a cart trailed by five dogs, all of mixed breed. He had the appearance of a wild man or an eccentric miner from the west, his hair flying all over and unkempt, his beard just a continuation of the hair framing his entire face, what little one could see of it. As if that weren't enough to catch your attention his pack animal, pulling the cart, was - by God! - A moose.

A Moose!

Hitched with a full harness to the cart, a rack of antlers that would do the biggest bull in the swamp proud, and pulling the cart along next to the mountain man just as calm as you please.

A moose's rack - the term often used for its antlers - is largely a function of the animal's diet. Even though Thomas' pack animal was by all accounts of average size, his rack was outsized and thus gave the appearance of a massive bull. He was obviously well fed, though Thomas's gaunt frame gave one the impression that food was not his priority.

So this was the Mooseman.

Herbert and Michelle were not alone among those who had joked about this legendary character for years - neither one believing that he actually existed. Whenever they packed up to go on a fishing trip up north they would always make a show of packing their cameras and tripods, remarking that they might see the Mooseman, but they never believed that it would actually happen - yet here he was in the flesh.

The Mooseman was an enigma; a ghost who roamed the part of New Hampshire's North Country known as the Great North Woods. North of the White Mountains, the Great North Woods is a vast, fertile area where earth and water are braided together in a tapestry of streams, rivers, lakes and land. Like the rivers, streams and air that weaved their way through and above the tapestry it was not bound by human made geographic boundaries, even barriers imposed by language. So the northern region of Vermont, the Carrabassett region of Maine and even Canada were part of both the natural and human ecosystems of the region. Cemeteries were populated with family names that bridged geography, race, and religion. Roads, rail lines and well-worn Indian trails conjoined states; and legends - like Metallak, Chocorua, Moll Ockett and Roger's Rangers, were shared across boundaries.

This was the haunt of Thomas, The Mooseman - Where he came and went - largely unnoticed. Many a young journalist had tried to track down and interview the Mooseman but he had always managed to evade them; in part by having more homes than John and Cindy McCain or other representatives of the uber-rich who breathed the rarified air of the one percent. But unlike John and Cindy, none of the residences would be listed in the Realtors MLS or the tax roles of the local community. Some were shared, by virtue of their status as public buildings - like the cabin atop Mount Cabot. Most were simply woven into the fabric of the region: A longhouse built of saplings, bark, leaf litter, and branches, well hidden on the second Connecticut Lake and another in the area of Metallak point on an island of Lake Umbagog; a cave on Roger's Point, named for the famed scout and warrior Robert Rogers, whom the Indian people called the "White Devil" though they both despised and admired him; a fishing camp deep in the woods of Vermont along the Connecticut River with escape routes by land and water.

The locals insisted he was real but most folks chalked the Mooseman up to the legends and lore of the Great North Woods and didn't give it any more credence than the Loch Ness Monster or a similar critter that locals claimed plumbed the depths of Lake Winnipesaukee - "Winni" they called him . . . or her.

But at long last, here he was; and Thomas was his name.

Thomas . . . no last name, just Thomas, like Cher or Sting or Bono; (at least that was all he cared to share with his neighbors).

The legend was that Thomas was a direct descendant of Metallak, an old Indian who was said to ride into town on a moose that he raised from a calf given to him as a gift after he went blind in his nineties. In fact, it was said that Metallak continued to ride that moose until the moose died at the ripe old age of twenty-five, leaving Metallak broken hearted and eventually claiming him, too.

Metallak, the "Lone Indian of the Magalloway".

The "Lone" Indian . . . not because he was the only Indian, but rather because he was the last of his tribe, a branch of the Abenaki Nation known as the

Androscoggin or the Cowasuck. Androscoggin, being the more poetic moniker, it became the name attached to one of the big rivers running through the region. Cowasuck, for obvious reasons, never caught on.

Despite the common assertion that Metallak was the last of his line, Thomas claimed that he was in a direct line of descent from one Molly Susup, reputed to be the love child of Metallak and Moll Ockett, a famed Indian healer of the region. Both Metallak and Moll Ockett traveled in intersecting circles and both moved easily between the worlds of the native peoples and the white settlers.

Thomas, circling back, named his moose Metallak. His pack of mongrel dogs were similarly named for many of the more widely known historic contemporaries of Metallak and Moll Ockett.

And so Thomas meandered into town drawing surprisingly little attention. Given his motley entourage, one might have expected that his arrival would have caused quite a stir but it was midweek and it seemed as though Thomas' comings and goings had become of little consequence to the local folks and he avoided the weekend crowds for that very reason.

As he drew nearer to the town core Thomas started to pass by a parked truck sporting a Polaris Electric logo.

Not knowing Michelle and Herbert were observing him from the safety of their Jeep, he glanced around.

Herbert watched as the Mooseman bowed his head and reached down.

"What the . . . " Michelle whispered as he pulled down his zipper.

"Shhhhh" was Herbert's reply.

Stealthily Thomas removed the gas cap and then he stood, stretching his right arm above his head as if he were yawning and using the opportunity to assess whether he was still unobserved, he proceeded to urinate into the gas tank.

Perhaps it was just the quiet of the moment or the neck of the nearly empty gas tank created just the right sine wave to amplify the sound of his stream but as Herbert and Michelle struggled to keep from laughing, the thunderous sound of Thomas' piss cut through the afternoon air and the tempered glass of their car, stopping for a moment and then resuming loud and proud, over and over, until relief was at hand, and with a groan Thomas completed his business.

Without bothering to re-trouser himself, Thomas reached into his pocket and produced two packets of sugar, shook them, ripped them open and added them into the tank for good measure, a sly smile spreading across his face as he did.

Having completed his purposeful task, Thomas flipped his member back into his jeans and zipped up, adding a little gleeful jump at the end of the motion, and with a spring in his step turned toward Metallak and winked.

The moose was nonplussed.

"On Dasher" he said in a bit of a historic play and the old moose resumed his shambling pace, passing the jeep where Herbert and Michelle sat motionless, hidden behind tinted windows.

As they passed by Herbert noticed that the back of the cart was filled with grade stakes, trailing pink ribbons.

It was an odd coincidence that the newspaper he had grabbed on his way out of the store, had fallen from the bag, revealing its headline: "Vandals Hit Granite Skyway Survey Site" blared out above the fold.

Part 2 The Gathering Storm

Chapter 7   Rattlesnake Mountain

"Wow! That was amazing! Linda exclaimed as she collapsed in a single motion to the pine needle covered ground at the top of Main Cliff on Rattlesnake.

"I know," replied her climbing partner Zach Roy who had led the three-pitch climb. "I've been wanting to get back to this one for months, but you can climb Rattlesnake for years and never return to the same climb, your phone call this morning was just what I needed to motivate my sorry ass to try it again."

The two sat quietly catching their breath and taking in the magnificent view of the Baker River as it wound through the forests and meadows below them.

Called "Asquamchumaukee" by the native people of the area, which translated into "Place of Mountain Waters" in Algonquin, and later renamed for Lt. Thomas Baker after the regiment he led attacked and massacred a peaceful village of native people hunting and fishing along the river near its confluence with the Pemigewasset River in the present day town of Plymouth. The Baker cut a unique path through the little valley that began in the Moosilauke region and descended to the Pemigewasset Valley in Plymouth. Unlike the Pemigewasset that ran nearly straight down a third of the state from North to South, through the White Mountains, before joining up with the Merrimack River and making its way to the sea, the Baker meandered through its valley, leaving behind oxbows and wetlands in the course of geological time that provided ideal habitat for the migratory birds moving south in the autumn and north in the spring.

Just to the south of them a ridge of mountains ran from Tenney Mountain to Mt. Cube in the Northwest. These mountains were the foothills of the White Mountains, high enough to make for a challenging day hike but paling in comparison to the rugged peaks of the Franconia Range and the mighty Presidentials that included the highest peak in the northeast, Mount Washington.

"I'm betting you know the name of every one of these mountains." Linda said to Zach, still trying to catch her breath. Noting a line of wind turbines along the ridge she asked, " and what about those turbines? I don't remember them from the last time I was here".

Zach pointed to the northernmost mountain with a scar running the length of its summit. "That's Mt. Cube there. A fire, opened up the summit back in the 1930s, I think. Could have been after the 1938 hurricane that came through here like a freight train - leveling millions of board feet in trees creating a fire hazard everywhere you looked.   Cube's claim to fame is that it lies along the Appalachian trail and on the other side of it is a sugar bush . . . that's a large stand of Sugar Maple trees . . . currently belonging to the Thomson family. They fled the south in the mid 1900s and moved to Orford where they tried to bring their own brand of southern politics north. In the 60s the patriarch of the clan Meldrim "Mel" Thomson got elected Governor with a cornball but effective branding campaign around the phrase "Ax the Tax".

Zach continued. "Ol' Mel, he was his own unique brand of southern redneck crazy - sloe as a gin fizz and sly as old Brer Fox. He ran the state for 6 years. Pretty much all anyone remembers about him is that he use to lower the flag to half mast every time he got a bee in his bonnet; and he wanted to arm the National Guard with nukes. It was a national sideshow - sort of '*Deliverance* meets Planet of the Apeshit'."

"The turbines have been here for two years," he continued, "clearly you have not been climbing here enough lately," he said wryly. "Beautiful aren't they? Almost like a work of art, a sculpture on the ridge."

Linda looked at him quizzically, "No, but I've been keeping up. " she replied. "There's been a lot of controversy about these turbines and the proposed Granite Skyway project. That's what makes your comment so curious. I haven't asked you but I'm assuming that you aren't a fan of the Granite Skyway proposal based on what I've read about it. Isn't it a bit hypocritical to find these big turbines beautiful and to see the towers proposed by Polaris otherwise? And what about the opposition to wind turbines along Newfound Lake and in other places?" She asked.

"Whoa! Slow down," he said laughing. "That's a lot to bite off. "

Picking up a piece of quartz from the ground he held it up. "This piece of quartz is beautiful here on the ground and when it adorns a big granite, or schist, boulder; but if every stone was quartz and every boulder as well, the beauty would be eroded by its commonality."

He laughed again, "I don't remember exactly, but I believe it was Ben Franklin who said that 'a foolish consistency is the hobgoblin of small minds.' In other words, simply always being consistent may not be the wisest approach to any challenge.

"But how do you decide when it is right to demand consistency or to eschew it?" Linda asked.

"Dad use to tell me that when in doubt, he had a code that he tried to live by. Asking himself and answering these questions:

1. Is it sustainable (or in this case renewable)?
2. Is it consistent with our values?
3. Does it make us safer, freer, more or less prepared to face the future and protect the planet?

He says, 'if it meets this test, or comes close then you embrace it. If it does not, you oppose it. The degree to which you oppose it is commensurate with the degree of the threat you perceive.'

"This wind farm is, to me, beautiful," Zach continued. "It is a renewable energy source, it is small and sustainable, and if a terrorist takes it out, it won't throw the state or the country into the dark. However, we don't want to see a turbine on every mountaintop. Wilderness is also an important value to us. This wind farm came in under the radar and ironically it raised the alarm about others taking up other ridges. As a result, while we may consider this wind farm to be beautiful we still have the right - even the duty - to consider what the consequences of more such farms are. That debate has been joined and we will be asking ourselves the tough questions about this as we seek to balance the interests of all those affected."

"And the Granite Skyway project?" Linda asked.

"To compare these graceful turbines with massive electric towers is to equate the work of Claude Monet with that of an Orangutan", Zach replied, "There is not one reason for me to be in favor of Granite Skyway. First, it is a private venture. By definition this means that there are no controls in place for protecting the public interest with respect to the cost of the power. It is purely defined by the market and the company's control the market because it is a public utility not a freely traded commodity or a product that the public can choose to consume or not."

"These companies will take every opportunity they can to pass along the costs of development to the public, and any cost associated with the project that is not born by the investors in the project is, by default, borne by the public. It's hard to argue that 150-foot towers are beautiful, except to some very specific engineering types. In every place where a tower can be viewed, or a massive scar mars the land, there is a negative impact on property values. There is also a negative impact on the landscape - particularly what we call the 'viewscape'. Those negative impacts show up as a positive cash flow on the other side of the ledger flowing directly into the pockets of the investors."

"As a comparison, before the Clean Air Act began to punish companies for polluting the air, companies willfully polluted the atmosphere passing the costs of cleaning up their act along to the people who breathed the unsafe air and paid for it with higher infant mortality, more lung disease and other costs. These companies used the air and the water as free waste disposal vehicles and we all paid for it."

"But the source of the power, Hydro-Quebec, is renewable water power. Isn't that in its favor?" Linda asked.

"A renewable source of power is not, by definition, sustainable. First, reliance on one power source in two countries sets up a situation where a power shortage might create the necessity for the producer to choose who would receive power and who would not. I doubt that the US consumers would be protected in that case. More important, however, is the danger inherent in over reliance on a very large power source that is vulnerable to acts of terrorism that might very well throw the entire eastern seaboard into the dark and its ensuing chaos."

"And that doesn't even begin to touch on the issues of land taken from native people to build these monoliths and the environmental effects of flooding thousands of acres of land and releasing large quantities of mercury and other toxins into the drinking water and the wildlife that native people, and other families rely on as a food source."

Linda stood, dusting the pine needles and dirt from her climbing shorts, "well that's that then."

Zach replied, "No. That's only the beginning of that, we can talk more about the loss of forests that serve as a carbon sink for the planet but if we are going to get another climb in we better move on."

Chapter 8 One Commercial Plaza

The monolithic black building of One Commercial Plaza in Manchester, dominates both the skyline and the footprint of the downtown area in the financial capital of New Hampshire. Like New York City, or Lagos, Nigeria or hundreds of other such cities around the world. This is not an official designation . . . it rarely is. Rather, it is the unofficial gathering place for financial power, separated by a healthy distance from the political Capital, in this case, Concord. Manchester rocks the clock whereas Concord rolls up the sidewalks at about 6pm on an average day. The rarefied air of Manchester gives the power brokers a sense that they are above the fray in the day-to-day job of keeping the wheels of government turning.

On this particular evening, a gunmetal grey sky cast an ominous shroud over One Commercial Plaza. Like a view in some dystopian, post apocalypse movie where one expects a monstrous military vehicle to roll up carrying storm troopers to enforce some hated code laid down by the powerful, unelected and unloved . . . empowered through sheer force. This, of course, was not actually the case . . . at least not as far as the public knew.

Yet an unsettling darkness prevailed.

On the 10th floor of One Commercial Plaza the lights burned despite the fact that most of the rest of the floors were dark in the post-workday hours. These were the offices of Polaris Electric, the state's largest utility company.

Polaris Electric was a subsidiary of a larger company based in the toney suburbs of Connecticut, the shotgun marriage a result of Polaris' investment in a nuclear plant that drove them into bankruptcy and ultimately spawned a sweetheart deal in the legislature. A deal that protected those holding junk bonds while creating the nation's highest electric rates for consumers who had nothing to do with the poor decisions made by the managers and bean counters at Polaris or the spineless bureaucrats in the capitol, who year after year continued to give aid and succor to the poor utility company piling one bad decision onto another and blaming it on the previous administration.

Inside One Commercial Plaza a small group had gathered around the conference room table at Polaris. None had signed in at the front lobby, nor had they even used the parking garage where there would have been a digital footprint of their visit to the building. Instead they had each parked inconspicuously nearby, in an alley, in another corporate parking lot, on a side street.

Likewise, upon their exit, each member of the cabal would make a stop somewhere in the "Queen City" that would provide the cover just in case someone had recognized their vehicle and thereupon held a piece of the puzzle in their minds.

This was the Granite Skyway's dark team . . . the "shadow cabal".

Not one of them was a known commodity in either political or business circles in the state. Nor did the members of the media know whom they were in any more than a passing way. The media was watching the big dogs, not these wraiths, these ghosts.

A public steering committee composed of the "C-Level" (CEO, COO, CFO, etc . . .) players from the various investors in the project provided all the window dressing needed to keep the public's eyes off the Shadow Cabal. The C-Level "suits" were the public face of Granite Skyway. They provided a squeaky clean front for the public relations effort and the head feint needed to prevent anyone from suspecting that any other power center existed. The members of the Shadow Cabal were well compensated, though none but their leader knew how well. More important, they were invisible.

There were many others on the Granite Skyway payroll, drawing a salary and working to make this project happen; hundreds - perhaps even thousands - all employed, openly or surreptitiously, in the efforts to see that Granite Skyway received approvals and moved forward; but in the quiet recesses these five, the Shadow Cabal, were the operating system for the dark machine at its central core. They crafted the sub rosa message after the PR folks were done creating the happy face. They figured out who was with them and who was not; who could be bought and who could not - and therefore belonged on the enemies list. They paid off the right people, made generous gifts to public radio and public television to secure the last word in any substantive debate, purchased ad buys on the private media, and laid the groundwork for discrediting those who could not be bought. In short, they did the dirty work.

Not one of them was what you might consider a "player". They were once, and sometimes twice removed from the players, providing what the political system termed *plausible deniability* . . . a plausible reason to believe that they were rogue operators, should their work ever come to light.

The media and the public believed that the power was vested in the Steering Committee but it was in the Shadow Cabal that the power truly resided.

James Enright was de facto leader of the group by virtue of his control of the very generous purse and his direct contact with Conrad Fleming, the CEO and President of Polaris Energy. Enright had put himself through college dealing pills and playing in the grey areas of collegiate life at the University. In high school he'd been voted as "most likely to do time" an honorific surreptitiously created by teachers in the school hoping to forewarn those who crossed his path in future years without finding themselves in his sights or those of his less-than-honorable parents.

Enright had spent the last ten years in a third level position in the public relations department of Polaris. Like a CIA agent assigned to USAID he did little to pull his own weight and everyone of substance not only steered clear of him but largely denied him unless pushed to the wall; Even then they only acknowledged that they knew him as they quickly retired from whatever conversation was drawing them into the line of fire.

Enright was Conrad Fleming's mad dog. In political lingo, he might have been referred to as a hatchet man but that moniker was far too kind for Enright. A hatchet man usually had limits, if only for self-preservation. Enright did not know the meaning of the word - - thus the allusion to a rabid animal, foaming at the mouth, looking for something to bite and snapping at air. He went by JEn, pronounced like J - N but no one ever knew how it was spelled because JEn's first rule for the Shadow Cabal was that nothing was ever put in writing. He was fond of quoting Earl Long - the infamous Louisiana politician - on the matter: "Don't write anything you can phone. Don't phone anything you can talk. Don't talk anything you can whisper. Don't whisper anything you can smile. Don't smile anything you can nod. Don't nod anything you can wink." Enright lived by those words.

JEn had made his bones during the battle over the Old Saybrook Nuclear Plant when he made a particularly effective up and coming leader in the anti-nuclear movement disappear mysteriously without any fingerprints. The anti-nuke forces eventually petered out but the veggies at the University research farm had an odd growth spurt and the cows, record milk production.

Kayla MacIntire, who had known Enright in College and could - it seemed - still stomach him, was the erstwhile number two of the Cabal. "Mac", as she was called, was a lobbyist in Vermont. She knew all of the players in New Hampshire but she was able to circumvent the laws governing lobbyists in New Hampshire by virtue of the fact that she did not officially represent any New Hampshire business or organization and she did not prowl the halls of the Statehouse as a hired gun on legislation. Among her many clients in Vermont was a venture capital company that was a junior investor in Granite Skyway. She was also the Governor's girlfriend - though the Governor's husband hadn't been read-in.

Hers was a delicate situation, the Governor didn't know about her position in the Shadow Cabal of course, because she did not know about the Cabal. In fact the Governor believed that the red line drawn by MacIntire - not lobbying in NH - was the surest way to protect them from exposure. That and the fact that she was a woman and the wags of the Republican dominated legislature weren't imaginative enough to make up a story this good; and since the Republicans were ostensibly her allies, in her political party, she figured they would keep the Democrats busy enough to keep them quiet as well. Thus, Mac walked a tightrope between her very lucrative role in the Shadow Cabal and her pleasurable and useful relationship with the Governor.

If called upon to make the choice she was too invested in the river of cash flowing her way from the Granite Skyway project; but she really did care about "Mags", her endearing name for Governor Margaret Gallow, and she would be very sad if she had to make the choice. She sincerely hoped the day would not come, but as her father use to say: *"hope in one hand and piss in the other and see which one fills up faster."* . . . despite her hopes, she suspected that day might come.

Mac's assignment with respect to the Governor was to gently move her in the direction of supporting the project by using their relationship to keep her "open minded" as the process moved forward. "Open Minded" in this case was favorably disposed to the project, not actually open-minded. Eventually, the theory was, she would come around to the utility's position. Mac's job was to keep the Governor happy and distracted and to make sure the Cabal was not blindsided by a decision that they were not expecting. Though Mac didn't know it, James Enright was prepared to out the relationship between his number two and the Governor if it came to that, even if Mac was a casualty of the outing.

The final three members of the cabal rounded out the team providing experience and loyalty borne of their gratitude to Enright for providing them with a job when they were toxic to almost anyone still taking air:

Will Duggan, a former news director for the Seacoasts most prominent newspaper, *The Seacoast Emblem*. Duggan was disgraced in a scandal in which he had personally accepted money in exchange for stepping on a news story about a businessman whose company was secretly dumping toxic chemicals into the Piscataqua River through a drain running directly from their warehouse into the river. Duggan was ruggedly handsome which made at least half the population willing to give him the benefit of the doubt on almost anything and he was not at all shy about using his good looks to his advantage.

Susan Wilson, the daughter of a prominent New Hampshire physician, who had written prescriptions for her underage lover on her father's prescription pad and later through his electronic identity, and was caught only when her lover died of an overdose brought on by a switch from Oxycontin to Heroin when the Oxy just lost its edge for him. She had only escaped jail because her young lover had turned 18 only ten days before his overdose and while she was universally scorned by the public, a first rate defense attorney was able to get her a slap on the wrist largely in deference to her much beloved father, who had, as a family doc, delivered a high percentage of the most prominent members of the community.

Now in her late forties Susan spent a good deal of her disposable income on Botox treatments and plastic surgery to keep her in the kind of shape she needed to continue to attract young boy toys and she had a stable of them because she was less concerned about their looks than she was about their stamina and ability to service her. She was able to maintain her stable by taking full advantage of the hormonal impulses of young men and her generosity. More than half the stable was receiving life subsidies from her to keep them responsive which was not cheap. Between her personal care needs and her stable upkeep she had a healthy monthly nut so her work on the Shadow Cabal was not just helpful, it was paramount. Which made her particularly useful to Enright who always was aware of the little things that made his people most useful. He was also aware of his vulnerabilities and a man or a woman with Wilson's proclivities was always a risk when it came to the danger of an employee who decided to play double agent for the money.

Fortunately, in this case the opposition didn't have enough money to be a risk in that department. This liability came into play in the inside game, with investors and other partners that might be looking for an advantage over other investors. He'd have to bear all this in mind if somehow the field of operations broadened, as they got closer to the finish line. For now though, he wouldn't need to be concerned he just needed to make sure that she was not spending all her time and all the cash that he was providing on her extracurricular activities and kept her head in the game.

Finally, there was Harry Echo. Echo was what Enright quietly referred to as the Shadow Cabal's tampon - behind his back of course: small, able to fit into tight places, not really very noteworthy, and, above all, disposable. Echo had come to this place through sheer self-immolation. 20 years prior he had started off well, getting elected to the New Hampshire House of Representatives at the tender age of 19.

Echo's election was no great feat or sign of talent or perseverance. Twenty years ago if you were a Democrat in New Hampshire your party affiliation was announced aloud when you took your ballot on Election Day because they wanted to shame you into changing your registration. Naturally Echo chose to register as a Republican - though he didn't have a clue about either party, it just seemed like it would be fun to run and his only friend had told him he'd be a shoo in as long as no one else ran on the Republican side. He watched the notices coming out of the town hall and on the last day, when no other Republican had registered, he ambled into the town hall and paid his one-dollar registration fee.

The District he was running in was known as a floterial district, part of a very smooth redistricting maneuver by House and Senate committees after the 1980 census. Where the numbers did not work just right they would add a single Rep here or there by taking towns that already had been placed in a district and creating another district layered on and composed of multiple towns. Almost invariably these floterial districts were composed of towns that were overwhelmingly Republican assuring that a Republican would be chosen by the citizens who were either voting a straight Republican ticket, confused by the fact that there were two elections for the State House of Representatives, or just plain ignorant.

Echo's great good fortune was that he was from a district where a raving lunatic could get elected as long as he had an R after his name. Once elected he immediately began to sell his position to any bidder. He would start his day off driving to Concord, signing in to make him eligible for about $55 in mileage reimbursement, then hustling over to Mount Sunapee, where his legislative pass entitled him to a day pass at the, then, state owned ski area. After he quietly scalped his ticket to an out-of-state skier - who would never remember him even if he were caught - he then headed north to Cannon Mountain where he repeated the process. Then he would usually just drive the fifteen minutes home and call it a day.

Though this busy schedule meant that he didn't have much time for his committee assignment at the legislature he was netting about 600 to 800 dollars a week and really had a good thing going when a lapse in judgment prompted him to throw a trash can through the front window of a Cumberland Farms because he needed a case of Bud and Cumbies was closed.

He was so sure that he would not be caught that he didn't bother to try and wipe the scene down. It was just plain bad luck that the week before he had - in his official capacity - accompanied his brother, a part time police officer in Laconia, to a fourth grade classroom where everyone, including the adults, were fingerprinted as a hedge against a child being abducted by some predator. The prints had accidentally been sitting on the desk of the Laconia Police chief when a clerical worker noticed that the prints just brought in from Cumberland Farms matched a set on the Chief's desk. Though every parent and adult at the school function was assured that the prints would not be mingled with the real criminals, the Chief couldn't just ignore the match with one Lawrence Echo. "Accidents happen" was the official explanation for it. In any case, it led the police right to Echo and while eventually the charges would be dismissed because of the print fiasco, by the time all that played out Echo had been dogged by a dozen reporters who managed to dig up the goods on some of his other activities and he was forced to resign from his position as State Rep to prevent the media from finding out about his deal with a rookie Police officer in Wagner with whom Echo would ride on select nights when they would stop young ladies for driving too fast or too drunk and then trade their freedom for accommodating them in the back of the cruiser.

Unlike Duggan, Echo was as homely as the day was long and even the power conferred upon him as a state lawmaker was not likely to get him laid, he saw this as his just rewards.

This was the Shadow Cabal. Called together in the gathering darkness to plan the next stage of the sub-rosa campaign for the Granite Skyway.

The news had just come through that very day that an important preliminary hurdle had been passed in the process of gaining state approval for the project. The opponents had fought to immediately stop the project in its infancy. They had done so by making the case to the Public Utilities Commission, which provided state oversight, that the power was not needed and therefore the project should be denied. The PUC, however, came back with a decision that the project was not in their jurisdiction because it was a private project which was to be funded by private entities and therefore did not need to demonstrate a "Public Good" or a demand or need for the power. Never mind that Polaris controlled much of the land through right-of-ways established as a public utility serving the needs of state ratepayers.

The opponents of the Granite Skyway tried valiantly to kill the idea in its cradle, so to speak, but in the end, like the Old Saybrook nuclear plant that would seemingly forever drive the price of electricity, the state skids were greased in favor of the utility company and while they might have to provide some window dressing before the final approval was granted they were well on their way. Sure, maybe they would have to bury a little of the line but the vast amount of the powerline would be above ground where reduced home and real estate values for everyone within sight of the project would subsidize the private corporate venture by substantially reducing the costs of construction. To many, this was a direct transfer of wealth from the pockets of average homeowners directly into the pockets of the elite investors of Granite Skyway but it was just devious enough to be successful.

Enright opened the meeting informally with the news about the Public Utilities Commission decision. "The opposition is going to begin turning up the heat," he said. "We have to be ready."

Chapter 9 NH Business Digest

Jim Kitchen browsed through the latest business news from the AP. He was looking for something that would catch his attention. Actually, he was looking for something that would "rock his world". It was so long since he had a story that would really challenge him, giving him the opportunity to examine important issues locally - better yet, something with a national flavor, something that smelled like Pulitzer.

Drought didn't begin to describe the state of affairs for Kitchen. Something in the back of his brain had told him that the Granite Skyway project was going to be his way back to the big leagues but it sure wasn't feeling that way right now.

At 5 ft 8 inches and a rail thin 160 pounds, Kitchen kept his girlish figure by a steady diet of coffee (cream and 3 sugars) and American Spirit cigarettes. Though it was harder and harder to be true to the diet because there were a dwindling number of spots available for him to indulge his tastes. For every coffee shop that opened nearby four or five spots to sneak a smoke disappeared. He had tried carrying an eCig for those moments when he couldn't find a spot to have a smoke but the thought-police were actively pursuing even electronic alternatives to cigarettes as a public enemy and fewer and fewer places were willing to spot a break to those who were sporting the blue dot. Fortunately for him, his boss was willing to let him work from home liberally and his landlord had not yet drawn the shades on smoking in his apartment . . . though he figured it was only a matter of time before he pulled that trigger. Jim just hoped he would reach retirement age before he did, but his confidence in that was fading faster than the color photo of Eugene McCarthy that hung on his office wall in the only spot that the sun hit. If Granite Skyway was going to blossom into a real story with real implications it had better happen soon because all of these other deadlines and car crashes were closing in on him fast.

This story . . . it had all of the right stuff: a really bad idea with powerful monied interests behind it - willing to do whatever it took to get their way against a group of committed opponents with little or no juice or clout. It hit all of the right buttons in terms of current issues. He ticked them off in his head: energy, international intrigue, climate change, terrorism, sustainable power, environmental protection, public interests vs. private greed, It made for the classic David vs. Goliath story but at this point neither David nor Goliath had done much of anything, or so it seemed, to give it any traction.

You would think that the public and even the politicians would have realized that they were on the verge of being twice burned; first by the nuke that tripled electric rates and served up golden parachutes to the junk bond holders and inept management. Now here they were about to launch their second boondoggle in their short corporate history. Their hubris was beyond compare.

This one really took the prize when it came to lame ideas. First, on the heels of 9-11, the worst terrorist attack in American history, Polaris Electric was proposing one of the largest single power transmission projects in the country, dependent on transborder cooperation, demand centered politics from two separate nations, anti-terrorist challenges that would be next to impossible to manage - should it come to that - and opportunity costs that would stifle innovation and small power production for a decade or more.

With the rest of the developed world moving toward smart grids and decentralized small power production, dispersed across geographic regions to enhance the reliability, security and sustainability of power production and distribution, this proposal was a dinosaur right out of the gate. With the marginal costs of power production dropping everywhere except those places where sweetheart deals between government and private industry had hard-wired costs, Polaris Electric was making one last play to set in stone a long-term obligation that would stay on the books no matter what happened to electric costs.

In theory at least, this should be lighting up all of the marquees and big screens, screaming "Over here! Look this way!" so why were things so quiet on the Northern front? Had the opposition been so cowed that they weren't going to put up a real fight? Or was this what activism and opposition had become since the Twin Towers fell and the country had drawn itself into a paralyzed ball of fear and paranoia; had activism become nothing more than an endless shuffling of papers, murmurs of committees, and droning of judges?

Let's face it, Kitchen perambulated through his thoughts, what Thoreau and Martin Luther King had termed Civil Disobedience, was now labeled as "terrorism" by those who wanted to crack down on dissent. He had watched as the culture drifted to the right on these security issues, even as it became much more tolerant and progressive on other fronts: endorsing same sex marriage, acknowledging global climate change, even electing a black man President.

If there is a truism in politics it is that the middle is defined by the margins in any debate. The radicals of the abolitionist movement, like John Brown, shifted the ground of the debate so that Frederick Douglass, Abraham Lincoln and Daniel Webster came to occupy the middle. Likewise Malcolm X, the SDS and Weatherman; and the Black Panther's of the 60s and 70s provided a new fulcrum point for the debate over civil rights and the Vietnam War. But since 9-11 the security debate had shifted dramatically to the right and the country was debating the finer points of torture while giving up the ground on the freedom front. Ben Franklin had called it exactly right; we were hell bent on sacrificing freedom in the name of security.

Kitchen did not hold out much hope that there would be a robust debate over these issues. There was a chance that somehow the media could step into the void but the chance was slim at best. In the last decade the media had become more and more the captive of corporate interests itself. The independent media that the founders had envisioned was in danger of becoming extinct with more and more consolidation leading to media monoliths that were either part of a corporate family themselves or so dependent upon corporate largesse that they tried to steer clear of alienating powerful corporate interests.

All right It was quiet . . . too quiet, he realized as he turned it over again in his mind - - Like the lull before the storm.

Chapter 10 Jack Carrigain

The old chair creaked as Jack Carrigain leaned back from his massive oak desk, where only moments before he was banging out a happy tune on his old Underwood typewriter. He put his feet up as he responded to the ring of the rotary telephone, placing the vintage phone against his ear. "Carrigain here . . . "

Carrigain was as savvy with a computer as the next guy but there was something about vintage hardware that bespoke comfort and dependability. Jack was the great grandson of Philip Carrigain who had not only been Secretary of State for the great state of New Hampshire but had also been the first person to develop a detailed map of the White Mountains - - a map still known as the "Carrigain Map" in antiquing and historic circles. One of the last of the original printing hung on Jack's wall in his home office and he took great pride in showing it off to anyone who had an interest.

Jack, however, was famous in his own right. Having grown up in New Hampshire he had achieved near-folk hero status during his years reporting for National Public Radio from various war fronts, particularly the Middle East and Eastern Europe. His hometown friends would never have predicted that this skinny and timid little kid would become a lion of war reporting but something happened over four summers at a camp on Newfound Lake . . . Something life-changing. Where he had arrived as a wisp of a boy, a self-confidence had taken root born of backpacking trips into the White Mountains and rock climbing and a program that emphasized both fun and rigorous learning. Mowglis was one of the last summer-long camps in the northeast. Based on the Jungle Books of Rudyard Kipling the camp had built a strong tradition gathered from the metaphor rich stories of the jungle boy and his brothers and sisters in the Seeonee wolf pack. The camp had struggled with the changing times. While other summer camps fell to the developer's dozers or had gone to shorter sessions at twice the cost, Mowglis had held fast to the belief that only a summer-long experience offered the kind of character-building that was truly meaningful and, if Jack Carrigain was even close to the rule, they were right. A pair of worn old copies of the first and second Jungle Books sat in a prominent place on his desk and had never been far from his reach no matter where life had taken him.

When a chopper carrying Carrigain and five other reporters was shot down during one particularly fierce battle in Eastern Europe his reputation was further burnished when he single-handedly dragged his injured companions to safety as bullets and mortars whizzed around them. Later, when he was assisting with their recovery he would sit by their bedsides and read the Jungle Books to them, taking a special care to bring the characters to life with a well-rehearsed retinue of voices and calls.

By the time he and his companions were headed home to the USA, Carrigain was already working on a reputation approaching legendary status; So it was quite a surprise when this young man, seemingly bound for glory in the upper reaches of the media constellation threw it all in and returned to New Hampshire to take the job as editor of a small North Country newspaper.

Though it was not the expected career path that others might have surmised, surprisingly it made Carrigain even more of a national folk hero.

New Hampshire's First in the Nation Presidential Primary didn't hurt either. A steady stream of hungry young journalists and presidential wannabes made their way to his door stoop and, while Carrigain took seriously his responsibility to mentor the journalists and vet potential national leaders, he was not above having a little fun with it from time to time.

Most notably was the national prank he played in his first year back. It was early in the primary campaign when he got a call from a California reporter. The reporter was looking for an interesting angle so he called Jack Carrigain and Jack told him about a new candidate who seemed to be gathering steam in the New Hampshire Primary. The early winter blues had given way to a spring surge by "a fellow with bright orange campaign signs", according to Carrigain. "His name is Heaves, Frost Heaves".

Carrigain expected the punch line would result in a hardy laugh and was, frankly, not quite sure what to do when the reporter seemed to take him completely seriously and asked further questions about Candidate Heaves. A combination of curiosity and sheer embarrassment over the fact that the reporter had fallen for the prank prevented him from disclosing the joke, yet he was sure that between the phone interview and the publishing of the story someone in the newsroom would straighten out this young cub reporter.

Much to his chagrin, the afternoon wire carried a UPI wire story about Presidential newcomer Frost Heaves, whom they were attempting to contact for a quote. Carrigain was at first horrified and began trying to come up with a plan for damage control but then decided to just go along for the ride. He didn't grant any further interviews, didn't stoke the rumor, after all, it had a life of its own. It might have gone on for weeks had it not been for William "Billy" Gardner, New Hampshire's longest serving Secretary of State, who, upon hearing about the rumor, promptly declared that the Emperor had no clothes!

By the time the rumor reached Secretary Gardner though it went through a long process akin to the children's game called "Telephone" where one child in a long line whispers a phrase to the next and the phrase is passed from child to child down the line. By the time it reaches the end of the line it has so completely morphed that the person originating the phrase doesn't even recognize it. Gardner held an impromptu news conference to squelch the rumor and had some fun with it himself - bringing in half the employees of the NH Department of Transportation and conducting the news conference from the driver's seat of a huge orange snow plow.

He later called Carrigain after he had traced the story back to its roots and had a good laugh with him.

Through humor, a sharp wit and a keen bullshit detector, Carrigain established himself as a local and national oracle. So it was not unexpected that both sides in the Granite Skyway debate would approach him to solicit his support. He withheld judgment immediately though he was pretty sure where he would come down on this one - - he would play it out and give both sides the opportunity to make their cases - - after all, that's the job of an oracle.

Part 3 The Sacred Trust

Chapter 11 - Moll's Rock

The water barely rippled as Michelle's naked body slid noiselessly beneath the surface of Lake Umbagog, Her years as a competitive swimmer allowed her to enter the water almost without a splash and she followed her graceful dive from Moll's Rock with a hundred feet underwater just to prove she still had it going on.

Herbert paused from gathering wood at the forest's edge to watch her. She was a country girl to the core. She'd finish her swim and within an hour or so she would have a stringer of bass ready to be cooked up for dinner. He would go out with her to fish but it was mostly to provide the company. Despite years of trying, Herbert was still in the "fishing" phase of the sport. MIchelle, on the other hand, had long ago graduated to the "catching" level. She knew just what lure to use in what conditions and just how to spot a bass nest in the broad shallows of the lake.

Umbagog is a shallow lake, formed by the receding glacier in the last polar epoch some ten thousand years ago. By its nature, a shallow lake is prone to developing some healthy waves in response to even a slight wind. Herbert, the scientist, explained to her that it was because there was less depth to moderate the effects of the wind. While it was calm now, when they had set out a few hours earlier there were some nasty white caps on the lake so they had decided to paddle in to Moll's Rock from the Southwest end of the lake where it formed the headwaters of the Androscoggin River.

Moll's Rock was only a short paddle from the Errol boat launch and didn't require hours of fighting the wind to get to the destination. A beautiful little half-acre field carved out of the surrounding dark green and blue forest with a large rock outcrop at the water's edge. From a distance Moll's Rock site was an artist's canvas of intersecting lines. The straight lines of the rock stood fast against all comers, and when the air was still the tall grasses of the field reflected the rock, providing a parallel carpet. When the wind blew, though, the tall grasses crafted a complex and beautiful tapestry drawn from different angles, weaving together the grasses and the season's flowers into lines splashed with color and rivaling the finest work of Manet, Degas and Pissarro.

Legend held that this was one of the famed Indian medicine woman Moll Ockett's favorite basecamp sites during the part of the year that she spent here in the Umbagog area. Beside its proximity to the headwaters of the Androscoggin river, it was also far enough from the actual convergence of the lake and the river that the wetlands and their prodigious mosquito population was not likely to be a factor in getting a good night's sleep or enjoying the campfire for a few hours after dinner. Herbert was a relative newcomer so he wasn't aware of the issue but Michelle recalled stories from her older brother, a mountain and river guide in the Whites during the 70's and 80's who had recounted one sleepless night when he claimed that the mosquitoes were so thick it was like sleeping on a runway. In fact the party had ended up abandoning their attempts to sleep and spent the night paddling and hiking around the wetlands in search of various kinds of wildlife, ending the night with a crayfish roast, having gathered a bucket full of plump crayfish drawn to their shore by a few errant noodles washed from a camper's dinner plate.

During the height of the summer most of the camping sites on Umbagog are reserved and even the locals are careful to check in with the overseers at the eastern cove of the lake to be sure their site of preference is available, but after labor day most people simply assumed that the sites will be vacant. In most cases the worst that could happen is that they would have to either share a site or paddle another half mile to an alternate one.

Herbert and Michelle arrived at Moll's rock in the early hours of the afternoon, so they presumed it was still possible that they would not be alone.

Sure enough, Charlie Stonebridge paddled up just as they were headed out to fish. Herbert had just pushed off from his position in the stern of the canoe and Michelle had done a quick draw stroke to aim the boat north toward the cooler waters of the feeder streams and rivers. They were hoping to catch a mixed string of trout and bass.

"Greetings folks" Stonebridge said, paddling his C1 up next to Herbert's Lone Wolf canoe. "I was hoping to camp here so I could get an early start to the Errol rapids tomorrow morning. Mind sharing the site?"

"No problem" Michelle responded. We didn't have a reservation either, as long as you don't mind sharing the fire and you can stand it when Herbert here starts snoring like a freight train . . ."

Herbert gave her a look of feigned shock and broke in "She's just giving you her cover story. If the earth starts to shake in the middle of the night it will be a gift from her, not me."

Stonebridge laughed. "I sleep like a log, and I'll set my tent up at the edge of the grass so there's plenty of privacy for everyone."

"You can actually get a tent in that Kayak?" Herbert asked looking at Stonebridge's covered boat. "It looks like it barely holds you!"

"Actually, this is a C1, a covered canoe, you kneel in it and paddle it with a single bladed paddle, instead of the double bladed paddle they use for a kayak." He held up his paddle to show them.

"You'd be surprised at how much I can get in under this deck, even with my flotation bags." He patted the surface of the boat for effect and headed it to shore, leaning back slightly as he approached the landing and executing a long reverse sweep that brought the boat parallel to the shore as he reached out to place his hand on the grassy shore. He pulled at the release loop on the front of his spray skirt, freeing himself from the boat and as he rose you could see that he paddled from a kneeling position, as you would in a canoe, unlike a kayak where your legs push out in front, limiting the amount of room available for cargo.

Though he never bragged about it, Stonebridge was one of the pioneers of modern day wildwater (aka whitewater) paddling and boat building. Of course the native peoples, particularly the Inuit of the north, were building kayaks and using them for hunting and fishing for thousands of years and both the military and the recreational community had adopted kayaks at the margins, but it was only in the early 1940s that they began to capture the imagination of the leading edge of the adventure and recreation community. At first it was only the hardiest souls who could build their own boats and scout and chart their own rivers and rapids, but as the sport began to catch on boat molds replaced the hand-crafted boats. Soon mass production of kayaks and the design of longer and wider boats, both singles and doubles for lake paddling and recreational use, created the beginnings of the vigorous industry of today.

Stonebridge's earliest boats were made by his own hands, using fiberglass and cloth, and he found that his 6 foot 6 frame was more comfortably accommodated by a C1 than a kayak, or K1, so he stuck with the C1 style of boat even though it meant many more years of building his own boats as kayaks ascended the ladder of popularity and mass production much more rapidly than the covered canoe. In 1972 Wildwater Slalom became an Olympic sport for the first time. Stonebridge tried out for the team and was selected to represent the United States but the joy of his selection was overshadowed by the terrorist attack on the Israeli team in Munich. As a result, he rarely even mentioned the event.

Stonebridge pulled his gear bag from the bow compartment of his boat and in one swift motion lifted the C1 onto his other shoulder and loped off across the small meadow that surrounded Moll's Rock to select a spot that would comfortably accommodate his tent and went to work setting it up.

Chapter 12 Big Island, Lake Umbagog

Hank Algren was just about to give up for the day when he came upon a school of rainbow trout in a shoal just off the shore of Big Island on Umbagog. He brought in four nice size fish in a five-minute span and he was just getting ready to cast his line in again when a huge barge loaded with timber came around the eastern end of the island. The barge was ferrying timber, mostly white pine apparently from Big Island, where it was clearly being logged, and headed to a landing point on the Western side of the lake for transport - probably to a local sawmill.

"Son of a Bitch! What the hell are they doing logging on an island where my raptors nest?" Hank's love of raptors, especially the Bald Eagles and the Ospreys, was legendary among his friends and made him more than a little possessive about them. Other than his deer, they were closest to the heart of the big man. He had coffee tables and bookshelves filled with books by Galen Rowell, Nick Brandt and Laura Dyer. His favorite photographer though was Clyde Smith Jr. - - not because he was the best wildlife photographer, but because he, above all others, had taught Hank to love the outdoors.

Smith was a National Geographic photographer who photographed the outdoors in all its splendor and a native son of New Hampshire with whom Hank had grown up. Known to his friends as "Micky", Smith had grown up on Mount Cardigan, literally, where his father Clyde Smith Sr. served as the fire warden and ranger as an employee of the NH Division of Parks and Recreation. Micky lived with his mother and father in a small cabin just down from the summit of the mountain during the Spring, Summer and Fall; hiking down the mountain every morning - outside of summer vacation - to attend school in the valley and hiking back up the mountain after classes ended for the day. In the winter, the family lived in Bristol where Micky would take the bus like all the other kids and he and Hank would often sit together. Hank loved to hear stories about life on the mountain and Micky never tired of telling them.

His favorite was the story of a sunny afternoon picking blueberries on top of Cardigan. Micky had told his father that he was going blueberry picking and his father had given him strict instructions about how far he could stray from the summit where the tower stood. Micky found a large patch of blueberries not far from the tower and began to pick berries, eating more than he saved in the grand tradition of children everywhere. About an hour after Micky left Clyde stepped out onto the deck that surrounded the cabin of the tower. He walked around the deck trying to spot Micky. He had just rounded the corner onto the north facing deck when he spotted a large black bear eating berries from a patch just to the north of the tower. The patch of berries and land was the size of a large building, round, with a diameter of about 100 feet. Directly across from the bear was Micky picking and eating away oblivious to the danger just on the other side of the patch. Unable to call out, for fear that startling the bear would cause it to behave protectively, Micky's dad could do nothing but watch and as he did the most wondrous thing happened. Micky and the bear never moved relative to one another. They remained at 12 and 6 o'clock, relatively, as they moved clockwise around the berry patch. When the bear had eaten its fill it wandered off, as did Micky shortly afterwards . . . neither the wiser for the presence of the other.

Micky had captured the raptors of Umbagog in his final shoot for National Geographic and Hank had gotten him to sign the cover shot before he had it framed for the space above his desk. That was fifteen years ago, when they had first declared that the bald eagles were officially back. Hank was not about to let this rogue operation stain the memory of his friend. Someone would answer for this.

Hank had left his truck and trailer at a boat launch about 15 miles east of Errol, just over the border in Maine. He was planning to spend the night camped at Moll's Rock but wanted to get in a few hours of fishing before he motored over to the campsite. Just to be safe he had made reservations for the site for two nights, even though he planned to only be there tonight. But right now he was headed for the landing point where the timber was unloaded. He didn't hold the poor bastard driving the barge responsible, he was just feeding his family. However, someone was behind this logging operation and if he didn't act quickly they would wipe out the raptor habitat on the largest island in the lake.

He docked his boat directly across from the cabin of the barge and hailed the driver.

Chapter 13 Prelude to a Potlatch

Sarah Brandt and Daniel Roy paddled around the bend from the headwaters of the Androscoggin toward Moll's Rock at about the same time that Hank Algren motored into the cove where the campsite was. It was getting late and Hank was not happy to see three people already inhabiting his reserved campsite in addition to the two he could see dead ahead aiming for them as well.

Hank carefully nosed the bow end of his boat into a small break in the shore bushes and reached into his front pocket to extract the reservation sheet they had given him when he paid his fee earlier, making a bit of a show opening it up as Stonebridge approached his bow and took hold of it to lend a hand.

"Uh-oh" Stonebridge said, "looks like we're poaching your spot for the night eh?"

"Two nights," Hank replied, "I have Moll's Rock campsite reserved for two nights, according to this document and I . . ." Just then Herbert and Michelle emerged from their tent and Hank saw two of his best venison customers and a major reason for his Middle-East antler market, grinning from ear to ear; as his own jaw dropped along with his heart.

"Why if it's not High - Ronny Mus Algren," Herbert said playfully. "You didn't need to come all this way to sell me some venison. I would have been down in a week or two to place my order for the winter! Or has the Prince cut back on his order and you're tracking me down for some muscle?" This in reference to the equally inconvenient fact that Herbert had introduced Hank to his friend Prince Faud Ramaladi, who was now his Middle East partner in a thriving Supplements business with customers running from Saudi Arabia to Turkey, providing a whole host of products to the region that made his little operation the most sustainable deer farm in the United States and opened up the lecture circuit from Maine to Hawaii for Hank.

"Herbert!   . . . err and Michelle!" Hank exclaimed, hoping that his show of good cheer would mask his disappointment at not finding Moll's Rock quiet and empty. "I was just wondering how I was going to possibly eat all these beautiful trout and here you are. Seems like you, Herbert, have a way of showing up at just the right moment when I have a problem that requires a solution. I hope you're hungry."

"As long as you don't mind sharing our Bass", Michelle said holding up her stringer of largemouths and smiling broadly. "Good thing we have Charlie here to help us out and maybe even support three more carnivores," she said with a slight tilt of her head toward the canoe bearing Sarah, Daniel and a weaving, panting, white wolf named Cochise.

Chapter 14 The Campfire

Cochise was happily munching away on an uncooked trout as the five Homo sapiens lounged in various poses of satisfied stupor around the campfire.

"Isn't it dangerous for him to eat that bony fish?" Michelle asked Sasha.

"Not at all" she responded. "In the wild Cochise wouldn't have anyone to fillet his fish for him or do similarly with any kind of meat. In fact, as long as the bones are raw, dogs and wolves can eat pretty much anything. We feed him raw chicken and fish and anything that we can buy or catch because it's both healthy and safe. It's a whole lot less expensive than commercial dog food, and if things get particularly tight we can dumpster dive at a grocery store and almost always find some meat that has hit its expiration date. Truth is, most of the time the meat is perfectly good for humans as well. Federal regs require an expiration date that errs on the side of caution, so if you find meat or any other consumable that's only a few days past, it's likely that it's perfectly safe.

"I can't believe how stuffed I am." Daniel Roy groaned "and we even had a nice big trout for ol' Cochise here."

Making the assumption that Cochise was Daniel's dog, Henry said to him "That's one big dog, must weigh more than Sasha here. He a hybrid?" referring to an abbreviated term used to describe a wolf-hybrid, created by crossbreeding a wolf and some kind of domestic dog.

"Yeah," Daniel replied, "I'm guessing he's about a buck and a half." Sasha cut in making it clear that she was going to be at the center of this conversation.

"Just under that. Cochise here is my longest male relationship and he's not a hybrid, he's full-blooded Timberwolf from Isle Royale on Lake Superior. I tell people he's a hybrid because it's less scary to a lot of them and in the US it's not legal to have a domestic wolf, but on the Rez where I live, it's perfectly legal. Cochise was orphaned when he was just a few weeks old."

"Normally the researchers on Isle Royale would have let nature take its course and he would have starved to death but since I was going to be taking him off the island and it would not in any way affect their research by doing so, they allowed my two brothers and I to each adopt one wolf. I guess you could say he's mine or I'm his!"

She paused thoughtfully, "Truth is though, no one owns Cochise. He chooses to hang with me but he's free to come and go as he pleases. He usually hunts for himself and while I'm happy to have his company, I'm aware that the time may come when he goes off to do more than hunt."

"Isle Royale," Hank said, "I've read about that place. It's an island on Lake Superior where there is a population of Wolves and Deer . . . "

. . . "Moose" corrected Sasha.

"Right, right, right, moose" Hank continued, "seems at some point the lake froze enough to create a bridge from the island to the mainland and a small herd of moose with wolves - following their scent - made their way out to the island and got stranded there when ice-out came."

"Technically," Sasha corrected again, "there's no 'ice-out' on Lake Superior because there's no 'ice-in'. The lake is so large it effectively creates its own climate system and never freezes completely. That's why the moose and wolves on Isle Royale remain there.

"Turns out," Hank continued, breaking in like a tag team wrestler tagging back in and jumping into the ring, "it's a near- perfect ecosystem for studying the relationship between wolves and moose in their natural habitat. Because no one lives full time on the island and there are no human factors to interfere with the relationship it becomes a nearly pure ecosystem for studying the population dynamics and other cycles affecting both the wolves and the moose. As the moose population grows, the wolf population follows and when the wolf population gets too large and begins to eat more moose reducing the herd size, then the wolf population begins to decline as well in response to a lack of food."

"Every once in awhile an ice bridge forms that's strong enough for an animal or two to make their way to the island. Turns out that's good because it serves to enrich the genetic pool just enough to keep the health impacts of a shallow gene pool from creating existential threats to the population. As long as the change in population is only one or two wolves or moose making the adjustments to the study is simple enough but a big change would be problematic, throwing all of the scientific findings into question. Luckily, there have not been any large changes.

Sasha chimed in again, "During the winter of 1997, a wolf from Canada immigrated to Isle Royale. He crossed on an ice bridge that occasionally forms between Isle Royale and Canada. We knew him as 'the Old Grey One'. For fourteen years his presence was known only to our elders and a few members of the tribe known as the 'Keepers of the Wolf', responsible for maintaining the legends and lore of wolves among our people. He became one of the most successful wolves ever to live on Isle Royale, and he revitalized the population's genetic diversity. By the time the scientists and researchers figured out what had happened the Old Grey One had successfully sown his seed all over Isle Royale and the genetic health of the various packs dramatically improved. Our keepers of the Wolf have turned this into the story of how the Old Grey One saved the Island and his story will be told for generations making him as much a hero to our children as any great warrior. Perhaps the day will come when saving the island evolves to saving the world"

"Wow! Wolf porn." Herbert said, " I wonder if Big Island here on Umbagog has a similar thing going on?"

"This lake freeze completely," said Hank, "so the moose, deer and coyotes are free to come and go from year to year."

"Wolves too?" Michelle asked, punching Herbert in the shoulder for his wise-ass porn remark.

"Now that depends on whether you believe that wolves have moved back into New Hampshire," said Daniel. "If you ask New Hampshire Fish and Game they will tell you that there is no wolf population, except for those snuck in here by wild Iroquois women," he said winking at Sasha. "But they said that about coyotes for a very long time and then Mountain Lions too. We know there's a very healthy population of coyotes now. Much bigger than the western brand because they bred with ol' Cochise's kinfolk on their way across the country before they repopulated the Northeast. The Mountain lion is still a subject of debate in New Hampshire but the Fish and Game departments of New York, Massachusetts and Vermont have admitted to having a small population, though there is still some controversy over whether they've been here all along or have only recently escaped captivity or wandered over. I think it's just a matter of time before New Hampshire comes around."

Daniel continued, "There are those of us who want to give Fish and Game the benefit of the doubt on this, not about whether they are here but when they'll tell the public. The theory is that they won't admit they are here until they have a healthy enough population to sustain themselves and the Legislature is forced to pass legislation to protect them. Otherwise they would be hunted to extinction again before they had time to get a foothold."

"So by giving them the benefit of the doubt, as you say, you mean giving them credit for knowing but hiding the truth? Devious as opposed to stupid?" Sasha inquired.

"Something like that," Daniel responded, "though they would call it caution and an insistence on absolute proof of life."

"I like to think the wolf is here," he continued, "and I would sooner have Fish and Game deny it than to open it up before our conservation efforts can catch up. I wouldn't want to invite trouble. I guess it's the romantic in me. I want my North Country to be a place where eagles fly and wolves howl."

There was a slight pause as the group let that sink in but it was broken when Daniel let go a long mournful howl.

Cochise responded with a quizzical look and a tilt of his head and promptly joined in the chorus. Before long the entire crew was howling together joyously until Cochise had enough and he stood up, stretched his big front paws out, bowed slightly and then repeated the action rolling into a stretch of his back legs then trotted off.

"Speaking of Big Island," Hank said after the cacophony had ceased, "I saw a barge hauling huge white pine logs from there today."

Daniel leapt to his feet "They can't do that! They will endanger the raptors just as they're getting a foothold."

Hank continued "Well I followed the barge operator back to the shore and spoke with him, he's just trying to feed his family, doesn't even know who he's hauling them for; but I'm guessing he's the poor schmuck who will pay the price if he gets caught."

"I told him that he should cut and run while he can, but I don't know that he will. The money is very tempting for a guy like him."

Daniel was beside himself. "We've worked for too long re-establishing nesting pairs of Bald Eagles and protecting the small population of Peregrine and Osprey. This could ruin everything we've worked for."

Herbert chimed in, "If the Granite Skyway project goes through you won't have to think about that. Logging will be the least of your worries. With a trail of 150 foot steel towers crossing the border out of Canada and bisecting the state, the raptors will need to do some very fancy flying to avoid being fried by those high tension wires."

"Unless we do something about It.," a disembodied voice said.

The entire group looked at one another trying to figure out who had said this.

"If we don't stop Granite Skyway it won't just be the raptors who will be destroyed," continued the voice.

By now everyone had figured out the voice had come from the shadows just outside them in the darkened woods.

"Our entire way of life will be changed."

Thomas emerged from the woods looking like Jeremiah Johnson and the grizzly that stalked him all rolled into one.

"What the hell?" Stonebridge uttered as the others expressed similar sentiments of shocked surprise.

"Jesus H. Christ . . . Thomas!" Hank bellowed as he heaved himself off the ground. Walking toward the figure that had emerged from the woods and throwing his arms around the "Mountain Man" who had just scared the hell out of everyone.

"I figured you weren't going to show your pretty face with all these people here Thomas".

"I've been sitting against a tree for about an hour listening and trying to decide," Thomas said quietly, "but when the talked turned to Granite Skyway I knew that I had to put aside my natural aversion to crowds and say something."

"You know this guy Hank?" Herbert said with amazement, thinking about the scene in the parking lot.

"I've never known anyone to sneak up on Cochise," whispered Sasha in amazement as she watched her wolf who had quietly emerged from the woods along with Thomas, whose long arm reached down to scratch between the animal's ears.

"Yeah, we made friends about five minutes ago," Thomas said smiling; further shocking Sasha with the realization that he was able to hear her whisper, "The two of us have been sitting in the woods listening to all of you."

"Thomas and I were in the Rangers together. He was the brains and I was the brawn of the team," said Henry. "When we returned stateside he moved to the Great North Woods and I returned to the family farm. I see him whenever I come up this way but he doesn't do much traveling, what with Metallak and the dogs.

The puzzled look on the faces of the group with the mention of Metallak and the dogs made Henry realize that he was confusing everyone even more and he said "Well never mind, I'll explain everything to you later. Are you hungry Thomas? We've got plenty of chow, let's get you some."

Thomas said that he was, indeed, hungry and Michelle and Herbert hustled off to fix him a plate of food as he settled himself down on a log by the campfire and the group drifted back into quiet conversation.

As one of only two of the group from outside New Hampshire Charlie Stonebridge wanted to know about Granite Skyway. Sasha Brandt concurred and Michelle got the ball rolling as the most active member of what could be generously referred to as the opposition.

"Granite Skyway is a private project proposed to build a large electric transmission line from the Hydro-Quebec system of dams - including some newly proposed dams - it's intended to bring electricity to New York City and the southern regions of the megalopolis running down to Washington DC and Baltimore. The backbone of the project is a proposal to build a line of 150 foot transmission towers running straight down through the heart of the White Mountain National Forest and taking advantage of the public right-of-ways controlled by Polaris Electric, a partner in the project, even though the right-of-ways were purchased and maintained with taxpayer dollars over the years.

The proposal had cast a pall of uncertainty over the real estate business according to Michelle and in at least one instance had probably been responsible for the bankruptcy of one of the largest real estate developments in the state, a PGA quality golf course with its attendant homes and condominiums. "It's easy to understand why people are reluctant to make even a modest real estate investment if the view you are seeing today may become steel towers and humming transmission lines" Michelle said.

"But you did say the source of the electricity was hydropower didn't you," said Charlie Stonebridge. "It is, after all, renewable energy, at least, isn't it?"

"Well, yes and no," said Daniel Roy, who had just graduated from the University of New Hampshire in the Earth Sciences and Engineering program. "Not all renewable energy is created equally. Every form of energy - renewable or not - has its assets and liabilities and some is just more sustainable than others."

"My people are still having their land stolen from them in Canada for the development of those dams", said Sasha "and the growing incidents of cancer and mercury poisoning caused by the development of the dams is an ongoing tragedy."

"In the Rangers we'd see this big ol' transmission line as a fat easy target. Wouldn't we Thomas?" said Hank.

Thomas agreed, "I'm afraid terrorists and those who wish us ill would see it the same way."

Thomas went on to say that he was doing his small part to try and forestall the effort. "Yesterday I spent the evening pulling up grade stakes and removing ribbons that were placed by a survey crew in the region adjacent to the national border, but they will just bring another crew up and eventually they will have their way."

Herbert laughed as he thought about Thomas' wagon loaded with grade stakes. "Yeah and we saw you sabotage the utility truck parked along the road outside the IGA."

Thomas laughed sheepishly and said "It'll take a lot of us pissing in the gas tanks of Polaris trucks to make a dent in that fleet, and I think the job will be doubly difficult for the women. They aren't really built for it."

Chapter 15   The Trust

"So what do we do?" Herbert said.

"We fight," said Michelle, "we organize and we fight. There's already several groups organized. "

"Look", Herbert said, directing himself to everyone but Michelle, " Michelle and I have been debating this for a while now. She still believes in civic action. She thinks if people band together they'll be able to stop this travesty with their voices alone."

"Not their voices alone," Michelle protested, "They need to reach out to their elected leaders, to engage the public in the process, all that. Herbert, if you are going to air our dirty laundry publicly, at least get it right."

Herbert interjected, "Our debates on this aren't what I would consider 'dirty laundry' Michelle." He said. "I admire your optimistic viewpoint on this. Babe."

"Short of moving away, it seems as if nothing can be done to stop these people. They are the one percent and the ninety-nine don't stand a chance as near as I can tell. I have been planning to sell my place before the real estate values plummet - there is already a low hum and it's getting louder. Pretty soon the hum will be a dull roar. Real estate will be harder and harder to sell and people will start walking away from their homes. "

"I've already seen the signs," sighed Michelle. "Last week I was in the Citizen Guaranty Bank and watched as one of my neighbors, who has been trying to sell his house for a year now, walked in and just dropped his keys on the desk of a loan officer. 'It's your problem now', he said. It was heartbreaking. Tears were running down his face and his shoulders slumped as the sobs wracked his body. He and his wife raised their kids in that house, he was a volunteer coach for the elementary school's girl's basketball team and a volunteer firefighter and I never ran into a field trip where she wasn't a volunteer, sometimes with him."

"I can't imagine the bank can sustain too many of those hits either," Daniel said, poking the fire to stir the flames in the darkening void. "So the tragedy will roll through - and over - the community."

"The bigger banks can probably sustain the hits," Said Stonebridge, "But the community banks may be in trouble. I wouldn't be surprised if you saw them move to limit their losses in some way."

Hank was watching Michelle as she described the family and knew immediately who she was talking about. "Well there's only one community bank left in my town and they just announced that they were selling out to a much bigger bank."

" I repeat," Herbert said standing to his full 6 foot plus stature as the reborn flames rose from the hearth casting an orange glow on the scene - - "What do we do?"

"Well we have a problem," Thomas said scratching his beard thoughtfully. "The dynamics of the current debate favor the bad guys and if nothing else changes they'll get their approvals and railroad this through. Oh sure, they will have to make a change or two in their plans but they were already counting on that. "

Sasha had been very quiet as the discussion around the campfire became more animated. She was sitting with the wolf's big head on her lap, scratching that favorite spot between his ears. Now she spoke. "I'm not sure what you mean, Thomas."

"You can bet that they announced their intentions to construct this steel monster well into their own internal process. They surely built some things into the design and the payout that they knew they would have to give away or that they could sneak past us."

"We know they designed it as a hydra with a public utility, a group of private investors, and separate private business entity. That's not a coincidence. " Thomas continued. "You can bet they will be using the public utility to access public rights. They already tried to use eminent domain but the legislature and courts beat them back, but there will be other things they will try to slip into the mix down the road if they aren't already there."

"Of course!" Daniel exclaimed. "They knew there would be a huge public outcry when they announced this so they planned it through in advance. They loaded the initial plan with goats they never wanted or expected - things they could give away to make it look as if they were compromising; made it seem as if they were honest brokers in the process. But they were really red herrings disguised to mask the issues that really mattered to them. "

"They are already spreading money around." Said Hank. "Between advertising in every publication, making ad buys and donations in the electronic media and the Web, plus some well publicized donations to various groups trying to create jobs in the region to buy some 'good will', they are trying to give people the impression that public support is with Granite Skyway."

"They will make some concessions and there will be a well orchestrated movement in support planned to follow those concessions."

Herbert had remained quiet, almost sullen, for a while, clearly troubled by Michelle's reference to airing dirty laundry. When he spoke he spoke to everyone but to Michelle in particular.

"Michelle has made a strong case for getting involved with the existing groups," he said. The fact is I long - desperately - for the days when I believed the same thing. I long for the days when my glass was half full - not half empty. But I just don't feel that way any more. I feel like the world has changed, the ground has shifted under our feet and we are running out of time to stop it. "

Daniel chimed in "You mean to stop Granite Skyway Herbert?"

"That, yes, but much more than that, Daniel."

"The efforts of a handful of wealthy individuals and businesses to use lands procured through eminent domain with taxpayer funds for the purposes of running a massive electricity transmission system that they control, and they alone benefit from, is only one symptom of a much larger problem."

"In the past 30 years there has been a massive transfer of wealth in this country and despite what the wing nuts in Congress and Fox News try to foist on us, it HAS NOT been from the 'Haves' to the 'Have Nots'. It's been exactly the reverse. The wealthy plutocrats in this country have used political sleight-of-hand to stir silly debates within the public discourse while they proceeded to download the wealth of the nation into their bank accounts. While we were arguing about flag burning amendments to the Constitution, they were using the tax code to pay fewer and lower taxes. While we were fighting about English as the official language, they were hijacking the political process and electing people to Congress who would carry their water and extend their power."

Herbert continued, "In less than a generation the Republican party has purged its centrists and used the state directed redistricting process to gerrymander a nearly unstoppable majority position that virtually guarantees they will control the US House of Representatives for the foreseeable future. It's been so effective Stalin would have been proud. The Democrats were no better when they were in power."

"Oh yes, they were very good at it. Slick in fact." interjected Thomas. "As wages stagnated and taxes that fell more heavily on the wealthy were eliminated, more and more of the burden of everyday life fell upon the shoulders of those who could least afford it. Cities and towns that once received revenue sharing from the Federal and State governments were forced to rely almost exclusively on the property tax to fund everything from schools to repair of roads and bridges. Property taxes are the most regressive form of taxation and fall most heavily on the middle class and the poor. Take New Hampshire as an example. We live in a state that claims the lowest tax burden in the nation, but that is only when you average all income groups together. If you removed the wealthiest citizens from the equation leaving only the poor and middle class, New Hampshire citizens have one of the highest tax burdens in the nation. This is true in many states where the property tax is the primary revenue source for local needs. So there is little wonder that in many places citizens organize to control property taxes."

"Then when people call for cuts in government spending because their taxes have become unbearable, the plutocrats have their minions push for cuts to agencies that protect the purity of our water or air and protected companies that want to go even farther."

Thomas was on a roll now. "They would tsk tsk about the shame of it all as they cut funds for public education and state colleges and universities; They made it an act of treason to question the billions poured into advanced weaponry while homeless veterans went without adequate food and medical care. Families that once could afford to help their kids with college and take a yearly vacation found themselves forced to work two jobs just to make ends meet as their disposable income declined year after year."

"And now we face the prospect of a planet warming while they deny the role of humans in the process. It is a giant game of power chess. For years they have denied the reality of climate change and then as the scientific evidence turns overwhelmingly against them, they use the opportunity to propose a "green" power transmission system. Pointing to the use of renewable hydropower to give them the appearance of the moral high ground. It's the ultimate bait and switch. With generous helpings of hypocrisy washed down with a pint of hubris. "

"Granite Skyway is only one example of all this, there are similar proposals popping up all over the country", Herbert said, "but this is the place we can have an impact."

"Archimedes said *give me a place to stand and I will move the world* Granite Skyway is our place to stand and maybe in fighting this battle we can - in fact - move the world. But what I have been saying to Michelle," Herbert added, "is that speaking our minds is not enough. We can't stop them with words alone. We have to move the gravitational center of this fight to win. We have to be willing to take risks, maybe even go to jail. Are we willing to do that?"

"I can't hurt anyone," Michelle said, almost as if to herself.

"I would never ask you to," Herbert replied. "And it would turn people against us and our cause."

"Thomas replied, "Sometimes these things get away from us . . ."

Herbert reached for Michelle, "Michelle's right though, God knows I've hurt plenty of people in my past but it was always an act of self defense or war. Besides if we lose the hearts and minds of the people we won't have achieved anything. No, when you get right down to it, this is all about money. We have to be creative - to open up a new front in the battle that strengthens the hand of the opposition without alienating the public. We have to make Granite Skyway bleed money, and we have to bring the fight to the front page."

"The landing page," said Michelle, ever the millennium,

"Above the fold," said Stonebridge, himself a boomer,

A Loon's bittersweet cry echoed across the lake at that moment and found complete purchase in its path, for it had grown silent around the campfire at Moll's Rock. Each soul was taking the measure of its worth in a world where steel towers and humming transmission lines became the object of a child's awe.

"I'm in." Sasha said with quiet determination, not wanting to break the silence but feeling herself being drawn, as if by both feet, to this place. She stood as she said it, Cochise rising beside her.

One by one, wordlessly, the others rose until all of them stood around the fire.

Chapter 16 Songs of the Night

Daniel zipped the tent door as Sasha removed her sneakers. Cochise had curled up under the extra large fly that covered the tent and provided cover space for cooking in the rain if necessary. Generally he liked to be closer to Sasha but he didn't like the cramped space in the tent; and, after all, nights were for hunting. At some point he would steal away quietly and find something to supplement the trout and the scraps from the evening meal, something warm and filling.

A week had passed since Daniel and Sasha had met at the base of Mahoosuc Cascade. Sasha was hiking alone - well, with Cochise - joining up with Daniel to hike the Mahoosucs was a natural thing to do. Until now, though, the two had kept it light and friendly . . . friends with benefits as they say. Neither one, it seemed, was in the market for a partner but tonight Daniel rolled onto his side reaching over he brushed the hair out of Sasha's face and looked deep into her hazel eyes.

"You were incredible tonight Sash."

Sasha looked puzzled "What do you mean Daniel? I was just a part of the conversation. Nothing special."

His hand played through her hair and rubbed her cheek softly as he spoke: "No Sasha, I was mesmerized by you. Your words may have been few, but when you spoke, people listened . . . and I think it's more than your heritage at play. You are so sure and so focused . . . and when you and Cochise stood at the end. I was so proud of you, so inspired."

"I think some day your people will tell your story."

Sasha wrapped her arm around Daniel bringing his lips to hers, her tongue lightly running across his bottom lip. "Maybe it will be OUR story they tell Daniel." She said, a throaty whisper that reached deep into Daniel's soul. And then there were no more words.

****

Hank had set up his tent but the night was so clear and cool that he had decided to sleep under the stars. He was pulling his bag and his mattress pad out onto a grassy spot when he noticed Stonebridge doing the same. He called over, "Hey!

Charlie, I got a great spot here for doing some star gazing while you are drifting off, you're welcome to join me if you don't mind the company."

"Stargazing is always better when you have someone to share the moment." Stonebridge said, carrying his bag and pad over to join Hank. "Where did Thomas disappear to?"

"Thomas is not really the sleeping type, Hank replied, "more the napping type and he has a raft of animals including his moose Metallak that will need to be fed and watered. I'm guessing Metallak was tied up somewhere near the campsite here waiting for Thomas and he'll ride that Moose home if you can believe it." Just then they heard a crash in the thicket and the sound of something very big running through the bush . . .

"That would be him right now." Hank said.

With no light pollution to spoil the view, the stars were as bright as Hank had ever seen them and the Milky Way shown clearly overhead, as the two got comfortable. It was the perfect night for sleeping under the stars . . . it was September and the mosquitoes were practically gone. The moonless sky broadcast the light from the stars as crisp and clear as a laser light show, bringing the constellations into sharp relief on the inky backdrop. Stonebridge looked up at the Big Dipper pouring its black night into the cup of the little dipper and smiled. Certain things in life were constant - but damn few of them. This view of Ursa Major, at least from the standpoint of a mortal human, was a constant and he took great comfort in it. The two lay quietly for a time until Hank spoke.

"Feels a little weird to team up with all these lefties," he said. "Don't get me wrong, I'm in with both feet and my hands on my ass, but I guess it's weird to find myself in this position. Usually I'm trying to find a reason why everything they believe is a flaming pile of dog shit. Yet here I am. "

"I think the older we get, the more we begin to see there's a lot of gray area in our belief systems. This seems to be especially true when it comes to the environment - maybe it's because our shared experiences are so much the same when it comes to our world. A lot of other issues are viewed through a prism of life experience and social status or culture. They're harder to find common ground around." Stonebridge observed. "New Hampshire is my second home. I grew up in Pennsylvania but spent my summers here on Newfound Lake. Eventually I landed in West Virginia, mostly for the paddling I suppose. West Virginia has a pretty broad spectrum of beliefs but the one area where the ideological spectrum seems to be conjoined is when it comes to protecting the environment. "

"Guess that's true," responded Hank. "I was watching an eagle fish today when I was out doing the same. I have to admit that the feelings I got when I saw that handsome daddy deliver a wriggling trout to his nest of eaglets made me forget any of the rational notions that normally govern my life."

"I grew up with a fellow who often spent time here in the Great North Woods documenting the fight to restore nesting pairs of Bald Eagles. He used to say that he never felt closer to God than he did when he watched the flashing of an eagle's wings and talons as it skimmed over the water and snatched up a fish and then repeated the action as it delivered the fish to its eaglets."

"He traveled all over the world photographing for National Geographic, saw some of the most beautiful places you can imagine but always made his way back here. Here and his farm in Vermont. God he loved that old farm. Happiest I ever saw him was riding his old John Deere as he cut hay for his Percherons. "

"You couldn't be talking about anyone else but Micky Smith," Stonebridge said, "though I didn't know he owned Percheron draft horses."

"You knew Micky?"

"Knew him and admired the hell out of him," Charlie said. "I never saw his farm but the Percherons make sense, I'm betting they were just pets to him."

Hank responded, "Yeah, kind of the Hummer model of a lapdog. In the summers they would be on the farm where Micky could hang out with them. He had a summer office in the barn - - sort of a circle in the middle of their massive stall. If they weren't out grazing in the fields, chances are you would find them with their heads over the rail watching Micky at the computer. He would carry on a running conversation with them as he worked on his images on a big Mac, breaking every now and then to walk around and let the horses explore his pockets for hidden carrots and apples. They would smell them and then poke and prod him until he gave them up."

"He'd get such a kick out of telling people about how the massive dappled grey draft horses would spend their winters at another nearby farm where they had goats, emus, llamas, alpacas; and adopted burros and horses from that program out West where they save them when their population reaches over-capacity. He'd wrap up the story by saying he had traveled the world and this was the only place he knew of where a noun usually used to describe a season - winter - was used as a verb. He'd take a long piece of hay from a nearby bale and put it in his mouth and then, in his best Vermont old timer's impression, he would say: "Aeeyup, the boys heya spend summa' with me but they winta at the Merrill faarm and home for unwed, unwanted and unambiguously well-loved crittas."

Charlie laughed. He liked this fellow . . . a lot. And while there may be an ideological gap between them, he had a sense that he could trust Hank. They were wading into some unknown waters, or about to, and he suspected that trust was going to be a commodity that was both precious and critically important.

****

Herbert placed his hands under his head and stretched his arms to the side as Michelle pulled out her sleeping bag and fluffed it. "Should be good sleeping tonight," he said, "it's nice and cool."

"Herbert," Michelle said, "I'm scared. I know this is the time and a place for me to go outside my comfort zone. I feel it with every ounce of my being, but I'm just scared. I'm willing to take the risk of going to jail to stop this, but I've gotta know that you're with me to the bitter end. Gotta know that you won't fight this fight only to end up moving away when it's over - or before it's over."

Herbert reached over and brought her to his bare chest and as she laid her head down on him he said," Michelle hun, I lived a big life before I even came here. Most of it I can't even tell you about. Then, at the top of my game, I was laid low by a fucking tick the size of a pinhead. Not the Russians, not the Afghans loyal to the Kremlin, not some spook out for vengeance, a fucking tick! "

" When I came here I was a walking cauliflower, for chrissake, but you saved me. Your love saved me and this place saved me. The smell of pine needles on the drive on a spring morning, the feeling of the sun on an Indian summer day in Fall, the taste of a just-ripe Macintosh apple right off the tree, maybe as I watch the high school football game."

"This is my spot on the porch babe, as Castaneda said, and as much as I sometimes seem to push you away because of our age difference, the truth of the matter is - it's only right if you're here with me . . . and if we can grow old together with the sun setting over the Whites; the way they should be, wild and free, unscarred by 150 foot monstrous towers. I'm willing to risk more than jail for this, I'm willing to risk my life. Of all the things I've risked my life for this is by far the most important. I'm not doing it because some jarhead with more stripes than me ordered me to, or some bureaucrat. I'm doing it because my heart is telling me to save this place that God made."

He paused a moment and took in a deep breath. "If these are my last moments on this planet, I plan to love you as hard as I can, to live like I have never lived before, and to fight like I plan to return; Reborn from the cosmos in the warm embrace of God . . ." He paused for a moment and continued "Sasha's Great Spirit that watches over this sacred place."

Michelle looked at him, almost puzzled, and then she smiled, "Not a peach inspediment in sight," she said. "I feel as if I have waited my whole life to hear someone say something so beautiful and powerful to me."

She kissed him deeply and in one motion threw her leg over him and drew him into her.

Chapter 17 Stumbled Upon

"Hello at the campsite!"

Linda Levy paddled her kayak closer to land. She was staying at the Balsams Hotel while she was doing some research for a book she was hoping to write. On a whim she left Max lounging on her bed back at the hotel with a "do not disturb" placard on the door to prevent him from attacking the maid and she drove down to where the Androscoggin River flowed out of Lake Umbagog for an early morning paddle while most of the world was still asleep.

She had paddled up the river from the Errol dam where she thought she had recognized Herbert Johannsen's Jeep parked. It would be a weird coincidence if Herbert and Michelle were up here too she thought. She had met the two when Michelle had rented her a little cottage on Stinson Lake a few summers ago and ever since she had tried to spend time with them whenever she was up in New Hampshire.

But before long all thoughts of her two friends took second place to her sense of wonder at this deep green wonderland. The thick boreal forest surrounded the river, black fading to green into blue, with only a wetland here and there marking the entrance of a small tributary. Kingfishers with their undulating flight paths darted from river to bank and back again among massive dead trees that seemed to grow out of the water in unexpected places. She made a mental note to ask someone how this happened. The trees also provided nesting spots for herons, eagles and hawks that were busily flying back and forth from their forays for food to their nests as their noisy clutches came alive with the rising sun. Mergansers, Wood Ducks and Mallards plied the waters with their ducklings in tow, while a momma Loon cruised down the river, close to the bank in case she needed to make a fast exit. As Michelle got closer she noticed the Loon chicks were riding on the back of their mother. She had heard about this but had never seen it before and the sight of it sent a jolt of electric joy through her.

She had barely been on the water ten minutes when she came upon a bull moose up to his withers in the river. The big fellow would sink his head into the water and come up with a mouthful of water plants and munch away unconcerned at her approaching boat. Several long strands of what looked like water lilies or maybe pickerelweed hung from his huge rack making him look whimsical despite his massive size. Given that it was the beginning of rutting season she would not have wanted to meet this big guy in the woods, she thought to herself. However, immersed in the water it should be a safer situation. Still she gave him a wide berth. No need to prove anything.

She paddled on and turned east then slightly south into the lake heading toward what the map labeled Moll's Rock. She had packed breakfast and planned to sit on the rock and eat before she turned around to head back to the hotel to shower and get ready to visit some folks who she hoped could confirm a story she was chasing down. As she got closer to Moll's Rock she realized the campsite was occupied. Then she thought she saw Herbert's tall frame among them - - she took a chance and called out to the shore.

"Well if it isn't Officer Levy." she heard in a distinctive voice, part panther, and part wood sprite with just a little drunken leprechaun thrown in for good measure; as Herbert's head peered over Moll's Rock at her. "I should have known you'd show up when we started to cook", he said, a crooked grin lighting up his black eyes and devilish face.

"I thought I saw your Jeep back at the parking lot Herbert, but then I figured Michelle wouldn't dare take you some place where your wild man instincts would be summoned forth. Or did she bring you out here to set you free? I hope Fish and Game doesn't catch her releasing non-native species in the White Mountains. She'll end up in the hoosegow for sure."

Michelle's voice sang out from behind the rock. "I was planning on calling those guys from *The Search for Bigfoot on Animal Planet,*" she said. "I was pretty sure there was some serious coin in it for me, especially when they hear him howling in the woods. They would declare Bigfoot found. Come to think of it, they might be right."

Michelle came out from behind the outcrop, smiling broadly as Herbert waded into the water and steadied Linda's kayak while she stepped out and scrambled up onto the shore. Linda scanned the campsite and saw what looked like a small jamboree in progress.

"It's a bit of a story," Michelle said casting a look that was a mix of uncertainty, fear and anxiety toward Herbert.

Herbert jumped in "We'll fill you in as we get breakfast Linda, but for now pull up a log and tell us what brings you to the Great North Woods."

Linda sat on a log facing the fire and Michelle, glad for the chance to escape to gather her wits, headed off to begin the process of gathering breakfast donations from all the members of the group. Herbert meanwhile began making a fire by balling up a handful of very small dry pine branches and placing them atop a pile of birch bark he had gathered from the ground before Linda had arrived. He avoided the subject of the group's new raison d'être by conducting a running commentary on his fire building process.

"We call this a tinder ball because it catches very quickly and in conjunction with birch bark will burn even if it's pretty wet. Then it's only a matter of picking the right wood from the forest floor to create the perfect cooking fire. "Birch bark will burn no matter how wet it is if you peel it thinly enough"

He paused and looked at her. "You'd think that maybe I learned all this in the service but they never took the purist approach when a gallon of white gas was just as effective and didn't take a tenth of the effort; No I learned it from Zach Roy who had to be able to build a fire in the pouring rain to graduate from the camp he went to over on Newfound Lake.

"I was just climbing with him yesterday," Linda said. "He's 18 and climbing circles around me and most of the folks out there. He's just a natural. I heard he was the same paddling a kayak too. Funny thing is, he doesn't care . . . he's in it for the pure joy of it. "

Reaching into his pocket Herbert extracted a dollar bill, gazed at it for a moment as he flattened it out and then handed it to her. Linda gave him a puzzled look and then said "Uh-oh, I stumbled on something, right?"

"Let's take a walk counselor." Herbert said.

Chapter 18   The Breakfast Club

By the time Herbert and Linda returned to the cooking circle most of the crew had gathered around and were busily engaged in the process of turning four or five individual breakfasts into a group meal. Michelle had given everyone the heads-up about Linda and there was a sense of anticipation coupled with anxiety.

"Good morning!" Herbert greeted the group. "For those who don't know her, this is Linda Levy. Linda is a Boston police officer and an Attorney licensed to practice in New Hampshire and Massachusetts, among other states. She has something to say to the group."

"Good morning everyone," Linda said smiling broadly. "The first thing you should understand is I have no law enforcement authority as a police officer in New Hampshire. I do, however, have the authority to practice law in New Hampshire and I have agreed - at least tentatively until you all have the opportunity to discuss it among yourselves - to represent your group. I agree with you, the construction of this transmission line, as proposed at least, would be an existential threat to New Hampshire's scenic beauty and tourism appeal. I believe I can make a competing harms case on your behalf, if necessary, but of course I can't guarantee its success.

"It wouldn't be Civil Disobedience if you could," Daniel said.

"True enough," Linda said. "However, you should understand, I may not succeed if called upon and ultimately I'm probably the only one here who is not in danger of being arrested and sentenced for what you are - in theory - contemplating, and even I, may not be immune."

She continued: " I suggest you talk it over and make a decision, today if possible, and let me know.

"No need for talking 'far as I'm concerned," Hank said, "If Herbert trusts you, I trust you, though I make it a policy not to trust lawyers generally."

A murmur of agreement spread through the group.

"Then let's break bread! " said Sasha, and she moved toward the fire and took up a casty with a scrambled eggs mixture that included various donations from the crew and started dishing it out.

"This is great Sasha," said Michelle "what's the orange leafy thing here? It has an interesting flavor, sort of nutty with a hint of perfume.

Sasha pointed to a plant growing off to the side of the grassy area.

"The last Day Lilies of summer" Sasha said. They have, as you said, a light nutty flavor with just a hint of perfume and they add color to a dish that's mostly in the brown range." Then summoning up her best Julia Child voice she said, "if only we had a little sherry to add it would be just perfect!"

Daniel laughed. "Now I've seen it all, the Iroquois Julia Child. Next thing you know Hank here will be playing Jane Fonda and doing workout videos with his deer!"

"Fat chance of that." Hank spat. "Hanging out with you pinkos is 'work out' enough."

"Oh-oh " said, Linda. "Do I sense some discord?"

"Not even a whiff." replied Hank. "Just keeping them honest Counsellor. If this one's for the history books, I don't want them reporting I lost my marbles and veered left in the final moments."

"There will be NO final moments Hank." Linda replied in mock seriousness.

Once again . . . from the woods: "Sometimes these things get away from us." Thomas said as he emerged from the bush. Sasha handed Thomas a plate and introduced him to Linda.

While Sasha was making the introduction, Linda began to grow restless and look around. She surreptitiously pulled Sasha aside. "Where do I pee?" she said.

Sasha pointed to the woods. "Pick a tree, any tree," she said. And Linda beat a hasty retreat.

Suddenly there was an ear-piercing scream from the woods and Linda came running out before anyone could respond. She ran up to the group breathlessly. "Mmmm . . . Moo... Moose! There's a huge Moose in the woods right there!" she said pointing to the spot from which she had just emerged.

Thomas who had watched Linda heading into the woods to take care of business smiled with anticipation as he watched her dance with Metallak unfold. Finally, after he had wrung as much delight and humor from the moment as he could, he stepped forward and said, "it's ok, nothing to worry about, just old Metallak. He's my companion and my ride."

Linda looked at him as if he had just told her the trees were made of green cheese. Thomas took her hand and she reluctantly followed him back into the woods. The others, who had heard tales of this moose but, with the exception of Herbert and Michelle, had never set eyes on him, all followed in procession. "Linda, everyone, meet Metallak."

Sure enough, tethered to a tree just inside the tree line, was an immense bull moose with a 12-point rack that must have been five feet across. Metallak stood almost six feet at the shoulders his huge head adding another foot or two onto his frame.

"I rescued Metallak fifteen years ago when his momma was killed by a logging truck", Thomas said. "He was so young he could barely navigate around on those spindly legs - if you think they look gawky now, you should have seen that little critter. He would have died for sure if I'd just walked away. So I took him back to my cabin and made a deal with my neighbor for enough milk over the next six months to get him to where he could eat solid food.

"He's named after the last member of the Megalloway tribe who lived here among the white settlers as an old man. He was reputed to have a moose that served as both his ride and his Seeing Eye service animal during the final years of his life - they say he lived to be well over a hundred. Some accounts say 125 years but there were no birth records among any American Indian tribe at the time."

"By the time my Metallak was eating solid food, I realized I was not going to be able to teach him what he needed to survive the woods on his own; and he and the dogs had become pals which did not bode well for giving him a natural aversion to coyotes, wild dogs or wolves. So I trained him to pull my donkey cart and later fitted him with this makeshift saddle and bridle and began riding him around."

"Can I touch him?" Linda asked giving voice to the question on everyone's mind.

"He's a love hound," said Thomas "Nothing he likes better than attention. He especially loves to be scratched under his chin." He demonstrated and Metallak stretched out his neck in obvious pleasure, making low, soft chuffing sounds.

The entire crew gathered around the moose, each picking a spot and caressed him from every angle. "I'd say that's about the closest he's ever going to get to heaven," Thomas said, beaming.

Gradually the crew drifted, one at a time, back to the cooking area and helped themselves to coffee and tea that had been set up by Sasha.

"Daniel drifted over to Thomas. "Doesn't Fish and Game give you a hard time about having a moose as a domestic pet?"

"Nah," Thomas replied grinning broadly, "they would have to admit they could be domesticated and believe me that would be more trouble than they want to take on. Sometimes those guys do the right thing for all the wrong reasons."

Daniel and Thomas returned to the group in time to hear Herbert ask Linda what she was doing up north so far from her usual haunt around Rattlesnake Mountain.

"The short answer," she said, "is research for a book I'm writing. Don't ask me to explain it too much because I'm still looking for the unified field theory that draws all of the stories in my book into one thematic compendium but in short I'm working to tell interesting stories about politics and rural life at the grassroots level. It all started with a visit to the Rumney Historic Society Museum, where I saw a photo of a bunch of people in coveralls standing in front of a steam engine and train."

"According to the docent - I guess that's what you call a historic society volunteer - back in the early nineteen-hundreds a State Representative from the Baker River Valley had conceived of this idea of asking everyone in town for the Old Home Day celebration to dress up in coveralls to pose in front of a huge railroad engine. Everyone thought it was a great idea and for some time they talked about how Representative Hill had set up that Old Home Day Photo. That is, until they found out he had taken that photograph and made copies he then spread far and wide throughout the State of California where he claimed it was a photo of the employees in a new mining company in which he was selling stock. He had concocted some story about a mine that had the richest deposits of Beryl in the world and they already had a contract with the US Government for all the Beryl they could mine. Since it was the Federal Government it was somewhat classified information and they would probably have trouble finding out much about it, that's why he was hired to sell the stock."

"What happened to him?" Michelle asked. "By the time word got back to the folks in his hometown, he had sold several million dollars of stock and simply vanished. They never did find him, he just took off with the money."

"That story sort of whet my appetite and I began to look for leads to other interesting stories and follow them up. I'm following up a story here that has been passed around the Boston PD for almost 40 years so the trail is pretty cold, and I don't know how much of the story I can get confirmed, but I'm giving it a shot.

"Well don't keep us waiting," Hank said. "Let's hear it."

"Yeah," Sasha said, "Dish girl!"

"Well, I guess I can tell the story without names since that will protect the innocent or guilty, as the case may be. This story came down through the force in Boston because the young state police officer from New Hampshire ended up in Massachusetts and use to tell the story to his new comrades in arms, they loved re-telling the story and it was about New Hampshire so they wouldn't get into trouble telling it."

She continued. "During most of the twentieth century Concord's biggest hotel and the watering hole for legislators, lobbyists and the "in-crowd" was a place called the Highway Hotel. If there was a deal made, a bureaucrat paid off, a Senator or member of the House banging boots with an intern - as we would say in the cop shop - chances are it was happening at the Highway Hotel."

One evening after the legislative session a group of about five Senators gathered for dinner at the Highway Hotel. They began with a couple rounds of drinks bought for them by two lobbyists. Then the House Majority Leader, who was not so surreptitiously sleeping with the lobbyist for one of the last remaining railroad companies, decided he would buy them a couple more rounds. Possibly so they would forget to watch them when they slipped up to their room a little later."

"At this point it was about 10 and dinner seemed like a waste of a good buzz so they just kept drinking until 1am when the Highway Hotel bar closed. Now, by this time they were feeling no pain and enjoying themselves too much to quit over a little thing like *last call* and closing time, so one of the Senators said he had a well stocked bar at his house in Berlin. He suggested they move the party north. Normal folks, especially ones not half in the bag, would have taken stock and decided that Berlin was a bridge too far for them - after all it's a two hour drive - but these guys were too drunk to be rational."

"The five Senators packed into a van and headed north . . . on the southbound lane of Interstate 93."

"Hollllly shit!" said Hank.

"They could have killed someone," said Sasha.

"Did anyone stop them?" asked Daniel.

"This was well before cell phones," Linda continued, " so by the time someone had gotten off the highway and found a phone to call the police, they were well on their way and apparently still unaware they were traveling in the wrong lane. The State Police received a series of calls from folks who had called to report a van traveling north on the southbound lane so they were able to track them but, as you might imagine, catching them without creating an even greater danger for people driving south on 93 was not a simple task. They couldn't just put a bunch of cruisers in the southbound lane chasing them. Instead, they had to time it so they could make a roadblock safely in one spot to stop them. This way they could place a few cruisers

83

with their lights flashing in the breakdown lanes to slow down the traffic and then scoop them up safely at a prearranged spot. After a couple of near misses, in more ways than one, they got the hang of the timing but they didn't manage to catch up with them until they reached Ashland, exactly in the geographic center of the state. They stopped the van and arrested the lot of them. "

Linda continued, "They took them south to Tilton and locked them up in the one cell the town had."

Hank was looking skeptical. "I was not do young that I wouldn't remember this if it had happened, he said. "It would have been the biggest scandal in a long time."

"True," Linda responded. "This would have been fodder for the papers in Boston even. But, as it happens the Senator who was driving used his one call to reach out to the Chairman of Senate Finance who was in his car and on his way to Concord within minutes. And he wasn't abiding by the speed limit. He was driving that winding Rte 10 like a bat outta hell when he, too, got pulled over by a State Police Cruiser. "

The Senator was out of his car before the police officer and he was holding a large piece of paper in his hand. He pointed a finger at the young 'Statie' . . . who must have known he was in for a pile of shit when he stopped the car with Senate plates going almost a hundred mph.

" '*You get the Commissioner on the horn right now.*' The Senator yelled at him."

"The surprised young State Police officer decided he had best comply with the Chairman of Senate Finance. So he did, although they had to patch him through to the Commissioner's home where he was still asleep at 4am. "

"When the officer had the Commissioner on the line he reached out to hand the radio handset to the Senator who promptly waved him off."

" '*I don't want to talk to him,*' He said, '*I want you to tell him what I have in my hand.*'"

"The officer clicked his handset on and said '*It looks like a blueprint . . . PAUSE . . . of the new Police Standards and Training Academy building, sir . . . and your new Headquarters building,*' he added. At this he seemed to almost smile, though he quickly composed himself and became serious."

" '*Now you tell him what I'm doing*' the Senator said, raising his voice a few more decibels. He proceeded to rip the blueprint in half, once, then twice and then again. He stood there, red faced, as the torn sheets fluttered to the ground."

" 'Now you tell him those Senators had better be out of jail, with no charges filed, by the time I get to Concord, or I'll see to it his precious buildings will be nothing more than a wet dream by the end of the day.' "

Linda wrapped it up with a bow. "At 1 pm when the Senate was gaveled into session, everyone was present and accounted for and not one member of the press was any the wiser. Later that afternoon they passed the bill for the new Police Standards Academy and the Commissioner's Headquarters."

"Jeeezzus" Stonebridge half-whistled, half-whispered. "How the hell did they keep that quiet?"

"I doubt they could have pulled it off nowadays", Linda said. "But back then there was no Internet, no social media, no Buzzfeed or Drudge Report. They were a mix of Democrats and Republicans so there was no political advantage to be had. And if anyone can keep something secret, it's the police - - Especially back then. "

A hush fell over the group no doubt accompanied by each member thinking his or her own thoughts, until Linda broke the silence.

"I'm up here to verify as much of the story as I can and then I'll have to decide how much artistic license I will take with what can't be verified. This one is particularly hard because it happened so long ago and it's a fairly lengthy story with a lot of moving parts."

Some stories are long and complex and some are quite simple." She continued, hoping to get everyone's brain working in a different direction.

"Like the story of Steffan O'Farrell who was running for Boston City Council when he was accosted on the street by an older Boston Brahmin woman who chewed on his ear over something completely inconsequential. He stopped her in the middle of her rant and said, 'Excuse me ma'am but are you registered to vote? She said 'why no' and was about to launch back into her complaint when he flipped her the bird and said, 'Then Fuck you!' "

"This story," said Linda, " was pretty easy to confirm because he was so forceful that people heard him for several city blocks. Steffan had already developed a little bit of a reputation, as it happens, so a core of legends had begun to grow around him. There was the time he apparently got tired of being hectored while he was standing on a street corner with a campaign sign and waving at the traffic. They call this a 'visibility' event." Linda said. " At some point his patience wore out and he dropped trow right there and mooned a car full of teenagers who had come around to heckle him for a second time."

She continued: "So, here I am in the Great North Woods looking for answers to something that happened almost 40 years ago. I've always wanted to stay at the Balsams, so I made a reservation for a few nights there and decided I would pamper myself a little. As good luck would have it, while I was in the Spa I ran into a woman who was there because Polaris Electric and the partners in the Granite Skyway project were having a meeting there tomorrow night. They had come up early so her husband could play eighteen holes at the Balsams golf course and she was going to be spending her time immersing herself in spa treatments and massages."

Linda was about to continue with her mission description but she realized something she had said had gotten the attention of the group and they were excitedly talking among themselves.

"A meeting tomorrow night eh? Sounds like just enough time for us to put together a special reception for them," Herbert said. "Hank! You reserved this spot for three days right?"

"And it was going to be a nice quiet retreat until I found you granola munchers squatting on my spot!" Hank said with a wry smile. "If you lefties don't mind taking marching orders from someone who leads with his right foot and carries a little more common sense in his bag-o-tricks, I think I have an idea for our first dance with the devils."

Linda was already grabbing her paddle, "This is where I get off folks," she said. "I don't want to know in advance what you are doing unless it's absolutely necessary. Besides I have an appointment with a genuine hero. A fellow named Carrigain who I used to listen to on National Public Radio doing reporting from the war in Kosovo."

The group gathered around the embers of the breakfast fire and listened as Hank outlined his idea. They had a little more than 24 hours to pull it all together so with some discussion they divided up the tasks and by noon they were all engaged in the preparation.

Chapter 19 The Day Before Tomorrow

The morning sky lapped into the cloudless dark night in silvercast waves, unfolding from the night sky, yielding to the light, as Daniel slipped the canoe into the water and Cochise bounded into the bow position. He smiled as the white wolf took up a position in the front, like the figurehead of an ancient mariner's ship, as they moved out onto the lake. Sasha was still sleeping in the tent and Daniel felt the need for some quiet time. He had a lot to think about.

Only a week before he was the prime architect of his future.
Just out of college he was planning on taking the next twelve months to travel the world, the way the kids from Australia and New Zealand did.

They called it Walkabout, adopted from the Maori and aboriginal traditions when a young man would venture out into the world in search of his place within it. Today, both men and women in the lands "down under" regularly did it. Daniel was introduced to Walkabout a few summers before when he was a hutsman in the Appalachian Mountain Club system of huts in the Presidential Range, the most dramatic peaks in the White Mountains. He had met a small group of people traveling through who were from Australia. Some of them had been traveling together for months and others had only just joined them. The more he learned about Walkabout the more he came to see it as an almost organic extension of the countries from which they came - young people branching out around the world coming together here and there into larger elements and then dividing off and moving in separate directions. Dividing, morphing, joining, like huge bacterium glimpsed from space.

The idea of living the life of a vagabond was incredibly exciting to him. He would be like Whitman, adventuring, writing, and living large. Of course he had the same dreams most young men did of starting his own life, with his own place and a mate, eventually even kids, but he wasn't in any great hurry on that front. He had some living to do before he moved onto that phase of his life. Thus, the idea of an unencumbered adventure across the globe was thrilling and until that fateful day beneath Mahoosuc Cascade that is where he was heading.

Now he was staring down the barrel of an entirely different future.

It scared the hell out of him.

It was also the most exciting thing that had ever happened to him.

Things were moving very fast with The Trust and with Sasha.

A breeze rippled the water as he dipped his paddle in and propelled the boat forward. He was captivated by the pure power of the moment and the flow of power within him. He was in a state of FLOW.

Flow is one of the newest words in the lexicon of psychology. Everyone is familiar with the traditional definition of flow, equivalent to movement. But the Term "Flow" now also had a new theoretical meaning - - that state of being where a person was at the peak of their performance. Where a nearly trance-like state envelops the individual putting them fully and totally in the moment and the experience.

Flow is the mental state in which a person performing an activity is fully immersed in a feeling of energized focus, full involvement, and enjoyment in the process of the activity. In previous years actors, artists, and athletes, who most often experienced FLOW, referred to it as "being in the zone" That special place where mind, body and experience become one and all else is swept aside.

Usually Daniel found himself in this state of Flow when he was rock climbing or kayaking. . Something requiring all of his attention and focus; something that placed him on the edge, where he was more fully alive than he was at any other moment of his life. But here he was paddling placidly on Lake Umbagog and fully engaged in the moment as if he were on the most difficult ascent of Cannon Cliff or running the Basin at high water. It made sense when he thought about it. The state of Flow did not require he be staring death in the face. There were also occasional moments when a state of Flow was achieved on a purely psychological or mental level, the way a Yogi might achieve a higher level of thought through meditation or the peace he felt when he was hiking and experiencing each moment completely as the peak baggers went panting by, oblivious to the pure joy of the experience.

A shadow passed over him floating across the water and drawing his attention upward. He shaded his eyes from the low slung morning sun and looked up to see a bald eagle, perhaps 100 feet above him. Despite the fact the Bald Eagle had made a miraculous recovery here in the Great North Woods it was actually the first time he had ever seen one in the wild and the excitement of the moment nearly caused him to lose his balance in the canoe.

It was so much bigger than he had imagined, bigger than the turkey vultures and hawks he often saw when he was hiking or the ravens that hung out at Madison Hut on the side of Mount Adams in the Northern Presidentials.

Both he, and now Cochise, watched transfixed as the massive bird rode the air currents, never once flapping its wings. One moment it would be tacking like a schooner to the left and then it would simply tilt its body and catch an updraft from the warming waters of the lake and the next moment it would have risen 50 feet higher and started carving a second graceful arc in another direction. Daniel had heard friends and his father speak reverently about the way this bird would ride the wind and he was raised on the ballads of John Denver and Dan Fogelberg celebrating their dominion in the Rockies. But nothing could have prepared him for the near religious experience of actually seeing one.

At this moment the graceful movements of this minion of the morning seemed to have but one purpose, to track the movements of this strange craft and it's even stranger contingent. Glancing around, Daniel realized they had paddled into an area that contained the bird's rookery and this was the first protective action of a concerned parent. He couldn't tell if it was dad or mom running the protective play, for unlike many other birds where the males and females sported different plumage making them easy to differentiate, the distinctive plumage of the Bald Eagle - its head of white feathers - was found on both sexes.

Carefully, Daniel used a sweep stroke to bring the stern of the boat around the bow pointing it away from the nesting area. He took two powerful strokes to give the boat some forward momentum and then shipped his paddle so he could continue to observe the eagle as it continued to ride the wind. His mind wandered to Sasha and her stories of her grandfather who often spoke of the "oneness" of things in nature. Surely he would have described this eagle as one with the air and the wind. At least an hour had elapsed since he and Cochise had first seen the eagle and Daniel was yet to see its wings move except as rudders in the air, carrying the bird across the arc of the sky and lifting it rapidly up to again harness gravity and the currents of air to its purpose.

Daniel lifted his paddle and took a few more powerful strokes, bearing them still farther from the nest, and then in the time it took for him to take his strokes the eagle was nothing more than a dot on the end of an exclamation point.

Cochise made a yip that caught his attention and Daniel saw Sasha waving to them from the shore so the "boys" headed in.

"Nice paddle?" Sasha inquired catching the canoe as they came in to land.

Daniel was shaking his head and smiling as he looked at this beautiful woman who had come into his life - a lot like an eagle on the wind he thought. "I saw my first Bald Eagle in the wild today Sash. It was magnificent. I had gone out to do some soul searching and never had time to do anything more than to watch as he - or she - rode the wind. But I think somehow what I was seeking to find - found me instead."

"Cryptic" Sasha said "but I have learned never to be surprised at the speed with which brother eagle can deliver a message. You were given the rare gift of a sign. The Bald Eagle is considered by my people to be a very good omen."

Earlier on the day of the meeting, as they made their way from the Moll's Rock Campsite to the landing where the logs were stored before they were picked up and delivered to the mill the group had pulled their boats up onto a grassy river bank and ate some sandwiches as Hank reviewed the mission plan and Stonebridge described the plan for getting everyone out after their mission was completed. The plan was to creatively re-park the vehicles belonging to the investors and attendees from the Polaris Electric meeting at the Balsams to an opening on Big Island where the illegal logging operation was conducted. This allowed them to both carry off their own mission and to expose the timbering operation at the same time.

Hank had been trying to come up with a plan for exposing the logging from the moment he had come across it. When Linda Levy had come to them with the information about the investors meeting he saw an opportunity to expose the logging operation and save his beloved raptors and - at the same time - blow a lot of smoke into the air that would serve to mask their own identities. A call to the driver of the barge and one other quick call to a local friend who had a car transporter and he was ready to unveil his plan to the members of The Trust. He outlined the plan as they sat eating their lunch . . . sure to include contingency plans in the event they were interrupted before they were able to complete the mission. He had broken the responsibilities up into parts based on timing and location. Daniel and Sasha would replace the two kids who were serving as valets at the Balsams and would be responsible for seeing to it the vehicles were loaded onto the transporter, to be driven by Herbert who had some experience driving similar vehicles in Afghanistan. Hank and Thomas would supervise the lakeside landing and the transport of the cars from the landing to the island. Stonebridge would be responsible for the exit strategy including contingencies if needed.

After wrapping up his briefing Hank turned to Charlie who explained the exit strategy.

Hank would leave his boat parked at the loading area in case they were forced to make a water retreat because the world had gone to shit and the authorities were closing in. Hanks bass boat was really only certified for three so if they ended up making a water retreat they were going to be like a tub of immigrants coming ashore in Miami. It would be dicey, but it could be done.

Three cars would be left at the landing area. If they were forced to make a water retreat the owners of the cars, Herbert, Daniel and Stonebridge would claim they were among the people who had lost their cars to the thieves. They could only speculate that the scoundrels were forced to evacuate before they were able to move the last three vehicles to the island. It was risky but it was only in the event all else failed and they had to go with plan D. D for DEEP. DEEP for "deliver each and everyone's (ass outta' here) pronto."

If everything went according to plan everyone but Hank and Thomas would exit by car, drop Sasha at her car at the boat launch in Errol, and then head home with a plan to regroup in a week at Zipline Adventures in Lincoln for some fun and a strategy meeting. Hank would take Thomas back to Moll's Rock where he had left Metallak and he too would return home, wherever that was. Hank would get some sleep and then spend one more day fishing and one last night alone at Moll's Rock - to make sure no one was able to track them to the campsite - playing the part of cleaner; triple checking for any clues they might have left behind.

Part 4 - Beginnings

Chapter 20   The Balsams

The entry to the Balsams was bathed in a warm golden light, a combination of effects from gas lamps, warm incandescents and solar lighting, throwing an early evening glow on the paths and stairs leading into the hotel as darkness descended on the town of Dixville. The dark outline of Old Speck Mountain, the last in the Mahoosuc range (or the first depending on your direction) loomed in the distance as the last rays of sunlight reached the Great North Woods, bathing the summit in purple hues fading to black beneath. From a bird's eye view, the lights of the Balsams filtered through the wilderness, a golden glow in a sea of blackness, like the last embers in a dying fire.

Dixville, though only a small, unincorporated town of eleven full time souls, cast its own unique glow on the national political stage as the first town to vote in both the Presidential elections and the storied New Hampshire First-in-the-Nation Presidential Primary.

By special dispensation from the legislature, Dixville was allowed to vote before everyone else in New Hampshire and the Nation. It wasn't because a special law was written for Dixville that would cause a small constitutional crisis. It was, simply, that the change in law permitted any town - and ONLY those towns - whose residents had ALL voted, to close its polls once all residents had voted. While the laws governing polling hours and election days were all within the purview of the individual states, the real basis of the legal issue resided with the United States Constitution - specifically what is commonly referred to as the "Equal Protection Clause". In short the Equal Protection Clause, the fourteenth Amendment, declares that no law shall apply unequally to different citizens or groups of citizens. Passed in 1868 it was - at first - a response to the emancipation of slaves, but the language of the clause was not race specific and before long the broader interpretation had taken root and the accepted norm was it applied to all citizens and all groups that could be identified. Accordingly, New Hampshire's Legislature passed a law applying to all citizens but could, as a practical matter, only be exercised by the smallest and most organized of towns.

Thus Dixville, presuming all its residents were healthy, present and accounted for, was able to cast its votes and be counted before any other town at 1 minute after midnight, or thereabouts, on Election Day. This put them on the map every four years and made them one of the towns almost every candidate for President wanted to visit. The vote occurred in a special room designated as the "Ballot

Room" and the Ballot Room as it happened was located in the Balsams Grand Resort.

The Balsams Hotel is what is known as a "Grand Hotel". The Grand Hotels are a dwindling group of large and majestic old hotels around the country - most often found in resort areas away from the maddening crowds.

While they are found in many states, the Grand Hotels of New Hampshire were unique in that they were, for a time, the most numerous and well known such hotels in the country. They were castle-like, beautiful buildings located mostly in the rural regions of NH and served as the respite for the wealthy of an earlier day.

Built in the waning days of the era of Grand Hotels, the Balsams was among the last of its kind. Historians would later designate this era as the "Gilded Age", borrowing on a term coined by Mark Twain, who was describing a very rapid redistribution of wealth into the hands of the Robber Barons and Plutocrats of the late nineteenth century.

The first Grand Hotels were created as summer sanctuaries for the elite, who would pack their steamer trunks as the cities began to heat up into sweltering centers of sickness and virulence. The summer would find the refugees of New York, Boston, Philadelphia and a hundred cities, headed north by train and carriage to spend their summer lounging on shady verandas attached to rambling colossal porches, stretching from one end of the massive hotel's facade to the other. It was believed the cool mountain air had a healing effect on those who were ill and for those who were not it simply provided them with the comfort to which their means entitled them.

The early days of summer would be dominated by women and children who often fled the cities ahead of their husbands but as the days grew shorter after the solstice, the number of men would grow as well, with husbands winding up their work and heading north to join their families for the last vestiges of summer.

The verandahs and porticos of the Grand Hotels provided cooling shade and protection from the summer rain as the inhabitants whiled away the hours sipping manhattans and sloe gin fizzes or cape cod ice tea from tall glasses with ice chipped from huge blocks, harvested in the dead of winter for their comfort and pleasure in the heat of summer. The ice blocks were stacked in special rooms, often below grade, and insulated by wood chips, sawdust and hay carefully stacked and utilized so they would last through the summer and fall until the last cool drops of melt would correspond with the first flakes of snow heralding the season for their harvest once again. As they melted in the ice rooms the hotel's residents would while away the summer hours playing cards, reading, or watching the lightning flashes from a late afternoon thunderstorm over the White Mountains.

Daily outings would take hotel guests to high country meadows and mountaintops by carriage, foot and even aboard the famed Cog railway. On mid-summer mornings families would pack a picnic, take a carriage to the boarding station, board the Cog and chug to the summit of Mount Washington. From there they would hike the short distance to the Alpine Gardens of Tuckerman Ravine for a picnic or to the Bigelow Lawns of Mt Jefferson for a leisurely afternoon of croquet at 5000 feet.

Most of the Grand Hotels rose up in the late eighteenth and early nineteenth centuries. Construction of the Balsams came at the tail end of the era, first opening just after the Civil War as the Dix House, a 25-room summer inn established by George Parsons. In 1895, it was purchased by Henry Hale, an inventor from Philadelphia, who was rumored to have gotten into a pissing contest with the owners of the Mount Washington Hotel where he was spending summers with his family in the 1880s. They say Hale hired a carriage to carry him on a scouting mission along the Old Coos trail where he found the Dix House sitting at just the right spot at the height of land past Dixville Notch, near the border between Maine and New Hampshire. He renamed it "The Balsams", and by 1918 he had doubled the resort's capacity to 400 guests thus entitling it to be considered among the firmament as a Grand Hotel.

Over the years since then the number of Grand Hotels had dwindled. The Pemigewasset House in Plymouth, where Nathaniel Hawthorne had breathed his last, succumbed to fire. The Profile House at the base of Cannon Mountain was rebuilt after being razed and then it too succumbed to fire. The Crawford House, quite possibly the Grandest of the Grand, had its own glory days but it closed in the mid 1970's, before its abandoned shell fell to fire.

The Balsams was among a small number of Grand Hotels that survived, along with the Mount Washington Hotel in Bretton Woods and the Mountain View Grand Hotel in nearby Whitefield.

On this night, the Balsams was the setting for a meeting of investors in the Granite Skyway project. Usually they would meet closer to the center of power and money - the New York or Connecticut areas - but on this particular night the stars had aligned so the investors, the corporate heads and the power producers along with the surveyors, engineers and lobbyists all found themselves pulled into the swirling vortex of the Great North Woods for a host of reasons, not the least of which was the chance to play a few rounds of golf at the award winning Balsams Resort Golf Course.

The Balsams Grand Resort Golf Course is, to a golfer, something quite special. Designed by the great Scottish-American architect Donald Ross, who designed more than four hundred courses during the span of a nearly 50 year career. The Balsams was a purist's wet dream. First because Ross had not only designed the course but also had personally supervised the process of laying it out and building it - something he rarely did. Ross built his reputation on envisioning each course in the context of the existing landscape, trying to move as little earth as possible in the process of building the course. Imagining Ross standing at the highest point of land and watching over his project one can understand why subsequent owners of the resort have eschewed the temptation to tweak the course in favor of duffers who might be staying at the resort, or the modern world. Best of all, the fairways are still natural without the garish homes that line the outskirts of most golf courses today.

Chapter 21   The Roundup

Attendees arrived for the meeting one by one making their way up the drive into the resort. They arrived in their BMWs, Mercedes and Lexus sedans, lining up impatiently, windows closed and air conditioning on high, not because the day was too hot but rather because they did not care to mingle with the unwashed masses gathered around the entrance to the resort and along the drive to protest.

The protesters had gotten word, last minute, of the meeting. They lined the drive carrying placards and chanting "No Trees for Towers". The valets politely received the keys to their cars and drove them away, disappearing around a hedge of American Yew that formed a tight wall of visual security, then reappearing - on foot - in a timely way to receive the next car.

Under normal circumstances, to keep the line moving and the correct rhythm required multiple valets working as a well oiled machine; however, the Balsams was in the shoulder season and college kids who spent their summers servicing the well heeled at the Balsams had all gone back to school for the fall semester. They were, instead, operating on a skeleton staff with only two valets available, a brother and sister team from one of the area families.

Tonight the rhythm for servicing the incoming traffic was a one/one song in two part harmony - one valet coming and one going at all times, sporting their Balsams windbreakers and ball caps.

Thus it was that Daniel Roy and Sasha Brandt were able to casually slip into the roles - implementing the "The Balsams Roundup", Phase One of the "Androscoggin Stampede".

The two had come prepared to taize and tie up the twins if necessary but found them to be willing co-conspirators who would happily allow themselves to be tied up and left in the breaker room, where the night watchman would come to do the midnight shutdown of the lights not required for overnight security.

Cochise was hanging with Thomas back at the lake to avoid drawing too much attention to the pair.

Chapter 22 The Meeting

Conrad Fleming, CEO of Polaris Electric Corporation, stood in a darkened corner of the rambling porch adjacent to the entryway, talking quietly with James Enright. Enright, his back to the attendees filing into the hotel provided sufficient cover for Fleming as well; assuring an over-eager investor would not try to buttonhole Fleming before the meeting and possibly recognize Enright whose visage was familiar enough to warrant a second look and subsequent compulsion to recall "who that guy was".

"Look," said Fleming, " I want you here so you know what's going on within this group but you can't be at the meeting and you should leave discreetly as soon as the meeting is over so we don't risk having someone recognize you. I've arranged to have my laptop setup to allow you to see the room and hear the conversation from the comfort of my hotel room. Keep your eyes peeled for any weak links in the group. We can't afford to have anyone getting all squishy on us, there's a shit load of money at stake."

Enright nodded his assent. He knew he had to fly under the radar and frankly didn't need this idiot reminding him. How was it that such dim bulbs managed to find their way into the corporate suites of these big companies? They were like fucking black holes in a firmament of stars, sucking all of the life out of anything that came within their orbit even though they exerted power in inverse proportion to the light they shed.

Enright stepped off the porch onto the lawn, darkened by the long shadows of shrubs and hedges, silently congratulating himself for the quick trip around the cosmos he had made in that little mental exercise and feeling quite content with his own intellectual capacity, confident that he was safe from the inevitable double-cross that would come when Fleming was successful enough that only Enright himself remained as a threat. He'd be ready then and the only question was whether the final payment would come in dollars or flesh.

Fleming assured himself Enright was gone and spun on his heels and stepped into the brightly lit foyer heading for the Ballot Room where the meeting would take place. He strode to the front of the room where his techies, two interns from Saint Anselm College were finishing their set-up. It was a stroke of good fortune that the attendees were still milling about getting themselves coffee and pastries when one of the techies inquired about who was at the other end of the network he had just finished assembling. Enright shot him a look that could have ignited green oak in a winter ice storm and the matter was closed with no further discussion.

Opening the network link Fleming stepped up to the dais and brought the meeting to order. "Let's get started here," he said, "we have a lot of ground to cover before we can all go home or to our rooms."

He began by providing a summary of where the project was in the State and Federal approval processes. At the conclusion Enright announced that Polaris Energy had just completed a long-term power agreement with Hydro-Quebec of Canada that would guarantee the power supply for a twenty-year period. This would, he concluded, allow them to provide evidence of the reliability of the power supply down the road.

A hand shot up from the crowd and an investor queried: "Given how fast things are changing in the energy field and the plummeting cost of solar cells and wind power, why would you want to be locked into a rate twenty years from now that might be completely uncompetitive?"

Enright glanced around the room. He was looking to see if any of the media had slipped through the screening they had done with attendees. Though he could not be absolutely certain of course, he had specifically scheduled this meeting at the Balsams because it was so far out of the way that most of the media would not bother to make the trip. Like most people in the upper echelons of the corporate world he knew the vast majority of the traditional media were just plain lazy when it came to making the effort to travel four hours to a meeting. They would just wait for the news release. In days past, reporters were hungry for a story and would make the local school board meeting in East Bumfuck if they smelled even the whiff of a story, but with most of the media now in the firm control of major corporations there was a disincentive to write or report anything that might rock the boat so reporters had grown increasingly lazy or justifiably discouraged. In fact, new hires in the PR department at Polaris spent more time learning how to spoon feed information to reporters than they did in actually learning how to write a grammatically correct release or report.

When he was reasonably confident no media were present he answered the question. "For those of you who may have wondered what the advantage was to having Granite Skyway developed by a private group of investors which included a public utility, you will understand now when I tell you this arrangement allows us to act like private entrepreneurs when that is most advantageous and like a utility when that is to our advantage."

"In this case we are using Polaris Electric - the utility company - to make the power purchase. As a utility company there is a little-known provision of the law that says a utility can define certain costs as "stranded". This means, in essence, they aren't subject to market forces with respect to cost."

"This allows us to pass the costs along to ratepayers even when that cost is considerably higher than the going market rate for electricity. We have the ability, in the future, to define major parts of the Granite Skyway project as stranded costs if the costs of power in this agreement become uncompetitive. That means we are protected from more competitive rates and we can assess the ratepayers here in New Hampshire, rates that allow us to subsidize the overall cost of power to the markets downstream making us competitive where we need to be competitive and allowing us to make up that subsidy in our stranded power costs where ratepayers have no protection.

Chapter 23 The Androscoggin Stampede

Sasha drove the Lexus up the rear ramp of the massive car carrier hidden at the very back section of the Valet parking lot and debarked off the side of the carrier, between girders, to buy her a few extra seconds. She caught a glimpse of Daniel's ponytail, tucked carefully into the back of his shirt as she prepared to exit the car. By the time she was rounding the Yew hedge, Daniel would be wheeling the next car around the corner and up onto the carrier.

Darkness was descending and should provide the needed cover for the carrier once it was filled. The trip to the landing area for the logging operation was just over ten miles, but the last two were deep in the woods over muddy terrain. Making three trips, as the team had planned, was going to be cutting it close even if everything went perfectly; but they didn't want to leave any of the cars behind so they were determined to try.

Everything had to be precisely timed right down to the 5 minutes required to tie up the two actual valets who were taking a few hours off and would arrive in time to be secured in an empty room where they would be found just after nine pm.

Daniel climbed down from the carrier and swung himself around the cab where Herbert was checking all the instrument panels. "Ready to roll!" he said and as Herbert started the engine Daniel leapt down and headed back to the valet area. Herbert glanced at his watch. Seven o'clock, right on time he thought. Reaching down he released the emergency brake and lightly feathered the gas pedal as he let out the clutch. Employing as much stealth as a massive car carrier could, he slipped out the back entrance of the Balsams headed toward the Landing.

Chapter 24   The Log Yard

Looking at his watch Hank pulled the ramp into place creating a smooth glide path for moving the cars from the carrier to the barge that would serve as a ferry for three loads of cars coming from the Balsams. It was 7:30 pushing things a bit on the early side though the days were getting shorter. The barge driver was finished his work, though only about 1/10 of the harvestable timber had yet been cut. Hank had persuaded him that no one was likely to come after him for the money he had already been paid to move the entire load of timber once the illegal timbering operation was discovered. The rats would all be running for cover and would not be worrying about trying to get his money back. He was a little crayfish in this swamp and Hank had told him how to clear any evidence incriminating him from the scene. As long as he followed Hank's directives, it was unlikely he would see any personal fallout. Even if he did, he could simply tell the police he had found out about the illegal nature of the operation and walked away. He might get a slap on the ass but that would be the extent of it.

Hanks - and the rest of The Trust - were counting on this as well. They figured that once they discovered this illegal logging operation the authorities would not worry about a prank to move a few cars from the Balsams to Big Island. But just to make sure Michelle would put in a call to U.S. Fish and Wildlife to report the logging operation. By daybreak the log yard would be swarming with a mixed bag of Federal agents and local authorities who would see the mystery of the missing cars as a secondary offense to the illegal logging operation.

Between the driver and The Trust the agreement was simple - silence. As long as everyone kept the vow, no one would be the wiser. In fact, with only a few barges available for hire on the lake the driver might even have a shot at getting Polaris Energy to pay for his services retrieving the vehicles. He decided he was not going to mention this to the crew calling themselves The Trust.

The driver recruited his wife to drive him out to the landing and then she headed home. He had not filled her in on the plans. She was dead set against the plan to build this powerline but that was all the more reason not to tell her. If he gave her something to talk about when she got her hair done at "Curl Up N Dye", the entire town would know what happened before nightfall. Which wasn't saying much since there were only ten voters to begin with. But it was still ten too many people.

He knew he wasn't much better. He would be tempted to tell the story at Clarence George's barber shop in Groveton but he would have to wait until he was reasonably sure he would not be prosecuted for his part.

He made himself comfortable on a bed of white pine needles, it would be a few hours before he could get his barge back from The Trust after they had moved the cars out to Big Island. Then he would ship out, headed for his dock space on the other side of the lake, up near where the Dead River flowed into Umbagog. The only person who might be able to put two and two together was his neighbor Jack Carrigain, who had a fishing cabin next to his . . . but whom would he tell anyway?

Just then Hank let out a war whoop as the car carrier rounded the last bend in the dirt road leading to the landing with Herbert behind the wheel, grinning like a monkey with a bunch of bananas. As he drove by Herbert, headed for the loading dock, stuck his head out the window and yelled at Hank.

"I love New Hamster! Live Free or Fry!"

The first load of cars in the Androscoggin Stampede had arrived!

Michelle, Hank, Stonebridge and Herbert drove the cars directly from the carrier onto the barge, with Thomas serving as the guide, and within 15 minutes Herbert was headed back toward the Balsams on his second run.

Chapter 25 The Second Run

Herbert drove through the night, headlights cutting through the darkness. The toughest part of the second run would be the final half-mile to the hotel. Herbert knew he had to run dark to avoid calling attention to the massive carrier as he pulled into the hotel's back entrance.

If he had known he would be ferrying three loads of cars between the Balsams and Big Island, Herbert would have brought along the night vision goggles that were sitting in the drawer of a side table back at his cabin, but instead he would have to go freestyle. "Commando" they would have called it back in his earlier days but - like a lot of things - the phrase had taken on a whole new meaning in the modern era.

A half mile from the entrance he pulled over onto the side of the road and doused his lights. He paused and his heart quickened. This was one of those moments - - when the old ghosts came screaming back in unsettling ways. He recalled taking a hike into Welton Falls with his friend Dan only a few months before. Dan was a second generation Asian American who had served in Vietnam more than 20 years prior. They had barely gotten onto the trail when he noticed something had changed in his friend's demeanor. Every crack of a branch, every change in the undergrowth or cairn on the trail caused Dan to flinch, or pause or jump. It wasn't until Dan had asked Herbert if he could take Taffy's leash and walk with her - creating a calming effect - that Herbert finally put it all together. It was Dan's first time in the woods since 'Nam and he was reliving the experience in mind numbing detail. Dan hadn't just been a grunt in the army; he was an Asian-American grunt in the US army, fighting an Asian enemy. It just was terrifying to think about on a dozen different levels. Thinking about Dan's ghosts was a whole lot easier than obsessing about his own - - but almost invariably led there anyway.

Herbert's own ghosts were of a different type. Instead of jungles and thatched huts his leapt from mud huts and sand hills but they were no less powerful than Dan's were.

Just for a moment he found himself back in Afghanistan reaching up to adjust the black turban on his head. The Taliban, our allies in this earlier conflict, were moving weapons through a pass for the Afghan resistance. Three previous efforts had failed when the Russians had attacked the caravans of trucks; the first after the lead vehicle broke an axle on the rocky terrain preventing the rest of the vehicles from moving ahead and making them an easy mark for a Russian recon plane flying down the Khyber. The second and third caravans were compromised when the Russians wised up to the plan and planted sound activated alarms along the pass. The trucks were incapable of moving through the pass quietly making it a simple matter for the Russians to intercept the shipments - until, that is, Herbert had called an old friend from Wyoming who raised mules and ordered up "five string" of mules shuttled to Afghanistan in a pair of old C41 cargo planes. Herbert, mounted on the lead mule, could have just closed his eyes and allowed the mule to find its own way and everything would have been just fine, but he just could not bring himself to trust the animals that much. This time they succeeded and the reinforcements allowed the Afghan resistance to push back the Russian invaders. "If we had only left well enough alone," he thought. But the truth was these people were not going to stop when they drove the Russians out. Even then he knew - or sensed at least - that we had not heard the last of this guy Bin Laden.

He did, however, learn a trick from one of the guerillas on that caravan - - if he closed his eyes tightly for a minute and then opened them he could see better in the darkness. Better than simply letting his eyes become accustomed to the dark or squinting. Later on he would mention this to an old mentor, who explained that the trick fooled the neurons and receptors in one's eyes into sensing it was completely dark thus signaling them to open up to their maximum receptivity. It wasn't night vision goggles, but it was a damn sight better than squinting into the dark. It would not have prevented that Muscovite from planting his combat knife into Herbert's side a few weeks later, but it had helped him escape after the attack.

Herbert closed his eyes. Willing away the ghosts of Afghanistan and Vietnam and then, opening his eyes, buying himself just a few lumens of advantage; with lights off, he eased the carrier back onto the road. He should be able to make it back to the driveway in about 2 minutes; God willing and the moose don't cross.

Chapter 26 End Around

Cindy Fallon looked at her smartphone sitting face up on the passenger seat as she drove through the night heading home. She was running late and her boyfriend was going to meet her at her parent's house. It would not be good for him to arrive before her. He was not a particular favorite of her father and giving them quality time alone was not an idea Cindy felt would lead to anything good. If she kept moving she would be late but might be able to intercept Jamie before his orbit intersected with her father but safety dictated she should pull over to call or text. That would be the safest approach however if she were unable to reach Jamie, it would virtually assure that he and her father would cross paths, and, quite possibly, swords.

She reached for the phone. Picked it up, paused, then put it back down. She was passing by the Balsams, which meant the next few miles would be through spruce fir forest with very little traffic likely, texting while driving should not be a problem under the circumstances. She picked up the phone and began to type in a message to Jamie.

Chapter 27   A Flash in the Pan

Herbert rounded the last bend before the rear entrance. Directly ahead he could see a small car straddling the centerline of the road. It was too far over for him to pull off discreetly - - he was going to have to make a decision. Pull over and take a chance the car would miss him, or, hit his lights and reveal his position.

If he pulled over and he was wrong, the driver - who had done him no harm - would be right in the line of impact with the truck. It was a fatal risk and one he was not willing to take. He hit the lights and leaned on his horn. Almost instantly Cindy's car swerved, overcompensating and swinging onto the soft shoulder of the road. The car swerved again, fishtailing back and forth as Herbert held his breath. Then miraculously the driver regained control and pulled back onto the pavement just as the two vehicles crossed safely. As the car and the truck passed, with Cindy finally back in control, Herbert looked directly into the eyes of the driver and saw Cindy - cell phone to her ear and fear in her eyes.

"Shit! Shit! Shit!!!!!" Herbert slammed the driver's wheel with each utterance as he shut the lights back off, hoping not to add to the problem by drawing further attention to himself as he navigated the last few yards and pulled into the parking area. Dan and Sasha were lined up waiting for him to arrive. He leapt from the truck before it had even come to a full stop.

"We've been made!" He hollered, "Get the cars onto the carrier as fast as you can."

In five minutes they had loaded all but two of the remaining vehicles.

"You guys drive these last two and follow me." Herbert said. "If we're lucky, the woman who saw me will be put through to the State Police because the locals won't have someone on duty this late. That should mean it'll be 45 minutes before someone responds . . . time enough for us to get our asses outta here and hopefully outta sight on the other end."

In seconds they were on the road - lights on this time - as they pulled out all the stops to deliver the last of the vehicles.

Herbert was not holding back a thing as he barreled down the road. If he got stopped a speeding ticket would be the least of his worries. He was hoping he would hit the turnoff to the dirt road before the cops met him coming from the other direction. He wasn't worried at this point about anyone spotting the carrier truck. By this time the truck's owner had called in a report that the truck was stolen from his front yard while he and his wife were enjoying dinner at the Rainbow Grille in Pittsburg. Hank had arranged to toss the extra keys to the truck into the lake before they left and pull the wires that would have been used for hot-wiring the vehicle to make it look like a legit theft.

Behind Herbert, Sasha and Daniel drove Enright's Town Car and a convertible Hummer whose owner was, as yet, unidentified. Daniel had just opened the sunroof on Enright's Town Car as they whizzed along behind Herbert when Sasha saw the brake lights flash on the Town Car. She mashed down on the brakes of the Hummer and the ABS braking system went into action, but by the time she had started to slow the brake lights had gone out and Daniel had pulled off onto the dirt road right behind Herbert and the carrier. She took her foot off the brake pedal and pulled in behind him and was just beginning to bring her Hummer up to speed when Dan hit his brakes again, this time pulling over.

Through his rearview mirror Herbert saw Daniel stop but he couldn't stop the carrier, he'd have to hope Sasha could do whatever was necessary to help out Daniel. He steeled himself and kept driving. Daniel jumped out of the Town Car and ran up to Sasha's window where she had pulled off after passing him.

"I just need a minute Sash," he said.

"What the hell Daniel?" she said.

"Trust me, this will be worth the risk." he said.

Sasha sat back impatiently as Daniel ran back toward the main road. In a few minutes she saw him closing the winter gate to the road and assumed he was trying to buy them a bit more time, making it appear the road was closed, though it was way too early for the gate to be closed for the winter. Summer was hardly even over. Then she watched as the trunk to the Town Car opened, completely blocking her view of Daniel. In just a few moments more Daniel closed the trunk and jumped back into the Town Car passing Sasha with a quick beep of the horn. Then she was on the road behind him and in another five minutes they pulled into the landing area where a relieved Herbert smiled at them and jogged over to fill them in on the plans for getting the second load of cars out to the island.

With six of them available to drive, it was only a matter of moments before the cars were on the barge and Hank was steering it out into the water toward Big Island. Herbert made a small ceremony out of disposing the keys to the carrier truck in the middle of the lake where no diver would ever be searching for them and the team huddled together for the brief ride to Big Island.

They arrived at the island and began to unload the vehicles, driving them into the open area prepared for holding logs. The first load of cars had already been moved by Stonebridge, Hank and Michelle, so the second load seemed easy by comparison. Sasha was just bringing up the rear in the Hummer and as she got out Stonebridge said, "Where's Daniel?"

Sasha looked around, "he was right behind me a minute ago. I don't know where he went." Then they heard a horn sound as they turned in unison to see Enright's Town Car rounding the grove of trees beside the parking area. Daniel was seated in the shotgun position with a grin painting his face from one ear to the other. Beside him, in the driver's seat, sat a big dead buck. His rack, all 12 points, and his head sticking out the sunroof and his hooves positioned on the steering wheel.

"This should give them something to talk about " Daniel said as he stepped around the Town Car and adroitly snapped a picture for posting to an anonymous Instagram account. We'll track down a list of the cars registered to the corporate leadership of Polaris and post it with an invitation for interested citizens to join the 'Roadkill Rangers' and donate a carcass to a member of the Polaris team. Hank gleefully remembered he had spotted a pile of carp, caught by a fisherman and left down by the water for scavenging critters. "Those should be good and ripe by the time these folks arrive to pick up their rides!" he chuckled as he headed off to gather them for distribution.

Chapter 28 The Treasure Hunt

The first group to leave the meeting at the Balsams stood waiting at the valet stand. It was 9:30 and no Valet was in sight. More attendees filtered into the area and suddenly there seemed to be a rush of staff flitting around the stand and hustling toward the parking area but never pausing long enough to be buttonholed by one of the waiting patrons. A curious patron wandered up to the valet board where normally the keys to the vehicles would have been hung. He noticed there were very few keys on the board, relative to the number of people lined up awaiting a valet. Then he noticed an envelope on the board, addressed 'Granite Skyway attendees'.He opened it and read it aloud to the gathered crowd.

"We regret to inform you that your cars have been moved to an alternative parking area. You are advised to make new plans for the night permitting you to resume your search for your vehicles in the light of the new day. You are also advised to make more sound investments in the future."

Beneath the note was what appeared to be a clue from a childhood treasure hunt.

There's more than a decade 'tween the guilty and fruit
Though labor is not what produced this fine loot.
No sweat or tears brought your chariot score
Simple entitlement, nothing more.

The trail to your wheels begins right now and right here
But rest a night - on the Skyway - let daylight appear.
Find a clue to the East, where the river runs fast
This is just the beginning, this fight's to the last.

It was signed . . . "The Trust"

"Great!" Sighed Dexter Mathies, a portly man in his mid forties who had made the trip up to the Granite Skyway meeting from his hometown of Greenwich, Connecticut. " I'm going to have to hire a sitter for my Yorkies for another day now." Mathies was standing curbside in a pair of madras Bermuda shorts, a banana yellow sports coat and argyle knee socks extending from his buckled patent leather loafers. "So what do we do now?"

Just then Conrad Fleming's assistant, Donna Barza, hastened up to the group. "Fortunately", she said, "since the summer rush is over, there are rooms left at the hotel; so we have secured rooms for everyone. We hope to have all this resolved by morning so you can be on your way home."

Elizabeth Schniewind, a tall matronly woman from the Beacon Hill area of Boston pushed her way to the front of the crowd addressing Barza in a tone so condescendingly sweet it suggested a concoction made of equal parts marzipan and paving tar.

"Miss Barza," she said, "Perhaps it is unclear to you that our vehicles are missing, any of which has a value greater than your entire net worth, even if you include the value of your new augmentation surgery as an unencumbered and obviously tangible asset. Furthermore", she said haughtily, "we appear to be stuck in this hell hole of a town populated by toothless hicks and tick infested moose, which, for some unknown reason your citizens seem to have an unhealthy fondness for."

She continued, "Do you suppose we could focus our attention on the matter at hand?"

Barza turned away and muttered under her breath, "which matter would that be? The missing cars or the fact that a snob from Beacon Hill seems to have also lost the subject after the preposition that was supposed to come at the end of the sentence. She had half a mind to turn back to her and say," I think what you meant to say . . ."

"Ms. Barza?" Schniewind repeated in the demanding tone of a Brahmin on Newbury Street, addressing a street vendor.

Barza lost it. "Ms. Schniewind, we are doing the best we can to try to find your cars despite the fact you think insulting us and suggesting we have an unhealthy fondness for our state animal will somehow magically ingratiate us to you. I'm not a huge fan of your project to begin with, but since you and my boss are allied in this effort it may be that my job is dependent on my cooperation. Don't mistake my cooperation for anything more than an act of self preservation and don't, don't, don't dangle your participles when speaking about our state animal, someone may think the unhealthy fondness is your problem!"

With that she turned on her heels and headed back into the building where she came upon a local police officer, Darren Pullman and her boss Conrad Fleming. The two were speaking in the foyer just off the entrance to the hotel.

"I expect you and your officers to get on this immediately." Fleming said. "These are important people and I don't want them here any longer than they have to be to get their cars back and go home. Do you understand?"

Yes sir. Pullman answered.

"Can I count on your entire department?" Fleming demanded.

"Yes sir."

Fleming: "How soon can they be here?"

"Immediately sir."

"They are already here?"

"Yes Sir."

"Well where are they then?" Conrad asked with exasperation.

"You're looking at 'em, Sir." Pullman answered with a grin. He loved this moment. It was like doing stand-up comedy on open mike night. You pulled them along slowly, simply and deliberately, playing the hick to their highbrow, until the moment of the great unveiling.

Fleming blew out a long breath and took a moment to compose himself. Then he spoke.

"I want these cars found. I want them found and found fast."

Dexter Mathies wandered into the foyer looking around and saw Conrad Fleming speaking animatedly with police Chief Pullman. Flushed with excitement he hastened over to them and presented Fleming with the note he had found. Fleming palmed the envelope as he handed the letter to Pullman. He figured the letter would be evidence but if he could spirit away the envelope, Enright might be able to get a print off it. He wasn't going to hold his breath hoping for officer improv to solve the case. In fact, even now he was on the phone to the Governor's office to ask her to dispatch the State Police to help. He was pretty certain the crime had occurred between towns so there were plenty of jurisdictional issues at work here and that would allow the Governor to assign it to the State Police.

In the meantime Chief Pullman had read the note and thought he knew where this clue would take them. He was about to head out to follow the lead when Fleming suggested Ms Barza would be very interested in riding along to see how he solved a crime like this. He wanted eyes and ears on the Chief and Donna Barza couldn't get away from this scene fast enough for her part. She hopped into the cruiser and they pulled out of the hotel entrance with lights flashing and siren blaring. It was probably overkill on his part but Chief/Officer Pullman did not often have the chance to use the bells and whistles on his cruiser so he took advantage whenever he had an excuse.

Chapter 29 Exit Strategies

"Let's move it people!" Stonebridge yelled. He was in charge of the exit strategy and was beginning to worry that keeping this group on a schedule was going to be like herding cats. It was already after midnight and the group was little more than a bunch of bobbing headlamps from where he stood, floating about in the dark like so many giant fireflies. It would take 15 minutes to motor back to the log yard on the mainland and then he had to get everyone into their vehicles and off.

Hank was putting the finishing touches on the out of state cars, opening the hood and tossing in a couple of big dead carp and closing it up. He didn't monkey with the engine otherwise since he wanted the owner to get in and start up the vehicle without incident. This would assure the dead fish would remain undetected until they began to really ripen. Maybe some of them would even be caught in the fan and spread through the engine block. That would make the task of cleaning next to impossible.

Hank ran to the barge just as it began to pull out, with Thomas at the wheel.

"Were you just going to leave me here?" Hank asked breathlessly.

"I figured starting the engine was sure to get the lead out of your ass," Thomas replied.

Daniel clapped a hand on Hank's shoulder as Sasha placed her hand on his arm just above his elbow. "Nice work Hank, there's gotta be a good million in cars here, if not more. I'm betting these investors are going to be looking at Polaris for the full value of their cars after they try to get the stink out."

"Too bad it'll probably be paid by some insurance company." Hank said.

"Don't count on it." Michelle said," I have some ideas about that, let's just watch and see how things play out in the next few days."

"As long as it doesn't end up in the rate base." Hank replied.

Thomas pulled the barge into the landing where it's owner waited anxiously. He waded into the water and held off the boat while the others debarked. Cochise bounded off ahead of the crew and within moments everyone was ashore and the barge was pulling away headed for home.

GO! Stonebridge yelled. "We need to be out of here as fast as possible."

With the exception of Hank and Thomas, the members of The Trust headed for their vehicles and, one by one, pulled away, headed south for some well-deserved rest.

Chapter 30 Errol Rapids

At 2am Chief Pullman pulled into the parking lot across from Saco Bound Kayak center and hit the brakes hard enough to make the rear of the cruiser to swerve in the dirt. The high season was past but some of the hard-core paddlers were still out and about and a few campfires burned around the campground, even at this late hour.

Pullman took a deep breath, pulling the air almost reverently into his lungs, eyes half closed. He loved the smell of a wood fire on a crisp autumn night. It was one of the many reasons why he had moved here from New York City. As a fresh air kid he had first spent a summer in New Hampshire. Luckily for him the family that had sponsored him had taken a shine to him and he returned every summer through elementary school in the program and afterwards to a job that not only paid his college tuition but also filled his heart all summer long. The way he saw it, this place had saved him. Most of the kids who he grew up with were dead or in prison. He himself had only managed to escape the jaws of the neighborhood gang because of a priest, Father Montrone, who was the Fresh Air contact for Brooklyn and Yonkers.

The Father had taken an interest in him and helped keep him on the straight and narrow. It wasn't easy. Gang activity was like a flesh eating bacteria, growing in leaps and bounds and consuming almost all who were caught up in its path, without regard to race or ethnicity.

Pullman headed toward the message board outside the Saco Bound office and picked up his pace when he saw a piece of paper similar to the note he was handed at the Balsams.

Sure enough, it was another clue.

Let the river run
Pay it no heed
Your aim is the source
The fruit of your greed
Left five from high noon
Right three, then Left 6
Then it's back to three finally
And you're done, take your lift.

"What the hell?" Pullman said.

He look quizzically at Barza, "does this make any sense to you?"

"Well . . . " Donna said, "the first part is fairly self explanatory. Don't pay attention to the river, or its downstream course. We're looking at something associated with the lake which is its source."

"Yeah! Right!" The chief said. "OK so starting at twelve o'clock - high noon - we go left five . . . but five what? Five degrees? Five miles? Five minutes?"

"It can't be degrees, too hard to calculate without some pretty specific equipment and minutes isn't precise enough. Too dependent on the person and the mode of transportation."

"Do you have a map?" Donna asked.

Pullman went to his car and returned with a State of New Hampshire road map. He spread it on a picnic table and aimed his flashlight at it. The two stared silently. "Not enough towns in the area for it to be towns and it doesn't seem to relate to route numbers."

After a good twenty minutes Pullman folded the map and with a sigh put it in his shirt pocket as they began walking back toward the cruiser. When they were almost back they passed a campfire where a group of campers were still awake. One camper strummed lazily on his guitar while a compatriot tried his best to accompany him on a harmonica. Two others were looking at a US Geographic Survey map, apparently scoping out an itinerary for the next leg of their trip.

"Hang on a second," the Chief said as he walked over to the campers looking at the map. Pullman spoke quietly with the group and soon he was huddled together with them examining the USGS map.

Suddenly, Donna heard a yahoo from the Chief and hustled over to join him to see what all the commotion was about.

"Look at this Donna," the Chief said, pointing to the northern tip of the lake. "The roadmap didn't show all these small gravel access roads. This could be the answer to our riddle," he said. He began counting the access roads to the left until he reached five. Then in a clockwise direction he counted three and then six roads counter clockwise. Pausing for dramatic effect, he placed his finger on the access road that was three to the right of the last road he had counted out.

"Here." He said definitively. "It goes all the way from the paved road, Rte 16, to the lake. This has to be what we are looking for. There might be some roads too small to even show up on this USGS Map, but they wouldn't be able to get the carrier down them. Even if we're wrong, it's pretty likely this will put us in the ballpark if not exactly on the spot."

"We can take a look now," the Chief said, "but we won't really be able to confirm it for sure until daylight . . . it's a nearly moonless night and we won't have anything but our headlights. We might get lucky and catch them still there. We really don't know how much of a head start they have on us."

Donna replied, "Let's drive in and see what we can. If the headlights don't give us what we need, we can close our eyes for a couple of hours and be ahead of the game when the sun comes up."

The Chief called dispatch and gave them a message for Doris when she returned to the office the next morning, then slapped the mic into its cradle, pulled the shift into drive and headed north.

Chapter 31   Exit Stage Right

Hank and Thomas quickly went about the task of cleaning the scene. Making sure they did not leave any clues that would allow the members of The Trust to be identified or tracked. They had to work fast, not knowing how much time they would have before the forces of the Granite Skyway, in whatever form they took, found their way through the brief series of clues to the landing site. It was already almost 4am by the time the team had departed so - unless they were extraordinarily lucky - the Skyway folks would not be far behind. The sun would be coming up in less than an hour and the opportunity for stealth would be greatly diminished.

Hank checked the cab of the truck to make sure Herbert hadn't left anything behind, but it was clean. He hadn't expected anything less; anyone who was engaged in covert activities in the Middle East would have been well trained in covering his tracks.

Thomas' primary task was to try to cover any obvious footprints. What he hadn't counted on were the prints left by Cochise. If anyone who knew their stuff came with the Granite Skyway folks they would notice his prints. He grabbed a spruce branch and began dragging it over the tracks - - both human and wolf.

"Hank" he called, "gonna need your help covering the wolf tracks. Grab one of those spruce branches and rake anywhere you see an obvious track."

The two old friends were furiously raking the area when they heard the rumble of a vehicle and saw headlights bobbing along the access road.

"Shit! Let's go Thomas!"
They dashed for the bass boat.

"We can't risk starting it!" Hank said when they reached the boat. "We're going to have to wade away with the boat and wait for an opportunity to start the electric trolling motor so we can get the hell out of here without making too much noise."

Thomas waded into the water followed by Hank. The sun was just starting to come up but there was still some cover of darkness left. Hank moved to the front of the boat, grabbing the bow painter and pulling the boat north along the shoreline.

"Get closer to the boat," Thomas said in a hushed tone, "Try and hide your body against it if you can." As they waded with the boat, making their best effort to hug the shoreline, Thomas grabbed any deadwood and branches he could reach, piling them on the boat to create makeshift camouflage.

Looking back, Hank saw headlights train across the water from the spot they had just left moments before. Just as Thomas found a huge white pine bow and placed it over the stern section of the boat.

"Headlights!" Hank said through labored breath.

"We need to get her a little farther away Hank, start looking for a spot where we can lay low for a while."

"There's not a lot of cover here," Hank said, "gotta keep moving and hope they don't see us."

Thomas moved to the front of the boat. "I've got the back hidden pretty well, let's hug the bow and swim it along, hope we find a little pull off spot."

The cold water of the lake in autumn weather was beginning to take a toll on both of them. But the countervailing force of their exertions kept exposure at bay. Hank looked at Thomas who was shivering and decided as long as he was still shivering he was going to be okay but shivering was the second stage of hypothermia; they needed to get out of this water soon or they would both be in trouble.

Chapter 32   East on Umbagog

The morning sun crept over the horizon, hanging low over the lake. Donna Barza held her hand up to shade her eyes as she looked eastward across Lake Umbagog.

The Chief leaned up against his cruiser and he spoke into his radio hand mic."This is the spot all right. There is a big landing area where they have been holding logs from what is clearly a timbering operation. There are more tracks from vehicles than they could possibly have required for the operation. I'd say 20-30 vehicles have passed over the ground here in the last few days. But there's nothing here now except a truck and car carrier . . . no doubt the one reported stolen last night."

Barza wandered up as he was speaking on the radio and listened in on the conversation. The Chief paused and said, "hang on a second Doris," as he palmed the mic, and then to Donna he said, "we can get a boat to begin the search for the cars but it may mean another night at the hotel for all those folks. Otherwise I can reach out to Chet Wincowski in Newport, Vermont, who has a chopper and probably spot them in an hour or less . . . but he doesn't work cheap."

Barza replied, "I'll call Conrad and get him to approve the helicopter," she said of her boss.

"Not with that," the Chief said nodding his head at her cell phone. "You'd have a better chance of reaching him if you started to bang on that tree trunk over there. You may have noticed by now, cell coverage up here is spotty at best."

Donna glanced down at her cell phone and sighed as she put it back into her hip pocket. "I should have guessed," she said.

"Looks like you are going to have to make a command decision Ms. Barza." and thought he might just enjoy watching Fleming squirm when he heard about this. He conferred a few more moments with Donna when she said "I may be looking for a job after this, but you had better get the chopper."

"Don't worry Ms. Barza, I'll be right by your side when you explain it to him."

Donna was buoyed by his support but somewhat puzzled by the smile on his face as he said it.

Chief Pullman put the mic back up to his mouth. "OK Doris, give Chet a call and tell him we have a live one. Give him our coordinates and tell him there's plenty of room to land his bird then get back to me and let me know his ETA please."

He paused a moment and added. "Listen Doris, let's also check on whether there's any authorized logging operation in this area. I don't remember seeing anything come across my desk, do you?"

He waited a moment for her response and then signed off.

Chapter 33   Disraeli Gears Revisited

The thudding of the chopper provided ample warning to Hank and Thomas, who were huddled together in only their underwear under a tarp and sleeping bag in the camouflaged bass boat, as Chester Wincowski drew near the landing area. Chet pulled his Red Sox cap off to improve his field of vision, revealing a mop of red hair bright enough to act as a landing beacon and brought the bird down smoothly. Hunching low as he got out and replacing his cap he hustled over to the Chief who was engaged with a small group of state troopers and some crime techs, who had just arrived on the site. Donna Barza looked on, sizing up Wincowski noting he wasn't wearing a wedding band.

Just about a mile up the lake Thomas and Hank, who had found a small notch in the shoreline to pull in to wait out the search party, were about to emerge from their cocoon. The sun had come up and the two had opted to stay in their underwear, rather than put on their wet clothing.

Hank sized up Thomas who already looked like the wild man of Borneo with his clothes on. He was pretty sure the man's father was Bigfoot, and he was considering the ramifications of telling him so, as Thomas stumbled around the boat in what probably passed for underwear on some other planet.

"If you ever mention this to any of those granola munchers in The Trust, Thomas, I'll grill Metallak and sell his antlers to fat Japanese sumo wrestlers to make their peckers hard enough to find." Hank said.

"Don't you worry a bit about that! I was none too happy to be rubbing balls with you under that tarp pal. " Thomas replied

"Balls? Really?" Hank replied. "There was no rubbing balls that couldn't get past our bellies to begin with!"

"I happen to like living alone and if we weren't half dead and heading home, to the sweet hereafter, I would've started swimming for Moll's Rock rather than cuddle up with you. There were at least a few times during the last hour when I thought you were getting ready - as a famous rocker from the 70s would have said - to give me your dull surprise." Thomas said.

"I think you got that wrong," said Hank. I think it was "dawn first prize."

"Now let's beat feet. The chopper is making plenty of noise, enough to cover our exit. Let's make some time and get out ahead of these guys."

"We're not done with this discussion Thomas, but I'm gonna err on the side of caution, " said Hank, starting the electric trolling motor. "We'll have to substitute quiet for speed until we are confident they won't hear us. Then we can start up the Evinrude and really make time."

"I think we should keep going north for a mile or two before we start cutting back toward the campsite. In fact, let's hug the shoreline and follow around until we can find an island or a bay that allows us to head south unnoticed."

"Right," replied Thomas. "The last thing we want to do is let anyone see you in your underwear. That will be a dead giveaway . . . and scare the shit out of any normal person who sees you."

"I'll scare them?" Hank said incredulously, "If they see you they'll think a Yeti has attacked a bass fisherman and stolen his boat. And speaking of underwear, do you pound birch bark into britches or have you just failed to change your drawers for the last five years?"

Thomas' face grew red and Hank was afraid he had gone too far. He wondered if his old friend would really lose his cool and do something physical so he prepared to fight back if it came to that when Thomas let out an enormous guffaw, slapped Hank on the back and said, "OK amigo! Man have I missed hanging out with you. Let's get outta here."

Within five minutes the pair was motoring north, hugging the shore.

Hank was driving and had not said a word since they had started the engine, when suddenly he threw back his head and laughed as he began to sing, well more accurately to perform since he didn't know lyrics from a hole in the ground: "It's getting near dawn - do dooo do dooo do do.I'll soon be with you, do dooo do dooo do do. I'll give you my dull surprise - do dooo do dooo do, do." Thomas chimed in, standing up in all his near-naked glory and striking a non-existent air guitar as their voices joined together and the two hollered out: "IN SUNSHINE OF YOUR LOOOVE . . ."

Fortunately, the sounds of the chopper covered their reverie.

Chapter 34   Search and Recovery

The Chief and Donna Barza climbed into the chopper as Chet passed them helmets that served as both modest protection and communications devices, allowing them to converse in normal tones without being drowned out by the sound of the rotors. Chet pulled on his own helmet, tested the communications, flipped a few switches and prepared to begin their search of the lake.

"Let's hope they aren't on the bottom of the lake." Chet said.

"Unless I completely have these folks wrong Chet, they aren't going to do something harmful to the environment. They are trying to send a message.

"This is a bit beyond sending a message," said Chet, "If I didn't know better chief, I'd think you'd gone soft on them"

It was Donna Barza who spoke next and she confirmed what the Chief had said. "I'll deny it if you tell my boss", she said, "but I agree with the chief. If I lived up here and someone was planning to make me look out my window at 150 foot steel towers I'd be looking to do more than complain too."

The chief and Chet looked at one another quizzically.

"OK then, not at the bottom of the lake," said Chester, "we can do a grid but before we do, have you got any ideas that might be a shortcut?"

"Well, these folks took advantage of a logging operation - an illegal one at that, according to Doris, who did a search of all logging permits in the area. It was smart thinking because it provided them with nearly everything they needed to pull this off with very short notice. I'm betting they wanted to expose this illegal operation as well so I suggest you look for an area that's been logg . . . "

"Jesssusss" Chester said, interrupting the Chief in mid-sentence. The three looked down on a devastated Big Island, stripped of its tall pines. The carcasses of raptor nests scattered on the ground where they were left, along with the branches of the massive trees.

"Those bastards!" Chet said.

"This wasn't the work of the people we're after," said the police chief.

"I know," said Wincowski. "In fact they led us right to the spot . . . I'd give them a medal instead of arresting them."

Chester tapped his headset and called in to dispatch. "We have a serious situation here he said. Call US Fish and Wildlife, enforcement division, and get them over here as fast as possible. Better let New Hampshire Fish and Game know as well. While you are at it," he continued, "call Audubon and the Forest Society and give them the heads up. We're going to need their help with damage control and abatement."

While he was speaking with dispatch Wincowski was scanning the ground in the vicinity of the cutting, then he pointed to a clearing just back from the water. "There they are." he said, pointing to a field full of cars and SUVs.

Tapping his headset, he called dispatch back. "Martha, see if you can reach one of the folks on the lake who has a barge and tell the first one you can get to come right now. We're going to need someone to move about 30 vehicles from Big Island to the mainland."

The pilot paused and then said thoughtfully "wait a moment, we are going to need drivers for all these vehicles. Call the Balsams and have them bring the owners of these cars down to the landing area and have the barge make its first order of business to pick up the owners and deliver them to Big Island."

"We can make shorter work of this if we just let them pick out their own vehicle and drive it onto the barge and then out."

Donna Barza held up her hand to signal Chet.

"Hold on a second Martha, Ms. Barza has something to add."

"I was just thinking . . . maybe we should check out the scene before we bring a bunch of pissed off people onto the site. I mean if we do that and the keys are at the bottom of the lake, or these jokers have broken them off in the ignitions or done anything else to gum up the works, we could be in for a very long day while we wait for secondary assistance."

"Good point," said Chief Pullman, "I'm thinking it wasn't lost on you that your boss would have to hang out with all these pissed off people while we waited as well."

Donna shrugged, "that goes without saying. When he's not under stress he comes off as a very regular guy. You know, a guy who'd do anything for the working man or woman."

"Ah I see, said Chet. "He'd do anything for the working man - except sit down and have dinner with him. He won't perform well if he has to play the role for too long with an unhappy audience."

"Right," said Donna. "I need to try and control the situation so he doesn't do something dumb . . ." she paused for a moment and then added . . . "and he can't know that's what I'm doing."

"Guess we know who the brains of this outfit are." said Chief Pullman. "Better put this bird down Chet and we'll summon folks only after we are sure the coast is clear."

"Roger that Chief." Chet winked at Donna, "I think you just saved us a lot of headaches Ms Barza."

"It's Donna, please," Barza said.

"OK, Donna it is."

Chapter 35 Bucks and Scents

The Chief, Donna Barza and Chet Winkowski confirmed the cars and SUVs all had keys in their ignitions.

The last they came to was Conrad's Lincoln Town Car with a dead buck in the driver's seat and its head and rack sticking out the sunroof.

"Now that is a sight!" said Chester. He took off his cap and placed it back on his head tilted back as he surveyed the scene.

Donna Barza put her hand over her nose and mouth and stifled a laugh. "Wow!" she said, "it's a bit ripe."

"Yes it is," said the chief. "I think we better let the techs take a look at the scene and see if they need to photograph it and gather any evidence. Too bad too, this Buck is going to get a lot more rank if we do that." he smiled.

"I'm guessing you think Conrad will need to remove this critter himself so it doesn't damage his Town Car any further . . . right?" Chet said.

"Right you are Chester. It's an insurance matter . . ."

Chapter 36 The Reunion

Conrad was pacing the area around his Town Car, muttering and swearing as he prepared himself for the extraction. Whoever placed this buck in his car had really gotten it in there tight.

The chief had given him some kind of song and dance about insurance company riders and ancillary damage waivers when he had informed Conrad he would have to remove the dead buck from his vehicle himself. He was pretty sure he had noticed the chief smiling as he walked away.

The southwest end of the island was crawling with people as the Fish & Wildlife investigators went about the business of gathering evidence, along with a team of techs from the State police.

What annoyed Fleming was that most of the energy expended was focused on the illegal timbering and not on the theft of vehicles from the parking lot at The Balsams.

Just as he was about to tackle the buck in his driver's seat, he saw a determined, young wildlife Conservation Officer walking briskly up to his commanding officer.

"Sir", the young officer said. "Something weird over here."

The commanding officer followed him to a low area near the water's edge. Conrad followed them both, not bothering to be discrete. The game officer squatted down and pushed aside a low hanging branch from a patch of sheep laurel revealing a print.

"I've been all over this area twice now trying to figure out if I was crazy . . . but I'm pretty sure I'm not."

"What is it?" The commander asked impatiently.

"I'm pretty sure this is a wolf track, sir."

Chapter 37   The Battle is Joined

Jim Kitchen was bordering on gleeful when he opened his smartphone and saw a new posting on Instagram featured a 12 point buck, seemingly driving Conrad Fleming's Lincoln Town Car, its long tongue lolling out - a common post mortem characteristic - now seeming to taunt Fleming from its position of power. Two photographs were featured in the post; one from the front looking directly at the Buck's head sticking out of the sunroof, the other from the passenger's side showing his hooves on the steering wheel. The photographs were linked to a blog post describing the "creative re-parking" of 32 vehicles from The Balsams Hotel; vehicles belonging to investors and corporate executives associated with the Granite Skyway project who were meeting at the hotel. The post included the information that the investigation had also revealed an illegal timbering operation on Big Island where the cars were "re-parked". The illegal timbering operation threatened efforts to restore nesting pairs of raptors in the Umbagog Lake region, as did the proposal for Granite Skyway, but the utility company was not responsible for the timbering.

Kitchen smelled that familiar scent. A story. A story that would put him back on the pathway to glory. Now the Granite Skyway was taking on a new life. It had, seemingly overnight, morphed from a dull battle of the attorneys into a full out fight for the future of the State and maybe with national implications.

In addition to the questions about sustainable energy, smart grids and the nuanced differences between massive hydropower projects and small sustainable renewable energy projects, there were the questions about civil disobedience and terrorism.

Where yesterday the country had seemed to be tumbling out of control toward a black and white - unnuanced - view of civil action that lumped everyone who took any action outside the law against established interests into the broad category of terrorist; today, there was a chance - albeit slim - to redraw the board. A chance to make it possible for civil disobedience to serve the public interest without being rebranded as "terror". Here was a story worth telling and he suspected a story a lot of journalists would be ready to tell if someone took the risk of being the first to tell it . . . the first man over the fence so to speak.

There was no time to lose. He was climbing the fence.

Chapter 38   The Gazetteers

Conrad Fleming stepped out of his Town Car and headed toward Tea Bird's Cafe in Berlin. The headache of the events at The Balsams was over for him - of course he had insisted, as CEO of Polaris, that the Lincoln be the first car transported from the island - which meant that everyone at the meeting was witness to the deer sitting in Fleming's driver's seat. Fleming's arrogance gave the local police all the excuse they needed to make the extra effort required to present his car to him exactly as it was. Giving everyone the pleasure of having a big laugh at his expense. A few of the police even took their own photos for posting on their favorite social networking sites. Word spread very fast and soon the entire state and beyond was watching the events unfold with rapt attention.

By the time the authorities had ascertained where the stolen cars were parked, found a boat capable of transporting them back to the mainland, assured themselves that Granite Skyway would be responsible for the $50,000 cost of recovery the boat's captain had requested, the road killed Buck had grown quite ripe and had spread the scent of death throughout the CEO's car. As if this weren't enough of a headache, a whole new headache was about to unveil itself. As he entered the cafe he saw a brochure case for visitors. Standing out at the top of the case was a stack of pamphlets in a section marked "No to Granite Skyway - Trees NOT Towers", stood a pamphlet that caused him to pause and snatch up a few copies. He stopped and read the first page before entering the Cafe. When he did, the look of rage on his face was apparent.

"What the hell is this?" said Fleming, slamming the pamphlet down on the table in front of Enright and Mac who had been discretely waiting for him - - no more. The pamphlet had old English font on the front with the title "A Sacred Trust" covering most of the page. By all appearances it was written by someone named T. Crawford Paine.

A Sacred Trust
The Case Against Granite Skyway
By T. Crawford Paine

The arc of history reveals itself to us as a great tapestry; its lateral weft and vertical warp woven in the interplay of people and events. The weft: the lives and deeds, successes and failures of countless generations. The warp: the flow of history, running north to south in a never-ending journey, so we hope.

Behind us it stands in sharp focus and relief, known to all; before us, shrouded in fog and mystery, presaging the future, yet to be revealed but still within our power to control.

Tug on any single strand within the weft and you will find revealed a series of threads, reflecting one or more lives, woven clumsily and lovingly by men and women, seeking their own path within this great tapestry. Transecting the rivers of the warp - a thousand, thousand, tributaries cast in the flow of human and natural events, sometimes flowing together in vast floodplains and sometimes distinctive and solitary, charting the flow of time and the course of history across the reach of space and time;

Among the lives enshrined, some shine bright and golden in the sun: the lives of Mohammed, Christ, Siddhartha, and Mother Theresa;

Among the epochs: the Renaissance and the Civil Rights movement gleam transcendent.

Still other lives and periods are as dark stains upon the tapestry. Where the tributaries and floodplains of time and events are measured in the blood, sweat and tears of generations of men, women and children: Slavery, the centuries of genocide visited upon the American Indian, the Jews and Armenians; Rwanda and the Aborigines of Australia.

These rivers of the warp are shaped and molded from the events that flow from humanity's relationships with itself and with the planet.

How deeply the wounds are embedded into the tapestry - how large the floodplain of their existence and persistence is a measure of the reach they will have in the future. Yet, even a relatively small event - like the construction of a 180-mile long power transmission line can have lasting impacts creating an environmental debt lasting for centuries.

This is the question we face with Granite Skyway. Will the shrouded mystery of the tapestry before us open to reveal a massive permanent scar upon the land we love and for which generations to come will pay the environmental and psychic cost?

Each generation has asked itself the timeless question: How will our children remember us? What legacy will we leave to them? And so we are faced with the question, how will we be remembered if our children and grandchildren inherit a massive, antiquated skeleton of steel snaking its way through the most beautiful parts of our state?

For all but the few who seek profit built on our collective loss, the answer is clear. We cannot allow the greed of a small group of people to outweigh the needs of the many.

Today we stand on the precipice of a new era. So much of what we have hoped for in our country may be taking shape. The shame of slavery and racism - while still echoing - has begun to fade. A new era of tolerance and opportunity and sustainability seems to be unfolding before us, giving shape to the unknown warp and weft.

A new generation of citizen activists is setting the stage for a more sustainable future. Ready to play their part in this new emerging economic and social paradigm.

Among the paths extending from this paradigm is a path leading to an energy future where citizens function as both producers and consumers of a sustainable stream of energy. Creating lateral, overlapping energy grids capable of providing power to the grid, even under less than perfect circumstances.

Yet, in contravention to this, a small group of people is attempting, in the most cynical way, to mortgage our environmental and economic future. Scheming to profit by controlling the distribution of energy and thoughtlessly creating an open door for every terrorist bent on doing us harm.

While Europe and most of the developed world are creating sustainable, decentralized power transmission and delivery systems with safe and secure, laterally scaled, green energy sources to assure no terrorist will be able to successfully attack their power grid, this cabal - motivated largely by greed and avarice - is attempting to maximize their profit by creating a single source transmission system obligating us to power purchases long past the time in which we can make rational projections and with no effort to create a smart grid with overlapping sources. The net result will be to create a 180-mile window of opportunity for every terrorist who wants to destroy the American economy with one or two well-placed explosives, capable of plunging the entire eastern seaboard and the nation's economic brain and nerve center into darkness.

A dark cloud looms over us. Threatening not only to stain our tapestry but to tear it asunder. Obliterating the fabric. This existential threat weaves its way through our tapestry and masks the hope that glimmers in our American dream.

We cannot permit this to happen. As the flag of the patriots acknowledged we must "Join or Die."

In recent days a group of environmental patriots has formed, known to themselves as "The Trust" in deference to their sacred bond with the earth. They have pledged to use all non-violent means, including civil disobedience in the spirit of Thoreau and Alinsky, to stop this travesty.

Their recent gambit, moving the entire retinue of cars belonging to the Granite Skyway investors meeting at the Balsams, from the hotel parking lot to Big Island in the middle of Lake Umbagog, represents their first shot. An erstwhile warning of things to come and the imagination and energy they will bring to the task.

In playing this hand, The Trust also exposed an illegal timber harvesting operation, removing trees representing the prime-nesting habitat of Bald Eagles, Peregrine Falcons and Osprey. Only the Granite Skyway itself could create a greater danger to the raptors of the Great North Woods. The Trust has struck a blow against both.

Their creative use of road kill gave the story that little extra kick and, unless we miss our mark, we predict others will join the campaign.

We, the Gazetteers, pledge to lend our pens and keyboards to the effort, to provide our modest support to the work of The Trust. Detailing the reasons from environmental, to economic and scientific why such an abuse of human rights and the public trust must be stopped and why a responsive and responsible alternative is essential.

In defense of their efforts we will employ the doctrine of competing harms, recognizing that only an economic impact - in conjunction with the public support we hope will be engendered - will be sufficient inducement to those who are use to getting their way by simply throwing money at the right people.

It is our fervent hope that by our efforts the Oligarchs of the Granite Skyway will find no purchase in their quest to trespass upon this generation and those that follow, but have no voice in the matters at hand.

Just as the oligarchs of times past enhanced their bottom line by despoiling the waters and air - using the public commons as their dumping grounds to avoid paying the real cost of their products. So too does this generation of offenders seek to use economic power and perverse interpretations of law to avoid paying the real cost of the debt that will come due and be payable for years to come by every citizen of this great state. Granite Skyway must be stopped.

The Gazetteers
T. Crawford Paine

At the bottom of the page was this note:

As the words of patriots helped spark a revolution more than 240 years ago, we have chosen to write these pamphlets under pseudonyms. We do so because we believe stopping the Granite Skyway is not just important but an existential necessity - requiring that we be willing to sacrifice, everything if necessary, to protect future generations from their treachery. We realize our actions may very well put our livelihoods and perhaps even our lives at risk and while we vow to respect human life in our actions and to hold the members of The Trust to that same standard, we do not share a similar confidence they - The Granite Skyway investors - will do the same. ~ The Gazetteers

---

Quite unlike the days of the colonials when a scribe would have to rely upon word of mouth and hand-carried missives, this pamphlet was in the ether within moments of its production and already journalists from across the country had grabbed onto the story and were running with it.

-=-=-=-=-=-

Enright and Mac had missed the pamphlet completely when they walked into Tea Bird's 30 minutes earlier. What they had noticed at the time was that a good 40% of the people in the Cafe were looking at and sharing the posts of the Buck driving the Lincoln Town Car when they sat down.

Feigning ignorance, Mac had asked the owners, Heather and Scott, who greeted them when they sat down "What's everyone so excited about?"

Heather answered, " Some people opposed to the Granite Skyway absconded with 32 cars from the Balsams last night. The cars belonged to investors in the transmission line project which is as popular around here as herpes so everyone's getting a kick out of sharing one of their posts showing the CEO's car with a dead buck in the driver's seat."

Scott continued, "We also heard they spread a couple stringers of about 40 dead sucker fish in the engines of all the cars too. By the time the owners find them they will probably be unable to get the stink out of their cars."

Scott chuckled, "wait until they try to collect insurance on cars that have absolutely nothing wrong with them except a God-awful smell." He shook his head, as if trying to clear it, as he pushed out the phrase "God-awful" crinkling his nose as if he were smelling the dead fish right then.

"I'd bet none of the policies cover that. Those bastards will be months, if not years, fighting with their insurance companies to get them to cover the loss. Even then the insurance company will try to claim the smell can be cleaned - though I sincerely doubt it. Especially if the fish fell into the fan and got pureed and blasted throughout the engine."

By the time Conrad Fleming had entered the Cafe they knew another shoe was about to drop, they were just unprepared for this particular shoe. Now Conrad Fleming was fired up and the two were not sure they were ready to call his attention to still another piece of footwear. Conrad was not in a mood to take prisoners.

"I hired you people to stay ahead of this shit. How is it we seem to have cascading crises with absolutely no forewarning? Who the hell wrote this?" Fleming asked Enright and Mac.

"This is the first we've seen this Conrad," Enright said. "Mac and I will take this back and analyze it. If we can figure out the author we will get back to you right away."

"Look," Conrad said, "I am not in a mood to tarry here with you two. I have just had two days from hell. It was bad enough I had to do a briefing for all those people but the theft of all these cars and everything that followed; it's too damn much to take. Let's get ahead of this damn thing."

Almost as an afterthought Enright said, "You find your car smelling worse than when you parked it, you may want to check your engine."

Fleming looked at him quizzically then heading out of the Cafe he paused once again at the brochure rack. Grabbing the remaining pamphlets and shoving them into his pocket he speed dialed his office. It might only be a stopgap measure but he needed to keep those pamphlets out of as many hands as he possibly could. He ordered a team of people onto the road to confiscate as many of the pamphlets as they could find. Then he headed for the Town Car and Manchester.

Chapter 39 Lancaster

Up in Lancaster the first cool days of autumn were met with the warm glow from the woodstove in Jack Carrigain's office as he put away - well, hid was more accurate - his laptop. Jack was eager to maintain his "Underwood" reputation. He placed the old typewriter back on top of the desk, inserted a sheet of paper, and rolled it into position.

"Seems like an interesting combination - politics and road kill - a marriage made in Hell," said Jack Carrigain to his old beagle 'Publisher' - 'Pub' for short. Who seemed rather nonplussed despite his companion's obvious excitement.

Back when Jack had picked the runt of the litter from a neighbor's newborn "bevy of beagles" (He made up his own collective noun for them) Jack had chosen the name "Publisher" as something of an inside joke after several days of pacing and smoking his grandfather's old Meerschaum pipe. Now, ten years later, he still got a perverse pleasure from being able to meet the demands of disgruntled readers or impatient politicians with the response "well, of course I need to run this by my publisher. He may have something more to add before I give you an answer."

Despite the fact he was a non-smoker for almost a decade now, Jack kept that old pipe in a burlwood display rack on the top of the fireplace mantle. He had loved being a pipe smoker. Loved the way it smelled, loved the little buzz he got from smoking - especially that first bowl in the morning with his first cup of coffee.

He smiled as he remembered the day he got the pipe.

His grandfather, Alexander Gottig Carrigain, was admitted to the hospital after an accident. He was lucky he wasn't handcuffed to the bed. At 92 he had stolen his own car from Jack's brother's driveway where it had languished since the state had revoked Al's driver's license when he failed his eye test.

After "stealing" his car, Al had driven directly to visit his wife Charlotte, who was confined to a nursing home in North Conway after a diagnosis of Alzheimer's confirmed what they were avoiding and denying for nearly four years in the quiet secrecy of their Bartlett home.

Al made it to the nursing home just fine and had a splendid visit with the love of his life, though she did not have a clue who he was. Then, as he was backing the car up to leave, he sideswiped four cars in the executive section of the parking lot.

It wasn't the car accident that had landed him in the hospital though. While they were waiting for the police at the nursing home; as half the administration of the nursing home was pacing the lot, cursing and mourning their fancy cars, Al had managed to slip away and was walking backward along busy Route 16 with his thumb out, when he tripped over a tree limb and broke his hip.

That afternoon Jack had gone to visit his grandfather in the hospital where he was presented by the old man with his prized pipe.

"Doc told me I had to quit," he said definitively. "Said smoking would kill me!"

Jack took the pipe.

It was a remarkable piece really.

Composed of the shells of tiny sea creatures that fell to the ocean floor millions of years ago and with the surrounding mud had fossilized, the combination created a medium ideal for handcrafting. At some point, a craftsman from Eskisehir, in central Turkey had set to work on a chunk of it, coaxing a bowl, a shank, a stem and a bit from the raw fossil. Meerschaum in a pipe gives the tobacco a very unique, cool smoking flavor; absorbing far more moisture than a briar pipe. When Al first acquired the pipe it was pearl white. Over the years the pipe developed a beautiful deep-brown color.

It was the only pipe Al owned. Jack on the other hand had a small collection of pipes from a corncob made especially for him by a local farmer to a few different clay and burl pipes. That day Jack had abandoned all his old pipes and adopted the Meerschaum.

Now an ex- smoker, Jack had created the special case for the pipe and it occupied an honored space above the mantle of his office fireplace, which now was itself occupied by a Vigilant wood stove from Vermont Castings. Jack had filled the firebox, the place where one builds the fire, with this mid-sized wood stove because it was more efficient. As he aged, Jack, who cut all his own firewood, placed a premium on efficiency, especially when it meant he needed to harvest three cord of wood instead of ten.

He missed the sight of a fire crackling and burning in the large firebox of the fireplace, but the vigilant did allow him to open the front of the stove in order to give one the aesthetics of a fireplace and, from time to time, when he was in the room, Jack would open it up and - efficiency be damned - burn the fire brightly like old times. Today was just one of those days and, occupying his space in this aesthetic tableau was good old Publisher.

Jack bent down to pet Publisher. The soft hair on his muzzle had some time ago turned to gray and his old bones were pretty creaky these days, with good reason. The two of them had hiked almost every Four Thousand Footer in New Hampshire together. "Almost" being the operative word. No, Jack and Pub were not "peak-baggers". They had skipped Owl's Head and Mt Field and a few others where there was no view - no reason to hike, save bragging rights - and they were not in it for the bragging rights. They were in it for the wind, the smell of Balsam fir and views that went on forever.

Don't tell Jack Carrigain that Publisher didn't appreciate the views.

Jack knew Publisher was in his final chapter but he also knew that for the rest of his own life he would remember the way Publisher looked as he gazed into the distance from a mountaintop.

Whenever they reached a summit old Pub would take a lay of the land and pick a flat rock in the highest location. He would then proceed very deliberately to that rock and sit quietly gazing into the distance - often with the wind causing his big ears to flap like a sheet, blown by the wind on a washline. His eyes expressing a wisdom that could not be only from his own brief life but from a deeper understanding; one that came from the ties that have bound men and women to dogs down through the ages. What Jack would have given to be able to know what his old friend was thinking - because he clearly was thinking something as he sat there.

Eventually Pub would lay down, his head planted firmly between his front feet as he continued to look out on the mountains. Slowly he would allow the sun and the breeze to lull him into a sleep that Jack envied.

Now, as he lay in the warm glow of the wood stove, Jack felt that bittersweet realization their time together was near an end. "Think you're ready for one more adventure Old Man?" Jack asked Publisher softly. As if in response Publisher opened one eye, looking directly at Jack, expelling a quiet breath and closing his eyes once again.

" Well, we've set the fire. Now let's see if it takes," Jack said.

Chapter 40 Roadkill Rangers

Like the speed of sound in seawater, word spread. Someone coined the name "The Androscoggin Stampede", presumably a play on the famed rodeo of Calgary, in the Canadian Province of Alberta, and it caught fire, pushing the communication envelope to even greater levels. From major media to local blogs it seemed as though almost everyone was weighing in.

Acting on Enright's counsel, Conrad Fleming had tried to get ahead of the wave by issuing a statement calling the members of The Trust "Eco-Terrorists, bent on denying the people of New Hampshire the power Granite Skyway would provide to them." But the media was quick to remind him that the project was intended to provide electricity to the urban areas far south of the little rural state that would have to pay the environmental price of servicing them. All the same Fleming continued to beat the "Eco-Terror" drum on the theory if you repeat a lie often enough people may eventually mistake it for the truth.

As the actions of The Trust caught the imagination of the public, so too did the words of the anonymous essayist capture the attention of the media. The words of the essay "A Sacred Trust" served as a self-sustaining brainstorm setting free a flood of ideas and theories from small town bloggers, to big city radio and TV producers, writers and camera crews; the kernels gathering momentum and lighting a flame of recognition and a sense of personal power in both opinion makers and the consumers of their ideas.

On the lighter side a host of new groups had sprung forth on Instagram, Twitter and Snapchat all with the words Roadkill Rangers as the basis of their themes and memes.

Roadkill_Rangers_in_Yellow_Trucks was a favorite because the bright yellow trucks and cars of Polaris Energy were an easy target. The first posting to RRIYT (RIT for short) was titled "flying squirrels love yellow trucks" and it featured some eight dead squirrels plastered on the windshield and side windows as if they had all flown into the truck at a high rate of speed. The artist who set this one up went out of his way to make it interesting, going so far as to use a pair of sticks to prop up one squirrel carcass so it appeared to be hanging onto the antenna with the wind and motion of the truck holding it horizontally.

Several contests evolved among the posters. There was a contest challenging people to post the most interesting roadkill (humans not permitted), a contest posing the roadkill in the most creative way, and a contest challenging entrants to create a posting with the largest number of roadkill animals in one vehicle. Among the more unique species to be posted were a huge opossum and a bear seated in the back seat of a limo with a half empty bottle of beer to his lips.

A few entrepreneurs saw opportunity in the act of civil disobedience. One began selling manufactured skunk tails. They were to be placed hanging from the trunk as if the animal itself were inside and its tail was caught in the trunk as it was closed. The tail came with a bumper strip that said, "Granite Skyway - Something stinks here."

Chapter 41   The Posse

Mac poured herself a cup of coffee from the pot on the counter at Enright's house and added a thimble of Bourbon despite the fact it was only 9am. It was right there on the counter after all. Bourbon had become her drink of choice over the years - sometimes with a good cigar - and it helped make JEn more bearable, especially when he was on a tear, as he was today.

She'd been summoned to help him plan their response to the Androscoggin Stampede. She didn't call it that in front of him because he would go ballistic, yelling at her for letting "those hoodlums" define the terms of the battle. She had tried to argue the point that this was a name given to the action by the media, not The Trust, but Enright was having none of it.

Enright was on the phone in the living room, pacing as he spoke loudly. Mac listened in and guessed he was on with Conrad Fleming - - even from the next room she could hear Fleming yelling at Enright through the handset.

"Look," Enright said, " We have some leads but they covered their tracks pretty damn well Conrad. The prints the police lifted have led only to three "black ops" types who are very well protected. We're trying to break through with the Army and CIA but so far they aren't playing ball with us."

"Black Ops?" Fleming said. "You mean like Rangers or Seals? NOT GOOD. NOT GOOD!" Fleming shouted," This is not good JEn. The last thing we need is to have a bunch of super patriots in this group. Don't you let the cat out of the bag on this one."

"Unless I miss my guess Conrad, "we may not have anything to say about this. I suspect they are intent on letting cats out of bags everywhere they go. And you have a sackful of 'em!"

Enright continued, " I have Duggan, Wilson and Echo up in Berlin and Errol right now trying to track down a lead. We are starting by trying to figure out how the hell they knew about that illegal timbering operation to begin with. The Feds are so fired up about the lumbering operation we can't get them to pay any attention to our outlaws; and the local cops, hell, they think it's all a great joke. They're taking selfies with Roadkill put in Polaris trucks and telling stories in the local bars about these guys like they are legends."

"Some local musician has even written a song called "Roadkill Rangers" and you'd think the guy was John Lennon the way the local folks have taken to singing along with it. Christ! If they hadn't made smoking illegal in bars they'd be holding up lighters as they sang. I guess we can be thankful all the politically correct nanny state types have made it easier for us on that count."

"JEn I need you to put together a posse and track these bastards down. I don't want them lionized as a bunch of environmental patriots. We need to smear them, make them into terrorist outlaws. If they're trying to avoid crossing a line to keep the public on their side, push them across it."

"How much do you want to be looped in on our activities Conrad? After all, every moment I am worrying about keeping you informed is a moment I can't concentrate on the task at hand."

"JEn, I'm paying you a lot of money to keep my hands clean and to get the job done. I want to be kept up to speed on your progress, but I want deniability if you screw up and get caught. And for Christ's sake keep control of that bunch of thugs you have working for you. I was in the House of Representatives when Echo was dipping his wick in speeders and litterbugs up in Wagner and without any provision for removing a guy like that we had to shame him into resigning. There were a lot of very nervous State Reps, wondering if their own set of peccadilloes would be revealed by that loose cannon . . . especially the Majority Leader. For a while there was even a rumor he was going to call on his old pals in the CIA to help him take care of the problem."

There was a long pause on the line and then JEn said, "I'd forgotten about the fact our esteemed Majority Leader was a career spook. Is he still burning the midnight oil with your lobbyist? "

"He is", said Fleming, but if you are going to ask for his help you had better let her handle it. He's a survivor and if he knows who you are and the shit hits the fan he'll give you up in a heartbeat. He'll protect her if for no other reason than his wife will have his balls in a vice grip if she finds out he's been "christening the yak" with our lobbyist - and it won't help us either."

"Christening the Yak? Now that's worth the price of admission for this phone call Conrad." Enright said.

"I thought you'd like it. Now get to work Enright. Find those damned outlaws."

Conrad was just about to hang up when he recalled the conversation between the young conservation officer and his commanding officer. "JEn, one other thing to check out. A young conservation officer at Big Island was sure he had stumbled upon a track from a wolf. I'm not sure why he thought that was important, but he did."

"Probably because wolves have been extinct in this area since the early 1900s." replied Enright. "Did it just occur to you we might find this information useful Conrad?"

Enright hung up the phone and called to Mac. "Tell those guys up north to ask around about someone with a wolf as a pet. We may have just caught a break."

Chapter 42 Who's in Charge Around Here?

Duggan, Wilson and Echo walked through the front door of Tea Bird's Cafe in Berlin with just minutes to spare before they stopped serving breakfast.

Wilson immediately noticed a new "Essay" from the Gazetteers had been released and was in the magazine rack just inside the front door. She surreptitiously snatched up the entire stack of them and slipped them into her jacket. As the three took a table she withdrew a copy and photographed it with her smartphone, sending it directly to both Enright and Mac. Mac would no doubt want to send it along to Governor "Mags" who was still operating under the illusion she was of an independent mind on this and Mac needed to treat her with kid gloves until she was turned.

She shared copies with Duggan and Larry Echo and the three sat stoically reading the essay.

Giving Away the Store
A Free Pass and an Extension Cord
Politicians and Bureaucrats Sell Out the State's Future with Granite Skyway
Patrick H. Stark

No matter the state, politicians have a long history of tough talk and slight of hand. Whether it's Kansas or Georgia, Alabama or New Hampshire we have all heard a line of Governors, Senators and Representatives talking tough about protecting the interests of their state only to cave in to the first comer with a bag of money.

All too often the tough talk is not meant to protect us but rather to distract us from what is really going on. This allows the politicians to seem as if their interest coincides with ours when actually they are aiding and abetting a "bait and switch" that leaves us digging around in our pockets and wondering how someone made off with our keys and our wallets.

Virgil and Wyatt Earp have the rest of us watching the OK Corral while the thieves are sneaking into the bank and stealing all the money and a horse or two on their way out for good measure.

Such is the case with Granite Skyway. Our current Governor was elected on a pledge she would not support the project unless the entire length was buried. Yet since her election all talk of burying the lines has evaporated like so much hot air and now she has moved on to wringing her hands about making sure the long-term power needs of the state are met.

Leaving aside the fact that no politician ever gave a rip about what was going to happen 20 or 30 years hence, unless it fit the needs of their current agenda, it's worth noting that the Granite Skyway project is proposed at a time when electricity demand has been flat or falling for more than a decade. Not because we have been in a recession - we have in fact had one of the longest periods of sustained growth in US history - but because of new technologies, particularly ones that allow us to reduce electricity demand through efficiency and conservation, are employed by more and more individuals and businesses.

Additionally, though only a modest number of homes and businesses have been able to take advantage of net metering laws, the electricity generated for the grid has demonstrated the promise of expanding rooftop, business and home solar arrays in the future. Most projections for the future indicate conservation and technological advances will continue to exert a downward pressure on the need for large new power facilities and transmission lines. Allowing older plants to be retired without the need to construct new large facilities.

This is not to say new sources of power and new transmission will be completely unnecessary. However, the changes needed will be more along the lines of upgrading existing systems and taking advantage of new ideas like smart grids and more green, renewable energy sources, decentralized and scaled laterally, built by joining together locally developed resources and linking them together through a smart grid.

A recent report from the highly respected Marcy Institute for Public Policy at the University of New Hampshire, indicates no additional transmission or power production is necessary for the foreseeable future and the creation of such is likely to create unanticipated costs to the ratepayers from unneeded stranded assets.

When viewed in this light the Granite Skyway project can only be described as . . . well . . . DOWNRIGHT STUPID.

A theft of public resources for private greed.

Ask yourself this: If a group of experts representing a broad diversity of residents and expertise had been brought together to design a power generation and transmission system in keeping with our best interests, how would it look?

Certainly not like this.

This is the biggest betrayal of all: At a time when we need our primary state utility to be planning the transmission grid of the future, advocating and advancing the generation of renewable power in a post-carbon era and standing up for the values that define our beautiful natural state, they are wasting their time and resources on a glorified extension cord with no future value to our state whatsoever.

All around us states have begun planning - even constructing - smart grids that meet the challenges of the future and support distributed energy sources - - but not here.

It is malpractice, malfeasance of the highest order. Over the years Polaris has grown fat, dumb and happy - with particular emphasis on DUMB - in its enviable position of a publicly sanctioned monopoly. If it had to compete with other utility companies in an open marketplace, it would have been long gone, but it has benefitted from a lack of assertive oversight and now we are paying for it.

In essay number 1 Gazetteer Paine compared them to the Oligarchs of old, who despoiled the air and the waters of our country rather than finding ways to produce their products without polluting the public commons - pocketing the difference and leaving us to breath the air and drink the water poisoned by their greed.

If the proponents of Granite Skyway have their way, they will repeat this travesty again and we will pay the price for the next 5 generations. They will start with thousands of acres of clear cuts, creating massive scars upon the land we love, and they will leave behind a trail of towers and tears that will be our legacy to our children, our grandchildren and their grandchildren.

Yet the politicians and bureaucrats are not standing up to them . . . Not demanding they go back to the drawing board or go home! Demanding, if we are to have a transmission line, let it be OUR transmission line not a privately owned one over which we have no control.

Polaris Electric exists by our forbearance. They are a <u>Public</u> utility. They can only hide behind a cadre of investors if WE PERMIT IT. If they wish to burden our grandchildren with a transmission line, let them bring us a proposal designed to cherish and respect our heritage, our land and our interests.

<u>We have been played for a bunch of chumps</u>. Handing over the public rights-of-way and the viewsheds to a cabal of investors, led by a utility company bent on ignoring its moral and economic obligation to us, whose only interest appears to be "making a buck".

Granite Skyway investors are bent on creating a transmission system that privatizes profits and socializes the environmental, social and economic costs and consequences.

As proposed The Granite Skyway Project began as nothing more than a glorified extension cord, bringing power directly from Canada to the suburbs of Philadelphia, Boston and New York without so much as a kilowatt finding its way into a home here in the Granite State. Little has changed since then.

For too many politicians this is just fine. They are willing to throw open the doors and let the home invaders have their way with the entire family.

We are not.

When the British came to enforce their authority over our land, their soldiers wore red and marched in a straight line. We hid in the woods, fought back from behind stonewalls and took the battle to them on our own terms.

This war will not be waged with guns and cannons but we will surely fight it on our own terms.

The Gazetteers
Patrick H. Stark

Scott Gregory was behind the grill making the last of the breakfasts as he watched Susan Wilson pocket the pamphlets. He discretely continued to watch the entire scene transpire while he cooked. Rather than confronting the trio, he decided he would simply watch them. Something wasn't entirely kosher but he was going to arm himself with all the details before he decided what to do. After all, he could always order more of the essays.

Heather was clearing tables when he hit the bell on the counter to indicate an order was up. When Heather turned Scott motioned with his head for her to join him.

"Don't look over there," Scott said, "but those three who just arrived are acting very weird. The woman took the entire stack of new essays from the Gazetteers and stashed them in her coat but for one each for herself and the other two, then she photographed hers and texted someone - probably sent the piece to them."

"What should we do? Should I make her put them back?" Heather said.

"No" Scott said. "Let's see if we can figure out what they're up to. If we figure out who the members of The Trust are maybe we can provide them with some useful information."

"Okay, I'll bring them menus and water."

"Be careful Heather. We don't want to tip them off."

Heather hugged him, "This is exciting! We get to play spies for the good guys."

"We're not playing Heather. This is serious business."

"Oh lighten up Lancelot. Your Guinevere knows how to handle this."

Heather walked over to the table and poured water into the glasses that had already been set there after the last patrons had departed. She passed out menus with her characteristic good cheer and said "Hi I'm Heather."

"We're still serving breakfast but only for a few more minutes. Can I bring you some coffee or juice while you're deciding?"

Will Duggan ordered coffees all around and just as Heather was about to walk away, he said, "hey we're up here scouting for a movie location and we're looking for someone who has a wolf we might be able to use in some of the scenes . . . Know anyone?"

Heather seemed genuinely interested. "A movie! WOW! How cool! What's it about?"

Duggan hesitated; he should have thought this through a bit more. He was improvising on the fly and now he had to come up with something he had not planned on. "Err. . . well . . . it's kind of a secret. You know intellectual property stuff. But it has a wolf as one of the characters. Does that sound like anyone you know? It's pretty good money."

"Wolves have been extinct here in NH since around 1900," Heather said, "and it's illegal to have a purebred wolf as a pet" There are some folks who have wolf-hybrids - - that's a dog that might be up to 50% wolf - - but I don't know any of them personally. There's actually a sanctuary down in the Ossipee area and one near Keene as well. You might check there."

"Ready to order? Or do you need a few more minutes?"

The trio ordered breakfast and Heather walked away, heading for the kitchen, trying not to be too obvious in her excitement.

"Did you learn anything?" Scott asked.

"They claim they're scouting a location for a movie, said they were looking for someone with a wolf; but something was hinky about their answer when I asked what the movie was about."

"Daniel Roy was here with that Canadian woman the other day, didn't he say something about a Timberwolf?"

"That's right. I caught a glimpse of him, the wolf I mean, and his big head was sticking out the car window when they drove in. I told these three I didn't know of anyone with a wolf. Do you think we should warn Daniel?"

"Whether we need to or not." Scott said. "He needs to know someone is asking around."

Chapter 43   Cruising the Boreal Forest

Thomas and Metallak cruised through the woods like a giant thresher navigating through a bay of icebergs. Thomas had learned early on, after training Metallak, that the border between the US and Canada had no real meaning for them. As long as he was well away from any highway he and his furry friend could cross back and forth across this artificial barrier at will. The dogs usually tagged along with them but if stealth were required Thomas would leave them at one of his many abodes.

Living by himself, here in the Great North Woods, was the life he had chosen. He had his reasons. It certainly wasn't that he was lazy. Thomas had made arrangements to farm plots on the property of more than ten local families. He would plant and nurture the garden and share a portion of the bounty with each family. This form of agriculture wasn't exactly anything in the lexicon of sustainable agriculture or even subsistence agriculture. It was one part sharecropper, one part subsistence farmer and one part entrepreneur. He called it Co-Farming. Had he been the least bit concerned about his legacy, he might have tried to copyright the term, just for the record books, but he didn't give a damn about such trivialities.

His efforts with The Trust had, of late, taken a serious bite out of his time. Luckily, he was at the tail end of the growing season and as long as he could handle the harvesting, he would not be in danger of harming his relationships with landowners. Harvesting was of course not a "one and done" kind of thing. It required regular visits to the plots to pick the veggies that were ripe so they did not go to waste. So far he had managed to both fulfill his obligations to The Trust and landowners but he was concerned; concerned both for his day-to-day obligations but also about the big picture. What if he was arrested and held for an extended time? What if he was hurt or worse? It wasn't a concern that incapacitated him but it was enough to move him to secure a safe deposit box at the Colebrook Savings and Loan. In that box he placed his contracts with local landowners, a map of the plot locations and general directions for fulfilling his obligations to them. He also placed a map of his "abodes" and a bill of sale for his few possessions, his dogs and Metallak, naming Hank Algren the "buyer".

Thomas felt weird about creating a bill of sale for warm-blooded creatures he himself viewed as his family but he set aside those views for a pragmatic approach that would guarantee their interests would be protected. Two keys were provided for this safe deposit box, one he retained and the other he gave to Hank Algren.

Hank had pooh-poohed the gesture at first, assuring him this was overkill but he accepted the key in deference to their long-time friendship.

The peace of mind Thomas felt from doing this could not be overstated.

As he wove his way through the woods, streams and boreal forests of the area Metallak was like a living all-terrain vehicle.

This was voyageur country. Where French trappers had used the interconnecting ponds and streams and rivers to ferry their furs to markets in the lower continental region and to ports where they could be shipped to Europe. A person on foot would have been wading through bogs and streams almost constantly. Being dry would be, at best, a state-of-mind. But for Metallak no stream was too wide or deep, no bog too mucky, no woods too dense, though Thomas tried to encourage him to avoid the densest of the wood simply because he, himself, was not scratch proof.

Today they were on a mission. They were scoping out the final transmission substation in Canada before the border. He would have preferred focusing on one of the many dams generating hydroelectricity in the Hydro-Quebec system but since all of them were located in the more remote northern regions of the province, he was going to have to focus on the substation instead. This substation would be the source of the Canadian power supplying Granite Skyway.

Hydro-Quebec had announced plans to add more than twenty additional dams in the coming years, the largest and most controversial - the Romaine River Dam - all built anticipating the demand from points south would exceed their current surplus requiring them to create additional capacity.

Security around these substations was almost non-existent, mostly a series of cameras, positioned to allow them to be monitored remotely. The cameras were all located in a very short perimeter and oddly no one had made any effort to conceal them so careful observation allowed him to avoid them as long as he kept a reasonable distance. When he couldn't avoid the cameras completely he had a secret weapon, copied from the Plains Indians. Four deerskins stitched together to make a camouflage he could pull over himself as he hugged Metallak's prodigious neck and head and buried himself behind the hump at the base of his neck. The sight of a moose in this country was no big deal. Chances were a video operator would not waste more than a moment on a wandering moose and certainly would not expect someone to be riding on its back. Thomas knew this wasn't fool proof but so far it had held him in good stead and he hoped his luck would hold.

Today Thomas needed his luck to hold because he was going "off book" on this one . . . "going rogue" as they said. He knew the other members of The Trust would not condone sabotage but taking a page from his Ranger days he was scouting out all the options. If it came down to it . . . if things went sideways . . . if things got away from them, he wanted to know what his options were and be able to execute one of them.

Sabotaging the final substation was the surest way to cut off the power that would be transmitted into New Hampshire. Since the power was not generated by a specific dam in the Hydro-Quebec system, a shutdown at any one dam in the system would simply be addressed by increasing the output of one or more other dams. However, cutting the power at the very point where it crosses over into the United States would create chaos.

Chapter 44   Local Power

Sandra Manes answered the phone on the second ring. She used a special ringtone for unknown callers, and this was one. She and Peter Brahms were working late on a Friday getting ready for a Local Power Raising.

Sandra at 45 was thin and athletic despite a sweet tooth she claimed was a genetic defect. Peter was a hale fellow with a ready smile and dark intelligent eyes framed by a pair of glasses that rarely came off. The two were friends since they had met while attending college at the University's northern campus in Plymouth. Each had gone their own way professionally since graduation but, like a lot of people in this rural state, had remained actively involved in the community. In the last few years much of their energy was focused on building a local grassroots organization aimed at putting solar panels on homes and taking advantage of the Net Metering law they had helped pass through the State Legislature.

Net metering is a process where solar panels on a home were not providing power for the home but instead directly linked to the grid. A meter on the home keeps track of the power produced and credits the electric account of the homeowner who would then only be responsible for the "net" cost of electricity at the end of each month. If the home produced more power than it needed, the surplus was "banked" with the local power company and could be drawn upon if the home used more power than it produced in the future.

"Sandra, it's Jack Carrigain, we met at one of the Appalachian Mountain Club events in the North Country when they were holding hearings about hikers and bikers sharing the trails. I've been watching your work with the communities down that way with great interest and I really admire the way you have pushed the envelope and the power structure by making things happen locally."

Surprised a North Country icon like Carrigain even remembered who she was, Sandra responded tentatively. "Hello Jack, very nice to hear from you and thank you so much. We're pretty proud of what we've been able to accomplish." She silently mouthed 'Jack Carrigain' to Peter, who had developed a knack for reading her lips after over a year of being completely annoyed by her penchant for doing this.

"Listen Sandra, I have a request but it's a little bit sensitive and I have to ask you a few questions before I lay it out for you. I just have to be sure we're on the same page in order to make my request."

"OK Jack," Sandra answered tentatively. "But what is this about?"

"I know you're opposed to the Granite Skyway project because I saw a photo of you at a protest in the NH Guardian last month. Have you been following the news about this group that calls itself The Trust? They are the ones who made all those cars vanish a few weeks ago at the Balsams."

"Jack, hold on a second, I'd like to bring my partner Peter into this discussion, since I would not want to even try keeping anything from him, if anything he's even more adamant about stopping Granite Skyway than I am."

Jack tried to object, unsure he wanted to have anyone else in on this conversation, but before he could voice his objection, Peter was on and Sandra was explaining that this was a call about the Granite Skyway transmission line proposal. Jack held back on his objection as they were already too far along.

"Jack it's a real honor to speak with you." Peter said. "Please tell me you are going to come out against this damn thing."

Jack paused for a moment. He was not sure he wanted to step into the breech on this just yet and besides he needed to maintain his neutrality in order to stay below the radar with the Gazetteers. Slowly he explained.

"Peter, Sandra, I think you will know, from the nature of the request I am making of you, my answer to your question. But before I go any farther, I need to know that if you can't help me you will, at the very least, promise to keep our conversation confidential . . . at least for the next few months. After that it's likely to be public knowledge anyway, but for right now we need to be under the radar if we're going to be effective."

"Well Jack," said Sandra, "Pete and I are cheering for The Trust and hoping they can move the debate in a saner direction. Right now it looks like the Polaris folks have all the advantage and that can't be good. So if you want us to do anything that hurts The Trust's cause, we'll have to politely decline before you go any farther."

"I'm glad to hear that Sandra, because I am looking for some people to help support their efforts. Now, can I count on your discretion?"

Peter and Sandra looked at one another. Each nodded to the other. Then Peter answered.

"Let's hear what you've got Jack; as long as you aren't prankin' us of course!"

Jack laughed and the tension seemed to drain from the conversation with Peter's lighthearted jest. "I assume," he said, "you have also seen the piece written under the aegis of *The Gazetteers*, by someone with the pen name of Paine."

"Sure", Peter said, "although I thought taking the name of that particular patriot was a bit over the top."

"Perhaps so," Jack responded thoughtfully, "although at the time I suspect Tom Paine had no more of an idea of how far reaching "Common Sense" would be than we have now as we are engaged in this fight. Even now there are more than a dozen similar projects proposed across the country, all with the intent of somehow halting the movement to a more secure and sustainable energy future. It may be what we are engaged in is much bigger than any of us realize."

"Ok" said Peter "I can buy that. Let's hear what you have to say."

"The Gazetteers is a small group of people who have agreed to write essays in support of a more sustainable approach to providing power in the future. While we are not specifically and directly defending The Trust, the ultimate result is that we are defending the righteousness of their cause and we are trying to leverage their efforts to bring attention to the larger issues at stake here. And, as you know, there are a lot of them. After all, the payback for projects of this magnitude are measured in decades, yet the advances in technology are coming at us exponentially. By employing today's technology to this problem, and wedding ourselves to those technologies, we are forgoing the opportunity to bring new technologies to bear."

Carrigain continued, " There are other issues of course, not the least of which is that this monstrosity will mar the landscape for a hundred years or more. Once it's up they'll surely be looking for ways to continue to use the infrastructure and we'll never be able to develop the public support to remove it."

"We are with you one hundred percent Jack," Sandra said. "How can we help?

"I need a writer who can make the case for a more sustainable approach to generating and transmitting power. Someone - or ones if you are going to do this as a team - who can inform the public about the cutting edge approaches being employed in other places and even speak to the issue of advances likely in the near term."

"We need to help the public understand where things are trending and what kind of technologies would be better to employ for future power production and transmission. And just as important, we need to set the tone for the media who will be reporting on The Trust and looking for ways to tie it into the debate over both the Granite Skyway proposal and the future of energy production and transmission in general - as well as climate change issues."

We recommend you write under a pseudonym because we just don't know how these people are going to react. There's a lot of money at stake and when that's the case, people can be pretty testy about opposition. For your own personal safety we feel you will want to mask your identity.

Sandra responded now, "OK Jack, we've got it. We will come up with a name and get working on a draft for you. Give me your email so we can keep in touch."

Jack gave her the address and added, "Also, if you happen to know anyone who can write an essay from another viewpoint - a terrorism expert for example, or an economist or futurist, let me know and I'll follow up. Don't ask them yourself, ok? We are trying to keep this circle very tight so I need to be the one to do the asking."

"We? Sandra asked. "Who else is on the team Jack?"

"My point exactly Sandra." Jack said. "When the battle is over we'll raise a glass together, but not until then."

Chapter 45   Smoke 'Em if You Catch 'Em

Linda Levy lifted and dropped the big cast iron knocker, shaped like a moose, on the door of Jack Carrigain's home in Lancaster. The boom of the sound rang through the house and brought Jack Carrigain to the door almost immediately.

Publisher, on the other hand, barely reacted. In his younger days he would have announced the presence of a visitor on the upward swing of the old door knocker, before it was dropped or rapped on the hard oak door; his beagle bay reverberating throughout the house.

Today the old boy simply raised his head, glanced at the door and saw Jack was on his way. He gave a small soft "woof" just to let Jack know he was still on his game; but, determining there was nothing to worry about, at the moment anyway, he set his head back down on his paws. He'd keep one eye open just to make sure Jack had everything under control but mostly he'd just rest.

Jack introduced himself to Linda and led her into his great room with huge picture windows that looked out on the Kilkenny Range. Linda was mesmerized by the view.

"Are you a hiker?" Jack asked her.

"A hiker and a climber." She responded.

"The Kilkenny Range is one of the great secrets of the White Mountains. Other ranges in the Whites get so much traffic they have to require hiking permits and fire permits and advance registration if your group is bigger than four or five people. None of that is an issue on Kilkenny. There's even a cabin you can stay in on Mount Cabot. It's rustic but a welcome spot in bad weather. There's also a great little high country pond, called "Unknown Pond" that is a "fly fishing only" pond. I bring my fly rod with me and sometimes I even camp there so I can enjoy my catch cooked over a nice little fire. If I catch my limit - and I often do in these high country ponds where there isn't a lot of competition - I'll smoke a few of them overnight and nibble on them the next day during the hike."

"You smoke them over the fire?"

"Yeah, I learned to do this while I was paddling in the Boundary Waters Canoe Wilderness in northern Minnesota with my college friend Christopher. It was a pretty amazing experience. We fished a little every day but didn't catch much most of the time. Then one day we hit the jackpot and caught 12 beautiful rainbow trout. That night we ate fish chowder prepared with dried milk, potatoes, onions and trout. We saved three trout for our breakfast and the rest we hung on a rack over the fire and smoked them overnight. They lasted us the rest of our trip, smoked just enough to preserve them for two weeks."

"When we were finished with our dinner we were leaning against a big old log by the fire when we heard a rustling in the woods behind us. We were both nervous about attracting bear with the fish so we watched with great trepidation as the sound grew closer to us . . . suddenly over the hill came this otter following the scent of the fish. He had his nose to the ground and was not really paying attention to anything except following the trail. I said "Well hello there little fella'!" and he lifted his head and spun around in one motion, like a little old man who had accidentally wandered into the ladies room. He started back down the hill but when we didn't give chase I guess he figured it was safe to venture back. We tossed him one of our fish and he just laid right down there and merrily munched away at his bounty."

"Anyway, Unknown Pond is a great trout fishery and the entire range makes for a good hike. There aren't any amazing views from the trails but beautiful forests and some nice vistas, just not 'knock your socks off' stuff. Publisher and I hike there regularly since we've both gotten older because the terrain is not as challenging as some of the other ranges in northern New Hampshire."

Linda bent down to pet Publisher and the beagle gladly accepted the attention. "His name's Publisher eh?" Linda said almost immediately grasping the utility of the name. "Guess I'll know what you mean if you tell me you have to discuss my request with your publisher!"

Jack smiled wryly, "not a lot of people catch that." he said. "But I suppose part of the issue is that I usually use his nickname "Pub" and they think he was named after a bar somewhere. I don't disabuse them of the notion for that very reason."

"Well Jack, I'm up this way because I am doing some research for a book I'm writing, I also just took on a new client - well more like a group and I was meeting with them as well."

"Where you staying?" Jack asked.

"Max and I are staying at the Balsams."

"Oh, so you are travelling first class then. You should have brought Max along, or is he playing golf while you work?"

"If he is, it's going to be the hottest cat video on the net!" Linda replied. "Max is a big ol' Maine Coon Cat, we sort of adopted one another a few years back when his Alley Cat days were drawing to an end."

"Ahhh, a Maine Coon Cat. Always seemed to me that was the only kind of cat I would ever want, they don't really think of themselves as cats, you know?"

"Ain't that the truth,"

"Me and Publisher, well, since my wife died a few years ago, we've been kind of a thing, you know. There's not a lot of space for a cat in our relationship even a cat that thinks of itself as a dog - or a person. It's just the two of us and from time to time my grand daughter, Jessie, who is the light of my life. She's coming to visit me in a few weeks so we can go to the Sandwich Fair together."

"By the way," Jack said, "were you at the Balsams when that group calling itself The Trust pulled off that creative parking gig?"

"I was, but I can't really talk about it any more than that without violating lawyer client privilege." she said.

"Ahhhh" Jack said, "I'll keep your secret if you'll keep mine."

Jack pulled out his copy of the first Gazetteer essay. "T. Crawford Paine here, glad to make your acquaintance."

"Jack! You are a hero! I can't tell you how much The Trust folks appreciate your support in this effort."

"Well, let's keep this between you and me for now ok? I'm less worried about my own safety than I am watching for the right moment to make my position public."

"You've got my word Jack."

"Well, you didn't come here to talk about me," Jack said. "How can I help you Linda?"

"Jack, this story is just so strange I felt as if I needed to get some insight from someone up this way. You were the name that kept coming up as I asked folks who I should speak with about it."

"Well, let's hear your story."

Linda launched right into the tale of the 'Wrong Way Senators' she had heard in the Boston PD. When she finished she paused and waited for Jack Carrigain to respond.

Carrigain was looking rather stunned. " Whhoooo eeee!" He said, "You know we talk about wanting Republicans and Democrats working together nowadays, but this is the other side of that looking glass isn't it? Damn, this is a story I had not heard. But from the way you told it to me I can almost put it together with names and faces, at least the main culprits."

"You can?" Linda replied.

"I can. But should I? More important should you use names at all? After the entire story is enough to raise the hair on the back of your neck without names and I don't think we have a way to verify the facts. None of them are alive at this point unless I'm mistaken about who the joy riders and their rescuer were."

"OK how about this," Linda posited. I will promise to leave out the names unless I can get absolute verification from at least two other sources. I won't include you as a source under any circumstances. Nor would I ever give up my sources!"

Jack thought for a moment. "I can live with that."

"You would have made a hell of a journalist Ms. Levy."

Chapter 46   Triple Threats

It had only been a few days since Linda's visit but Jack had thought of little else during that time. He guessed she was about ten years his junior but that wasn't such a big stretch these days. After all there was a nearly thirty-year gulf between the President and his First Lady right? He had no plans to run for office, so in theory he should have even more latitude in this matter.

At any rate, he was glad for the distraction provided by the arrival of the essay by Sandra and Peter to help him stop obsessing about the lovely Ms. Levy. He read through it hoping he would be able to get it into publication with a minimum of editing and a maximum of speed.

The Triple Threat of the Hydro-Quebec - Granite Skyway Nexus
Sandra and Peter Revere

Granite Skyway will encourage the continued destruction of Wild Rivers and Native lands in Canada; Discourage the production of our own home-grown renewable power; and create a nearly irresistible target for terror that could throw the entire Eastern Seaboard into darkness.

If you have ever wondered whether there could be a system for producing and transmitting electricity worse than the one we have here in the US, you need only look north to the Province of Quebec where government ownership of the corporate entity that both produces and distributes electrical power has led to a Crony Capitalism rife with institutional corruption and a government whose principal interest is profit, not the well-being of its citizens.

At a time when our own utility company should be improving our own grid, making it more resilient and capable of better servicing the needs of our own people, Polaris Electric and the investors of Granite Skyway are tying our fate to a gargantuan transmission line, little more than an extension cord for Southern New England and the suburbs of NY and Philadelphia, Baltimore and Washington DC.

While states all around us are creating smarter grids, capable of supporting the fast-paced growth in the development of microgrids of clean, renewable power created from the entrepreneurial development of small power production and linked net-metered homes and businesses, our primary utility is building a transmission line designed to specifically bypass these opportunities.

In other states the focus on grid improvement and microgrid creation is spurring homegrown businesses that will generate well-paying jobs, homegrown and sustainable. Here Granite Skyway will provide us a brief pop in employment that will disappear once the transmission line is built.

If Granite Skyway is built it will transmit only power produced in Canada. Power that is neither green nor clean. It is power developed at the continued expense of the Native First Nations people of Canada.

In the U.S., Indian people were moved onto reservations believed to be of no value only to have the treaties granting them the land abrogated the moment we discovered a resource we wanted to plunder . . .usually gold. In Quebec the gold that drives policy is hydropower.

Damming a river and creating reservoirs to hold the water used for electric generation could have been done along the border, closer to the source for the sale of surplus electricity produced by the dams. However, this would require Hydro-Quebec to displace and poison people who had political power . . . People who could fight back. Instead they have chosen to develop these power facilities by damming the wild and scenic rivers of the northern regions of Canada. Hydro-Quebec has flooded more than 9 million acres of land, largely in regions providing the principal sources of food and sustenance for First Nations tribes such as the Cree, the Inuit and the Innu.

The flooding required to create reservoirs for hydroelectric production builds dams on wild and scenic rivers, fills the surrounding valleys; and covers and kills the very forests needed to process the carbon in our atmosphere and for the generation of oxygen. The decomposing vegetation underlying the reservoir releases mercury, poisoning the fish and turning the once rich fishing resources of the native people into a toxic stew. The inundated vegetation produces both carbon dioxide and methane as it rots - some experts postulate methane alone asserts an effect on our climate 25 times worse than carbon dioxide.

If Granite Skyway is completed it will form a single central pipeline for electricity that will reach from northern Quebec down to the toney suburbs of the northeast United States. But the billions spent in the US to secure our own borders will provide no security whatsoever for the source of this power. We will be completely and irreversibly dependent upon Quebec and Canada, if we are fortunate and Quebec remains a Province. One well placed explosive from a domestic or international terrorist will cascade through the US grid and, quite likely, throw the entire Eastern Seaboard into darkness. Are we willing to place the fate of our electric grid in the hands of another nation?

The one ray of hope in this scenario is that our military installations will not go dark as well. Why? Because they are - right now - creating the same microgrids Granite Skyway will foreclose to the rest of us.

As our neighbor's seven year old would say: "Ain't that ironical!"

The Gazetteers
Sandra and Peter Revere

Chapter 47   Heading North

"Open a Goddamn window will you? You're killing me with those damn cancer sticks!"

Duggan was driving and the three were headed for the Canadian border where they were going to see if there was a record of a wolf brought into the state in the last month. They had split up after their stop at Tea Bird's and worked the street in Berlin and then a few of the surrounding towns trying to get a lead on the wolf. Each of them picked up bits and pieces of information that provided a series of clues to this mystery but nothing was definitive . . . not even close.

Several people recalled seeing what they thought was a white wolf-hybrid with its head sticking out the window of a Prius. No, they had not seen the Prius around before; it was unlikely it was someone local since they would remember that wolf dog and probably the car.

The next morning they stood outside of Tea Bird's and accosted people coming in for breakfast. It was here they caught a big break. Susan Wilson, who was less threatening to people entering the cafe, managed to convince a few people to open up and just like that the pieces began to fall into place.

One man she spoke with said he remembered the Prius with the white wolf. "The Prius had a "Trees Not Towers" bumper strip on it. Showing his age - and proclivities, he said "These damn hippies come up here and make us their playground but they don't give a rat's ass about us when they leave. Does it matter to them there aren't enough decent jobs for people who live here? Hell no!"

"I couldn't agree more", Wilson said. Egging him on, blowing smoke with the company line. "Granite Skyway is going to create a lot of jobs for people here in Berlin."

"Damn right!"

"What else do you remember?" Wilson pressed him. "Did you see anything more?"

The man thought a moment. "I remember the wolf, err dog; well, if that <u>was</u> a wolf-hybrid it was more wolf than dog." He said. "He - or she - was packed in tight with two big backpacks. They left the window wide open, I guess they figured no one was going to mess with their shit if they had to go through that critter."

"Do you remember anything else?"

Just then a burly man with a full beard stuck his head out the door of Tea Bird's. "Jesus Hal! How long are you going to make us wait to order here? Get your ass in here while it's still morning. Your coffee's getting cold."

Hal looked at him. "I hope you didn't order me one of them sissy coffees with the steamed milk and flavors. I'm coming now, keep your panties dry!"

He looked at Wilson, "I best be getting in there, the boys only meet on Thursdays and they get pretty prickly when they have to wait on someone." Hal headed for the door.

Just as he was about to enter the Cafe he stopped. "One other thing", he said. "One of the backpacks had a big Canadian flag sewed on the top. Damn Canucks they're just as bad as the Massholes. We're just a playground for them."

"Bingo!" thought Wilson.

Within ten minutes they had piled into Duggan's SUV and were headed for the border.

After they had been driving for about thirty minutes Susan Wilson lit up a Parliament cigarette from the pack in her belly bag. That's when Duggan lost it.

"I didn't hear you complaining when Larry here lit up that big doobie on the way up to Berlin," Wilson said defensively but she cracked her window and let the cigarette smoke escape, despite the rush of cold autumn air that filled the car.

"You want to spend a night in the Hoosegow? If we drove through these little towns wafting a trail of pot smoke some over-eager local cop would be only too happy to pinch us. JEn would be real happy with you then wouldn't he?" Duggan asked.

"I have a Cannabis Card," Wilson retorted. "So it wouldn't be my ass in jail now would it?"

"The hell it wouldn't," Echo said. "Do you know what happens to me if I get caught smoking dope with no card? I get a traffic ticket. That's what. But you, Miss High and Mighty, if you can't prove the weed came from your local dispensary you get charged with a misdemeanor, punishable by up to a year in jail."

"No shit?" Duggan said. "What the hell is the sense in that?"

"Your government at work." Echo said. "What they give with one hand they take away with the other. These dispensaries make up shit about the healing powers of various strains of dope and charge a hundred bucks for a dime bags worth of weed. Hell, I bet they take one bag of dope, divide it up into a bunch of jars and label them with a bunch of exotic names and sell the same dope to a bunch of idiots who think they are buying a special strain picked by brown skinned women with bare tits and Birkenstocks."

He laughed and went into his imitation of a dispensary employee. "Yeah man I'm a 'dispensary agent'. We call them 'Budtenders' among ourselves but when we are at the front of the dispensary, we go with the 'Agent' title, that's what my name tag says, and we refer to all those people looking for some good dank Kush as 'patients'. It's wild man! I skim plenty off the top so I am never without a ready supply of fine shit to meet my own needs. I sure as shit wouldn't pay what they're selling it for though. I can get dope from Warren Harding, my neighbor - though I don't think that's really his name - he sells all the same stuff for one tenth the price and he carries other products - if you know what I mean."

Echo pretended to take a big hit off an invisible joint, holding it in and then exhaling in a fit of coughing.

He smiled at Wilson. "Wow, you look pretty fine through pot goggles." He said.

Chapter 48 The Border

"I can't give you information about someone who came through Customs," said the US Border Patrol Officer to Duggan.

"But we are here helping the authorities," Duggan pleaded. "All we want to know is whether you let a woman with a white wolf-hybrid through in the past few weeks."

"Look", said the Patrolman. "You have no warrant, no shield, hell you don't even have any identification. I could just arrest you right now."

Duggan had told the other two to leave their driver's license and passports in the car - just in case they were asked to produce identification. They did not want to have their names AND faces on the radar of these folks. They were supposed to be sub rosa, undercover.

The Patrol Officer continued. " You expect me to just provide you with confidential information about a citizen of the United States . . ."

"We think she's from Canada."

"Doesn't matter. In fact, it might be worse. For all I know you three are stalking someone who doesn't want to be found."

Susan Wilson put her hand on Duggan's arm and said quietly, "Will, whether or not we have our ID with us, we are drawing too much attention to ourselves. I think we better just find out what he needs in order to talk with us. Let me see if I can figure it out."

Duggan acceded and Wilson said to the Border Patrol Officer. "We understand officer. We don't want to put your job at risk and we certainly don't want to be arrested. What do you need for us to be successful in making this inquiry?"

"I need a warrant and a shield," he said. "The warrant should have a very specific request."

"Very well, we'll be back with everything you need to provide us with the information." Susan Wilson said.

The three headed back to Duggan's SUV, backed out of their parking spot and headed back south.

The SUV was silent for a few miles when Duggan pounded on the steering wheel. "Damnit, Damnit, Damnit! What the hell are we going to do to get some information without tipping our hand to the cops?"

Susan remained quiet, she was thinking. Then she spoke. "I have an idea Will. We may not have to go back if I'm right. Head toward the Balsams."

Chapter 49   Hot Off The exPresses

Jim Kitchen's plane touched down at JFK at just after 6am. He had filed his first story since the Androscoggin Stampede from a hotel in Munich, Germany. His last stop on a whirlwind tour of Europe where he had gone for a first-hand look at the energy production, transmission and delivery systems planned and deployed in the European Union - especially in Monaco, Germany, Spain and the Netherlands. According to the energy geeks - who observed, researched and commented on trends, technology and global cost/benefit analyses, these countries were among the leaders in the EU movement toward a carbon-free energy future. The "Geeks" were not an organized group but, rather, the moniker self-described those experts who, by virtue of training or experience had a knack for analyzing new trends as well as a mountain of paperwork and data generated by the energy industry in an effort to ferret out truth from fiction and real capacity from public relations. In other words, they were the only ones who didn't have a dog in the fight, which left them free to call things the way they saw them. This made them a pretty dependable barometer of the current state of affairs, as well as future trends.

Kitchen had received special dispensation from his Editor to make the unusual trip as a means of highlighting the importance of the series he was about to write. In preparation for the trip he did a series of live interviews with radio stations, local newspapers and blogs to highlight the importance of getting a broader view of the issues. He had filed the first in the series from his Munich hotel room and had not seen the column in print yet.

It was silly he knew. After all, he had written the piece - a damn good one if he did say so himself - and he could go online to the Business Digest Website and see it there, formatted for his iPhone or iPad but there was something almost sacred about feeling the paper between his fingers, smelling the newsprint, and paging through it.

Having a story land on the front page, above the fold was not really anything new for him, but he was especially excited to see this piece as it should be seen, the headline searing into your brain and challenging the reader to jump in. He headed immediately for the Hudson News store where his Editor had arranged to have a copy waiting for him.

Jim was pleased his Editor seemed as excited about this series as he was. Excited enough to overnight a package to the Hudson News at JFK for him, even though this particular store carried the Business Digest regularly because it was the hub for

New Hampshire to New York commuters. His editor wasn't taking any chances the issue would be sold out; he wanted to stoke Kitchen's enthusiasm. After all 'Kitch' was the best writer they had ever had at the Business Digest and lately his work was just average. A sign there was an enthusiasm deficit.

Jim tore open the package and with barely enough time to make his connecting flight to Manchester he folded the paper under his arm, pulled out his boarding pass and passed through the gate on the final leg home.

He seated himself and opened the paper reverently. There it was, the headline.

Granite Skyway Proposal Creates New Firestorm.

A subtitle added more fuel to the fire:
New Opposition May Threaten Approval

Kitchen's byline was followed by the story, but a left margin sidebar contained a preface message from the Editor.

Note from the Editor: It arrived in a cloud of controversy but in recent months, following a series of concessions by the developers, had seemed to settle, appearing on its way to approval by state and federal regulatory and oversight bodies. Then last week, like a forest fire glowing and growing underground for months before erupting to the surface in an unexpected conflagration, the inferno was reignited.

It began with a still unidentified group of opponents, calling themselves *The Trust*, who staged a daring late night theft of more than thirty cars belonging to investors and C-level employees from Polaris Electric including CEO Conrad Fleming. When the cars were discovered twelve hours later, on an island in the middle of Lake Umbagog, The Trust had not only managed to pull off the most creative valet operation in local history but they had exposed a massive illegal timbering operation taking place right under the noses of authorities - - including Federal Fish and Wildlife officials, in the rural towns surrounding Lake Umbagog on the border of Maine and New Hampshire.

Fish and Wildlife officials say the discovery of the timbering operation halted one of the most serious threats to survival of newly established populations of Bald Eagles and other endangered raptors like Osprey and Peregrine Falcons.

Had the shenanigans of The Trust ended here, it might have been a story without legs, a sidebar to the bigger story. However, within hours of the discovery of the cars, a secondary fire broke out when a photograph was delivered via Instagram, Twitter and a host of other social media. The image of Polaris CEO Conrad Fleming's Lincoln Town Car "driven" by a 12 point buck, his tongue lolling out, seeming to taunt the powerful CEO. The photo was accompanied by a series of messages calling on opponents of Granite Skyway to join the 'Roadkill Rangers' in a campaign to sabotage Polaris Electric vehicles. A broadcast list of vehicles belonging to Granite Skyway investors invited recruits to include their vehicles in the effort. The photo and accompanying messages went viral and the story of both the rescue of the raptor habitat and the fight against Granite Skyway spread from coast-to-coast and beyond in the ether of the World Wide Web.

As if this was not enough for Polaris Electric - the embattled company and lead investor in the Granite Skyway - a second group of unidentified opponents, labeling themselves the "Gazetteers" and writing in the style of the authors of the revolutionary Federalist Papers - - even adopting some of the names of now-revealed patriot authors - - emerged, pledging to use their expertise and editorial skills and contacts to support The Trust by laying out the case against Granite Skyway.

Like a snowball rolling downhill after a late winter storm, the movement to stop Granite Skyway has suddenly become a cause célèbre. One local songwriter has written a ballad, aptly named *Roadkill Rangers* that is spreading like wildfire. The pilot of the helicopter summoned to aid police in the search, Chet Wincowski, who found the cars after they were surreptitiously moved, was even quoted in a local paper saying, "Catch them? If you do I'd like to shake their hands and give them a medal for saving our eagles and osprey. I didn't much follow all the controversy over Granite Skyway before, but I will now."

All of this has breathed new life into the fight to stop Granite Skyway. In the process it has opened up a debate with national implications and aspirations, over a series of questions yet to be answered.

Local and national observers say the debate is long overdue and - no matter the outcome - will serve us well.

It is in the spirit of this process the Business Digest begins a series of articles intended to explore many of the assertions made and questions raised.

To demonstrate our commitment to doing this correctly, the NH Business Digest recently sent our Business Editor James Kitchen on a fact finding mission to some of the states and countries on the cutting edge of generating and transmitting energy. These examples may or may not fit with the unique character of New Hampshire, but we can undoubtedly learn from them just the same.

Whether we will take a position on Granite Skyway or not remains an open question. It may be we come to a conclusion; or, it may be we simply play our essential role in examining the fundamental issues and questions which should be asked. In the spirit of fairness and good journalism we will put the horse before the cart, where it belongs, and trust that the journalistic interplay of our work, as well as the efforts of others, including those both for and against the proposal, will generate the dialog needed for making a decision in the public interest. - Editor in Chief

Examining Granite Skyway
Part I of a Special Series
James M. Kitchen
Business Editor

Munich, Germany - From my hotel room on the 8th floor of the George Hotel in Munich, the Alter Botanical Garden provides a peaceful and verdant view in the middle of one of Europe's busiest cities. It is a fitting place and landscape for my final night in Europe, where I have been receiving a crash course on energy demand, production and transmission in the European Union for the past eight days.

The trip, arranged by my editor, was intended as a means to expand my horizons in advance of this series of articles examining both the Granite Skyway proposal and its place in the energy future of New Hampshire, the United States and Canada - - all of which will be affected in some manner should the Granite Skyway transmission line come to pass.

There are times when we need to be shaken from our parochial dreams in order to better understand our place in the firmament. To my good fortune, and to the enduring credit of my editor, who recognized this was just one of those times.

My time in the EU, including visits to Monaco, Spain, France and the Netherlands in addition to here in Germany gave me the opportunity to examine how the EU, as a whole and these individual countries, are positioning themselves to thrive in a "Post-Carbon" world.

Before my visit the notion of a "Post-Carbon" world was unthinkable from my parochial view in downtown Manchester, New Hampshire. After all, the primary concern of energy policy was supply, demand and transmission - the ability to provide the power needed to assure a thriving economy, right? No politician of note in New Hampshire is talking about a post carbon economy. Even on the national level, especially in light of the recent success of a President who denies the reality of Climate Change, those who might be inclined to speak of anything as bold as a post-carbon economy have likely gone into hiding - - at least temporarily.

In Europe the effort to create post-carbon economies is now fully engaged; bound up directly in the efforts to create a thriving economy because they are committed to the Paris Accord on Climate Change and because renewable and sustainable energy sources now account for the fastest growing sector of the economy and have a competitive edge over older technologies which are heavily dependent on fossil fuels.

While politicians in the US continue to fight over whether Climate Change is real, the EU is moving ahead in dramatic fashion to lay the groundwork and to create the infrastructure for a Third Industrial Revolution.

The idea of a modern day Industrial Revolution is not new. Back in the 1980's Alvin Toffler alluded to this revolution in his much-heralded books "Future Shock" and "The Third Wave" in which he described the first signs of a new economic order; a revolution brought on by the information revolution. Today there is some disagreement about whether we are entering a Third or Fourth Revolution but this seems to be largely a matter of whether one considers the information revolution as a separate historic event, or simply the initial ripples of a tsunami-like revolution at the confluence of information and energy, bound up in both economic transformation and the sweeping cultural changes taking place.

It may also be a measure of whether you consider the roots of this revolution a natural progression or a direct response to a changing order, driven by the use of carbon-based fuels and the dramatic warming of the earth.

Toffler died recently. Today, these two schools of thought are best represented through the work of economist, author and activist Jeremy Rifkin (The Third Industrial Revolution, The Zero Marginal Cost Society, The End of Work), and Professor Klaus Schwab (The Fourth Industrial Revolution), Founder and Executive Chairman of the World Economic Forum. The intellectual battle between these two competing notions masks the fact that they are largely in agreement on the components of the Revolution and the competing ideas essentially represent a distinction without a difference.

Rifkin, however, seems to be making the most practical impact by developing relationships that span the globe, including close relationships with the European Union and China, among others. According to Wikipedia, he has advised the past three presidents of the European Commission and their leadership teams – President Romano Prodi, President Jose-Manuel Barroso, and President Jean-Claude Juncker. Rifkin has also served as an advisor to the leadership of the European Parliament and numerous heads of state, including Chancellor Angela Merkel of Germany, President Nicolas Sarkozy of France, Prime Minister Jose Luis Rodriguez Zapatero of Spain, Prime Minister Jose Socrates of Portugal, and Prime Minister Janez Jansa of Slovenia, during their respective European Council

Presidencies, on issues related to the economy, climate change, and energy security.

Rifkin is the principal architect of the verbosely named 'Third Industrial Revolution long-term economic sustainability plan to address the triple challenge of the global economic crisis, energy security, and climate change.' This plan has led to the EU's adoption of their 20-20-20 by 2020 strategy; setting joint targets of a 20% increase in energy efficiency, 20% reduction of CO2 emissions, and 20% renewables by the year 2020.

The concept of the Third Industrial Revolution (TIR) was formally endorsed by the European Parliament in 2007 and the plan envisioned by Rifkin, in consultation with these political leaders, is now being implemented by various agencies within the European Commission.

The concept of the TIR rests on 5 central pillars: 1. Switching to renewable sources of energy; 2. Transforming the building stock in each country to make each building its own power producer capable of both generating power and sharing it to the grid; 3. Deploying storage technologies to store intermittent energies; 4. Using Internet technology to transform the grid into a smart grid capable of moving energy to where it is needed; and, 5. Transitioning the transportation system to a fleet of electric cars, trucks, buses and other vehicles that can serve as power storage on a smart grid.

Among the most assertive and aggressive advocates of this concept has been the conservative Chancellor of Germany Angela Merkel. In the last few years Merkel has quietly made Germany a worldwide leader in efforts to create this new economic and energy paradigm.

Standing on the European continent and seeing the results of their efforts, I asked myself why it is the US was not forging ahead in the same manner? I asked this question of many leading advocates of green energy in Europe and the US and their replies we always some version of the same answer. A decentralized system for the production and distribution of power requires that significant investments in the creation of a smart grid must be made and the private sector and public sectors must be united in their commitment to building this system. In the US powerful private interests are aligned to maintain control over the distribution of electricity and for many it is a corporate life and death struggle.

Today, the US stands at a crossroads. Faced with the question of whether we will create a system that is an echo of the old order, where big new power plants, producing energy transmitted by privately owned power grids will continue to be the means by which we create and deliver electricity, or, whether we will create a new order with energy generated locally and shared across a smart grid laterally with our neighbors. Allowing each of us to become both producers and consumers of electricity in a new energy paradigm.

Granite Skyway clearly falls on the first of these paths. The electricity produced by one single source, Canadian hydropower, and transported across our state specifically to provide power to homes and businesses far from our borders. A different proposal might have taken a different approach but the choice we have is a binary one, "yes" or "no" to Granite Skyway. Each path has both benefits and hazards. We'll examine them more in this series.

In the next article we will explore the roots of distributed renewable power, the New Hampshire politician who made it all possible and the closest election in US history that brought him to power.

Chapter 50 Zipline Adventures

"Look out below!" hollered Michelle as she threw herself off the first platform near the top of Russell Crag where Zipline Adventures had built one of the most thrilling ziplines anywhere on the East Coast. She hurtled down toward the second platform at speeds approaching 50 mph, 75 feet above the forest floor, only slowing as she began approaching the platform where a safety guide awaited her. It was his job to make sure she alit from her descent as gently and safely as possible.

The Trust had gathered together for some fun and a quiet place to do some strategizing where they could be relatively confident no one would be listening in on their conversation. They had chosen Zipline Adventures because their reputation for both safety and excitement was unrivaled in New Hampshire and because Daniel had worked there on and off during the previous summer. He knew the safety guide and knew he could count on his discretion.

"So far, so good." Hank said to the group, referring to the fallout from the Androscoggin Stampede. "No one seems to be onto us yet, and so far the public seems to be on our side. Even the local police are disinclined to put any effort into finding us and the Gazetteers were an unexpectedly pleasant surprise."

"I'd like to give the guy who wrote the first piece a big ol' bear hug," Stonebridge said.

"I wonder if they'll put another one out soon," said Sasha.

"Have you read the opening piece in the series by Jim Kitchen in the Business Digest?" Daniel asked his compatriots. "He seems to be looking at both sides of this but I feel as if that means we win ultimately because we have the best story to tell and we have right on our side. He's certainly asking the relevant questions."

They were on the third platform of the trip down to the base when Daniel said with a sly smile "I have an idea for our next caper."

"Caper" said Hank, running the word around in his mouth like a taste of wine. "Now I like that. It has just the right amount of fun associated with it and a bit of zing at the midpoint. As if he were critiquing a work of art he held his arm out and swished his hand from side to side, imitating a Grande Dame in full snob mode.

Daniel laughed and said, "Sasha and I've been talking about it but I need to involve my cousin Zach and his African "Uncle" Osita who's visiting from West Africa. I'll need your permission to involve them."

Thomas, who had thrown caution to the wind and left home in the great North Woods for the first time since moving there after returning from Iraq, had accepted a ride from Daniel and Sasha to join The Trust for their zipline adventure. Watching him leap into the air and ride the line from platform to platform was a sight to behold for the others. They were all having fun, no doubt, but Thomas was like a kid on his first roller coaster ride. He would whoop and whistle and yell all the way down each section, with a grin that took up most of his face, his wild hair and beard blowing crazily at all angles. When Daniel mentioned bringing in two more people, however, he was the first to respond.

"Daniel, Amigo, I don't have to tell you how important it is for us to keep the circle tight here. The more people who are involved, the greater the chances we'll be exposed. And as I've said, these things . . ."

"Have a way of getting away from us," chanted the entire group.

The team was laughing and enjoying the moment, however, Thomas was not sharing in their merriment.

"Listen," he said, "there's a pretty good chance at least some of us are going to get caught no matter how careful we are. You may all think because I live in the woods, and go from habitat to habitat with Metallak, that I have less to lose than you but I happen to like my life and if I end up in jail, some asshole from Fish and Game is going to put old Metallak down because he's too much trouble for them. Then he'll turn his rifle on the dogs who will be half-crazed with grief and fear because he's just offed their constant companion. It's not a pretty thought."

"The saving grace of this group is that, beside me, none of us have little kids or sick parents who would be abandoned if we ended up doing time - or worse. But to me Metallak and my dogs are full-fledged members of my family. I love them like they're my children and I need to protect them."

The group grew very quiet until Hank broke the silence. "Hell Thomas, I'm sorry. I think we're all spending some of our quiet moments thinking about what might happen to us, but since you gave me that key to your safety deposit box, well I've tried not to think too much about how it might affect you and that's my bad."

"Hank, you had my back through our entire tour in Iraq. I know where your heart is. The rest of you have welcomed me into The Trust without a question asked. The truth is, for the first time since I've been back stateside I have a purpose" . . . he paused then added . . . "a human family". Thomas took the time to look at every member of the group now. "I have all of you to thank for this. I just want us to be aware of the dangers of bringing in more members into The Trust."

"Let's hear your plan Daniel," said Michelle. "Maybe that will set Thomas' fears to rest. If not we can talk it through and decide what to do."

"First though . . ." said Herbert, " . . . I have a nuisance plan to keep them all busy for the next few weeks."

Michelle put her hand softly on Herbert's shoulder. "Let's hear what Daniel and Sasha have in mind first Herbert. I think Thomas would feel better knowing and we can share our idea for a distraction afterwards."

For the remainder of their "Zip", Daniel and Sasha shared their idea with the other members of The Trust. Each one asked questions provided ideas and made observations and by the time they had arrived at the bottom, they had fleshed out The Trust's next move and each knew their respective role in bringing the caper to life.

Chapter 51   Putting the Knee Back in Jerk

Hank Algren was helping the safety monitor put away the last of the gear from their zipline adventure while the rest of The Trust was gathering around their cars in the parking lot. "Firearms Owners of New Hampshire (FAO NH) is - if it can be said - a local Gun Owners organization even more crazy and radical than the NRA. Which means they are also more susceptible to rumor and innuendo than even their hair-brained cousin." Herbert said. "My idea is to plant a rumor within their organization that sets their hair on fire over Polaris Electric."

"It just a stop-gap," Michelle said, "something to do while we plan and execute our next big escapade."

Daniel asked "aren't we asking for trouble by pissing off a gun owner's group, especially when they discover they've been punked?"

"Good point Daniel, but they're a small group."

" A small group with very big mouths," he added.

" . . . and bigger guns!" pointed out Daniel.

"Besides, who said anything about revealing ourselves? They may figure out they've been punked but they have enough enemies they'll have to go into circular firing squad mode before they actually figure this out if we do it right. They may never figure out the source of the rumors."

"What's the benefit of doing this Herbert?" Stonebridge asked.

"Its an old tactic we used in Afghanistan," Herbert replied, "Sowing disinformation to keep the enemy off-balance. If they spend the next few months dealing with both the fallout from the Androscoggin Stampede as well as coping with the flood of disinformation we create and feed, they never have time to go on the offense . . . or at least we keep them in defensive mode most of the time. It costs them time and money and doesn't allow them to gain a tactical advantage."

"I don't know, Herbert," said Daniel, "Our primary currency in waging this battle is truth. We don't want to do anything that undermines our own credibility."

"I'm not suggesting we sow disinformation about Granite Skyway, Daniel. I agree with you, we have to be as straight as possible with the issues around the transmission line proposal. The Gazetteers will be counting on us to do that as well. They can't be releasing essays making the case against Granite Skyway if we're muddying the waters by making false accusations about the Granite Skyway proposal. And we don't need to. Between what the dams are doing to the Native people of Quebec, clear cutting thousands of acres of NH, and the spine of huge steel towers as well as the pure foolishness of using 20th century technology for 21st century challenges, we have the arguments on our side."

"Besides," Stonebridge added, "all the other support we're already seeing and hoping for in the future, in order to bring attention to this travesty will disappear if we start making up shit and saying anything it will affect our credibility."

". . . or hurt someone . . ." Michelle added.

"Whoa, whoa," Herbert interjected, "I'm not suggesting disinformation about Granite Skyway itself. I'm saying we create disinformation of an ancillary nature that will have them running around putting out fires and taking their eyes off the prize in the meantime.

"Give us an example Herbert," said Daniel.

"Well, Conrad Fleming has been going around accusing us of Eco-Terrorism so it would be logical he might want to make sure that people opposing him weren't carrying firearms on public right-of-ways. Public right-of-ways of course are one of the most common routes for hunters to access the backcountry for hunting. If we find a way to float the rumor that Polaris is working with legislators to restrict firearms on right-of-ways, I'm betting Polaris will spend the next month, maybe longer, fending off telephone calls from rank and file hunters as well as holding news conferences to deny the rumors." Herbert speculated.

Linda Levy, who made the trip up from Boston to join the group but had not said a word other than her blood curdling screams at each station of the zip, asked "Is the proper plural term of art here 'Right of Ways' or 'Rights of Way?' I'm thinking it's 'Rights of Way.'

"Leave it to our lawyer . . ." Hank said.

"They'll figure it out pretty fast, won't they?" Daniel asked, still on the subject of the rumor.

"You mean 'Right of Ways' or 'Rights of Way' " Hank said, tongue planted firmly in cheek and grinning.

"You mean the Gun Owners or Polaris?" Herbert added.

"Both Herbert, but I don't know if this will have legs."

"Polaris will know right away," Herbert responded. "After all they'll know they haven't proposed anything but they'll also know they have to deny the story. They can't afford alienating such a big and vocal group. However, their denial will suck them right into the controversy. The gun owners on the other hand . . . well you can divide them into two groups: The rank and file, and the leadership. Remember this is the most rabid of the gun-owner's groups, we aren't talking about your salt of the earth hunter types, we're talking about the ones who see a pinko behind every bush and believe it's their God given right to own a tank and several bazookas . . ."

"Thomas, getting into the spirit of the moment placed his index finger on his nose and looked into the air as if pondering something very, very important before he asked: "Is it Bazooka or Bazookas? I mean if deer is the plural of deer, isn't Bazooka the plural of Bazooka?" This brought a hearty laugh from everyone - and a sense of relief that Thomas was with them.

"The rank and file", Herbert continued, "are sufficiently paranoid that they'll likely buy into the rumors enough to go into battle mode. The leadership, on the other hand, will probably see through it almost immediately, but at the same time they'll see a golden opportunity to bring in a flood of donations by fanning the flames. It will be impossible for them to ignore. I'm betting their greed will be more important to them than laughing off and squashing the rumor."

Stonebridge was listening intently and interjected, "Nothing like a good crisis to open up the wallets of your members eh?" he said. "Even if they don't believe the rumors, you think their greed will make them quiet collaborators?"

"That's the idea." Herbert said. They may even thank us, ultimately, for helping them fill their bank account. What do you think?"

"Might work," said Stonebridge, "but the trap needs to be laid convincingly."

Chapter 52   The White Wolf

Daniel got into the Prius and remembered to plug his iphone in to charge it. Had he thought of it earlier, he would have charged it while they did the zipline.

As he sat waiting for Sasha and Cochise in the Prius his mind drifted to their most recent trip.

He and Sasha had been hiking in the Carter Range for a week after the Androscoggin Stampede and his phone had run dangerously low just a few days into the trip so he shut it off, keeping just enough juice to use in an emergency. Not that he anticipated an emergency, just that he was always prepared if the worst came to pass. He tried to keep his phone off when he was hiking anyway. A call on top of a mountain was a bit of a buzzkill when you were reveling in the moment.

Backpacking with Sasha and Cochise was a humbling experience. He had never hiked with someone who knew more plants and trees than he did. He always thought of himself as a master woodsman and naturalist. Back when he was leading trips for kids it wasn't hard to be the smartest guy in the group but this was different. Sasha didn't herald it over him or anything but every few minutes there seemed to be a new revelation or observation.

He loved hiking along the trail and looking up to the next bluff as Cochise came into view, looking back at him. Cochise put in four miles for every one that Daniel and Sasha traveled, going back and forth, seeming to scout the trail then issuing the "all clear" from the front of the pack.

On the second night they were out they had just finished setting up the tent when he appeared with a big fat Spruce Grouse in his mouth. Setting it down in front of Daniel he sat back looking very satisfied with himself. Daniel looked at him quizzically. "OK what's this all about?"

"This, Daniel," Sasha said putting her arms around Daniel from behind and nuzzling her head on his shoulder, "is Cochise's way of saying you are officially a part of the pack. He wants you to share in his bounty!"

"So how do I do that?"

Sasha handed him her Buck knife. "First you dress the grouse and then you cut it in half. Give him his half raw, that way the bones won't splinter when he eats it. We'll cook the rest on a spit."

"I'm not a hunter Sash. You tell me to dress the grouse and I'm thinking it won't fit into anything I have."

Sasha laughed.

God he loved her laugh. It was big and uninhibited and . . . well . . . real, genuine. It seemed as if the Great Spirit himself, or herself - after all the Iroquois were a matriarchal society - was celebrating the moment. She sat down on the log next to Daniel, hung the bird upside down on a nearby branch and in two minutes she had gutted and removed every feather from the bird.

"OK" she said. "Next time you'll know what to do when he brings you a bird. Think you can figure out what to do with the knife?"

Now it was his turn to laugh. "Yeah but I'm thinking I need to cut it so we can put it on the spit and that may be different than what I would do if we were cooking it in an oven."

"Don't worry about that, the best meat, really the only meat on a spruce grouse, is the breast. Luckily, ol' Cochise would just as soon munch on the part that went over the fence - or I guess in this case the log - last. Cut it across the middle and you and I can enjoy the breast and Cochise gets his delicacy."

Daniel did as instructed then presented Cochise with the legs and tail and he trotted off to a spot behind the tent to eat in privacy.

"So he's an ass man, eh?"

"You're not going to fight him for it are you?" Sasha said as she slung her leg over his and sat on his lap facing him, bringing her lips to his in a soft, warm kiss.

"How long does it take to cook this over the spit?" Daniel asked, a gleam in his eyes.

"Long enough," she whispered not taking her lips from his.

Daniel stood up with Sasha's legs wrapped around him and headed for the tent.

"You aren't going to eat if we don't start the bird first, stud."

"I'll take my chances" Daniel said as he set Sasha down on the sleeping bag, climbed in and zipped up the tent flap.

-=-=-=-=-=-=-=-=-=-=-=-=-=-=-=-=-=

Just then the iphone rang, bringing Daniel out of his reverie. Looking at the screen he read the incoming call log: "Tea Bird's" he said to himself. "This can't be good."

"Hello?"

"Daniel, it's Scott Gregory. Heather and I've been trying to reach you for two days now. I've left a dozen messages on your cell."

"Hi Scott, sorry, we were hiking in the Carters and I generally turn off my phone and keep it for emergencies only so I don't run out of power. What's up?"

"Well, it may be nothing but there were three kind of suspicious characters in the cafe a few days ago and they were asking around about a wolf. I remembered you were with a woman - sorry I forgot her name - and she had a wolf dog of some sort. So we thought we should let you know someone was asking around."

"Her name is Sasha. Did you tell them anything?"

"Hell no! In fact we steered them completely wrong, but the next morning they were back, outside the Cafe asking everyone that would speak with them about a wolf. Then they piled into a black SUV and headed north."

"Listen" Scott said excitedly. "I know you probably can't tell me if you're part of this Trust group, but just in case you are, Heather and I want you to know we're with you. Feel free to call on us if you need anything up here."

"Sorry Scott. Can't confirm or deny but thanks for the tip. Keep this under your hat pal and let us know if you hear anything more. OK? Oh, and give Heather a big squeeze from me."

"You bet!"

" . . . And Daniel?"

"Yes?"

"Be careful. I don't know these people but I got a bad feeling. Heather too. Said they were claiming to be shooting a movie but then couldn't tell her what the movie was about . . . like it was a state secret or something."

"Thanks Scott. I owe you.

Just then Sasha opened the back door of the Prius and Cochise bounded in. Daniel brought her up to speed on his phone call with Scott Gregory.

"What should we do?" She asked.

"I have a plan that will let us lie low for a while."

"Should we tell the others, Daniel?"

"Not yet, let's charge both the phones on our way to Thomas' place, he needs a ride home anyway. We'll talk it over with the team after we have talked about it ourselves."

Daniel wheeled the Prius out of the parking lot after Thomas had jumped in. They headed for the northernmost town in NH - - Pittsburg. They would spend a few days with Thomas there while they restocked supplies for a trip to the Newfound Lake region where they could disappear for a few days into the backcountry on the Elwell Trail.

Part 5 Rumor Control

Chapter 53   The Presser

The media, both local and national, gathered in the Chambers of the Executive Council where the Governor was scheduled to hold a press conference - a "presser" if you were a hip young politico. New Hampshire's place in the national constellation always drew both local and national media because of The First in the Nation Primary.

The Governor was hoping to lend her support for a bill to require additional forms of identification for voters. Recent changes that required one form of identification had proven an annoyance to voters who found themselves having to provide a driver's license and verbally call out their name to neighbors, who had wiped their asses as a baby or chased them off when they were stealing apples from their trees - - but the annoyance hadn't deterred them from exercising their constitutional duty. As a Republican the Governor felt compelled to make voting more difficult, to suppress the vote - behind the cover of protecting the election from fraudulent votes and voters. She was proposing to step up their game.

What she didn't count on was that members of the media were waiting for the chance to ask about Granite Skyway, The Trust and the Gazetteers. Governor Mags had barely concluded her preliminary remarks when the first question was asked.

A journalist from HuffPost asked, "Governor, Polaris CEO Conrad Fleming has labeled the members of this group, calling itself The Trust, Eco-Terrorists. Do you agree with him? Does that make the citizens who are styling themselves after the authors of the Federalist Papers and writing essays in support and calling themselves Gazetteers, complicit?"

"I'm not ready to make a judgment on this matter yet. For now it's a law enforcement matter."

New Hampshire Guardian reporter Kevin Lanford followed up. "These people, The Trust, seem to have become folk heroes overnight. A local musician has written a song sung at open mike nights all over the North Country. More than a few random citizens are declaring themselves Roadkill Rangers and placing roadkill in Polaris vehicles, taking selfies with them and blasting them out over the web. There seems to be a renewed energy in opposition to the Granite Skyway project. Are you concerned about this?"

"As you know, I am very concerned about insuring New Hampshire has an adequate supply of electricity to meet the future needs of a healthy economy. I sympathize with some of our citizens who continue to have concerns about Granite Skyway." She said, playing both sides as usual, "but I don't condone the actions of this group. I don't plan to let their actions influence me one way or the other."

A Boston Globe journalist said "A source at Polaris told us their insurance provider is refusing to cover the nearly one million in damages to the vehicles of investors because CEO Fleming declared The Trust to be Eco-Terrorists giving them a reason to invoke a terrorism clause in the coverage. Do you think The Trust is trying to force the Granite Skyway investors to withdraw their proposal by making it so expensive they give up?"

"I can't comment on the tactics of this group or their results. I expect they will be apprehended and prosecuted for their actions. However, I would say it seems as though the Granite Skyway folks have made no effort to find common ground with legitimate opposition groups. I would certainly support any effort they make in this direction."

From the back of the room a voice came from an unknown journalist. "Governor, will you be supporting the bill being drafted in legislative services making it a felony to carry a firearm on public rights-of-way? Our sources tell us Polaris energy has asked an unnamed State Representative from Hillsborough County to draft the legislation on their behalf based on their belief their employees working on Granite Skyway are in danger from these people and their supporters."

Mac, who was seated in a chair appearing to read the Governor's statement, felt her radar come to full alert. She looked around but could not identify the source of the question. The Governor was just launching into another qualified denial when she slipped up to the Governor's Chief-of-Staff, "Did you see who asked that last question?"

But Michelle was already making her way down the stairs just outside Representatives Hall. She was less than halfway back to Herbert's farm in Groton when the story went viral.

Chapter 54 Terror and Civil Disobedience

Even as Michelle was winding her way home along the Pemigewasset River Valley the Gazetteers were releasing their next essay in print and in the ever-expanding flow of the digital universe.

Terror and Civil Disobedience
By Benjamin F. Einstein

Polaris Electric's CEO Conrad Fleming has been making a great deal of the so-called "Androscoggin Stampede" over the past few weeks. He has labeled members of The Trust "Eco-Terrorists" for their admittedly illegal and daring midnight theft of cars belonging to Granite Skyway investors, while the investors were meeting with leadership of Polaris for a briefing at the Balsams Hotel in Dixville Notch.

He fails to mention that The Trust used the Androscoggin Stampede as a means of exposing an illegal timbering operation which threatened the future of efforts to restore Bald Eagles and other raptors to the Great North Woods, a program with broad public support that has cost millions of dollars over the past decade.

While the real dangers of terrorism are far less than the purveyors of fear would have us believe - most citizens are more likely to be struck by lightning than subject to a terrorist attack - it is, nevertheless, a truism that perception shapes reality and in this "Age of Terror", when citizens are on edge. Accusations of terrorism or terrorist intent become a powerful tool with which to bludgeon political opponents or to justify the denial of constitutional rights in the name of safety.

The debate over the appropriate balance between freedom and safety is certain to occupy the country for the foreseeable future. However, we must not allow our fears to create an atmosphere where civil disobedience and terrorism are equated. To do this would destroy one of the most important and time-honored traditions of the American ideal. From the Boston Tea Party; to the voting protests of the women's suffrage movement; to the sit-ins of the civil rights era and the die-ins of the opposition to the war in Vietnam, civil disobedience has helped to shape and push the boundaries of the public dialog.

The First Amendment of the United States Constitution permits individuals to speak their minds and gather together in protest to address their grievances.

From time to time, citizens have felt compelled to answer a higher calling than the laws of the land and have engaged in what Thoreau called Civil Disobedience - - breaking the law because they consider the law to be unjust, immoral or contrary to the best interests of the people.

Civil disobedience comes with a price . . . often a high price. Those who engage in it face the wrath of the establishment backed by laws serving their interests, whether just or not. However, the willingness of those who engage in Civil Disobedience to pay that price also conveys upon them a moral authority that goes beyond the everyday protestor, acting clearly within the boundaries of the law. They act in the full knowledge they have stepped beyond the bounds of what is legal and their actions have consequences. Thus, they believe in their cause enough they are willing to pay the price for their actions.

This collision between the law and the civil offenders by its very nature draws greater attention to the object of the act of disobedience.

The red line that defines the point where civil disobedience crosses into criminal action or terrorism is wanton violence. Not even Conrad Fleming can make the case The Trust has crossed this line.

When Americans of all colors were acting together to defy the Jim Crow laws of the South they were engaging in civil disobedience. Their willingness to go to jail for registering black voters gave power and moral authority to their actions.

When Muhammad Ali refused to be drafted to fight in Vietnam and relinquished his Heavyweight Champion title, going to jail for his actions, his willingness to pay this price lent power and authority to his actions. Time has proven him to be a heroic figure for this sacrifice.

The members of The Trust are NOT terrorists. They are engaged in civil disobedience to stop harm far greater than the laws they have broken. To equate their actions with terrorism does grave moral harm to the hierarchy of protest we have honored over our long effort to extend the rights and privileges of citizenship to every American.

Martin Luther King Jr. assured us the "moral arc of the universe is long but it bends toward justice." and Barack Obama reminded us "the arc does not bend itself. We must bend it."

Sacred Trust

The members of The Trust are engaged in an effort to bend that arc. They may pay a price for those actions, but if they do, it will be a small price should they succeed.

The Gazetteers
Benjamin F. Einstein

Chapter 55 Carter & the Green Energy Revolution

Charlie Stonebridge was biding his time between gigs with The Trust by scheduling Whitewater Safety workshops. These workshops had become his bread and butter lately and it was a relatively simple matter to identify local paddlers associations and clubs and call them and offer to do a workshop. They almost never said no to him and even when they did, he could usually turn them around by offering to share the proceeds.

He had already scheduled enough workshops, from his campsite at Mollidgewock campground along the Androscoggin River, to keep him in the state for the next two months, after which he might need to make a trip back to West Virginia to clean up some matters at home before heading back north. For now he would focus his energy on helping his compatriots and putting together workshops for Norwich University, Dartmouth College, the Connecticut River Canoe and Kayak Club, Merrimack Valley Paddlers and the Saco Watershed Council.

He was still feeling the buzz from the now legendary Androscoggin Stampede. It was a long time since he had felt such purpose in his life. It was risky business, he knew. If they got caught, which was after all a distinct possibility, maybe even a probability, he'd probably end up doing time. But wasn't that what Thoreau had explained in his essay on Civil Disobedience? Without a price the action had no meaning. All of them had to be willing to pay the price for their actions. It was what gave their acts moral authority. Was he worried? Hell yes. But there was a spring in his step, asleep for a long time. That alone told him he was on the right path.

Today he was finishing up the first of these two-day workshops, with the Androscoggin Paddling Association, in Berlin, after which he was planning to drive north to hang out with Thomas for five days. He was on day two which was always the most interesting to him because it was the day "in the field" which is to say on a river practicing what he had preached the previous day.

Stonebridge was a legendary storyteller and he was in scores of scrapes, rescues and near death experiences and had reported on dozens of others for "Appalachia Magazine". He filled the first day with enough hair-raising anecdotes to keep the entire class on the edge of their seats for the six hours of the workshop without breaking a sweat. His somewhat awkward gait inspired stories about the many scrapes he was in himself, told by students, friends and admirers. Whether they were true or not did not matter because they believed them and each new story they heard was embraced, embellished and retold.

It wasn't just the stories - though they would surely be enough - but it was also his delivery. His facial expressions and the way he would modulate his voice as he described some half-wit who had tried to run Livermore falls from the top in an open boat; or a councilor showing off for his campers, yucking around near a fallen tree, ending up skewered on a broken limb when he looked back at the wrong moment. He would shake his head like a horse shaking off a bit that's too tight, often in connection with a drawn out curse: "it was just gawwwwd awful" or "Keee-riiist was he stupid!"

Day two was the day when he would give his charges the chance to practice a swift water rescue as well as to practice things like ferrying their boats across a stretch of river and doing an eddy turn; things that would serve them well when they were in a real life rescue situation.

Every now and then he would get lucky and find a boat swamped on a rock on one of the nearby rivers or tangled up in a deadfall allowing him to work with the group; perhaps to safely extract the mangled boat or simply to use the scene to emphasize the scenario that led to this situation.

"A canoe filled with water," he would tell them as he counseled them to remain upriver from a swamped boat, "weighs up to two tons. Imagine what it would be like to have an elephant take a flying leap on top of you. That's what it would be like to get caught between that boat and a rock or a tree."

The previous night, as he was scouting the section of the Androscoggin river where his workshop would be, he had found just such a challenge, a Grumman canoe, made of the same aluminum as their world renowned airplanes, wrapped around a rock in the middle of the river, water piling into it and holding it tight to the upstream side of the rock.

Now, the workshop participants stood on the shore as Stonebridge pointed out all of the mistakes that had gone into the creation of this tableau. "The first mistake probably was that the pair of people paddling this boat lost their alignment. Instead of keeping the boat pointed downstream, aligned in the same direction as the flow of the river, they allowed the boat to drift and the stern began to be pushed downriver faster than the bow, moving the boat from a position parallel to the current toward a perpendicular, or broadside, position to the current. This may have happened because the paddlers failed to follow the cardinal rule of white water: keep paddling. In order to control a boat in wildwater a paddler needs to be moving faster than the water itself. The minute they panic and stop paddling, the boat begins to lose alignment and if it's not corrected it is likely to end up pinned broadside on a rock."

"I can't tell you how many paddlers I've seen freak out in the middle of a rapid and either drop their paddle or just set it down and grab the gunwales of the boat in sheer terror."

"The next mistake they made," he continued, getting back to his description and drawing a vivid picture for the trainees "was to lean upstream when they went broadside on the rock. It's a natural reaction really. You literally are tempted to reach for the water expecting, in the back of your mind, to find a solid surface allowing you to push off to avoid swamping. Instead, you find your hands sinking into the water. You have to fight the urge to lean upstream in this circumstance. If you make a mistake that leaves you broadside against a rock, the first thing you do is lean into the rock. This means the water is plowing into the bottom of the canoe and then making its way around it. It has no way to fill the boat when it meets only the hard surface of the canoe's bottom. You may still be stuck on the rock but the boat has not filled with water and subsequently wrapped itself around the rock if the current is powerful enough."

"As long as your boat is still reasonably empty, you have a chance of getting free of the rock and continuing on. The minute you lean upstream, you're toast. If that happens, forget the damn canoe and get yourself to safety. The boat can be replaced, you can't."

A hand went up in the crowd. "What do you do once you are free of the boat?"

"The safest thing to do is to ride out the rapid, floating, feet first, to prevent you from hitting anything vital, especially your head, on rocks as you go down river. Do not try to stand up or touch the bottom until you are free of the fast moving water."

"Why not?" asked another student.

"Because your foot can become entrapped and you may not be able to get free.

I watched a man drown in two feet of water on a river in West Virginia because his foot became entrapped when he tried to stand up in two feet of water and the water rolled over him, pushing him under. A dozen people tried to reach him to save him and not one of them was able to get him loose before he drowned. He effectively drowned two inches beneath the surface of the water."

"If someone is able to throw you a rescue line, which is what we will be working on today, then you can continue to keep your feet forward and floating as you are pulled to safety. But if there is no one to throw you a line, or the rapid is short, riding it out, feet first, is best."

"We aren't going to try and salvage this boat. It's really not worth the risk in my opinion. At some point a high or low water event will either shake it free or expose it to the extent it can be salvaged, but that won't be us. It's not likely this canoe will ever see action again. When it gets wrapped around a rock like this, the keel is probably broken completely and is likely to be beyond repair, except maybe for lake paddling."

When the workshop was over, Stonebridge was tying his boat to the top of the Range Rover when a young lady came up to him. " I was thinking Charlie." She said.

"Well that's always a good start." said Charlie - being a bit of a wise ass.

"Its funny but your advice to always keep paddling. It's kind of good life advice in general isn't it? When things get dicey, don't drop your paddle and try to ride it out. Keep paddling."

Stonebridge stopped cinching his boat and looked at the young lady. "Very astute observation," he said.

After she had walked away he thought about how she had just described the last twenty years of his life. Too often just holding on and not paddling hard. In fact, the only time he was heeding his own advice was when he was actually paddling on a river.

He was glad to be paddling once again. It felt good. He finished tying the boat onto the roof of the Rover and headed north to the Second Connecticut Lake. His GPS wasn't going to do him any good on this trip; Thomas had given him a hand drawn map showing him the way to his abode in the woods.

The peninsula on which Thomas had built his longhouse was a fifteen-minute walk from a parking area at the small hydro-storage dam, owned by a company called Trans-Canada, off Daniel Webster Highway in the town of Pittsburg, New Hampshire. Thomas was not completely under the radar at this location because he had a co-farming relationship with the family that owned the land.

Shaped like the state of Michigan, the peninsula reached into the lake at its southern end. A very rough trail led from the woods just north of the parking area, where he could park more discreetly, to the tip of the mitt.

Stonebridge took the C-1 off the roof and put it into the Rover, locked it up and headed off, not completely sure he was on the right trail until he spotted moose tracks interspersed with the tracks from a Vibram sole hiking boot. He continued hiking for about fifteen minutes until he began to hear voices, one male and one female. Walking carefully, since he was not expecting anyone except Thomas, he picked his way until he rounded a corner and was confronted by a large white wolf standing right in the middle of the trail. Well, standing wasn't exactly the right description, Cochise was crouched on the trail, poised to jump, ready for anything.

"Easy Cochise, remember me, I'm one of the good guys."

Cochise clearly did recognize Stonebridge because his ears flattened against his head from the alert position they were in previously. Head low, he pranced over to Stonebridge who at this point had kneeled down to greet the big white wolf. He reached out and Cochise whined and barked joyfully as if reunited with a long lost friend.

Sasha appeared at the sound of Cochise's yips, recognizing their friendly sound. "Charlie!" She exclaimed. "What a wonderful surprise! Welcome to my new second home." She warmly took Stonebridge's hand and led him into the longhouse. "Can you believe Thomas has a Longhouse? I feel like I've been transported back home to Canada."

Stonebridge had to bend forward as he entered the Longhouse but once he entered there was plenty of headroom.

"For a minute there I was thinking I was going to have to crab-walk around his place but there's a good ten feet above my head once you get in."

"It's an old design . . . the doorway I mean." Sasha said as Daniel entered in behind them adding "The design was originally intended as a defense mechanism, if a person has to bend forward as they enter they're vulnerable to someone standing next to the door inside and taking defensive action, clocking them one by one as they come through. The entry design is found on almost all kinds of Native American homes and outbuildings.

Nowadays." Daniel continued," not all of them continue to reflect this defensive posture but the smaller doorway also has a practical purpose. The doorway is one of a very few openings on a longhouse, allowing cold air to enter in the winter and warm air in the summer. The smaller the opening is the more efficient the longhouse is, in theory at least."

From the outside the longhouse was covered with a series of tarps, Thomas' major concession to modernity inasmuch as a traditional Longhouse would have ash or elm bark shingles as its covering. The tarps made it difficult to see much of the actual construction that had gone into building the longhouse but once inside it was easy to see the house was built by placing a series of saplings, like ribs along a boat. In fact, though shapes vary in longhouses from tribe to tribe, nation to nation, a longhouse looks much like a giant canoe or ship turned upside down with its bow and stern lopped off or simply flattened. Across the top of the longhouse additional saplings are bent and lashed to create a bowed effect that assures rain and snow will run off, or slide off, and not threaten the structure. Additional saplings lashed perpendicular to these give the structure strength. In longhouses built for ceremonial use or as a meetinghouse for a tribal meetings, larger trees are often used as load bearing beams and posts, though Thomas' longhouse was only intended for a single family and did not require these internal structures.

Stonebridge was struck by how comfortable and homey the structure was and, in fact, given the structure was both a home and a storage facility for drying vegetables, herbs and spices Thomas had harvested from his numerous gardens, it was truly beautiful; filled with color and smells blended together, joining with the scent of wood smoke from the wood fires of two separate pits.

Running along the walls of the Longhouse were a series of flat shelf-like structures that doubled as storage space or bunks depending on the need. Sasha directed Stonebridge to one of these. "I think it's long enough to accommodate your height," she said.

They had entered the Longhouse at one end and were gradually making their way to the other end when Sasha said, "This is the area where Thomas spends most of his downtime, it's sort of his living area."

Stonebridge looked around and was struck by a series of pictures on the wall. The first was a graphic depiction of an Indian man, the second Robert Kennedy the third, to his surprise, was former President Jimmy Carter. Then there was one more he didn't recognize. Beneath his photo was the name "John Durkin".

"You will have to ask Thomas about his reasons for these," Sasha said, pointing to the photos of Kennedy and Carter as they headed for the east facing door, "But the first picture is one man's depiction of Deganawida, the Peacemaker who united the nations of my people, the *Haudenosaunee,* also known as the Iroquois confederacy, probably in the 12th century.

They exited through the east door to find Metallak eating some hay outside the longhouse and Stonebridge said, "Where is Thomas anyway?"

Sasha pointed out onto the lake and in the distance Stonebridge could see the flash of arms coming out of the water from what obviously was a swimmer. Charlie stood gazing out on the lake, shaking his head in amazement. "I can barely walk up to my knees in the water now it's so cold."

"Yeah," Sasha said "he doesn't make a big deal about it, just says he's acclimated, but I think it's more than that, it's a sort of internal strength he has developed living up here."

"Sash," Daniel said, interrupting Stonebridge's reverie, "Thomas asked me to brush Metallak while he was gone. He said you would know what to do and could explain it to me."

"Oh, ok, sure." she replied. She smiled as she told Charlie that Thomas had spent nearly two hours the first day she and Daniel were there, explaining the grooming process for Metallak. "For Thomas it's a bonding moment, an almost religious experience. He talks to Metallak and pets him, scratches behind his ears and inside the ears as he checks for ticks. Then he brushes him from head to tail all the while talking to him. It was really a beautiful thing to watch."

"When he was showing me this," Sasha continued, "he was also explaining what was happening to the moose population in New Hampshire and other places along the US Canada border. He's convinced climate change is the main culprit for the dramatic decline in Moose populations. Moose are vulnerable to a parasite called the Winter Tick. The shorter winters and warmer climates make it more likely that more ticks survive and they literally suck the life out of a moose, especially the young calves."

"Do other animals like deer get these ticks too?" asked Stonebridge as he scratched Metallak behind his ears, eliciting a happy grunt from the big moose.

"They do, but they have grooming habits that seem to allow them to remove the ticks better than the moose. Some of the moose researchers have checked during the last few years have had as many as one hundred thousand ticks, literally sucking the life-blood out of them."

"How does a moose get so many ticks?" asked Daniel.

"These ticks are different from the ones we pick up when we are walking in a field or hiking in the woods," Sasha said. Their front legs somehow allow them to link up, like a chain of paper dolls or a line of chorus dancers. They form a clump on a piece of vegetation, waiting for a moose or a deer to walk by and when one of them is able to grab onto the moose it brings an entire entourage of additional ticks that are linked to it onto the animal. You could have one encounter bring a thousand ticks onto a moose."

"I guess Metallak is lucky to have Thomas."

Just then Thomas came trotting up. "Stonebridge!" he shouted joyfully. "Wow! Hail, hail the gang's all here! So have Daniel and Sasha gotten you settled in ok?

"Yeah they have been great. There were a few questions they couldn't answer but I'll ask you later."

That evening after the four friends had made a communal dinner, including a couple of nice bass for Cochise, they sat around a fire inside the longhouse. "Thomas, about those pictures in your living area . . . " Stonebridge said.

Thomas was quiet for a moment. Then he spoke. "Well, you probably know something of the Peacemaker's story. There are a lot of folks who believe the Iroquois Confederation was the inspiration for the US Constitution. It's well documented Ben Franklin spent some time with the Iroquois during the period before the Constitutional Convention in Philadelphia. Even if it wasn't the source for the Founders, it is inspiring to think of what the people of the Confederation were able to achieve as far back as the 12th century."

"It's also interesting to note that the legend of the Peacemaker has it he was born of a virgin mother. That legend makes for some interesting discussion obviously."

"Bobby Kennedy, well he's my hero. I think the world would have been a much different place if he hadn't been killed in June of 1968."

Thomas paused for a moment causing Stonebridge to interject, "I understand those two, but the portrait of Jimmy Carter . . .?"

Thomas smiled. "I don't have a lot of visitors here Charlie, but the few who do visit almost all wonder about that." Most people remember Jimmy Carter for the Iran Hostage crisis, or his infamous "Malaise" speech; or even the fact he put solar panels on the White House that Ronald Reagan tore down after he beat Carter. I could give you chapter and verse on each of those events of course, making the case for why the American people misunderstood or ignored the important parts of what Carter was doing or how everything would have changed if the rescue of the hostages was successful."

"I could even make the argument that he is the greatest ex-president in American history or at least the greatest living ex-President. As important as each of these things were, none of those things are what I consider to be his most important legacy."

Stonebridge leaned forward, fascinated with where this all seemed to be going. "Really?" he said.

"In addition to breaking the news to the American people that we needed to make big changes to the way we generated electricity and the kinds of energy we were relying on, Carter's administration passed major legislative changes laying the groundwork for the revolution in renewables we are experiencing right now. This began with a sweeping law called the National Energy Policy Act, passed in 1978. The National Energy Policy included five separate section."

"The Energy Tax Act established tax incentives for citizens using solar, wind or geothermal energy at home; The National Energy Conservation Policy Act created mandatory standards for energy usage and incentives for conservation; most important of all was what they call PURPA, the Public Utility Regulatory Policies Act. PURPA was a game changer. It changed the relationship between public utilities and citizens and businesses and encouraged the use of renewables and cogeneration. A two line amendment, slipped into the bill at the last minute by New Hampshire's Senator John Durkin, with Carter's support, required that the utilities purchase electricity from any small provider under a certain size."

"Section 210 of PURPA required utilities to purchase electricity - at a fair price - called the "avoided cost" - meaning what it would cost them to make the electricity - to any generator of electricity producing less than eighty megawatts."

"This one short paragraph successfully wrested monopoly control over the electric grid from the utility companies and opened the gates for a flood of small alternative power producers and eventually individual homeowners and businesses."

"For the first time the American people, just beginning to experience a growing environmental consciousness back in the 70s, had a say in the kinds of energy we were using and could participate in the creation of that energy. We can thank Jimmy Carter, John Durkin and the 95th Congress of the United States for that."

Chapter 56   An Apple a Day

Michelle, returning from the Governor's news conference, made a snap decision to stop off at Hank's farm on her way back to Herbert's cabin in Groton. She wanted to pick up some venison steaks for Herbert as a surprise and she wanted to see if Hank had laid the groundwork that would enable her planted question to take root. She walked through the door to find Hank at his Power Mac.

He swiveled his chair around toward her as she came through the door. "Just so's you know, I'm going to be going to "handgun hell" for this. I knew you lefties were going to get me into hot water with my compadres. I just didn't know how deep I was going to get and how fast it would happen."

"I just finished hacking into Legislative Services and setting up an anonymous Legislative Services Request . . . called an LSR. The Title, 'Making it a Class A Felony to carry a firearm on a public right-of-way' will be anonymous for fourteen business days before the sponsor has to identify himself or herself publicly. Only the title is published. We have a little more than two weeks to stoke this fire before someone figures out there's no sponsor."

"Won't someone ask the lawyer who supposedly recorded the title about it?" Michelle asked, proud she remembered the process from her visit to the Statehouse when she was a chaperone for the fourth grade the previous year.

"You won't believe how lucky we got with that," Hank said with a devilish grin on his face. "Each lawyer has a number that identifies who accepted the LSR request. It just so happens a friend of mine who works in Legislative Services told me about one of their lawyers who just checked into rehab for an opiate problem. He had a skiing injury this winter and then he got hooked on Oxycontin. When the Legislature went crazy over the "Opiate Crisis" his doctor told him he was going to be cut off and he could choose to go it alone or to go into rehab to kick the habit. He chose rehab. He'll be out-of-pocket - - unreachable - - for four weeks according to the rules of the Rehab facility. Not even his mother can speak with him."

"You used his number?"

"Right as rain amigo." Hank said.

"I didn't know you were such an accomplished hacker,"

"I'm just a piker really." Hank replied. "If we are going to do anything on a more serious level, we are going to need someone who has mad skills. Not a lightweight like me. The firewalls around Legislative Services are minor league compared with most. But if we go up against Polaris or one of the big boys, it's going to be like scaling the big green monster at Fenway by comparison."

"If we need to do that," Michelle said thoughtfully, "we had better start talking with Thomas about it now so we don't have another set-to with him about growing the circle."

"It's a good idea, Michelle. I was thinking another camping trip to Moll's Rock would be a good way for us to do some planning, relaxing and fishing at the same time."

"If we're going to do that we had better do it soon, the nights are getting colder fast. Maybe the first weekend in October, just before the Sandwich Fair. Herbert won't want to miss the fair. He starts talking on the day after the fair ends, around October 13 of every year, about going back to the fair for another one of those great éclairs . . . and he loves the Oxen barn, too."

"Sounds like a plan." Said Hank. "Let's start passing the word around. I'll get word to Thomas. I can also let Daniel and Sasha know when I meet with them at *Dot's Bread and Butter Bistro* next week. They are hiking on the Newfound Range right now."

"OK, I'll take the rest," Michelle said. "You free the last weekend in September as an alternative?"

"Affirmative. But let's try to push folks on October. It gives us more time to think about what we want to discuss . . . besides, the fish will be more hungry with all the bugs pretty much gone."

Chapter 57   Birth of the Renewables Revolution

As Thomas waxed philosophical around the fire of the longhouse in Pittsburgh, James Kitchen was putting the finishing touch on his next article for the NH Business Digest. If two great minds can truly think alike, one might have thought a Vulcan mind-meld had occurred.

The Birth of the Renewable Revolution
How Two Votes Won an Election and One Vote Changed the World
By James Kitchen

Understanding the choices our nation faces as we struggle to build a new energy paradigm requires we have at least a basic understanding about how we got to where we are today and that journey - strangely enough - winds right through New Hampshire . . . in more ways than one in fact.

Most politicians and even most citizens in New Hampshire consider the place of our state in the national election process sacrosanct. The First-in-the-Nation Presidential Primary provides a jolt of cash to the state's economy every four years but most people, particularly the staunchest defenders of the Primary, will tell you there are more important reasons for protecting our place as first in the nation.

They will explain that only in a small state like New Hampshire does a candidate with limited money - but a great message - have a chance. In larger states, where the election is dominated by big business, big labor, and exorbitant media costs, a great candidate without deep pockets will never have such a chance.

New Hampshire folks take their role in the process of winnowing down the field of candidates in their primary very seriously. They study the issues, they vigorously question the candidates, and then, once they've made up their minds, they roll up their sleeves and get involved in one campaign or another.

To understand where we are today we need to go back to the mid-1970s. Richard Nixon had resigned, to avoid impeachment and Gerald Ford was our first unelected President. The Presidential Primary of 1976 saw a very crowded field among Democrats. Depending on who you count, there were almost twenty people testing the waters or outright campaigning for the nomination. From that process, an unknown Governor named Jimmy Carter emerged and swept to the nomination as the "un-politician". Carter won in Iowa and during the last three weeks of the New Hampshire Primary, capitalized on his Iowa win and zoomed from a 2% standing to over 30%, capturing New Hampshire. These two wins would serve to create a groundswell and Carter would go on to win the Democratic nomination. By the time the General Election rolled around James Earl Carter had sold himself as the first "outsider" candidate of the modern era and he won handily over Gerald Ford.

Carter's one-term presidency was roiled by controversy and crisis, from an Arab Oil Embargo to the taking of American hostages at the American Embassy in Iran.

Hidden in the layers of these controversies and crises is a legislative record that created the framework for the renewable energy revolution that has, of late, taken the country by storm. Carter's team shepherded through Congress the landmark National Energy Policy Act, including a section called PURPA - the Public Utility Regulatory Policies Act. These massive pieces of Federal legislation included the first national policies on renewable energy and energy conservation, among other things.

Two years before Carter ascended to the Presidency, New Hampshire held an election for a United States Senator to replace the retiring Norris Cotton. A close contest between the Democrat John Durkin and the Republican Louis Wyman led to two recounts; the first won by Durkin by ten votes and the second won by Wyman by 2 votes. Any citizen, who wonders if their vote counts, need only look at the outcome of this election. Finally, at an impasse, the election was decided in the US Senate and Durkin was seated. Two years later, as the Carter Energy policy was moving through the congress John Durkin slipped an amendment into PURPA. The amendment required utility companies to purchase power - at market rates - from any producer of electricity generating fewer than 80 megawatts.

Durkin originally believed he was helping establish a foothold for wood to energy biomass and trash to energy cogeneration. He was, but the door he opened with his amendment turned out to be big enough for every dreamer and entrepreneur, with a viable idea for generating electricity renewably, to walk through. Soon proposals for small hydro (called Low Head Hydro), solar power, wind power and other renewable resources were on the drawing board or underway.

The Energy Policy Act passed the Senate by 1 vote.

Over the years since then changes have been made to the Energy Act, but all moving the country toward the day when renewable energy would account for a larger and larger portion of the power produced.

The changes of the 70s represented the first step in a changing relationship between America's public utilities and the people and businesses that consumed *the energy. Utilities no longer held complete monopoly power over both the sale and the purchase of electricity as well as its transmission.*

Granite Skyway represents a well-planned effort to reverse the evolutionary chain of events leading us to this place. Polaris Electric and a large group of investors, both individuals and institutions, have joined together to build a private transmission line. Not subject to the same constraints of public utilities, allowing them to circumvent many of the requirements Polaris Electric would be subject to had they proposed to do this alone, as a public utility. At the same time, because Polaris is an investor in the project, they are able to make side deals between their company and the Granite Skyway project that gives Granite Skyway access to the Polaris Electric utility rights of way - - perhaps even - - a backdoor to allow Granite Skyway to use state laws providing protection from losses that result from so-called stranded assets, to assure that if the investment made turns out to be uncompetitive as the cost of renewables continue to go down, Granite Skyway will still be able to charge New Hampshire ratepayers for a portion of the costs of the transmission line.

From the Canadian Border to a terminus in Southern New Hampshire, the only electricity that will flow through the transmission lines of Granite Skyway will be what it purchases from Hydro-Quebec in Canada. This will effectively limit the number of renewable energy projects possible forcing the state backwards relative to our surrounding states.

The motivation for Polaris that brought on Granite Skyway is, despite all this, understandable. The changes that have taken place over the past twenty years represent an existential challenge to many utility companies, including Polaris. They are casting around for ways to generate more profits in an era of shrinking opportunities.

In the next article we'll examine why this is so.

Chapter 58   The Guns of Social Media

Conrad Fleming sat in the back of his new Lincoln Town Car. The old one, the one last driven by an unlucky buck with a big rack and memorialized on every form of social media known to humanity, was on its way to an auto recycler. This was the final verdict of a detailer who, though he gave it his best effort, said he could not eliminate the smell of death!

Fleming was furious with Polaris' insurance company who had - at least so far - refused to cover the cost of replacing his car or any of those parked on Big Island. They had taken the position that a clause in the insurance policy, declaring it null and void if Terrorism was in any way the cause of the claim, had to be invoked after Fleming had publicly called the members of The Trust "eco-terrorists". His lawyers might be able to get the insurance company to reverse themselves but it would take months if not years, surely requiring a court decision because shareholders of the insurance company were calling to say they were watching and if the company buckled under to Polaris they would raise holy hell. At any rate, at four hundred dollars an hour it might end up costing the company as much to appeal the decision and play it out, as it would to just replace the cars. They would undoubtedly have to replace them anyway because the investors were not going to wait while they fought with the insurance company.

His cell phone rang, not a number he recognized, but he answered it. Mac on the other end, said, "Conrad, I know I'm not supposed to call you but JEn is tied up with some other business and he authorized me to call using a burner phone. I think we may have a couple of good leads and JEn wanted me to give you a report so you knew we were making some progress."

"Go ahead then."

"First, it turns out three, not two, of the prints we found on the cars led to classified identities."

"Jesus H. Christ!!" Conrad roared. "Isn't there some way to break through those classifications to find out who these people are?"

"There isn't enough probable cause to even make a request according to the State Police. We might be able to go around them by having your lobbyist ask her paramour, the Majority Leader, to call in some favors with his old classmates at the CIA, but that would create a lot of questions we may not want her to be asking. I think we should hold off for now and only use that relationship if we absolutely must. We have enough other leads to get to the bottom of this mystery and eventually we'll figure out who the super patriots are."

"Agreed, we don't want to widen the circle by asking Beth; I'm not even supposed to know about her relationship with the Majority Leader . . . and Mac . . . (pause) . . . If you ever call them *Super Patriots* again, you will be waiting tables in a St. Johnsbury diner, and don't you forget it."

"Yes sir." Mac, who was in the back seat of her own SUV, vigorously thrust her hand out with her middle finger extended in a silent salute. Conrad could be a real bastard sometimes.

She continued, "we have a lead on the wolf but got turned away at the border when we tried to get information from the Border Patrol. We think the woman came across with the wolf recently and it should be pretty easy to check. The State Police could get the information, or the Chief in Dixville, but we were trying to stay ahead of them so we're trying another angle for the moment. Susan Wilson has an idea she's going to follow up on next."

"What's that?"

"She didn't elaborate but she said it would either pan out or not within the next few hours and she'll let me know."

"It also seems the wolf is attached to a couple, one possibly from Canada and the other from the US - at least with a New Hampshire registered Prius. They appear to have been backpacking. We don't know if they are casual or a more formal couple but this gives us an excellent set of data points for identifying them."

Fleming's phone beeped signaling an incoming call, it was his office. "I have a call coming in Mac, gotta take this. He hung up without so much as a goodbye. Mac dropped the burner phone onto the seat and raised her other hand in a double salute.

"Conrad," came the voice of his administrative assistant, "The phones are blowing up here. Every gun nut in the state is calling to ask why we are treading - no stomping - on their second amendment rights."

"What the hell are you talking about?

"Yesterday at the Governor's press conference a reporter asked a question about Polaris getting a State Rep to sponsor a bill making it illegal to carry a firearm on a public right-of-way. When other reporters followed up on it today they found a

Legislative Services Request had indeed been filed but the Attorney who took the request is gone and can't be reached for the next four weeks."

"There's no way to find out who the State Rep was who filed it?"

"Not until we can talk with the attorney or after a two week period elapses during which the sponsor is allowed to remain anonymous."

"Oh for Christ's sake," Conrad growled." Have the folks in communications issue a denial. Make it clear we have not asked anyone to sponsor such a bill."

"In the meantime, what do I do about the calls? They're tying up every single line and blowing up the Internet! The office here has ground to a halt, nothing is getting done because no one can use the phones."

"Have Communications get that statement to me as soon as they can. We need to nip this in the bud as soon as possible. Also, get someone from Tech up there. See if there is a way to reroute the calls to the Bedford office in order to free up our phones for business, at least we'll be able to make calls out that way. Now, I have to call someone right away about this press conference."

Conrad hung up and immediately redialed the number from Mac's burner phone.

"Mac, why the hell didn't you tell me about the press conference yesterday and the gun thing?"

"I was just getting to that Conrad when you blew me off."

Not bothering to apologize Conrad asked "So what do we know about the reporter who asked the question?"

"Well the first thing we know is she wasn't a reporter, at least not from any news outlet we know. She might be a blogger, since we can't possibly keep track of all those. I got the Governor to call in her security detail from the State Police and they reviewed all of the security cams. We have a picture of the woman as she was exiting down the stairwell and security ran it with facial recognition software."

"And?"

"And she was not in the system. But we have her photo, so we'll identify her soon enough."

"Soon enough is NOW Mac. Do you have any idea of what is happening to our corporate communications system? I heard social media was blowing up as well."

Mac had hoped Fleming had not heard about this. She was watching her Twitter feed, Facebook and Linkedin accounts and the view from here was not good. The gun owners were pissed and most of their fire was directed at Polaris, Conrad Fleming and the Granite Skyway proposal.

Fleming continued, "I think we can assume someone is trying to sabotage us and it's likely to be tied to this Trust group. See if you can get the Governor to raise the security alert level and put the State Police on finding this woman."

"But aren't we trying to stay ahead of the police on this?" Mac asked, lifting her middle finger once again and shaking it in the air for effect.

"Think it through Mac. She hasn't broken any laws. The police will bring her in, ask her a bunch of questions and, unless she spills her guts, which is highly unlikely, they'll have to release her, but we'll know who she is and where she lives."

"Right," Mac said. "OK I'll figure out a way to get the Governor to issue the order without making her suspicious."

"Oh and Mac," Fleming said, "have Enright call me as soon as he can. We have some things to talk about."

Chapter 59   The Trailhead

The three members of the Cabal had left the Canadian border and headed, at the insistence of Susan Wilson, toward the Balsams.

As they neared the Balsams, Wilson said to Duggan "We're heading about three miles southeast, past the hotel."

Five minutes later she said, "Right here. Pull over in this parking area." Just three miles past the Balsams, on the right hand side of the road a brown trail sign indicated a road crossing for the Appalachian Trail was just ahead. Duggan pulled off into the parking area for the Old Spec Trail.

Susan got out and walked over to a trail board at the trailhead. A trailboard is a small structure built at the trailhead of a high-use trail. It is used to place important announcements for hikers and also serves as a place where hikers along the Appalachian trail leave messages for other hikers who may have fallen behind or planned to meet up with them. At certain key areas, like the Old Spec trailhead, there is often a logbook that records the comings and goings of the hikers. Here the many and varied hikers of this portion of Appalachian Trail record their names and comments for posterity.

Ironically, many of those making the long trip from Maine to Georgia, or Georgia to Maine, leave the longest entries in which they obsess for pages about the need to travel as many miles a day as they possibly can. Those here embarking on a shorter trip, a day hike up to the top of Old Spec and back; or a longer trip over the Mahoosucs, perhaps even continuing on to the Carter-Moriah Range with its magnificent viewpoints overlooking the Northern Presidentials, often just leave a brief message noting the weather or the trail conditions.

Susan waited as an AT hiker wrote in the logbook. Echo and Duggan stood by the car complaining to one another about wasting time at some trailhead in the middle of nowhere. After 15 minutes, the AT hiker was still writing and Duggan's patience ran out . . .

"Are you writing a Goddamn book?" he hollered out.

The hiker, sitting on the ground cross-legged, his pack serving as a back brace, did not bother to look up as he simply lifted his unengaged arm and raised his middle finger in response to Duggan's question.

Duggan started toward the hiker but was warned off with a withering look from Susan Wilson. He shuffled back to where Echo leaned against the SUV kicking the tire in frustration.

Finally, the hiker closed the book, stood and brought it over to the shelf where it was kept sheltered from the elements by a small roof over the trailboard.

Susan casually walked over and began to page through the logbook, working backwards from the last entry. After a few minutes she came upon a brief entry and caught her breath.

What is life?
What is life?
It is the flash of a firefly in the night.
It is the breath of a buffalo in the wintertime.
It is the little shadow, which runs across
the grass and loses itself in the sunset.
       ~ Crowfoot, Blackfoot warrior and orator 1830 - 1890

Beneath it was written: "Sasha Brandt and Cochise passed this way."

Just above Cochise's name and to the right someone, presumably Sasha Brandt, had drawn a paw print.

Susan tore out an empty page from the back of the logbook and jotted down the name of their quarry . . . Sasha Brandt.

For good measure she carried the logbook over to Duggan and Echo and showed them Sasha's entry.

Duggan promptly tore out the page on which Sasha had written.

"You didn't need to do that," said Susan. "I copied it all down."

"If you thought of it Wilson, how long will it be before the Chief stops by looking for the same thing?"

"That depends," Susan replied.

"Depends on what? Duggan asked.

"If he's smarter than you or has shit for brains too."

Chapter 60 The First Nail

Conrad Fleming had just pulled into his parking space at the main office of Polaris Electric, or rather his driver had, when the cell rang again. Conrad looked at the screen and saw that it was Enright. "Talk to me." he barked.

"We got a name for the girl with the wolf dog." Enright said. "Should I pass it along to the Chief in Dixville or the Staties? I'd rather not, mind you, not yet anyway."

"What's your rationale?" Conrad asked, pretty sure he knew.

"I think we should keep this a shadow operation for the time being. If we can stay ahead of them it may be to our advantage at some point. That's about all I should say - you can fill in the spaces."

Conrad smiled; he was one evil mother, Enright. Conrad wouldn't want to be on his bad side. "Listen JEn, I had one more thing I wanted to run by you. That first piece written by the Gazetteer pen named Paine . . . there was something familiar in the way it was written, especially the use of the term "viewscape" I think it may have been written by Jack Carrigain. He's one of the few people I know who uses that term. I thought he was still undecided on our project."

"Far as I know he hasn't come out one way or the other." Enright replied.

"If there is one person we want to neutralize on this it's Carrigain. He's a virtual folk hero up there in the North Country. If he comes out against us we're in real trouble. See what you can dig up on that, will you?"

"10-4 Conrad."

Fleming closed his phone and got out of the Town Car.

"I'll be back in 30 minutes Jim," he said to his driver. "Go grab yourself a coffee, you are going to need to stay sharp today."

As Fleming was giving Jim instructions, two cars pulled up two rows away from his reserved parking spot. The cars sported bumper strips that read "Official Member Roadkill Rangers." Beneath this was written "#TreesNotTowers."
Feeling the call of a Dunkin Donuts Coffee Coolatta Jim got out, locked up the Town Car and headed down the street. He failed to notice a young lady trailing just

behind him with what appeared to be a small laptop. In just moments she had cloned the signal from his key fob and sent the signal to the Rangers parked nearby.

The occupants of both cars jumped out and one went immediately to the driver's side door of the Town Car and pressed a button unlocking the Town Car instantly. Smiling he said "ain't technology great!" A second Ranger opened a back door and a third popped the trunk on his own car.

"I'm going to need a little help the third Ranger called out," and his friends returned to his car and joined him at the trunk.

"OK coast is clear", said the Ranger who had unlocked Conrad's car.

"Did you ever see the movie <u>The Longest Yard</u>?" He asked.

"Saw them both, the first and the remake, the first one, with Burt Reynolds playing the Quarterback, Paul "Wrecking" Crewe, was way better." answered Ranger number two.

"OK then, as Burt Reynolds said in the huddle - just after he had drilled a bullet pass into the balls of a defensive back, 'Worked once, should work again." He lifted the trunk revealing a large buck - discovered on the roadside that morning. They scooped it up together and loaded it into the back seat opposite the side where Conrad Fleming had gotten out.

"I suspect this is going to really piss him off. But just to be sure, hand me that empty Champagne bottle and the plastic glass on our front seat"

He placed the bottle and glass in separate cradles they had made with zip ties on the deer's front legs, and stood back gazing admiringly at their handiwork.

"We'd better get the hell out of here."

"Are you kidding me? I wouldn't miss this for the world. You guys get the cars out of here and I'll document it for us."

He took his iPhone out of his pocket and took a seat at the base of an elm tree shading the premium parking spaces outside One Commercial Plaza.

Ten minutes later he saw Conrad approaching from the building just as Jim was returning from Dunkin Donuts. He pressed the button and began to video the scene.

The two stood outside the car. "We're headed to the Statehouse first, said Conrad. "Then I'll let you know where we have to go after I have a meeting with the Governor. I'm so tired of holding that bitch's hand."

"Yes sir," answered Jim. He liked the Governor; she was a lot more respectful to him than his boss.

The two got into the car simultaneously.

The Ranger continued to discreetly train his iphone on the car.

Suddenly a roar erupted from the car as Conrad discovered his new, ripe seatmate. "God Damn it! He screamed as he jumped from the car, oblivious to the young man under the elm. "How the hell did they get into the car Jim? Did you forget to lock it?"

"No sir. I always lock then check. This car was securely locked before I left it."

"You stupid sack of shit! They could not have just done this unless you left the damn car unlocked!"

"Get this thing out of there before it stinks up another car. How many of these do you think the company is going to replace before I end up riding around in the back of a VW Beetle?"

Fleming stormed off, "I'm going back to my office to make a call, have this shit show cleaned up before I get back Jim, or don't be here. I don't need an incompetent hillbilly driving my car. Get with the program or I'll fire your ass."

At this point the Ranger handling the video was brazen enough to walk up to the Town Car. "He sounded pissed," the Ranger said to Jim. "What happened?"

Jim grabbed the handle of the door and opened it to provide a perfect video view of the deer. "This happened." he said.

Jim stood looking at the deer. Here, where he stood, with an autumn breeze rustling the leaves, he could smell that bad boy even now. What the hell was he supposed to do with it? "Screw this," he said, turning and walking away. "The bastard's on his own."

Chapter 61   The Unveiling

It took the Roadkill Rangers less than 5 minutes to upload their video to a dozen social media sites and within another ten the chatter among those who had viewed it, the clip already had reached every TV, radio station and social media site in the Northeast and was heading West in a wave.

It was hard to resist playing the video of "the CEO gone ballistic" on the evening news and most stations did not even try. By nightfall the entire 10 minutes of video was moving at lightning speed around the world and the death grimace of the buck was adorning thousands of emails and Facebook pages where it had replaced the headshots and avatars of anyone wanting to claim their place among the Roadkill Rangers. It was trending on Twitter, Facebook, and YouTube. Even Conrad Fleming's employees had to admit it was a hoot, especially when Fleming returned to the car to find Jim gone and promptly went crazy, kicking and screaming in hysteria as a crowd of observers gathered.

The Rangers ran the credits over the kicking and screaming Fleming with a final message that read "#TreesNotTowers".

That evening Seth Meyers, former Saturday Night Live Weekend Update anchor, and Manchester boy made good, played the entire 10 minutes on his show *Late Night with Seth Meyers*. When the camera came back to Seth at the end of the video he said "So, I have a message for Mr. Fleming too." He reached under his desk and donned a pair of antlers, sticking his tongue out for a moment and said. "Keep your hands off New Hampshire, take your Towers somewhere else!"

Just after "the Late Show" ended the telephone rang in Chester Wincowski's home.

"Hello" answered Wincowski.

"Hey! Uncle Chet, did you see Seth Meyers' show tonight?" Said the disembodied voice.

A big smile came over Chet's face and he replied, "Hell yes! You done good nephew. You struck a blow for the Wincowski clan and for New Hampshire. I'm proud of you.

"Thanks for the buck Uncle Chet."

Chapter 62   Wellington State Park

Daniel and Sasha arrived at the trailhead of the Elwell Trail just before dusk. They drove first into Wellington State Park to take a quick and bracing dip in Newfound Lake before they headed up the trail. The State Park was closed for the season but the entrance was left open so boaters and fishermen could access the only public boat launch on Newfound Lake. It also meant local folks could use the park and its long sandy beach in the off-season and on warm autumn days there was often a healthy contingent of them . . . especially on weekends.

Technically they were required to be out by dark but Daniel knew neither the state nor the town of Bristol had the funds or inclination to enforce the rule, so he and Sasha stripped and ran naked into the lake as Cochise joyfully ran wind sprints up and down the beach. Every once in awhile he would dart into the water and scare up a pair of ducks or wading birds. He wasn't really trying to catch them; he just liked to see them panic and fly off squawking, quacking or shrieking.

Daniel and Sasha took turns washing one another's backs, chest deep in the lake.

"Damn it's cold!" Sasha said.

Daniel put his arms around her and drew her naked body next to his. "This better?"

"Only moderately. And if you think you are going to do anything with that thing poking me from behind, think again. I'm getting clean and I'm getting out. I'm stunned it hasn't shrunk to the size of a wooly bear caterpillar; Besides, here's Cochise", she said as the Wolf paddled up and began swimming circles around them. "You don't want to get him all worked up or he may try to mount you from behind while you're working your magic on me."

Daniel laughed and pushed her away melodramatically. "You know I like it wild Sash, but THAT I can do without."

Newfound Lake is one of the cleanest lakes of its size anywhere. Daniel had grown up with adults always telling him it was one of the cleanest lakes in the world but he had spent more than a few summers traveling across Canada by train and the US by car and had seen more than his fair share of sparkling lakes in Glacier Park, Banff and the Wind River range of Wyoming. Still, with a turnover rate of several times a year, Newfound was remarkably clear and clean, despite the number of houses dotting the landscape.

Sasha looked up at the dark mountain looming over them to the west. "Is that where we're going?"

"Yup, we're going to hike one of my favorite trails, the *Elwell Trail*. It used to start halfway down the lake but in the mid-70's my dad and a bunch of other guys cut an extension from Nuttings Beach down to Wellington so folks would have the reward of the lake when they finished their hike."

Named after Colonel Alcott Farrar Elwell who died in 1962, the trail follows the ridge over Bear Mountain, Sugarloaf, Oregon and Mowglis Mountains all the way to Firescrew, which is actually a shoulder of Mt. Cardigan, the tallest of the range and the terminus of the trail. Unlike the other mountains in the range the summit of Cardigan is bare rock, burned off in a fire in the thirties.

As they toweled off on the beach, Daniel told Sasha about Colonel Elwell. "Elwell was a scion of a wealthy family from Boston who spent his summers on Newfound first as Assistant Director of Camp Mowglis and then Director after the original director, Elizabeth Ford Holt, died and left the camp to him. Harvard educated - he did his Master's Thesis on camps as a component of education - and spent one summer with the John Wesley Powell Expedition mapping the Yellowstone area. He was late signing up for the expedition and by the time he had heard about it all the jobs were taken except for cook - - so he signed on as the cook, even though he really was not much of a cook. He was determined not to miss the opportunity and with the blessing of Mrs. Holt he headed west.

"They probably could have just asked the Cheyenne, The Crow or Nez Perce for a map." Sasha said.

"Yeah but that would have entailed admitting the Indians were not subhuman," said Daniel, "and that was a bridge too far for a bunch of white guys in those days. In fact when they made the trip, there were still occasional skirmishes between the various tribes of the area and white settlers or people traveling through. "

"Good for them!" Sasha said.

"Elwell himself didn't have the same views about Native Americans."

"What makes you say that?"

"Well, because in the late 30's he hired a young Cheyenne man from Oklahoma, Wah-Pah-Nah-Yah or W. Richard West by his anglicized name."

"I don't know much Cheyenne," said Sasha, "but I think Wah-Pah-Nah-Yah means something like quiet, swift, runner."

"He translated it as 'Lightfoot Runner' " Daniel said.

"I was pretty close, eh?"

"Yes you were! Not bad for an Iroquois gal. After all they lived half a continent away from your folks."

"True, but most of the time you can't really tell much from that because your President Jackson, whom the current President seems to think was a "big-hearted guy" in 1838 forced most of the South-Eastern tribes including the Cherokee, Muscogee, Seminole, Chickasaw, and Choctaw to leave their homes on the *Trail of Tears*. The Cheyenne were moved from the Great Plains states to Oklahoma. Just some of the many "hikes" on the path to genocide our people have endured."

"That's right," Daniel said mentally kicking himself for not thinking about Andrew Jackson's systematic war on the Native people of the country and the *Indian Removal Act*.

"Jackson wasn't a big fan of those heathen nomads," he said in an effort to lighten things up.

"Ironically," Sasha replied, correcting Daniel again, "the Cherokee were more like "civilized" Europeans than most of the white settlers by 1830 when Congress passed the Indian Removal Act. Cherokee women wore gowns similar to those worn by European women. The Cherokee had established their own system of representational government, built roads, schools and churches, were farmers and cattle ranchers, all in an effort to assimilate."

"Historic documentation, in fact, shows more white settlers "migrated" to join Indian tribes than Indians joined white settlers during the years between Columbus and the end of the "Indian Wars". But the Cherokee were trying very hard to assimilate as a strategy for cultural survival."

"The Trail of Tears was not the last event in this nearly four hundred year struggle but it was one of the most brutal and cruel. In fact, one of America's greatest heroes of the day, Davy Crockett, opposed the Indian Removal Act, standing up for the Cherokee and lost his seat in Congress for doing it. He left Washington, headed for Texas, and you know what happened to him after that."

"I didn't know that story, Sash," Daniel said quietly.

"His parting words to Congress were 'I would sooner be honestly damned than hypocritically immortalized' " Sasha said.

"OK so I interrupted your story about Wah-Pah-Nah-Yah, Daniel. I really would like to hear the end of the story."

"Wah-Pah-Nah-Yah was a favorite among the boys and an extraordinary artist. He taught Cheyenne dances to the boys and Colonel Elwell purchased enough Cheyenne regalia so they could demonstrate the dances for the other boys and - from time to time - local communities. He also taught archery."

"Of course" said Sasha "whether he knew it or not" she said sarcastically.

"Oh he did. He was an excellent archer. There are stories about him shooting his bow from underneath a horse galloping across the athletic field and hitting his target. His most lasting memorial, though, was a series of murals he painted - renderings of scenes from Kipling's *Jungle Book*, on which the camp is based. Today Wah-Pah-Nah-Yah is considered one of the pre-eminent Native American Indian painters of the 20th century."

"But I'm getting ahead of myself.

By the time Elwell graduated Harvard, the US had entered the action in World War I so he joined the army where he rose to the rank of Colonel. When the war was over he came back to help Mrs. Holt run the camp again. After he took over, he actually closed the camp for two summers at the height of World War II because he felt it was his patriotic duty to get back into the action to stop Hitler. The army was, apparently, less enthused than he was - they had plenty of ranking officers - it was the "cannon fodder" grunts they were short on. Nevertheless, they accepted him back on the condition he accept a demotion to Captain, which he did."

"From what I have heard, Elwell had expected to see action when he re-upped but ended up working in an office somewhere far from the action. After two rather frustrating years he decided he would return to civilian life and moved back to New Hampshire and reopened the camp."

In the early 60s, after Elwell died the camp fell on hard times. In 1962, a group of ex-campers, including US Senator John Heinz and an FBI Agent named William Baird Hart formed a nonprofit foundation to save the camp. The old campers could not bear to see "the Colonel's" legacy tarnished and they knew how important the camp was to their own personal development so they formed the Holt-Elwell Foundation and purchased the camp. Bill Hart agreed to leave the FBI and take over as director and for more than two decades he ran Mowglis and established it as a non-profit powerhouse among camps.

The three walked back to the Prius and moved it across the road to the trailhead parking, where it would be less noticeable, and packed their backpacks by the light of their headlamps. "We'll hike in just far enough to be legal and camp for the night." Daniel said. Then we'll hike over Bear Mountain and Sugarloaf tomorrow and camp on top of Oregon Mountain."

"Not that I'm worried about breaking the law at this point," Sasha said, "but is it legal to camp on the summit?"

"This range gets quite a bit of summer traffic from day hikers," said Daniel "but very few backpack along it. So it's not highly restricted. I suspect we won't see a soul for the next few days until we get to the summit of Cardigan. I'm counting on finding someone, after we get down from Cardigan, who can give me, or the three of us, a ride back to the car." With supplies for the next four or five days, headlamps lit, the three set out on the Elwell Trail watching for a flat spot where they could put up their tent.

Chapter 63   Daybreak at Nubian Farm

Herbert started his day with a trip up the rope in his backyard and his regular breakfast - - a huge bowl of couscous. Michelle had already left for the day because she had a house showing at 8am in Plymouth. She'd been spending almost every night there lately and Herbert had to admit it felt good. They never had the talk they were planning to have during their trip to Umbagog and, though he still had some misgivings about whether he was doing right by Michelle, he was beginning to think all this was what his grandfather used to call "over-thinking".

"Don't over-think it, Herbert." he would say. "What does your heart tell you? If your heart says 'go' then don't say 'no'. Life is too short. Does it mean sometimes you'll make a mistake? Sure. Does it mean sometimes you get hurt? You bet. But mistakes and failures, well, they are often our best teachers. If you don't make mistakes then you aren't trying hard enough."

Herbert had never been particularly close to his father, who was cold and withdrawn, but his grandfather was a different subject altogether. He was a man of few words . . . but those words had the ring of wisdom and experience. Once, when Herbert was particularly young he was rummaging around in his grandfather's attic when he came upon a box that he opened to find a piece of old black felt with four different medals, two purple hearts and two star-shaped, one brown and one silver. He had brought them to show his grandfather who had gently taken them from his grandson and explained they were from his service during World War II.

Over the years Herbert would gradually piece together the story behind those medals. His grandfather was part of the Normandy invasion. One of the purple hearts was from a wound he sustained there. When he had pressed the old man for details he had simply said, "there's nothing much to say about getting shot in the ass boy. Nothing heroic about it." Later Herbert would find out he was shot when he went back to help a fallen comrade. He had been hoisting him onto his shoulders when a German sniper had hit his mark.

God he loved that old man!

When he was in high school, his grandfather had moved in with them full time, unable to care for himself any longer. Herbert would help him get out of bed every morning, bring him his coffee, give him his pills, sometimes massage his legs and feet, which were weak and painful from peripheral neuropathy, to help him walk well enough to get to the bathroom.

At night they would sit down at the dinner table and grandfather would always ask the same question . . . though it would take different forms. "What did you fail at today Boy?" He didn't ask the question to be cruel; he asked the question to challenge Herbert to push the boundaries of his imagination and courage. Herbert didn't always have an answer for the question but over time it had spurred him to fear failure less and less and to take risks others would not. It also made for some of the most memorable dinner conversations and a whole lot of laughter. Herbert had learned about courage and how to laugh at himself.

Now Herbert sat at the table in his cabin, looking north toward the Waterville Range out a picture window, lost in his thoughts. Taffy, perhaps sensing Herbert was lost in the past, came over and nudged him. Herbert reached down to scratch her behind the ears. "What do you say we ask her to move in with us Taffy? It's time to stop over-thinking it."

Chapter 64   Two Down

Mac mingled with the crowd of journalists in the Lobby of the Legislative Office Building. The President of Firearms Owners of NH had called a news conference for nine am. The crowd expected he would have something to say about the move to ban firearms on public rights-of-way. A news conference, or in today's parlance, a "presser" (short for press conference), remained the first line of defense or offense in any kind of campaign.

Mac dialed Enright's cell phone and he answered on the first ring. "Go Mac."

"The Governor's security has identified the woman who asked the question at the presser. The State Police told her, the Governor I mean, they would question the woman but they had no reason to do anything more, she had every right to be there."

"That's what I figured, but now we have her name right?"

"Right. Name's Michelle Kane, she has a real estate business in the Plymouth area."

"I want you to head up there Mac . . . see if you can get close to this woman and find out everything you can."

"I'm in Concord at the moment, Alphonse Ruger is about to have a news conference here about the Right-of-way bill. I figure I'll stick with this, then head up there after."

"OK." Enright said, "Call me if anything happens there of consequence."

"Will do."

Ruger stepped up to the microphone. The usual coterie of media were there, even though it was a Friday and usually a very quiet day in the hallowed halls of the New Hampshire Capitol building.

Tall and thin, his pale skin nearly translucent, with an adam's apple that bobbed up and down as he spoke, creating a distraction that couldn't possibly be ignored, Ruger looked as if he was held prisoner and fed nothing but bread and water in a darkened room for the last year. He could have been a character from a

Washington Irving novel or a runway model for American Gothic fashions. If his first name had been Ichabod it would have been downright perfect casting.

"Good day" he said. "I'm Alphonse Ruger." Mac was startled by his voice - - so startled she had to suppress a laugh. Where she had expected to hear the baritone of a radio announcer or an operatic basso profundo coming out of this ghostly figure, instead she heard a high pitched, almost screeching voice.

"I am the President of the NH Firearms Owners Association. I'm here today to call out the coward who has anonymously sponsored LSR 497, a bill making possession of a firearm on a public right-of-way a crime."

The voice definitely did not lend itself to the challenge issued . . . a little like Barney Fife standing in for Magnum PI.

Just as he finished his opening challenge, a reporter, late to the News Conference, walked through the door of the Legislative Office Building creating a gust of wind that blew Ruger's notes off the dais. He lunged to catch them and his own personal firearm slipped out of its chest holster and clattered across the floor. Members of the media gasped and looked on in horror as he casually strode across the floor, picked it up and put it back in his holster. "Not the first time that's happened here at the Statehouse," he said casually.

Back at the dais now, Ruger commenced his formal remarks. "This morning we mailed a letter to our entire membership asking them to donate as much as they possibly can to defend our constitution against this travesty."

"BINGO" Hank Algren said to himself as he watched the news conference from a chair in the waiting area, near the door. Herbert had called it spot on.

For the next fifteen minutes Ruger tossed out the standard red meat for the news media: A clear violation of the sacred Second Amendment; a slap across the face to every law abiding gun owner; the usual fare. Wrapping up he said, "Today I am calling for a direct action by gun owners; a protest at the headquarters of Polaris Electric on Monday of next week. Our goal is to disrupt the business of Polaris Electric and to call for the abandonment of the Granite Skyway Project which has been used to justify this outrageous assault on the Constitution."

Then he opened the news conference to reporters' questions.

"Do you really see this as a serious effort?" asked one reporter.

"Whenever someone sponsors a bill that's such a clear and onerous violation of the right to bear arms we take it seriously. I'm calling on every law abiding gun owner to contact his or her State Representative. I'm also calling on the leadership of Polaris Electric to withdraw their support of the bill."

"But the company denies it has anything to do with this." fired back another reporter.

"Which is just what you would expect them to do when they were caught with their hand in the cookie jar."

Hank had heard enough. He stood up and quietly slipped out of the lobby of the Legislative Office Building. The hook was set. Under ordinary circumstances he would simply have told his compatriots to just sit back and watch the fun but Ruger's call for a protest had given him an idea . . .

Chapter 65   If a Shoe Drops in the Forest

Michelle was scheduled to show a home in the nearby town of Plymouth. She had just arrived at the home where the client had requested to meet her when her cell phone rang. It was the office. She answered and her partner Wally spoke quietly into the phone. "Michelle, I don't know what this is about but there are two cruisers and state police here asking to speak with you. I'm just going to pretend that I am leaving you a voicemail here. They won't say what it's about. Just that they would like to speak with you."

"Listen Wally, tell them you aren't sure when, or if, I am coming back, since it's supposed to be my day off on Saturday. Then close up the office and go home. If they want to wait outside they can do so, but you don't know if I'll be back or not."

Michelle hung up and dialed Linda Levy. "Linda I may be in trouble here. My partner just called and said there were two State Police officers waiting for me at the office. What should I do?"

"I'm on my way up to Rattlesnake to climb this afternoon," Linda said. Do you have something you can do that'll make you hard to find?"

"Yes, as a matter of fact I was thinking I would . . ."

"Stop. Don't tell me what. I don't want to lie to the police. I'm going to call and tell them you are away until tomorrow and I will be bringing you in to meet with them in the morning. I'll try to arrange to meet them at a local station so we don't have to drive all the way to Twin Mountain or Concord. Let's try to get together tonight so you can bring me up to speed."

"Why don't you plan to have dinner with Herbert and I after you climb?" Michelle said. "I can fill you both in then."

"Ok. What time should I be there?"

"Well Herbert feeds the goats at 6pm sharp and then he takes care of Taffy and he's usually at his table for dinner at 6:30, give or take . . ."

"Give or take an hour or two?" Linda said.

"Give or take a minute or two," Michelle said. "Keeping a regular schedule helps keep his brain damage from acting up, so he says. He calls it 'strapping on the feedbag'."

"OK, I'll be there at 6. I haven't had the pleasure of feeding the goats before so I wouldn't want to miss that."

"Don't wear anything loose or they'll be eating you too."

Chapter 66   Asquamchumaukee Energy

Peter and Sandra hustled around the office of the Asquamchumaukee Renewable Energy Association offices - AREA for short - and for obvious reasons. Asquamchumaukee was a cool name but didn't exactly trip off the lips. It was the name the native people of the region had given the beautiful meandering river, now known as the Baker, that flowed through the fields and floodplain forests; its oxbows, ghosts of millennia past, provided peaceful and abundant habitat and food for critters of all kinds; those that made this place their home and those just passing through on the northeast flyway.

It was just that nexus of beauty and abundance that, more than two hundred years before, had drawn a small group of native women, children and a handful of old men left behind while the others hunted the forests on the nearby mountains for larger game. They had set up camp at the confluence of the Asquamchumaukee and the Pemigewasset rivers and were preparing the camp for what they hoped would be the fruits of the hunt when a group of soldiers, based in Northampton, Massachusetts and under the command of Lieutenant Thomas Baker unexpectedly came upon them. The soldiers attacked and ultimately burned the village to the ground. But not until they had scalped each of the dead and stolen all of the furs, pelts and meat the group had amassed.

For his efforts Baker was paid "40 pounds sterling" for the scalps and promoted to Captain. Ultimately, the poetic name of the Valley too was changed to 'honor' him.

Historians attribute Baker's blood lust for Indians to his own capture during the Deerfield Raid of the French and Indian Wars. The fact that he survived, however, probably indicates he was held by the French as a hostage and not by the Indians, who, for better or worse, rarely took male prisoners.

Over the years various groups, publications and documentaries have tried - if only for brief moments - to take back the name but none had succeeded.

Peter and Sandra were getting ready for the day's event when Michelle walked in. She introduced herself and said she was intending to get involved with the organization for some time but kept putting it off. She happened to be in town to show a house but the client had never shown up so she had time on her hands and decided to pop in.

"You're timing is perfect," Sandra said. "If you have time today we could use your help with our Energy Raiser."

"Energy Raiser?" Michelle said.

"Sure, you remember the old barn raisings where neighbors came together to help build a barn? Well, we've taken a page out of their book. The owner of the home buys the hardware for a renewable energy installation, usually solar but not always, we provide the volunteer labor and expertise to construct it and make it operational."

"That sounds wonderful" Michelle said. "Count me in - but I don't have any expertise in this area. I'm not sure I can be very helpful."

"You don't need any expertise." Peter chimed in, "most of the work that gets done is by people who are simply following orders from an installer or engineer type, in other words grunts like me. Hey, we're running a bit late so why don't you just tag along now and we can show you the ropes - kind of a baptism by fire situation!"

The three turned to leave and found Mac standing in the doorway. She was trailing Michelle since she arrived at the morning showing that Mac had arranged, never intending to show up of course.

"I've heard about what you have been doing here and was hoping I could help and learn the ropes along the way so I could do something similar over in the Burlington, Vermont area where I work", said Mac.

"Well" Sandra said, a bit hesitant to take on something quite so vague. Both Sandra and Peter had started this organization because it would make a real and tangible difference in the lives of people and to the planet. They'd had their fill of wild assed dreams and talking heads. "We've really got a lot on our plate, and I'm not sure we can take on something quite so big," she said.

"I work for Green State Power, I think I can get you a grant to do the training and probably a bunch of surplus equipment you could use for the installations." Mac said.

Now she had their attention. Running a small nonprofit was an adventure every day, but it had its ups and downs too. Most of the downs were associated with a lack of capital to help you realize your dreams. It wasn't every day someone showed up in your office ready to write a check.

Peter and Sandra looked at each other, shrugged and Sandra said, "why don't you both ride along with us to the site and we can talk about it on the way and see where things go. Are you available?"

Mac hesitated, waiting for Michelle; she wanted to make sure she didn't get split off from her quarry, not when she was this close.

Michelle pulled her phone from her pocket and said, "I just have to let my office know where I'm going to be. Let's go!"

Mac smiled. "Well, I said I wanted to learn the ropes right? Now is as good a time as any."

"I'm Sandra and this is Peter," she said, extending her hand to Mac. "Oh, and this is Michelle. She's just joined our group so stick close to her and you'll both get the cook's tour of our operations."

Sandra divided the load of materials among the group and they headed out the door. As they were walking to the car she said to Mac, "You know I've been thinking we should write a book, sort of a handbook, a how-to manual that other groups could use to launch their own organization. Maybe we could combine that with the training you are talking about and we could put a plug in for Green State Power, maybe even have them sponsor the book."

"Sounds very promising," said Mac.

Peter opened the trunk of an old Mercedes and began to pile the equipment in. As she was climbing into the back seat Mac said, "I was expecting you to be driving a Prius or an electric car. Not a big old gas-guzzler. Not exactly the best face of a green organization."

Peter laughed. "This baby hasn't tasted a lick of diesel in seven years" he said. "Mac and Michelle, meet Endora my veggie car. I run her on 100% vegetable oil, collected from every Chinese restaurant, fast food chain and pizza place in the area."

"Endora like the European tax haven for scoundrels?" Mac asked.

"Nah, like Samantha's mother in 'Bewitched'. Though I suppose I should not admit that. The other sounds so much more romantic and dangerous . . . and from what I've heard women love dangerous men."

"That's less true than you would imagine." Mac responded as if experience were speaking through her. Michelle, caught off guard by this moment of candor, looked at Mac and for a moment Mac thought she was blown. Then Michelle laughed and said "Yeah, overblown tripe! Brains . . . now that's sexy! And you've got brains aplenty Peter."

Embarrassed, Peter patted the seat next to him, "well anyway, Endora here, she's a beauty and you won't find a more comfortable ride anywhere in the White Mountains. Only problem is . . . her farts smell like French fries!"

"Would that we could all say that," said Sandra, who had obviously had this conversation before. She took up the shotgun position, closed her door and buckled up. "Ready when you are Cap'n."

Chapter 67   Demand and the Grid

The crew at AREA was putting the finishing touches on their latest Energy Raiser as James Kitchen was readying his next article for Sunday's newspaper. The New Hampshire Business Digest was released weekly on Mondays but a unique partnership between New Hampshire's only statewide daily newspaper had expanded the audience for Kitchen's series.

On the day following publication of his first article in the NH Business Digest, Joel Harmony, Editor of The New Hampshire Guardian, had contacted Kitchen's editor, Rosamond Finewood, to propose the Guardian reprint Kitchen's articles in the Business section of their Sunday papers with full acknowledgement of the NH Business Digest and James Kitchen. The point of the partnership, said Harmony, was they did not have a writer with the depth of knowledge Kitchen had and they believed the people of the state deserved to have the kind of in-depth coverage Kitchen was providing as they decided where they would come down in the debate over Granite Skyway. The two Editors agreed that sharing the content would be mutually beneficial. On most weeks, the Guardian's publication of the Kitchen article would follow the Business Digest's release but Finewood had agreed to allow the Guardian to have the first run on one issue in exchange for a full-page ad for the NH Business Digest on the facing page.

Both Editors were so pleased with the unusual partnership they agreed to consider doing a joint editorial either for, or against, the Granite Skyway Project after publication of the series. Neither was bound by the decision of the other but they simply decided that if they were on the same page they would consider using their considerable clout to issue a jointly signed editorial.

Electricity Demand, Transmission and the Grid
By James Kitchen

There are large disagreements over the direction power production and transmission is likely to go in the coming decades but there is one area of agreement. We are entering the "Era of Electricity", when few of the conveniences and necessities of life will be powered by other types of fuel. By the middle of the century, homes and vehicles will largely be heated and powered by electricity. Smart appliances will allow us to control everything from our refrigerator to our heating system thermostat, digitally through apps on our smartphones or in our homes themselves.

In the two previous articles I've described the two competing visions and directions energy production and transmission might take in the coming decades. The first, an extension of the current energy regime where large power plants produce the energy required for the population. This is the vision exemplified by Granite Skyway. The second vision is an interlinking laterally connected network of distributed power, generated by smaller plants and homes and businesses acting as both consumers and producers of electricity.

In the eye of this firestorm are the utilities.

If talk about utility companies, PURPA, NERPA, and a hundred other acronyms have made your eyes glaze over, consider yourself at home among the vast majority of the American people who find this area of public policy as dull as ditchwater. As David Roberts said in his article 'Utilities for Dummies': "Utility companies are shielded by a force field of tedium."

Utility companies are considered to be what is known as a "Natural Monopoly". In essence a natural monopoly is a company where the level of investment necessary and the cost of providing the product - in this case electricity - create a situation where multiple competing entities are not in the public interest. For this reason, back in the days of Teddy Roosevelt when many monopolies were broken up across the breadth of the economy's sectors, utilities were permitted an exception - along with a few other natural monopolies like railroads.

To protect the public interest, and to avoid many of the pitfalls characteristic of monopolies, the federal government and the states negotiated the creation of the 'regulatory compact.' - an agreement that continues to this day.

The regulatory compact grants each utility a monopoly to be the sole provider of electricity in an agreed service area. The utility company is allowed to charge rates that cover their costs and guarantee them a reasonable return on their investment. A Public Utilities Commission (PUC) was created to oversee the process of setting those rates. The presumption was this would assure the utility company provided electricity at a reasonable cost and, in exchange, it was guaranteed a "captive" customer base.

One of the problems with this method of creating electricity and determining rates is that the methodology for determining return on investment provides an incentive for utilities to spend money on both essential and frivolous "investments" and is rewarded equally for both. For example, the more plants they build, whether they are needed or not, the greater is their return. Spending a million dollars on creating a palatial office for the CEO generates the same returns as an investment that makes the grid more resilient or terror proof.

Just as important, when it came to the utility companies, return on investment was only guaranteed for building or buying things, for spending capital and generating more electricity. There was no incentive for efficiency or conservation. A dollar spent on office furniture would guarantee a return on investment but a dollar saved through efficiency or conservation yielded no return.

When the regulatory compact was created - during the progressive era of the early twentieth century - it was considered a very progressive reform at a time when demand for electricity was growing dramatically and when many had no access to electricity without the construction of new power plants, new transmission lines and the utility companies brought all of these things together.

It seemed, at the time, this growth in demand would last forever.

Then in the 1990s things began to change. It had become clear the natural monopoly concept was no longer up to the challenges and opportunities of the new digital era. The concept of simply tacking a return on investment for every expenditure made was easily managed but in no way reflected the complexities of the marketplace or the opportunities for creating a system of distribution and production in a time when rapid change and innovation was the rule.

The day had come for electricity to be created and distributed in response to market forces and to new technologies and innovations. It was time to reform utilities and the market tableau in which they existed. In doing this several things happened that have created an economic threat to the viability of utility companies. First and most important, in most places utility companies were forced by law to divest of their holdings in plants generating electricity. This removed a critical profit center from their domain.

The second consequential change was that demand for electricity began to slow largely because, while there was no incentive for conservation to the utilities, the incentive for individual customers and businesses was very real. Every kilowatt saved represented real dollars flowing to the bottom line of businesses and the pockets of individuals. In addition to this, a growing environmental consciousness in the eighties and nineties took hold of the public imagination. For businesses especially, this made saving energy not only good economics but good public relations. By the nineties companies were marketing themselves based on their success in reducing their "carbon footprint". Demand for energy has dropped dramatically, largely from increased efficiency and conservation. In addition, people and companies have begun producing their own electricity.

In fairness to Polaris and other public utilities the reason they continue to fight for this pathway . . . the "old way" is that - at least right now - it appears to be the only path leading to their survival in the long run.

Gone are the halcyon days of utility companies when they were not only monopolies, as sole provider of electricity; but monopsonies - a term rarely heard today that describes a company with control over the purchase of the product - electricity - granting them complete control of the market, in their specific service area, on both the supply and demand side. Changed by the two sentences inserted into the PURPA law by Senator John Durkin.

It is, of course, not the job of government to assure the survival of businesses. It is the job of businesses to innovate and respond to changes in the marketplace in order to thrive amid the challenges of the market. However, just as our nation recognized the unique nature of utility companies back in the early 1900s, resulting in the highly regulated arena of utility law, it is incumbent upon regulators and legislators to work with utility companies like Polaris to assure they have the flexibility and opportunity to innovate and thrive while delivering electricity.

Among the issues that must be resolved is whether the state will adopt a new paradigm similar to the Pentagon's model of intersecting microgrids, with small energy producers and net metered homes and businesses providing the lion's share of the power or whether they will stick to the existing system of reliance on a few large producers of electricity. In either case they will need to determine just how the company that carries the electricity will be paid for that service. This decision will define the character of the region for generations to come.

Chapter 68   The Elwell Trail

Sasha awoke and lifted her head to look out the tent. She had zipped the screen but left the flap rolled up when they went to bed the night before. It was a cool night but ey had both agreed that they wanted the cool air to flow in while they slept. Cochise was standing just outside the tent giving her the "wolf stare" . . . front legs splayed slightly as if poised to move swiftly in either direction, head bowed slightly creating a straight line from the tip of his tail to the top of his head, never taking his eyes off the target of his stare.

Sasha laughed, bringing Daniel out of his sleep. He sat up, his hair tousled - "bed head" he called it - and he smiled sleepily as he saw Cochise.

"The great protector", he said.

"That he is." Sasha replied. "I wonder how long he's been standing there staring at us?"

The two climbed out of the tent and sat together on a log and shared a few handfuls of trail mix as a quick starter breakfast. Sasha gave Cochise a bit of dried meat and some water.

Within a few minutes they had packed up the tent and their sleeping bags and were headed north along the Elwell trail up Bear Mountain.

It took them a few hours to hike from their camping spot over the summit of Bear Mountain to the top of Little Sugarloaf.

Pausing at the summit, Daniel said, "there used to be a trail here that shot up, short and steep, from the lake. It was called the "Carter Gibbs Escalator" named for the fellow who built it in the early 1900s. It has disappeared since development of a big condo complex on the water in the area known as Nutting's Beach. The development all but obscured the trailhead. Every few years I hear people talking about restoring it, but it doesn't seem to happen. He paused, looking out "what a view!"

Newfound Lake lay below them, seeming almost close enough to jump from there.

"The trail from here over to Cardigan is not used much. I think you'll notice as we hike along."

The two continued on and soon the trail was covered with a thick carpeting of moss, not something one sees very often as hiking boots have a way of scuffing this layer off the earth.

"It's beautiful," Sasha said." It almost seems a shame to hike on it."

The two paused, looking down the moss-covered path to where it bent in the undergrowth. Sasha removed her pack, sat and began untying her hiking boots. Soon she was barefoot and walking about gently on the path. Daniel followed suit but after he had bared his feet, Sasha upped the ante. Stripping off her shirt and then peeling down her shorts and panties until she stood naked . . . her hands outstretched, palms upward, her head lifted slightly, eyes half closed, a gentle breeze blowing through her raven hair. It was as if she were absorbing the energy all around her.

Daniel watched her. Suddenly Cochise was there too, standing next to her, his nose lifted, sniffing the air.

This was one of those times when everything yields to the moment.

Daniel would not recall what happened next, even as he searched his memory years later. He would only remember standing next to Sasha, one hand in hers, and one arm reaching out palm upward; feeling the breeze blow cool across his own naked body. All else seemed to vanish into a dreamlike quintessentialism, drawing him deeper into the moment.

Now the trio continued on, walking gently on the moss covered trail for nearly two miles. The ancient forest surrounded them in a warm embrace of rich browns, verdant greens and splashing blue highlights . . . nothing but the packs on their backs . . . embedded in the universe.

Then, as quickly as it came upon them, the moss covered trail was gone, subsumed by a tangle of roots, rocks and leaves as the trail began to climb toward the next summit. The moss, washed away by rains creating flowing water that took the path of least resistance, following the trail downward, summoned by natural law toward the waters of Newfound. Sasha and Daniel stopped to don their clothes and boots in silence, not yet ready to speak, then hiking on in silence until they sat at the summit of Oregon Mountain, drawn to another patch of moss covering the ground near the cairn marking the summit.

Daniel turned to Sasha. "Sash . . ." He looked at her. Tears were streaming down her cheeks. "Sash!" he said, more urgently now.

Sasha said nothing. She pulled him down on top of her. They made love right there on the last struggling patch of moss. Later, Daniel thought there was something life affirming and beautiful in the way they came together, but desperate too.

He tried to talk with Sasha about it. He wanted truly to understand the tears, but Sasha said trying to analyze the experience would only diminish the mystery of it. "We were given a gift Daniel. That is enough to know."

Chapter 69   The Sun Doesn't Always Shine

While Sasha and Daniel were hiking - and hiding - on the Elwell Trail, James Kitchen was preparing the fourth in his series of articles released for the following Monday.

The Sun Doesn't Always Shine; The Winds Don't Always Blow
By James Kitchen

Among the reasons why those who remain skeptical about renewables is the intermittent nature of the power they produce. The sun doesn't always shine and the wind doesn't always blow, and in periods when this is the case, the grid is denied the power they provide.

But demand for electricity cannot be turned on and off with the sun or the wind. The grid must have a constant flow of power to meet the needs of the businesses and residences of the people who rely upon it. When a ratepayer comes home and turns up his heat on a cold winter day or turns on her air conditioner on a hot summer afternoon, there is an expectation that the grid will be able to respond to the call for added electricity.

Until recently, electricity has been provided only by large plants, burning fossil fuels or producing nuclear energy. Utility companies used their most efficient plants to produce the bulk of the power and when needed turned to less efficient sources to fill the added need.

This is the power regime for which the grid was originally designed.

There is no doubt renewables put added stress on the grid.

The grid is a lot like a bumblebee. In theory the bumblebee should not be able to fly: its wings are too small, its body too large and not aerodynamic. Yet, it flies. With the grid, in theory it should not work, but in practice it does - mostly. The grid is not so much something we built as it is something that grew along with the country piece-by-piece, pole-by-pole, wire-by-wire, and transformer-by-transformer.

America has the highest number of outage minutes of any industrialized country and our outages are growing not declining, as is the case in most other nations according to Gretchen Bakke, PHd, author of "The Grid".

The grid was originally built only to accommodate a few massive power plants yet with the phenomenal growth of home and business solar generation, we have created tremendous new challenges for the grid because these solar installations are simply smaller scale power plants. It used to be the grid had to take power from a few large plants and distribute it to many people across the grid. Today, more and more, the grid must take power from everywhere to distribute it everywhere. It is the difference between multiplying 10x1000 and multiplying 10,000 x 10,000 and some would say that the real number is more akin to 10,000 squared times 10,000 squared.

As Bakke puts it, the grid is not just a technological system pieced together from 19th, 20th and 21st century technology but rather "a massive cultural system and the stakeholders: utility companies, power producers, investment firms, mining firms and too-big-to-fail multinational conglomerates will not go gently into the future's bright light. The grid is built as much from law as it is from steel" And the laws still lean in the direction of the monied interests - though that is the area of most dynamic change as well.

It appears we are headed toward a knock down, drag out, battle between the energy systems of the past and those of the future.

By 2050 nearly every single power plant that exists today will need to be replaced with new sources of power generation.

However, it may be we are not headed for this battle but already fully engaged.

In Hawaii, 12% of homes are equipped with home solar panels. On some days solar rooftop generates more electricity than the entire system requires. While too much power can be just as detrimental to the grid as too little power, nevertheless, the possibility Hawaii could generate all of the power needed for its thriving economy from solar, and other renewables, is clear and compelling.

Wind energy too is pushing through the veil of fossil fuels. In Texas, wind power accounts for 9% of electric production, Oregon 13% and in Iowa 30%.

Right now, variable generation of electricity - renewables - account for about 7% of electric production. The US Department of Energy has set a goal of 25% by 2025 from renewables. This goal was scoffed at when it was first announced, yet in only the last three years the amount of electricity generated by renewables has tripled and this does not even include the electricity generated by net-metered systems on homes and businesses. It seems - if anything - this goal is not ambitious enough.

The Grid needs to change if we are to generate the lion's share of power with renewables. However, according to most experts we are already far enough along this path that these changes are considered inevitable . . . unstoppable.

With a growing percentage of the electricity generated by intermittent sources the challenge of how to provide needed power at times when intermittent sources fail to generate power is the central challenge remaining to be conquered.

Work in process by Tesla, Google and several other cutting edge companies promises to yield the answers to this question before the need becomes too acute. The question is not if, but when, this problem too will be resolved.

Chapter 70   The Energy Raiser

"Grab that roll of insulation and carry it up the ladder to Tom." Peter said to Mac. She was sweating profusely from the exertion and wondering what she had gotten herself into as she proceeded to slowly work her way up the ladder on the side of the small Cape style house.

"So in addition to setting the house up with solar panels, you also do some weatherization as well?" Michelle asked Peter.

"If the owner has the insulation and we have the people power, we're glad to make the home more energy efficient . . . every bit helps. We often dream about what we could do if we had the money to help lower income people purchase their solar panels and then teamed up with the Community Action Program that has funds for low-income weatherization so the money for one leap in technology would leverage other funds.

"What a great idea." Michelle said.

Mac reached the top of the ladder and handed off the roll of insulation to Tom, who was poking his head out of the attic window. Slowly she began to back down the ladder as she worked to formulate a plan for drawing Michelle out. Mac was pretty certain she was connected to The Trust but what about these other folks? Were Peter and Sandra part of it as well? She needed to come up with some way to get to the answer, but she needed to do it discreetly. This was going to require she establish some level of trust.

Sandra was working with an electrician named Stephen Farrell, who had a solar energy business installing systems for companies. On weekends he volunteered his time to AREA. The two of them were installing the new metering system attached to the house. She motioned for Michelle and Mac and they came over to where the two were working. Introducing them to Stephen, Sandra said. "Stephen volunteers with us - otherwise the cost of doing this would make it almost impossible for our small nonprofit. We're installing a net metering system here so as electricity is generated by the sunlight it feeds the electricity into the grid and turns the meter here on the house backwards, reflecting the value of the power being generated by the system. At the end of the month the owners then only pay for the difference between what they have produced and what they have used. The owners of the home - when we're finished - will become prosumers instead of consumers. They will be both producers and consumers of electricity instead of just consumers."

"The term was actually coined by Alvin Toffler, you know the guy who wrote 'Future Shock'. The term was first used in a later book, not as highly acclaimed, but to my mind was much more important - 'The Third Wave'. Toffler was making the case we were entering a Third Industrial Revolution built around technology and the digital and communications revolution in which the lines between consumers and producers were going to become increasingly blurred."

"He was spot on," said Peter, walking up in the midst of the conversation, "except he didn't warn us about how hard the second wave companies would try to hold onto their control."

"You mean like the climate deniers?" asked Mac.

"Like the Granite Skyway proposal?" asked Michelle.

"That's just the tip of the iceberg," said Peter.

Sandra laughed, "Careful ladies! You wind this guy up and you may never get him to stop! Peter has a theory the Liberal vs. Conservative fault line is going to yield to a new Centralized vs. Decentralized paradigm and the first place that battle is going to be fought is over electric power."

"Well," Peter said, "it's not quite that simple. But Sandra's right about the first battle. You are standing on the front line as we speak. We are fighting the ground war in a battle to try and turn every home and office into both an abode and a power plant. Linked together in a web of decentralized production."

"You know" Mac said, "you just got me thinking. Jeremy Rifkin is going to be speaking at the University of Vermont next week. He's there to honor the President of Green State Power and the company that has just won an award for the work they've done integrating renewables into the grid in Vermont. If I can get us tickets, wanna go see him next Wednesday night?"

"That would be awesome," Peter said, "Rifkin is really the heir to Toffler's legacy in my mind. I'd like to bring my wife Robbin if you can swing that."

"Can I bring Herbert?" Michelle asked.

"Ok that's 7 of us. I'll get us enough tickets for everyone to have a plus one." Mac said, smiling. "Maybe I can find a date as well. In any case, let's make it an adventure. I'll even try to get us a ride. I have an idea and I'll try to put it into action.

Come ready to drive your own vehicles but prepared to leave it and ride together if I can make this happen."

Chapter 71   Feeding the Goats, Facing the Fire

Linda arrived at Herbert's farm at 6pm sharp still in her climbing shoes and shorts.

"Herbert, I forgot to ask Michelle about how Taffy would get along with Maxmillian, my cat, who accompanies me on trips that are going to last more than a few days. Is it ok for me to bring him in and feed him?"

"Oh sure," Herbert said, "When it comes to Taff you'll see he's more brain damaged than I am, but it's mostly from old age I think - although on my most recent visit to the vet I found out they are now encouraging us to vaccinate our dogs and cats against Lyme Disease - so who knows, maybe we've both been brought low by those damn deer ticks! It seems like every time I visit the vet there's a new disease we have to vaccinate our pets for. I never know if they're sincere or just taking advantage of our affections."

"But you think it's just age related dementia?" Linda asked.

"You'll see," Herbert responded. "The first time he meets Max he'll be like "oh a new friend!" then Max will disappear for a few minutes and when he passes by ten minutes later Taffy will jump up as if to say "Hey! Who's this?"

"Maybe he's just a goofball."

"Quite possibly. There's a lot of that going around."

Michelle, who had arrived mid-conversation, wrapped her arms around Herbert and said "Yeah, but you are a lovable goofball."

"We weren't talking about me."

"I was" . . . Michelle said, smiling broadly.

The three friends climbed the stairs to Herbert's cozy little cabin. Walking through the front door Linda was struck by the scent of apples and cinnamon in the air.

"Oh it smells delightful," she said. "What are you cooking Herbert?"

"Just taking the scent of canine and macho man out of the air, darlin'. Taffy and I took a hike today and gathered up the apples that have dropped off one of the wild apple trees just up the road. They are a little bitter for my taste but the goats love 'em. I gather them up in a big sack and dole them out for as long as they last. I take one or two of them, cut them up and toss 'em in a pot of water I keep on the woodstove to condition the air, then I add some cinnamon sticks and just let them do their thing. They keep the place smelling great for days."

The table was set for three but Linda got a sense Michelle had not yet broken the news to Herbert so she waited until Herbert was out of earshot and whispered, "did you tell him Michelle?"

"NO I was so worried it would upset him I waited to do it when we were all together."

Just then Herbert walked back in - "ah conspiring against me eh? I suspected Linda was paying us a visit for more than just a meal. After all Michelle knows I have the most boring pallet on the planet. If it were up to me I would just eat couscous every meal and be a happy camper."

"OK, let's have it. Did I do something stupid?"

"Oh Herbert!" Michelle nearly wailed. "They're onto me. Wally called today while I was at a showing to say that State Police were at my office and wanted to speak with me." A tear rolled down her cheek and she wiped it away. She was doing her best to be strong but she was scared.

Herbert put his arms around Michelle and said, "Well at least I didn't do something stupid."

"No, I did!" said Michelle, her resolve returning to her.

"Ok!" Linda said, "let's hear about it from beginning to end and don't leave anything out. Herbert do you have any Chiai?"

"My favorite brand, Stash Black Spice Chai," Herbert responded. "Want me to whip some up?"

Linda answered in the affirmative and Michelle proceeded to describe the plan to start a rumor about gun control legislation as well as Hank's role in the deception. Finally she described the Governor's news conference and her question from the back.

Herbert listened in as he boiled the water and prepared three cups of Chai and put them on the table.

Michelle finished and Linda sat quietly for a moment, gathering her thoughts and sipping on her Chiai. "MMmm I think I have a new favorite brand of Chai, this is great!" she said.

Then she began. "First, you're going to forget Hank has anything to do with this and that you ever talked to him. There is no way anyone knows about him in all this and if anyone did something illegal it was him, so we need to protect him and keep the bad guys from knowing any more than they already do."

Michelle was looking puzzled. Linda realized what she had said and corrected herself. "I'm not talking about the police, Michelle. They're not our friends in all this, but they aren't the 'bad guys'. Someone else is pulling the strings here and we need to try and figure out who."

Linda continued, "Let me ask you a few more questions."

"Have you ever blogged?"

"Why sure! I have my own real estate blog and I put new listings up and give people advice on listing their home or appealing their taxes."

"You ever write about shared access roads or wells or rights-of-way?"

"Of course. Those are all important aspects of real estate law."

"Great." Linda said. "Michelle, you did nothing illegal. For all the police know you are one of the thousands of Blogger's now providing news and opinion across the Web and it's true. You are going to stay as close to the truth here as possible without revealing anything that will give the police evidence to hold you."

"You heard about this proposed legislation and you were preparing an article on the legal rights of landowners if this bill becomes law. You heard about the Governor's news conference and decided to attend."

"Do I tell them I asked the question?" Michelle asked.

"Only if they ask you about it. The idea is to answer their questions and ONLY their questions. Be short and sweet, with no extra information. My guess is you will be out of there in a few minutes and the worst will be behind you."

"Will you be with me?"

"Yes of course, but it will be best if I do not try to direct you so it all seems sincere."

"What if they ask me about The Trust?"

"I don't think they'll connect The Trust with any of this, they really have no reason to do so. But if they do, try not to lie to them. You can say something like; you are just a real estate broker and blogger. You were following the story."

"Are you telling me I don't have to worry?" Michelle asked.

"I wouldn't go so far as to say you have nothing to worry about. The fact that they want to question you means someone wants to know who you are and what you are up to. The police will have no probable cause on which to hold you and certainly nothing that would stand up, even in a preliminary hearing. But someone wants to know and it's my job to try and figure out whom. So you leave that up to me."

"We are scheduled to meet with them tomorrow morning at the police station in Plymouth. I'm staying at the hotel right next to the station so I have a good view of the parking lot, why don't you come there, room 36, in the morning around 10 and we can make any last minute preparations we need before meeting with them."

"Now, let's get back to the issue of who is pulling the strings behind the scenes."

"Why do you think there's someone behind the scenes?" Herbert asked.

Linda answered, "There are too many steps between the Balsams and the Governor's news conference at the Statehouse. Someone - or more likely a group - is doing their own private investigation and were far enough ahead of the police to have someone monitoring the news conference."

"Also, we know a group of three people - masquerading as movie location scouts - were asking around in Berlin about a wolf and seemingly getting closer to the trail of Daniel and Sasha. Yet no police or investigatory agency has come looking for them or shown they were moving in that direction. I've used my sources at the Boston PD to see if any BOLOs, 'Be On the Lookout' advisories, or similar announcements regarding them have been broadcast and I've turned up nothing."

"All of this leads me to conclude there is a subterranean investigation being conducted outside of the official channels. This concerns me for a lot of reasons, most important because a group like this is not bound by law or protocol. They are, therefore, far more dangerous to us."

"Do you think Michelle is in any danger?" Herbert asked.

"I think you should stay as close as possible for the next few weeks, Herbert, and I think we should try and figure out who these people are."

Michelle began to protest when Herbert put his hand on hers.

"Listen, this is a conversation I had planned on having with you tonight anyway, but I didn't expect to have it in the context of this discussion . . . romantic as it may be," Herbert said sarcastically.

"Taffy and I had a long conversation this morning," he said with a silly smile on his face, "we'd like you to move in with us Michelle."

Michelle sat back and looked at Herbert. "Well, this is a horse - or maybe I should say a goat - of a different color . . . that might just make it bearable to have you hovering over me Herbert. Of course you're going to have to deal with my mother and father over this. They're pretty old fashioned about this sort of thing."

"I think I can put their minds at ease." Herbert said, wrapping Michelle in his strong arms. "I'll let them know I have only the most honorable intentions with respect to their baby girl."

"And if they disapprove?"

"We'll just move in with them, though I don't know how they'll feel about having goats in their garage in New Jersey."

Part 6 The Glide Path

Chapter 72 Performance Art

Dot's Bread and Butter Bistro was buzzing when Sasha and Daniel walked in. They had returned from their trip on the Elwell Trail the evening before and that morning they had left Cochise at Daniel's yurt to avoid drawing too much attention to them.

"Dot's" is located in Ashland, the geographic center of New Hampshire, and ground zero for gun owners. A week had passed since Michelle had planted the rumor at the Governor's press conference and the buzz was only growing stronger. It didn't hurt that the headline in that day's Guardian newspaper read "Source of Right-of-Way Bill Remains Mystery". The story, of course, included the denials from Polaris as well as the quote from Alphonse Ruger about the cookie jar. This served to stir the controversy all the more and the crowd at Dot's, while politically eclectic, was nonetheless nearly unanimous in its disdain for the idea of banning firearms from these public access points to the backcountry.

Michelle and Herbert had arrived five minutes earlier and found Hank sitting at a table in the corner with his back to the wall. "Wild Bill Hickok always said you take the table where you can watch the whole room and your back is to the wall." Hank said. "I always found that to be good advice."

Daniel was accompanied by his cousin Zach Roy and Dr. Osita Aniemeka an elegant black man wearing a "Fila", a type of soft fez, the traditional cap of the Yoruba nation made of hand-woven African fabric. Osita himself was from the Igbo nation, these two nations along with a third, the Hausa, account for a majority of the people living in Nigeria, a country created by British colonial fiat, today the economic powerhouse of West Africa. A colorful silk neckerchief completed his ensemble and certainly gave him the appearance of an artist.

Zach greeted a table full of local friends, clearly there with their grandmother on some special occasion as she sat looking happy and proud at the head of the table; though the group who were rather self-involved despite their good intentions largely ignored her.

While Zach bantered with his friends, Osita quietly pulled a chair over and sat next to the old woman, taking her hand. "Grandmother, I greet you," he said warmly.

Zach, noticing Osita, smiled and said admiringly, "There is a lot we can learn from my Uncle Osita. Beginning with his respect, even reverence, for his elders. Whenever we enter a room together he greets the elder in the room first. It's a cultural thing, but it's something we would do well to emulate."

Zach gave him a few moments and then called out "Uncle Osita, you have got to try the Eggs Florentine, it's the best I've ever had." Then he added hastily, "We'd better sit down before they give away our table."

Osita stood up, still holding the old woman's hand as she beamed. "Good day Grandmother. Thank you for the gift of sharing your birthday with me."

Sasha took Ostia's arm and led him to their table. "My people too have such respect for their elders," she said to him. "Maybe between the two of us we can teach these culturally impoverished people a thing or two."

"It would be my pleasure, m'lady." Osita said with a smile indicating he was in on the joke.

Daniel took a seat next to Hank and while Zach was doing the introductions he asked quietly, "Is the background cover all set?"

Hank, eyebrows raised in a look of mock shock, said to Daniel, "You need to ask me? You lefties always underestimate us. No one does fake news better than we do Daniel my man. You are just lucky I'm on your side and not theirs."

"Here's to that!" Daniel said, toasting him with a glass of freshly poured ice water. "I have to admit Hank, having you as part of the team has really opened my eyes to the absurd way we have of shutting off dialog between progressives and conservatives. We have much more in common than we have differences."

Hank returned his toast and winked at him as he leaned forward and got the attention of the group. "OK folks, we're 'live in five' so let's get a few things straight before the reporter from the Monitor arrives."

"For any of you who are feeling guilty we are creating a fake news story for the media let me disabuse you of that notion right now."

"Wow," Herbert said, "let me disabuse you? Hank you've been hanging with the weeds and seeds crowd too long, you are starting to talk like them."

Hank looked at Herbert as if he had just insulted Hank's mother and for a moment everyone thought there was going to be trouble between these two strong personalities. Then Hank smiled and said, "I'll give you a thumping later Herbert, but right now we have to get our story straight and there's no time for us to dance."

The entire table laughed and Hank continued.

"We may have created some fictional biography and background here but our friend Osita is going to pitch a very real artist's vision, and, if we can get a few approvals and some local support, he will take the lead in making the vision a reality. So, point of fact, this is no different than any other business pitch, we've taken some liberties with the narrative but the end result is going to be the real thing. You are all here to provide support and to help us have a sincere brainstorming session after Osita has described his vision. OK, Osita give us the "Reader's Digest" version of your pitch."

Michelle said, "I don't think "Reader's Digest" was ever standard fare in the waiting rooms of Nigeria, Hank."

"On the contrary," Osita said, "Reader's Digest is very popular in Nigeria!" he laughed and withdrew a folded paper from his pocket. However, asking me to give you the abridged version, that's the tough part! I'm very excited about this project and it's hard to be brief. I'll do my best though."

"I think most of you came down from the North today, so the view from the highway as you hit the top of the rise before the Ashland exit will be fresh in your mind. My proposal is to create a one to two mile washline in the valley following, generally, the Pemigewasset River. We will recruit people from all over the region to contribute clothing for our great work of art in celebration of a shared experience and as a clarion call to save the planet."

"Like the art of the incomparable 'Christo' our line will flow across the landscape but it will be the creation of hundreds, perhaps thousands of people. It will be a whole greater than the sum of its parts because it will contain many hundreds of small moments, memories, ideas and revelations - each a building block of the final product."

"Each contribution will reflect the individuals who have donated their time and clothing to the project. They can let the article of clothing speak for itself or they can alter the clothing in some way to make a statement - perhaps by writing on it, perhaps by altering the cut in some way. For example, if a family wanted to honor a relative that has passed, they might include an outfit belonging to that person with a memorial note. "

Though not an artist by trade, clearly Osita had the heart of an artist, thought Sasha and she shared her thought with Daniel who offered it up to the group, giving Sasha credit for the thought. His own confidence grew as he listened. This might just work and it would be great fun whether it did or not.

Just as Daniel was thinking about this, the reporter from the Monitor came through the door. Daniel stood and walked briskly to greet him, bringing him to the table to join the group. "Gary, I'd like to introduce you to the support team for Dr. Aniemeka's project."

He proceeded to introduce each of the members of the group to Gary, introducing him last to Dr. Osita Aniemeka.

"Zach maybe you can give Gary a little background about how we came up with this performance art idea and then Osita can lay out his vision."

"Sure. Well Gary, you know my Dad, and you know he has been working in West Africa with NGOs - non-governmental organizations - what we call nonprofits, for the Ford Foundation."

"Yeah," Gary responded. "I heard one crazy story about his team getting arrested by Sanny Abacha's secret police and held at gunpoint for six hours. That must have been pretty terrifying. We never really appreciate life here in the good ol' USA quite so much as when we get a taste of what it's like living under a ruthless dictator like Abacha."

Several people around the table had not heard the story and Zach promised to give them the full version later but he gently steered the conversation back to the issue at hand. "Well it was on one of his trips to Nigeria he met Dr. Aniemeka who was doing some unique performance art focused on Climate Change. Since then he's been raising money to bring Osita here to do something."

Osita chimed in with characteristic humility; "I don't want to represent that my performance pieces are as "unique" as Zach has suggested, although I thank him for the compliment just the same. I've really taken a page out of the book of the legendary artist known to most people as "Christo". Are you familiar with him, Gary?"

"He's the guy who, for lack of a better description, wraps the landscape with long ribbons of colorful fabric right?"

"Exactly," said Osita. "What I think IS different, is the relationship I create between the idea - the art - and the community. I don't just create a piece of art for the enjoyment of the public, I invite them to be an intimate part of its creation, even to participate in a way that allows them to bring their own stories to the work. To 'sing their own song', you could say. And from all those individual songs we create a rich and beautiful life-symphony, filled with unique stories, capable of engaging the public for endless hours as they explore the rich tapestry of individual stories."

Osita continued, and unlike the signs I see in many of the shops here in the US - - signs that say: 'please do not handle the merchandise', or 'you break it you buy it,' - - we will encourage those who view the artwork to experience it to the fullest. Our sign, though unwritten, will say, 'Please Touch'.

"That must make it a much more complicated process," observed Gary, jotting notes in his storied shorthand.

"Yes Gary. I usually need to spend quite a bit of time in advance of beginning the piece getting to know the community and how best to weave it into the art. But Gary, I never see it as work to do this. It makes the experience so much richer for the community and for me as well."

"So you are essentially talking about creating a massive washline or clothesline, right? What is the motivation behind this?"

"Well Gary, it's an homage to one of humanity's greatest shared traditions. You can travel anywhere in the world and you will find washlines painting the backyards of rural homes or weaving a tapestry of bright colors across every floor of a tenement. Most do it for practical reasons, an electric or gas clothes dryer is an unaffordable luxury for most people. Even here where electricity is more affordable and the middle class, at least, see a dryer as a necessity not a luxury, it is true. Many still have a clothesline in addition to their dryer. There are nearly as many reasons for this as there are people and clotheslines."

"I understand," Gary said. "Terri and I have a washline too. We love the way sheets smell after they've dried on the line. There's nothing quite like slipping into sheets that have dried in the sunshine and breezes."

"Fabulous! You must become a part of our symphony Gary. It will help you understand why this small community artwork can become a powerful message uniting people across the globe and making a statement about their connection to the planet and their concern for its future."

"When do you anticipate you will begin to construct the piece? " Gary asked.

"It will depend on how long it takes to get the approvals from the local towns and the land owners. If we are lucky we will be able to put it all together before snow flies, but it may be spring before we can begin. I will absolutely keep you informed as we get closer."

"What's the best way to stay in touch?" Gary asked.

Probably by email Gary," he said handing Gary a specially prepared card, but I'm doing a lot of traveling these days so if you have a question that requires an immediate answer you can call Zach directly. He is going to take charge on the ground here."

After Gary left, the group began to do some brainstorming.

"There is a lot of planning that will need to go into this" said Linda "and I'll be busy trying to figure out the legal piece, so we're going to need some help from people who can be counted on to help - without being privy to the big picture reason for this."

Michelle spoke up. "Sandra and Peter from the Asquamchumaukee Renewable Energy Association would be perfect for this, they can rally a big group of volunteers with just a quick email. Herbert and I are going with them to see Jeremy Rifkin speak at UVM next week so I'll speak with them then."

Daniel had a few of his own ideas. "John and Kathy Rocker would be perfect. Kathy is an activist and knows just about everybody in the area and John is a Surgeon at the hospital. Sasha and I can drop in on them today to see if they'd be willing to help.

Chapter 73 Mama Llama

It was 10pm when Daniel and Sasha finally put in a call to the home of Kathy and John Rocker. Their daughter Johanna answered.

"Hey Daniel! Mom and Dad are at the hospital. Dad said he had some unexpected surgery to perform."

Daniel said, "Seems an odd time to schedule a surgery. I mean 10pm is not when you'd expect to be going into surgery."

"You know, that thought occurred to me too," said Johanna, "but nothing surprises me when it comes to my parents. I just go with the flow. Why don't you go over to the hospital and see if you can catch them there?"

"If you don't think that would be a problem . . . "

"Oh no, they'll be glad to see you, I'm sure."

Daniel and Sasha headed over to the hospital. They tried the main door of the hospital but it was locked tight, closed after 10pm. A note on the door directed visitors to use the emergency room entrance after 10pm. As they walked around the building toward the emergency room entrance Daniel saw Dr. John Rocker standing with his back against the brick wall around the corner from the emergency entrance, a gurney against the wall with a sheet covering his apparent surgical patient. Rocker was thin and handsome, like an aging Harrison Ford, without the fedora.

"John!" Daniel called out. He was about to ask him what the hell he was doing out here when John Rocker put a finger to his lips and gestured for Daniel to be quiet.

"Shhhhhh . . . Kathy is checking to make sure the coast is clear before we roll into the operating room."

Daniel drew closer and saw what appeared to be a muzzle poking out from under the sheet. Suddenly it all became clear. Daniel lifted the sheet to see a llama laid out on the gurney, Sasha put her hand over her mouth to stifle a laugh and Daniel whispered to Dr. John. "You're sneaking a Llama into the hospital for emergency surgery?"

"That's about the size of it," Rocker whispered back. "Doc Allen called me from the Animal Hospital and told me he had a pregnant mama llama who needed emergency knee surgery and he didn't have the properly-sized instruments to do it. He asked if I had any ideas . . . so here we are."

Just then Kathy's head poked around the corner. "Now" she commanded in her most audible whisper.

"Latch on Daniel! Looks like you and your friend are coming along for the ride."

Like a scene from a Marx Brothers movie, the three grabbed the gurney and wheeled it around the corner and through the entrance to the emergency room, Rocker's white lab coat flew behind him as they rounded the corner. Daniel and Sasha held tight to the gurney and ran alongside.

As they wheeled the Llama down the hallway headed for operating room one, John Rocker said, "So what brings you to our fine hospital Daniel?"

They wheeled into emergency room one and John Rocker began putting on his surgical scrubs as Daniel started to describe the favor they had come to ask."

"I'm sorry. Let me stop you there Daniel," Dr. John interrupted. "This mama Llama needs surgery to correct a tear in her Anterior Cruciate Ligament - - ACL for short. Without the surgery she won't be able to continue to stand upright and that means she won't be able to carry her baby to term."

"The shot I gave her will keep her out for about another fifteen minutes and it's not safe to give her another shot in her condition, so I have to get this job done in the next fifteen minutes. You'd better pitch Kathy on this, while I make miracles. It's right up her alley I think."

Kathy was preparing the operating room for the surgery but she had also been listening in on the conversation as she did. When Daniel turned to Kathy to ask for her help, she tossed two sets of surgical scrubs at him and said. "You've both been drafted to help save Mama Llama. You can pitch me as we go."

Daniel and Sasha donned their scrubs, washed up and in three minutes they were huddled around Mama Llama, assisting Dr. John Rocker in his mission of mercy. Rocker began with a lecture to the unconscious Llama Mama about getting "knocked up" when she was having trouble walking. In twenty minutes they were finished and had a promise of assistance from Kathy and John. They also had a still dopey Mama Llama, standing now with a knee brace, made from the bladder of a milk dispenser John had pirated from the cafeteria adjacent to the surgical room.

"How are we going to get her out of here?" Sasha asked, holding the lead attached to Mama Llama's bridle.

Doctor John took the lead in hand. "The deeds done, what can they do to us now?"

With that he led the Llama out of the OR toward the Emergency room door, past a hallway full of shocked nurses, doctors and patients, and out into the night.

Chapter 74   White Devil

Daniel and Sasha had returned to Daniel's yurt after their adventure with Dr. John and Kathy Rocker. Completely exhausted, the two had fallen asleep on top of the covers of Daniel's bed without even taking their clothes off. It was almost 11am when Daniel awoke to the sound and smells of Sasha cooking breakfast on the propane stove.

Daniel walked over to Sasha and wrapped his arms around her from behind. "Now this is living," he said. "I could really get used to this."

They took a heaping plate of scrambled eggs, some toast Sasha had made in the oven and two tall glasses of OJ onto the deck facing Stinson Brook. They were just finishing up when Zach and Linda showed up.

Yurt living was just beginning to catch on in the area. Most people still didn't believe anything other than the traditional stick built house or mobile home was sufficient to provide year-round protection from the elements, but there was a growing murmur about tiny houses, yurts and other alternative housing.

Daniel was no stranger to alternative living arrangements. He had spent part of one summer living in a teepee with an Indian named Kemper Sackman, whom he had met on a train ride across Canada. A few years later, when he was coming up on his last year at the University and he realized he didn't have sufficient funds for tuition, room and board and living expenses, he found a quiet corner in the college woods, set up his dome tent and spent two semesters camping there. Of course it meant studying at the library and showering at the field house; but - as it turned out - all those long hours in the library paid off in the highest grade point average he had in all his years at college.

Looking back, the teepee had turned out to be reasonably comfortable - compared to camping anyway, but it was still not quite right for his taste. Camping in his tent had its own downsides. On the other hand, he was convinced there was a happy medium somewhere between a traditional home and camping or the teepee that would provide an affordable alternative for him, at least for now. That's how he came to learn about yurts.

The yurt was first used by the people of the Steppes in Central Asia and was designed as a portable structure to support their nomadic lifestyle. Over the years various modifications have made them less portable but more comfortable, especially for those accustomed to more traditional housing.

Daniel's yurt had a private bathroom with a shower and a waterless composting toilet. A set of solar panels provided most of the electricity needed but he was not completely off the grid, mostly because he could not live without wireless Internet service. After all he was in the job-seeking mode after graduating from the University.

A queen size bed folded down from a mount on the wall at night and back again during the day allowing him plenty of living space. All told, it was - in fact - a very comfortable abode. While small by comparison with a traditional home, it was every bit as comfortable as any other home. Two garden plots just outside provided most of the produce needed for delicious meals all through the later days of the summer. Corn was the only vegetable, among those he ate regularly, the plots lacked, although he did have four stalks of Indian Corn. The issue was not just space, for if you asked Daniel he would readily explain that the best corn in America was grown just down the road at Longview Farm and a near daily visit to the farm stand was not only a way to stock up on corn, but also a great way to stay connected with neighbors who came to the farm stand regularly.

The four stalks of Indian corn were both a planting intended to yield a decorative harvest but also as an homage to his own Native American roots. The term Indian corn was not, like so many other similar appellations, a pejorative but a fact he celebrated. Some visitors to his yurt regretted asking him about this because Daniel would use the opportunity to explain to them, in detail, the evolution of corn from the wild grass called Teosinte found growing in the region of what is now Mexico. He would also use the opportunity to explain that new evidence showed the Native American Indians of this region had civilizations more advanced than any other civilization in the world at the time. In fact, he would always say, the invention of the concept of Zero in mathematics is believed to have originated among the native people of this region.

Zach, of course, knew better than to go there. After all as Daniel's cousin the same blood flowed through his own veins and he was equally enthused, albeit less effusive. He had warned Linda not to ask about this if she wanted to actually get a climb in before dark.

"Hey, we're going to do a climb on Rattlesnake," Zach said. "Want to join us?"

"Awesome!" said Daniel. "I've been getting a little stir crazy since we got back from hiking. I'd love to."

Sasha looked at Daniel, "I'm really not feeling like a climb today Daniel. If you don't mind I'd like to stay here and just listen to the brook and relax . . . maybe pick some veggies and get a start on dinner. Will you two join us for dinner?"

"Love to" said Linda. "We should be back around seven if that's good for you."

"Perfect. It gives me plenty of time to relax and do the prep work."

Daniel ran into the yurt and emerged a moment later with his climbing gear and the three headed for Zach's pickup, bound for the 'Main Cliff' area of Rattlesnake Mountain.

Almost as an afterthought Daniel reached into his pocket and tossed a set of keys to Sasha saying, "Here's the keys for the Prius Sash. Just in case you change your mind or need to take a trip to Longview."

Sasha caught the keys and pocketed them.

Then they were gone.

Sasha went inside to find her iPhone. Daniel had created a playlist for her of his one hundred favorite tunes and she wanted to take a deep dive into the music that moved this beautiful young man. It had only been a month but Sasha was pretty sure she was in love with him. It exhilarated her . . . and scared her shitless.

Donning the ear buds she wandered back outside to the garden. She was thinking some summer squash, sautéed with onions would be a great vegetable dish for dinner and she had noticed there were quite a few of the little yellow buggers on the five plants in the garden. Salad made from spinach, lettuce and the abundant cukes and cherry tomatoes, dressed with some extra virgin olive oil and balsamic vinegar would really hit the spot after an arduous climb.

She was squatting next to the summer squash when a black hood came down over her head and two arms wrapped around her from behind pulling her, roughly, to her feet.

"Hand me that damn zip tie," the voice behind her said, tipping her to the fact there were at least two of them.

Sasha began to scream as loudly as she could. A voice in front of her laughed, "Not likely anyone's going to hear you way out here sweetheart."

Now she knew the second voice was directly in front of her.

As the source of the first voice continued to hold her arms waiting for his partner to provide the zip tie, In one quick motion, Sasha leaned back against him and kicked out hard with both legs and feet, sending a stunned Harry Echo flying backward.

"I wouldn't count on that," she said as a snarling, whirling dervish of white fur and snapping teeth, flew 4 feet above the ground right into Will Duggan's shoulder, knocking him sideways to the ground as well.

Sasha ripped off the hood and grabbed the zip tie off the ground where Echo had dropped it. She quickly zipped Echo's hands together, in front of him, before he had a chance to recover from her vicious kick and turning to Duggan, who was lying prostrate on the ground with Cochise's jaws clamped around his neck, she said, "who sent you here?"

Echo was attempting to stand when Sasha creamed him with another kick, this time to his knee, and he buckled to the ground screaming in pain and clutching his badly injured knee.

"Who sent you!" she shouted again. "One word to my friend here is all it will take and he will rip your throat out just to please me. Now SPEAK."

Then Duggan and Echo folded like the proverbial lawn chairs. "Please, please, don't . . ." Duggan struggled to say something, but with Cochise holding firmly it barely came out as a gurgled whisper. "Enright . . . James Enright, our boss. He told us to take you so we can find out who the others are in The Trust . . . well, he didn't exactly tell us, we just thought it would be the way to do it."

"Please, he'll kill us if he finds out about this." Echo said through clenched jaw, gritting from the pain.

Sasha pulled out her iPhone and snapped a quick shot of both Echo in his fetal pose and Duggan with Cochise's jaws clamped around his neck. "If you're right about that," she said, "the only thing preventing me from putting these pictures all over the Internet is the sure knowledge that you two flunkies are in the wind. If I ever see your faces again you can bet your boss and whoever's pulling his strings will see your faces in their nightmares."

"Now get the hell out of here. Head west and don't stop driving until you see buffalo."

She turned to Cochise, "Set Cochise," she said and the wolf released his grip on Duggan's throat and stood back, still snarling, still poised to return to the attack if Sasha were in any danger.

Duggan put Echo's arm over his shoulder and the two limped away through the woods to where they had obviously left a vehicle . . . and in a few minutes Sasha heard it start and drive away.

"Drive west until you see buffalo." she said, laughing at herself. That's gotta be one of my better lines!"

But as much as she was trying to be the brave Iroquois woman, Sasha was pretty shook up. She led Cochise over to Daniel's Prius and they headed for Main Cliff to find Daniel.

Duggan and Echo meanwhile had reached Route 25 and Duggan had made a left turn. "Hey this isn't west." Echo said.

"No shit Sherlock. Would you rather have JEn chasing us or take our chances with the Indian woman and the wolf? I think our chances of survival are better if we don't cross Enright."

Chapter 75 Main Cliff, Rattlesnake Mountain

Sasha and Cochise hiked the short distance into the area known as Main Cliff on Rattlesnake Mountain. There were more than 10 groups of people climbing different routes on the Cliff and it took a few minutes for her to find Daniel, Linda and Zach.

Daniel was on belay at the base of the cliff as Linda ascended above him.

"Daniel, I was just attacked at the yurt. Thanks to Cochise we got away but we've got a problem. They knew where to find me and that probably means they know you are a part of The Trust too."

Just then Linda called down, "Tension please Daniel! I'm not confident I can make this next move and I don't want to fall too far."

Daniel tightened the rope. Linda reached for her next handhold and stretched her left leg trying to gain purchase to move laterally over the cliff, and then she was falling.

Daniel reared back to maximize his resistance as Linda fell and in a moment she was floating safely in the air sixty feet above him.

"My arms are done," she called out. "I'm coming back down."

Daniel belayed her rappel style descent and in a moment she was standing at the base removing the carabineer from her Swiss Seat harness.

"Hey Sasha, did you change your mind? You can use my harness if you want to climb."

Daniel answered for her. "Sasha was just attacked by two men back at the yurt. It wasn't a random thing, they were after her because she's a member of The Trust."

"Maybe we shouldn't go back there - to the yurt I mean." Linda said.

"I'm pretty confident they won't be returning," Sasha said. The fellow who had Cochise's jaws clamped around his throat didn't look like he was up for another go round. We'll probably be safer there than anywhere else, at least for the time being."

Seeing the logic in that, the group packed their gear and returned to the yurt. Daniel got everyone a cold beer, except for Linda who preferred water and the four of them sat down at the picnic table outside.

Linda began. "OK, I think it's safe to assume they now know the identities of at least three members of The Trust, maybe four. What concerns me more, however, is why all of this activity against The Trust is coming from a shadowy group that has almost no connection whatsoever to legal authorities."

"Someone used the police to bring Michelle in for questioning but they never asked a single question about The Trust. They just wanted to know where the rumor about the "Right of Way" bill came from."

Zach Roy chimed in, "but that's good isn't it? I mean that the police aren't closing in on us?"

"I don't think so." came Linda's response.

"Whoever this group is, they're operating outside the constraints of the law - - that could have very dangerous consequences."

"But we're operating outside of the limits of the law too." chimed in Sasha.

"Yes, but you have committed yourselves to civil disobedience that doesn't harm anyone. The fact these people tried to put a bag over your head and kidnap you may indicate they do not intend to play by the same rules."

"We don't know who they are and they already know almost half the group."

"Wait! Said Sasha excitedly. The name of their leader is Enright, James Enright. I made them tell me while Cochise's jaws were clamped around the one guy's neck. I also took pictures of them both."

"Now we're getting somewhere," said Daniel. We can put the pictures up on Instagram, someone is bound to know who they are."

Linda thought for a moment. "Let's hold off for now Daniel. No sense letting them know we're onto them and I suspect they might figure that out if we post their pictures. Let's see how this plays out over the next few days."

Chapter 76   Moonlight in New Hampshire

Michelle and Herbert sat in Herbert's truck near the Smith Bridge parking area in Plymouth and watched the Harvest Moon rise over the Covered Bridge. The Smith Bridge is reputed to be the strongest covered bridge in the world. It is the result of an epic battle between the NH Highway Department and the surrounding communities which commenced shortly after an arsonist torched the original Smith Bridge, a nearly 200 year old landmark, beloved by the communities and documented in photos going back to just after the Civil War.

The Highway Department had seen the destruction of the bridge as a fortuitous event allowing them to erect a modern bridge on the Baker River crossing. The battle had ended when Zach Roy's father, then the Senator from District 2 had made it known he would hold up the entire Capital Budget if the Highway Department didn't back off and give the communities back their covered bridge. Having made the threat he then teamed up with the legendary Executive Councilor Raymond Burton to propose the new bridge be designed as a "Demonstration Project", requiring that it meet all of the size and safety specifications of a traditional modern day bridge. Burton was renown for such "Demonstration Projects" usually proposed as a means of getting around some bureaucratic roadblock in his district. The final result was a two-lane covered bridge that came in at half the cost of a traditional bridge and would have a life span of two to three times the modern day equivalent.

Michelle and Herbert were just preparing to step out of the truck when a very strange looking long black stretch limo pulled up. Mac got out smiling broadly and said "and you thought we couldn't all fit in a Prius!"

"Let me introduce you to the Prius Primo, a six door, eight seat, Prius limo. At better than 50 miles to the gallon this baby will take us to Burlington and back again on about 5 gallons of gas."

Herbert stepped up to the limo and ran a hand admiringly over the roof. "Where did this come from?" he said.

"It was built in Canada by a family that specializes in making limos out of unusual cars. Most of them are sold down into the US where there's more demand for limo services," said Mac.

Just then Peter's grease car pulled into the parking lot and Peter and Sandra, along with spouses Tim and Robbin climbed out.

"I knew it was you," said Mac, "I could smell you coming."

"Yeah, it's hard to make a discreet entrance. Endora sort of announces herself."

"She does indeed," said Mac.

"Nice ride" said Peter. "Guess an Endora led convoy is unnecessary tonight after all."

"You don't mind do you?" Mac asked, "I thought it would be nice if all of us could be traveling together."

"No, no, that's great." Peter said.

The group piled into the Primo and headed over the mountain on NH Rte 118 with the Harvest Moon behind them, headed for the junction with US Rte 89 and then straight to Burlington, Vermont.

Chapter 77 The Ride

When the limo had made it over the winding path of Rte 118 and was on the I89 glide path, the ride became more comfortable for the passengers and Mac broke out a bottle of champagne.

"I'm really looking forward to this," said Peter. "Rifkin has ideas that really give me hope for the future. Not just about renewable energy but also about our relationship to the planet and the ideological divisions plaguing our democracy."

Mac seemed genuinely interested. "What do you mean Peter? I mean, I do a lot of lobbying in Vermont and I have to say I am really tired of the black and white viewpoints politicians seem to have developed recently. Do you see that changing?"

"I warned you about this!" said Sandra jovially. "If you get him started there's no turning him off."

"It'll be worth it if it seems there is some hope at the end of the tunnel," said Mac.

"OK," said Peter. "I'm not saying all this is going to change overnight, nor even guaranteeing it's going to happen at all. None of us have a crystal ball after all but there is a real opportunity for the democratization of energy production and distribution right now and it may also mean the dialog over politics is about to undergo a shift as well."

"It wouldn't be the first time after all. Let's not forget that until Franklin Roosevelt's time the Republican Party was the progressive force in politics. Lincoln freed the slaves; Teddy Roosevelt busted the trusts, established the National Park system and fought for the working man. Hell the Democratic Party controlled the South until the Kennedy brothers and, later, Lyndon Johnson got the Civil Rights Act passed and the "new" Democrats turned their backs on seven or eight generations of Southern white supremacy under Democratic Party rule."

"Titanic shifts in politics have happened before, and they usually happen at a time when there is great upheaval, when the country has reached an inflection point of some kind."

"Like a tipping point you mean?" Mac asked.

"Yes, a growing social unrest leading to a cultural shift characterized by shifting alliances would be one way to describe it. The Civil War, The Great Depression, the Civil Rights Movement, all these things precipitated a shift that reversed the roles of political parties and the people themselves throughout the country. We're at such a point now in my opinion."

"Mind you, this isn't the case Rifkin makes. He's focused on other things but he too suggests the liberal vs. conservative divide is likely to yield to a centralized vs. democratized debate over the coming years. That debate is especially manifest in the fight over things like the Granite Skyway and the Smart Grid in general."

At the mention of "Granite Skyway" Mac became focused like a laser. "So what do you think of the Granite Skyway project Peter?" she asked.

"Well Mac, I'm not opposed to transmission lines, generally speaking. After all, we're entering the era of electricity and until we figure out ways to transmit electricity over large distances without lines we're kind of stuck with 'em."

He added quickly, "However, we're already starting to see the first stages that will be needed for this kind of development. When a village in Africa can turn two or three electric cars and their batteries, plugged into a microgrid, into the electricity source for a small village, it's only a matter of time before we find ways to link up multiple microgrids in a way that limits the wires necessary and eventually, perhaps, eliminates them entirely."

"But Granite Skyway's problems run much deeper than just towers and wires. It's the ham-handed approach they've used throughout the entire process that's gotten them into trouble. There's never been a point where the company has come to the people and said, 'These are your rights-of-way and this is your electric system, how do you want to move forward?' "

"If they had done that, the people would have told them how to proceed and the entire project would have probably been completed by now; or abandoned before the company sank so much money into it that turning back did not seem a viable option."

Mac asked, "What do you think the people would have told them?"

"Stick to the existing rights-of-way, reuse the towers already there; Go underground, even if it costs more; don't be cutting huge scars into the land we rely on for our tourist economy; most important of all don't bypass all of the work done on a community-by-community basis to make our electric production more sustainable and to create quality local jobs."

"Do you know that all of the homes and businesses producing electricity using net metering right now aren't even included in the estimates of solar energy generated for the grid?"

"THEY AREN'T?" It was not just Mac who was surprised by this revelation.

"No." Peter replied. " If you included them it would almost double the numbers but right now the folks who operate the grid have no way to measure them. Which also means they have no way to really take advantage of them to provide reliable flows of electricity."

"Could they?" Mac asked.

"The short answer is yes, but the long answer involves investing in a smarter grid, what they call resilience, which is just the opposite of what Granite Skyway does. Granite Skyway is really just a glorified extension cord that moves Canadian hydropower from the sources of its production through New Hampshire to the toney suburbs of the Northeast. It does nothing to make the grid smarter or more resilient, which is what experts say we need to be doing - and in fact is being done in places like Vermont, New York, Massachusetts and even in Maine."

"What's Vermont doing that New Hampshire isn't?" Mac asked.

"I'm afraid that discussion would take up a dozen of these rides," said Peter. "But for one thing, Vermont is encouraging the development of these community resources - including net metering and smart appliances. Their Grid is developed to take advantage of the growing number of microgrids and the individual homes and businesses contributing to the supply of electric power."

"Most important, though," Peter continued, is that Vermonters are talking with one another . . . Communicating, collaborating and envisioning their future. The communication and planning is occurring at all levels: Utility companies are working together to redefine their roles in this new Era of Electricity and Utilities, the state and consumers are working and planning together to craft a vision resulting in a resilient smart grid and establishes a win/win scenario where utilities thrive and help develop the infrastructure that will lead to long-term organic growth and quality, well-paying jobs.

"The relationship between utility companies and ratepayers as well as government varies substantially from state to state then," observed Mac.

"Where does all this leave the utility companies?"

"I'm glad you asked Mac. But I'm afraid my response is going to have to wait until the ride home because, as you can see, we've just taken the exit for Burlington."

Chapter 78 Burlington, Vermont

The Davis Center at the University of Vermont is a magnificent building that serves as the centerpiece of the campus. The Rifkin event, originally scheduled for a smaller room had been moved to the Grand Ballroom to accommodate ticket sales approaching a thousand people.

The UVM Campus is a testament to both the support of state government and the power of Patrick Leahy, Vermont's senior Senator, and more recently to Senator Bernie Sanders, both of whom annually manage to squeeze funding for one pilot project after another into the federal budget. Because of this, the University has, among many other things, busses that run on natural gas and a dormitory complex hailed as the greenest college residence in America, where even the rainwater running off the buildings is recycled.

The crowd making its way into the Davis Center was an eclectic mixture of students, local folks and Rifkin groupies who had traveled hours for the rare opportunity to see one of the great thinkers of the modern era.

The Ballroom buzzed with excitement as Mac, Herbert, Michelle, Peter, Robbin, Sandra and Tim entered and were escorted to seats at the front of the hall. "We have special tickets to a reception with Mr. Rifkin after the speech," Mac said. If we get separated let's plan to meet up at the front entrance and go to the reception in the Leahy Center together."

The crowd quieted as a young man took the stage, tapping the mike to check it. "We are very pleased to have Mr. Rifkin with us this evening. Vermonters have a unique place in the movement to change our relationship with the planet and we naturally take great pride in this. For example: When the country began to re-examine the role of utility companies and power production in the early nineties Vermont had already been engaging in this dialogue for more than two decades."

"There is much we can teach the broader world about cooperation and collaboration but we would not be Vermonters if we did not share a thirst to know more, to understand more and to reach for a higher plane with each generation. That is why I believe we will each take away from tonight's presentation a deeper understanding of the world we want to make together, and why we are grateful for our honored guest this evening."

"Mr. Rifkin has led the world toward an understanding that our industrial civilization is at a crossroads, that fossil fuel energies are antiquated and sunsetting; It is clear from the news nightly that the entire industrial infrastructure of our nation, built on fossil fuels, is aging and in disrepair."

"His warnings about rising unemployment; government and consumer debt; declining standards of living and the looming dangers of climate change are a clarion call for change."

"Dr. Rifkin's call for a new economic narrative - one that can move us toward a more equitable and sustainable future fits well with the Vermont narrative."

"For thirty years Jeremy Rifkin has been searching for a new paradigm to usher in a post-carbon era. In the mid 1990s the elements of that paradigm began to take shape in his mind and he has described it in his book 'The Third Industrial Revolution'."

The young man held up a copy of Rifkin's book. "In this book, he has outlined a vision where people, businesses and entrepreneurs produce their own green energy from their homes and businesses, sharing it with one another in an energy Internet just as we share information now. This dream of the democratization of energy presents an opportunity for a fundamental reordering of our relationships and priorities affecting the way we conduct business, educate our children, and engage in civic life."

"Fortunately he has been spreading this dream to all corners of the world and people are listening. That is why we are so very fortunate to have him here with us this evening."

"Ladies and gentlemen, please welcome, Dr. Jeremy Rifkin."

Rifkin took the dais and for the next two hours held the crowd at the Davis Center spellbound.

After the speech, Mac excused herself to make a phone call. Herbert, Michelle, Sandra, Tim, Robbin and Peter went outside and found a bench to watch the full moon over Vermont's Green Mountains.

Mac called Enright. "JEn, I'm over in Vermont with Michelle and her boyfriend Herbert. We also brought Sandra Manes and Peter Maas with us, they run the nonprofit that puts up solar net metering systems on homes in the area. I've been trying to get as much information out of them as I can without making them suspicious. Here's what I can tell you."

"Michelle is definitely part of The Trust, but you knew that. I'm pretty confident Herbert is too. I think he's one of the ones with a classified status and I've got a book he handled so we can cross check his prints. Sandra and Peter I'm not sure about. They just met Michelle at the same time I met them."

"That should mean they are not in on It.," said Enright.

"That's true, except I heard Sandra talking with Peter about something they were writing for someone named Carrigain. It sounded important and it sounded hush hush."

"Sonofabitch," Enright said. "They're Gazetteers and they don't know Michelle and her boyfriend are in The Trust. They're writing an essay for Carrigain. He's heading up the Gazetteers, Conrad was right."

After her call Mac headed out to join the group.

It was a beautiful night and they sat on the benches looking toward Mt Mansfield, its massive form lit by the full moon.

Mac sat quietly as the group talked excitedly about the future. They were filled with optimism and hope. Not the starry eyed, pie-in-the-sky type of hope . . . The steely-eyed, we-will-not-be-stopped kind. Mac thought fondly back to a time when she had that kind of steel in her own spine.

Chapter 79 The Ride Home

For the first fifteen minutes of the ride home the group was still talking about the Rifkin event but gradually the conversation began to wane and Mac saw her chance to refocus the discussion.

"Peter, you were talking about where all of these changes are going to leave the utility companies?"

Peter sat back crossed his legs and took a sip of water dramatically. " I think it's fair to summarize the situation, Mac, by saying it leaves them in an epic battle for survival. In fact, tonight you have really had a chance to witness two different responses to that. Interestingly, they fit right into the centralized vs. democratized paradigms we spoke of earlier."

"Do you remember the student who introduced Rifkin and what he said?"

"Vaguely." Mac said.

Well, he summarized the situation in Vermont by saying that the utility companies, the businesses and citizens of Vermont have been working collaboratively on these issues for over two decades, while most other states are just getting around to it. In those two decades the utility companies have developed a relationship with consumers in Vermont that has made them a central player in a cooperative effort. It hasn't always been easy but I would venture to say Vermont utility companies feel more comfortable with their long-term prospects for survival than almost any utility in the country right now."

"Vermont has chosen the democratized approach to its energy future and the utility companies have bought in. By buying in, they have also forced the other players to always ask the question, 'what about our utility companies? How do the choices we make strengthen their long-term interests?' "

"I'll wager it's not a question many are asking in New Hampshire, because Polaris Electric has chosen the centralized approach."

"It's not completely their fault, mind you. A heaping share of the blame for this can be attributed to political leadership - and I use the word loosely - politicians who have either missed the opportunities or turned a blind eye to them when they arose."

"What opportunities?" Mac asked.

"Well first there was a bankruptcy, then there was a national reorganization moving them from both generators and carriers, or 'wheelers', of electricity to transmission only. Each of those changes offered opportunities for developing a consensus about moving ahead and each passed without any real shift in the approach of New Hampshire's principle utility."

"What you're saying then, Peter, if I understand you correctly, is Polaris Electric could have found a way to respond to new challenges that the citizens of New Hampshire would have bought into, but they chose not to."

"BINGO! Chose not to and now they are trying to force the square peg of Granite Skyway's centralization, into the round hole of a developing democratization."

"But if they succeed?" said Mac.

"If they succeed, they may force a future of centralization onto the people of the State. For at least a decade or two."

"The good news is that eventually the people will win, but it will not be without pain. "For example, when enough renewables are produced that prosumers vote with their purses and begin a wholesale abandonment of the utility company for off-grid or extra-grid solutions causing rates go so high that either the remaining ratepayers foment a revolution or the company is forced to declare bankruptcy."

"Isn't that the bad news?"

"Surprisingly, no, because a reorganized utility company would be forced to become a part of a democratized system."

"What is the bad news then?"

"We'll have sacrificed our tourism economy on the altar of "steel towers"; The well-to-do will abandon the utility leaving only the poor to pay skyrocketing electric rates; businesses will flee the state in search of more affordable electric rates; and even after the system crashes, we will never restore our tourist economy because steel towers are forever."

Mac grew very quiet. For the rest of the trip she said almost nothing.

They arrived at the Smith Bridge Parking area and as the group emptied from the limo Mac said. "I'm going away for a while, but I will be in touch."

She handed each of them a card. "Here's my contact information for the future."

Mac got back into the Primo and closed her door.

As the limo pulled away she dialed a number and hit 'send'. Her driver was rolling up the privacy window when he heard her say, "Can we meet tomorrow? I have some things we need to discuss."

Chapter 80 Flashmob Alert

Hank Algren's hands flew over the keyboard. He was using his skills with social media to call for a flash mob protest at the offices of Polaris Electric the following Monday at 8am. He knew there was already a protest scheduled by the Firearms Owners of NH for the same day and at the same venue. He hoped to achieve some synergies by joining the two protests, which would mean they would draw a big crowd.

Thomas was the only one skipping this one. Even in a Zombie disguise he might stand out so they decided he would stick to sabotaging construction equipment with a mixture of sand and sugar in their gas tanks. He and Metallak would cover the rights-of-way in the northern part of the State, hitting any areas where Polaris had left equipment unattended.

All in all it seemed it would make for a good day's work for The Trust.

Hank sent out a Mailchimp alert email to over ten thousand people who had signed up to receive alerts from The Trust. He knew some people were too far away to participate but they might be able to let others know about the flashmob. The alert challenged supporters to be creative with their costumes and their signs. He even gave the protest a tongue in cheek theme. The theme was "Zombies for Granite Skyway." After all; you couldn't have Zombies on your side right? Hank had great fun thinking up ideas for protestors including encouraging participants to do things like dressing up as Zombies in an extra large tux or an evening gown and carrying a "Fat Cats for Granite Skyway" sign or "Towers NOT Trees" but he made sure to encourage them to come even if they couldn't come in costume.

He followed the email with posts to #"TreesNotTowers and #StopGraniteSkyway as well as the Facebook and LinkedIn pages he had created for The Trust. With each post he asked supporters to help spread the word. By mid-day, the Flashmob was trending on half a dozen social media sites and he felt confident enough to take a break - - he'd check later to see if there was anything else he could do to boost participation.

At six o'clock The Trust gathered together in Herbert's dining room. Zach Roy had officially joined the team so their numbers had swelled by one with the enthusiastic approval of Thomas.

Hank addressed the group "The purpose of this flashmob is to create a diversion that will allow us to break into Conrad Fleming's office to see if we can find out who this shadow group is that has been closing in on us. Herbert and Charlie, you'll be with me on this. Herbert, bring your lock picks in case they lock the office."

We'll need a secondary diversion, just to be sure that they don't figure out our primary intent. Daniel, Zach, Sasha this is where you come in.

"What about me?" said Michelle.

"I have a very special task for you tomorrow Michelle."

Chapter 81 Flashmob & the 2nd Amendment

At 7:30 am the members of The Trust pulled into two empty parking spots near the Polaris Parking garage. They wanted to be able to see the entrance to the building but minimize the chance someone might be able to identify them through video likely to be captured on the scene. The streets were empty.

Hank fidgeted nervously. What if they called a flash mob and no one came? Could they do this without the distraction? At 7:55 he was in full panic mode, drumming his fingers on his knees and panning the streets.

Then Michelle pointed down Elm Street. "Look" she said triumphantly, "Look!" A wave of bobbing and weaving undead had suddenly appeared marching toward Polaris Headquarters. The placards were, just as Hank had hoped - - very creative. One talented artist had drawn a caricature of Conrad Fleming dressed as a Doctor about to stick a tower into the ample posterior of what presumably was a patient. Beneath it was written,"Trust Me, This Won't Hurt a Bit."

Daniel was next to speak, looking down the street in the opposite direction. "Here comes the Second Amendment crowd too!"

With banners declaring "Hands off our Guns!" and "No Granite Skyway in our Granite State" The second Amendment crowd approached One Commercial Plaza.

"Okay!" Hank said "Everyone clear on what to do?"

Daniel, Zach Roy and Sasha were stuffing climbing ropes into their backpacks, donning them and pulling ponchos on over them to create a hunchback look that fit with their grotesque makeup. Hank and Herbert were dressed in full military camo and skull caps, their faces covered with fake blood and their fake teeth seemed to be falling out of the hole that once was a mouth.

Michelle looked like Little Bo Peep . . . with half a head. A very realistic brain oozed from the back of her head and her excessive makeup made it impossible for anyone to recognize her.

Stonebridge looked like Frankenstein himself, with a giant spike seeming to emerge from both sides of his head.

"Let's move people," Hank said.

Just down the street Linda and Max watched as the scene unfolded. "I'll be damned," she said quietly to Max as she stroked the big cats head. "They did it. Now let's see if they can pull off phase two. "

A thousand or more people were headed for the doors of One Commercial Plaza and the members of The Trust were carried along with the wave of anti-humanity.

Three unarmed security guards stood in front of the building looking panicked as the mob of zombies descended upon them and engulfed them in a frenzy of arms and legs, pretending to devour them but really only clearing a path for the others while gumming the guards to "death".

Daniel, Sasha and Zach were the first of The Trust into the building. Daniel said, "We need to move fast because I think the police won't allow this to happen without a response. Find a fire alarm quickly!"

The three scanned the walls as they headed down the hallway on the first floor.

Sasha called out when she came upon the alarm, pulling it and setting off a general alarm. The three Trust Zombies stood waiting to see if the alarm also set off sprinklers. When it became obvious the sprinklers were not tied into the alarm they breathed a sigh of relief and headed for the elevators as waves of employees swarmed out of the building - helping to build the crowd size in front of the building.

They met Hank, Herbert and Stonebridge at the elevators and headed up.

Michelle made her way through the crowd and ducked into the bathroom where she proceeded to remove her makeup and her oozing brain, tossing it into her backpack. She pulled out her iPhone, double-checked the charge and began to communicate with each of the groups over the Open Channel App on their iPhones.

Chapter 82 Fleming's Office

At the top floor both groups piled out onto the deserted floor. Daniel, Sasha and Zach headed for the door to the roof while the other three set off in search of Conrad Fleming's office.

Fleming's office was locked and Herbert pulled out his picks and set to work. Within a minute he had the door open and the three entered Fleming's office.

"Stonebridge, take the file cabinets. Herbert, take the desk, I'll take the bookshelves. We're looking for a file or a paper that has the name 'James Enright' on it, hopefully with other names as well. Try not to make a mess, it would be better if they didn't figure out we've been in here." barked Hank.

He set his iPhone to give him an alert in five minutes, then he held it to his mouth and said "Michelle give me the heads up if the police show up, we don't want to be here if they do." Hank then joined the other two, already at work.

At five minutes the iPhone alarm went off - - each of the three called out "Nothing here, NADA, Zip, Zilch".

"Dammit!" Herbert cursed.

"It's got to be here somewhere."

"We can't stay much longer, the police will be swarming this building," said Stonebridge just as Michelle's voice came over their iPhones, "Manchester Police coming through the door."

The door to Fleming's office opened and Donna Barza, Conrad's personal assistant who had rescued the cars at the Androscoggin Stampede, stood looking at the three Trust Zombies.

"You look like shit." Barza said, walking over to the desk. She lifted the Calendar blotter, pulled the bottom corners out of the triangular plastic holders and opened it to the December page, removing an 8x10 sheet of paper. "Follow me," she said sharply.

Completely taken aback, the three were unsure of whether to run or to do as they were instructed, but something told Herbert it was worth the risk. Barza walked briskly to the copier, made one quick copy and handed it to Herbert. "You never saw me." She said. "Now get the hell out of here and I'll put this back."

They didn't need to be told twice; as they headed back to the elevator Michelle whispered "Cops are headed upstairs. I'm going incognito. Everything ok up there?"

Hank came back on and said, "You wouldn't believe it if I told you. We're on our way down with the list."

"Take the elevator," Michelle said, "the cops are taking the stairwell."

In less than sixty seconds team one was back on the first floor, headed out the door and melding into the crowd of zombies, headed for the exit door.

Donna Barza went back into Fleming's office and replaced the sheet of paper with the names and numbers of the Cabal. As she was closing the door behind her she thought she saw a pair of legs outside the window but she didn't have time to investigate. She locked the door and dialed a number on her cell as she headed for the stairwell exit sign.

"You were right. They just left." Then she closed her phone and vanished through the door.

Chapter 83   Fleming's Return

Conrad Fleming was just dropping his second Town Car at the detailers as the news came in that the Zombies had taken over One Commercial Plaza. He climbed into the car that had followed him there and ordered the driver to take him back to the office. He was less than ten minutes from the office and the driver didn't spare a moment.

As Fleming jumped from the car he hollered to the driver "I don't want you leaving this car, do you understand? The last thing I need is another video on Late Night."

Fleming headed through the front door where only moments before a mob of Zombies and equally rabid gun owners had occupied the main entrance. The Manchester police had finally restored order with only a minimal number of arrests. The Police Chief met Fleming at the front door, along with Donna Barza and a small contingent of journalists. They took the elevator to the tenth floor and Fleming went immediately to his door and turned the knob. "Still locked he said with relief."

He placed his key in the lock and opened the door to his office. Looking at his desk and file cabinet it appeared everything was in order. Then he looked up. Where normally there was a large plate glass picture window affording a stunning view of the Merrimack River as it flowed through the City of Manchester, now there was a massive black silhouette of a tower top, spray-painted onto the window, obstructing the view. The tower top and cross beams were encircled with the International NO slash symbol. Fleming approached the window just in time to see three ropes that were attached to Zach, Daniel and Sasha falling from the roof as the three retrieved them after they had quickly rappelled down the building, stenciling each of the massive windows as they went.

Fleming did not stop to see if anything else was amiss inside his office as he ran from office to office on the floor, finding the stenciling in all three C-level offices. Cursing and flailing as the media followed, documenting the entire scene.

All the media that is, except for Michelle who, wearing a cap emblazoned with the word PRESS had joined the Fleming entourage as it entered the elevator on the first floor. By the time Fleming was lunging from office to office on the 10th floor, she was already on her way out of the building, iPhone in hand, with a delightful video of Conrad Fleming losing it as he entered his office. She shared her video with Hank, who sat in a nearby cafe taking advantage of the free wifi and sipping on a large hot latte. Hank hooked her iPhone to his laptop and with a dramatic flourish, hit send. Within a nano second the video was hurtling through space on the Information Superhighway, including a copy addressed to seth@LateNight.com.

"Don't tell anyone I was drinking this," he said, referring to the latte. "Wouldn't want folks to think you had infected my brain."

Chapter 84   Moll's Rock Redux

It was Thursday, a week and a half before Columbus Day, when The Trust gathered together at Moll's Rock. This time Hank had made reservations to be sure the site was available. The plan was for The Trust to spend three days relaxing and talking through their strategy for continuing the fight to stop Granite Skyway. This would allow them to get back home by Monday, which was, after all, a workday. The team would then regroup next at the annual Sandwich Fair on Monday a week later.

The last of the reds and oranges of Autumn in the Great North Woods were turning to brown. Most of the crowd of leaf peepers and gawkers had moved south to the Lakes Region or the Monadnock area where the colors of autumn were still vibrant. A few lone fishermen were still around, but the lake was largely quiet, abandoned to the eagles, the Peregrine Falcons and the loons - - providing The Trust both solitude and crisp nights, free of mosquitoes.

The group had split up upon their arrival; each assigned a task in preparation of their camp. Hank and Michelle, the primo fishers of the group, along with Zach Roy, who fancied himself one, had gone off in Hank's bass boat hoping to catch enough fish for at least the first night's meal. Herbert, Daniel and Sasha were assigned to gather wood for the fire. Thomas, and Charlie Stonebridge had still not arrived. They had invited Linda Levy to join them but she told them she needed to think it through before she made a decision. She wanted to come but was concerned about maintaining a professional distance from the group in everyone's best interests.

Daniel, Herbert and Sasha had just returned to the campsite to drop off their first armloads of wood. Daniel paused looking out at Lake Umbagog. "I love the vibrant colors of peak foliage,but this - - THIS" he said, sweeping his arms before him, "is my favorite time here in the North Country. I call it the "Golden Season". The birches, beech and poplars hold their yellows much longer than the maples and they appear as grand splashes of yellow on the brown and green canvas of the final day's tableau. Reds and oranges fading to brown amid the greens of every hue laid down by the conifers. It's one of the best-kept secrets, jealously guarded by the folks who live here. The crowds are gone, the days are usually sunny and warm and the hiking and paddling and fishing are fantastic.

Herbert stood beside him. "You know, no one has ever pointed that out to me Daniel. I think I sensed it after I was here a few years but . . ."

"That's why it's our secret," Daniel said smiling broadly. "You have to be here long enough that it just seeps into your heart and soul. Sounds to me like we can dub you an honorary native, Herbert."

"I'll do the honorary native dubbing around here." Sasha said.

Daniel held his hands up in mock surrender at this and headed back into the woods for another load of firewood. Sasha stayed behind and readied the fire and Herbert lingered to speak with her.

"Sasha, I think you should consider going home to Canada."

"Not a Chance."

"Thomas could smuggle you across the border on Metallak. Even if they have an alert for you at the border you should be able to get out safely."

"I don't intend to abandon The Trust, Herbert. Besides I've been looking forward to the Sandwich Fair. Hank calls it 'a slice of life'. How can I pass up my chance to witness a slice of life?"

Chapter 85 Planning the Work - Working the Plan

That evening, talk around the campfire began with a discussion about The Trust's plans.

"I wish Linda was here," said Hank, "She's doing the research on whether we can copyright the product of Dr. Aniemeka's performance art when it's finished. There is a chance we can block the construction of the towers south of Plymouth by having the work copyrighted and then fighting an intrusion from towers as a violation of the copyright."

"It's a longshot but it seems to be getting some traction in other parts of the country where local folks are trying it in similar situations, so we thought it was worth trying. It also makes for great optics." Daniel added.

"I also think we need to review the list of people we got from Fleming's office with everyone and talk about how we are going to approach it" Hank continued. Linda has the only copy of the list at the moment - I gave it to her after we escaped Fleming's office just in case we got arrested and the police confiscated it."

"Hey, by the way," said Michelle, "How did you get that list anyway? When you were talking with me as the Manchester Police were heading upstairs you said I wouldn't believe it if you told me."

"We promised we would not divulge the name of the person who helped us," said Hank. "Let's just say we seem to have an unexpected source on the inside. Maybe we had better keep it confidential for now in case we need help later on."

"Speaking of that," Herbert interjected, "I think we should talk about whether Thomas should help Sasha and Cochise get across the border where they're out of reach."

"Maybe Daniel should go with her," Michelle suggested, ever the romantic.

"There will be no talk about what Sasha and Cochise are going to do - with or without Daniel," Sasha said, "unless you want to tango with Cochise. He hates it when someone decides where and when he goes anywhere, any time."

There was a lull in the conversation and Thomas saw the opportunity to say what he was thinking over the last few days. "I know I have sort of said this before but I want to thank you all for including Metallak and me in The Trust. It means more than I could ever tell you."

"When I returned from Iraq I dropped out because I saw no hope against the tide of Oligarchy that had swept over our country while I was away."

"I was really in a bad place, angry and so hurt, thinking about my friends - so many of my friends - who had given their lives for a country that had changed while they were away fighting. I watched as so many others returned only to find their futures had fallen victim to a tide of selfishness."

"It wasn't just the growing inequity of wealth - that started long before we went - but the fact that those inequities had already led to a social inequality. What worried me most, though, was that social inequality was giving way to biological inequality, a sign the situation might soon be irreversible."

"I'm not sure I understand what you mean Thomas," said Michelle. "I feel like it's important. Can you elaborate?"

"In the past decade lifespan among working class people has begun declining for the first time in more than two centuries. I mean, it's always been true the wealthy have access to better medical care, healthier food and lifestyles - - But for two hundred years, if not more, the general trajectory for both men and women of all income levels has been a longer lifespan. It's only in the last decade this has reversed. When a social pattern like this becomes a biological fact, I think it becomes baked into the evolutionary equation."

"Anyway, the fight to maintain some chance to control our future, to fight for a sustainable world, for a democratic energy future, has given me new hope . . . and you - every one of you - have been the reason for that hope."

"It's not just the battle. It's the chance to fight side-by-side with you, to do battle with a group of people so good and decent."

Turning to Sasha, Thomas continued, "In some way, Sasha, it may be how your people must have felt near the end. When they knew the chances of victory were small but making their stand was the only way to stay true to everything that mattered."

I've thought a lot lately about how Chief Joseph must have felt in that final engagement of the Indians' sunset struggle as he led his small band of Nez Perce in their flight to freedom, trying desperately to reach Sitting Bull's free Lakota in Canada."

"With fewer than 200 warriors and a thousand old men, women and children he evaded and fought off over three thousand cavalry on horseback. The Nez Perce never killed anyone who was innocent, never took a scalp or committed an act that was against the moral code of either white men or Indian in their flight. All they wanted was to live out their days in peace and freedom."

From their example, they came to epitomize everything that is true and just and honorable. So much - we now know - that even the soldiers who pursued them secretly hoped they would succeed. Even many of the people of the country, following the news of the flight of the Nez Perce, watched the drama unfold on the pages of their local newspaper and hoped the Nez Perce would make it to Canada."

"When it became clear they would not make the last few miles, Joseph gave himself up, creating just enough of a diversion that the healthy and strong among his people could slip into Canada to join Sitting Bull in the dark of night, while Joseph remained behind with the sick and dying."

He turned to the others in the group; "if you haven't ever read Chief Joseph's speech - "I Will Fight No More Forever" - delivered when he surrendered to the army, read it. It is one of the most moving speeches I have ever read."

"Rebellion is a moral imperative. But you have shown me we can rebel with honor and to do that we must not resort to violence despite our frustration. We must respond to their violence with love and hope if we are to maintain the support of the people."

"We must, as Nelson Mandela said, 'surprise those who are against us.' "

"You all have shown me that hope exists in that place."

Part 7 Seatbelts Fastened

Chapter 86   Bloody Saturday

Herbert Johanssen was stoking the fire on Saturday morning when he looked out onto the water and saw Linda Levy approaching in her kayak.

"Hey! You decided to join us," he yelled out onto the water.

Linda waved and paddled to shore where Charlie Stonebridge, who had heard the commotion and wandered over, met her and held her boat as she climbed out.

"I'm afraid I'm not here for a social visit," Linda said. "A bomb went off this morning at a Granite Skyway construction site. Normally no one would have been working on a Saturday but it appears a site manager had gone over to check on the equipment and he was there when the bomb went off."

Michelle had joined them at the water's edge. "Is he ok?"

"I'm afraid not. He was rushed to Littleton Hospital in critical condition, but it doesn't look good."

"What the hell are they doing with a construction site to begin with?" said Daniel. The project hasn't been approved at any level."

"They're doing work on all of the existing rights-of-way they plan to use for the Granite Skyway in advance of the approvals. This will allow them to hit the ground running, if and when they get their approvals, according to the sources I've spoken with who are following the process. Unfortunately, they're within their rights to do this."

"We've got bigger concerns than work on the rights-of-way," said Hank.

Stonebridge finished his sentence . . . "They'll be blaming us for this. Someone sandbagged us."

"But we've all been here for the last three days, how can they make this stick?" said Sasha.

"They probably can't," said Linda, "legally I mean, but they don't have to prove you guilty to destroy your support among the people."

"What do we do then?" Daniel asked.

"Maybe we should claim responsibility for it. That would confuse the hell out of whoever did it," said Zach.

"People are counting on us to be creative and nonviolent," Michelle said. "We would destroy any public support we have if we take credit for it, even as a strategy."

The group grew quiet. This was a moment that would define everything that followed: How they would be remembered; whether they could stop Granite Skyway; what would happen to them personally.

"I think we all know what we have to do," said Hank.

The others looked at Hank, waiting to hear what he was thinking.

"We have to out ourselves."

Chapter 87 Monday Morning

Linda Levy walked up to the dais in the Hall of Flags at the New Hampshire Statehouse on Monday morning at 9am. She and Hank had spent the day on Sunday contacting key members of the media, blogs that were reporting on The Trust and emailing any supporters they had identified. They also sent out news releases to the broadest audience they could identify.

Linda had quietly slipped away and called Jack Carrigain. Letting him know what The Trust planned to do, he promised to alert his authors.

As a result of all this, the Hall of Flags was packed with people, media and gawkers.

"Thank you all for coming to this news conference on such short notice. My name is Linda Levy and I am the attorney representing The Trust."

"As you know, from the very beginning, the members of The Trust promised that they would employ creative and at times civilly disobedient methods, to stop the Granite Skyway. They promised, too, they would be non violent."

"I am here to tell you they have not broken their promise to you. They had nothing to do with the bombing that took place this past weekend. In fact they've all been camping together since Thursday at the Moll's Rock campsite, where they first met. Since all of the equipment involved in the bombing was used on both Thursday and Friday - the two days before the bombing - there was no way the bomb could have been planted before Friday night and therefore no way they could have planted the bomb."

"But you don't need to take my word for this."

As she spoke two people rolled a large screen monitor into the room. Linda pressed a button on the dais as she said, "It was important enough for you to know that the members of The Trust decided they needed to tell you themselves."

An excited murmur ran through the crowd. They were finally going to see this vaunted group.

The monitor flickered to life and the members of The Trust stood together in front of Moll's Rock. At the front of the group were Sasha Brandt and Cochise.

"There is a proverb shared among native people so ancient even its attribution is uncertain. Some think it was Chief Seattle who said this, but others insist the origins are even older.

"Treat the earth well: it was not given to you by your parents, it was loaned to you by your children. We do not inherit the Earth from our ancestors, we borrow it from our children."

"My name is Sasha Brandt and this is my companion Cochise, a Timberwolf from Isle Royale on Lake Superior. I am a member of the Iroquois nation. I have acted only on my own accord as a member of The Trust and not on behalf of the Iroquois. However, I have been moved to act in the name of my people and other native peoples in Canada who have seen their hunting and fishing grounds poisoned and their lands flooded by dams intended only for creating surplus electricity to be sold into the United States."

"Two months ago I met the other members of what we now call 'The Trust' right here at Moll's Rock, named for the legendary medicine woman Moll Ockett who is said to have camped here regularly as she traveled on the path between the worlds of the red man and the white man."

"Cochise and I were hiking on the Appalachian Trail when I met Daniel Roy, an extraordinary man with a deep commitment to our planet. The two of us came here to camp and fish and quite accidentally met the other members of the group who were also camping here. While getting to know one another we discovered we were all alarmed about the plans for Granite Skyway. We were also in agreement that the project was quite likely to receive approval if we simply relied on lawyers and protesters to stop it."

"Each of us has different reasons for our commitment to this effort but make no mistake, we are committed to stopping Granite Skyway and we are all willing to pay the price for our actions."

"Daniel and Zach Roy are cousins who grew up here. Their grandmother and grandfather were instrumental in the fight to close the paper mills spewing toxic waste into the Pemigewasset River, despite threats to burn down their home and to kill their livestock."

Today the Pemigewasset runs wild, free and clean. Both men were raised on stories about the night their grandmother and grandfather sat the family down around the table and told them of the threats. Their fathers and aunts urged their parents to keep up the fight. Fittingly, Daniel and Zach's Grandmother and Grandfather are buried on a promontory overlooking the river. That view will be of a trail of 150 foot steel towers should Granite Skyway come to pass."

"Michelle Kane moved here from New Jersey because New Hampshire was a place with clean air, crystal clear water and views that took your breath away. She says, despite growing up in New Jersey, she has always been a country girl in her heart. Today she is a successful business woman and she is risking everything to stop the construction of these monstrous towers."

"Charlie Stonebridge spent his summers on Newfound Lake and has made New Hampshire his second home since then. He is a legendary Olympic paddler who has climbed all of the four thousand footers in New Hampshire and paddled every navigable river in the state."

"Herbert Johannsen was a covert operative in a unit like the Navy Seals, 'only tougher' he would say with humor. He helped the Afghans repel the Soviet Union. He was also the first recorded victim of Lyme disease. When he emerged from his coma the doctors told him he would never recover his speech and would always need assistance walking. He moved to New Hampshire and began his own personal rehabilitation program, formulated in his mind as he lay recovering in his hospital bed, climbing a 35-foot rope with only his hands daily, hiking and tending his small farm. He tells me New Hampshire saved him, now he is determined to pay her back . . . to save New Hampshire."

"Hank Algren's family has been working the same piece of land in New Hampshire for at least eight generations. He tells me that back in the beginning his people and my people traded with one another; and they would not have survived but for the kindness of native people who helped give them their start. Today he has one of the most innovative and successful deer farms in the United States and ships product all over the world. He is a rock ribbed Republican who would sooner die than switch but today he stands proudly with The Trust. He's risking everything to save his beloved state."

"Then there is Thomas . . ."

Thomas walked into the picture from off screen leading Metallak. "My name is Thomas, just Thomas, like Cher and Sting" he said, a goofy grin on his face. " I grew up in the North Country where my family has lived for more generations than I can count. I joined the army right out of high school, right after 9/11, and then returned here after serving two tours in the Army Rangers beside Hank here."

"I'm not opposed to a transmission line. I am opposed to one built for the benefit of a few wealthy folks, ignoring the rights and the needs of the citizens of the State. We don't all agree on what should happen - but we all agree that Granite Skyway is not the answer."

"We did not plant the bomb that went off on Saturday. I saw enough killing during my years in Iraq that I would never be involved in anything that brought violence upon any other human being ever again. We had nothing to do with that bomb."

Then Thomas looked directly into the camera as it zoomed in on him and said "But we have a pretty good idea who is responsible and let me say something directly to them.

"We are coming after you. We won't rest until the only view you have is the bars separating you from the rest of humanity."

"Oh yes," he added lifting himself onto the saddle on Metallak's back," This is Metallak. Named for the last Indian of the Magalloway and the inspiration for a relationship that has developed since his mama was hit by a logging truck and he was just a knobby-kneed newborn. He has been one of our secret weapons in the fight to stop Granite Skyway. We hope you will join us in our efforts to stop this travesty."

Thomas trotted off screen and Sasha returned to center stage.

"Now you have met the entire team. That is, except for you," she said pointing at the camera. "Your support and efforts to help have sustained us over these last few months. We are especially grateful to the group of patriots who call themselves The Gazetteers. They have helped to define the terms of this struggle in ways we could not."

"We know that by revealing ourselves the risks now have become much greater for us. But we could not, in good conscience, do otherwise."

"You have believed in us and our struggle to stop this transmission line."

"You have joined in song to celebrate our efforts and you have kept the struggle alive in your words and deeds."

"We would never break faith with you by harming anyone. We ask for your help to bring the real perpetrators of this violence to justice . . . and to continue the fight to stop Granite Skyway."

"In the longhouse where I grew up my parents had four portraits: the first, Peacemaker who helped to unite the tribes of the Iroquois confederacy in peace and prosperity, the second Doctor Martin Luther King Jr., the third President of the United States John F. Kennedy and the fourth, his brother Senator Robert Francis Kennedy, who - even when it was not politically popular - stood up for justice for First Nations people.

It was Bobby Kennedy who said "Each time a man stands for an ideal, or acts to improve the lot of others, or strikes out against injustice, he sends forth a tiny ripple of hope, and crossing each other from a million different centers of energy and daring, those ripples build a current which can sweep down the mightiest walls of oppression and resistance."

"Together we can be centers of energy and daring. Together we can stop Granite Skyway and build a future of which we can be proud."

Chapter 88   A New Energy Paradigm

A new piece from the Gazetteers would greet The Trust as they entered the Sandwich Fairgrounds and at the same time would begin its journey on the Internet to every corner of the digital world.

Granite Skyway and the New Energy Paradigm
P. Samuel Adams

Throughout the history of our nation we have responded to the great challenges of our times by creating new paradigms designed to secure our future in the face of those challenges.

Often these new paradigms required we leave behind some long held cultural beliefs or biases, even those at one time considered sacred cows and protected, as a shroud, by the label "common sense".

The great Stephen Hawking said, "common sense is just another name for the prejudices we have been raised with."

Today we are faced with a global crisis unparalleled in human history. The warming of the planet, brought about by centuries of carbon-based fuel consumption, requires us to make a rapid switch to a carbon-free economic model. The common sense of two centuries has become the barrier to the next two and it must be relegated to the ash heap of history.

Making changes like these require us to embrace new ideas and technologies and to leave behind others. Carbon-based energy has given us nearly two hundred years of growth and - for the most part - prosperity. Yet even from the beginning a clock has been ticking. This clock has counted the minutes until the earth could no longer bear the burdens we were imposing on our environment.

A transmission and distribution system such as the proposed Granite Skyway project represents resources wasted and misdirected.

While other states and countries, including most of the developed world, are creating sustainable, decentralized power transmission and delivery systems with safe and secure, laterally scaled, green energy sources to assure that no terrorist will be able to successfully attack their power grid, the cabal of investors we call Granite Skyway - motivated largely by greed and avarice - is attempting to maximize their profit by creating a single source transmission system, a system obligating us to power purchases long past the time in which we can make rational projections and with no effort to create a smart grid with overlapping power sources.

The net result will be to create a 180-mile window of opportunity for every terrorist who wants to destroy the American economy with one or two well-placed explosives capable of plunging the entire eastern seaboard and the nation's economic brain and nerve center into darkness.

Granite Skyway is a vestige of a past best left behind.

Today we face a future filled with peril if we fail to change. The reality of climate change compels us to find a way forward that leads us into a post-carbon world.

Already we are seeing the signs of the possibilities of such a world.

It is a world where renewable sources of energy, backed up by new and old methodologies of energy storage, produce the energy we need to provide a safe, reliable and decentralized smart energy grid.

It is a world where even the poorest nations can create microgrids of electricity generation for the smallest villages. Given the speed with which it has been growing in only the last few years, it is closer than any of us think.

The Gazetteers
P. Samuel Adams

Chapter 89   The Sandwich Fair

In the days that followed the news conference at which The Trust revealed themselves there was a media frenzy. Biographies of every member of The Trust had appeared in traditional media outlets and Web publications and blogs. If the group had been folk heroes before, now they were approaching legendary status, individually and collectively. The downside, of course, was that now the police were in the hunt. They had to watch out for both the shadow cabal and the authorities.

This made a day at the Sandwich Fair a risky proposition but they all agreed they could blend into the huge crowd sufficiently to pull it off.

"I have to admit I'm looking forward to this fair." Sasha said as they drove toward the Town of Sandwich past the shores of Squam Lake. "Much as I hate to do anything except mourn on the day honoring the Italian fellow who was almost single handedly responsible for the start of the largest genocide in history," - - referring to the fact Christopher Columbus and his three ships were probably at least partially responsible for introducing a number of European diseases that spread, like a wildfire, through a population estimated to be as large as 100 million native people, leaving fewer than 10 million by 1700.

"I'm not sure you can call the accidental introduction of European diseases into the Native American population 'Genocide' " said Herbert. "But when you aggregate it with the intentional actions of nearly every European and Colonial contact for two centuries, or more, then you have a real conundrum."

Sasha was near a boiling point with Herbert at first, but as he continued his observations, she realized he was fair in his assessment. Influenza, smallpox, Bubonic plague, chickenpox, cholera, diphtheria, malaria, measles, scarlet fever, these were only some of the diseases introduced into the indigenous population of Native Americans during what would come to be known by some historians as the "Columbian Exchange".

If you were of European stock the Columbian Exchange was characterized by nearly two centuries of new products, new crops and new ideas flowing back to the European continent. It was a lopsided exchange at best, particularly if you were already living in the 'New World' when Columbus made his consequential voyage.

By the end of the first century after Columbus, European agriculture and palates were introduced to potatoes, tomatoes, corn, squash, pumpkins and tobacco to name just a few products that would revolutionize European agriculture.

If you found yourself on the Indian side of the exchange, the only truly important imports fell in the area of domesticated animals. Among them, and most consequential, was the horse, which, in fact, may have purchased a century more of resistance by the native people living, or driven to, the plains. Other domesticated animals however, particularly pigs and fowl, quite likely were additional vectors for the transfer of disease among the native people of North, Central and South America.

Herbert continued, "the greatest portion of the damage had already been done to Native Americans without a shot being fired. Then, adding insult to injury . . . No, adding further injury, disease began to be used as an instrument of warfare and genocide. Blankets infected with smallpox were employed against the native people during the French and Indian War, instigated by none other than Lord Jeffrey Amherst, for whom the illustrious University is named . . . and this was only the beginning!"

By now Sasha had not only cooled down but was feeling a real admiration for what Herbert had obviously studied and understood about the struggles of native people.

"OK" she said, "no more getting me down here. Let's focus on what fun we're going to have at the annual Sandwich Fair!"

"It really is a . . ." Herbert began to say before being cut off.

"SLICE OF LIFE" chanted the group.

Herbert, grinning, quickly embraced the opportunity to move off the genocide discussion. "I love the agriculture exhibits. Just the fact some farmer has gone to the trouble of bringing a squash weighing more than his entire family makes it worth the cost of admission."

"I'm heading straight for the giant éclairs!" said Michelle. Knowing these were the unspoken thoughts of Herbert, despite his words.

The Sandwich Fair is one of New Hampshire's largest state agricultural fairs held every year on the weekend preceding Columbus Day and on the holiday itself. It is a celebration of rural life and culinary excess.

While Daniel, Sasha, Zach, Herbert and Michelle were still making their way along NH Rte 113 toward Sandwich, at the East entrance of the fair, Jack Carrigain and his granddaughter Jessie were heading right for the midway, with an arms-length of tickets each. The day before the fair Jack had gone to visit an old friend who was a sailor and persuaded him to give Jack a scopolamine laced transdermal patch from his stash so Jack could enjoy the Midway rides with Jessie without getting so sick he vomited in her lap.

He recalled, with horror, the ride on what was called "The Roundabout" a few years back, at the Fryeburg Fair. When the ride broke down as he was hanging upside down he had showered a stomach full of half-digested onion blossoms, French fries, fried dough and lemonade onto the passengers directly below him.

Jessie had never let him live that one down. Whenever she had the chance to tell the story of his "mega-spew" as she called it, she would revel in the opportunity. Like Jack, she was a great storyteller so she would not hesitate to embellish it a bit - or as her mother would say "put a shine on it."

There was nothing shiny about the experience as far as Jack was concerned, so he was determined not to relive it.

"Let's start with something gentle, Jessie. How about the Ferris Wheel?"

OK Grampa," Jessie replied. "But don't forget the milking contest at 3:30. I want to try my hand at it this year."

"Don't worry Hon, if I'm still here on the midway at 3:30 it will be because I'm laid out in lavender."

"Oh Grampa!"

It wasn't the first time Jessie had heard her grandfather use this phrase and she knew it meant dead. The first time she had heard him use it, she had no idea of what he meant. Upon returning home, she had looked it up and determined it had come from the ancient practice of using lavender and other strong smelling herbs to cover the smell of a dead body prior to burial. This was not something she wanted to think about when it came to her beloved Grandfather.

Jessie took her grandfather's hand and led him to the Ferris Wheel where they paid their tickets and climbed aboard.

One of the advantages of making the Ferris Wheel their first stop was not only to start on the gentle side but to get a bird's eye view of the fair. The midway - the area where the rides and games were located - was on the highest point of land in the fairgrounds. From the apex of the ride they could look down into the valley where the competition arenas and food vendors were located. On the other side of the fairgrounds there were the livestock barns, including their favorites - - the oxen and draft horse barns.

As Jack surveyed the scene he looked down and just by chance spotted Linda Levy strolling under the Ferris Wheel.

Leaning out he yelled "Linda!"

Linda stopped and looked around her at ground level. Not seeing who had called out her name, she was about to begin walking again when he called again "Linda! Up here!"

Linda shaded her eyes from the sun and looked up toward the sound of Jack's voice. The sun made it difficult to see him, but she was pretty sure whose voice it was.

"Jack?" She called out. "Is that you? The sun is right behind you so I can't see much."

"Yes." He yelled, "we're almost done here, wait there for us."

As the two climbed down off the Ferris Wheel Linda thought she saw a hint of disappointment on Jessie's face. Here she was alone with her Grandfather and now she was going to have to compete with another adult for his attention. Jack introduced the two and Linda immediately said "Jessie, this is my first time here at the Sandwich fair and I want to go on the scariest rides they have! Will you be our guide?"

Jessie brightened immediately and said "well we have to be careful Grandpa doesn't spew on anyone, like he did a few years ago."

Linda took her hand and said, "I think we can team up so we don't repeat that, but you'll have to tell me <u>all</u> about it."

Jack Carrigain groaned and rolled his eyes. "Alright you two. I'm ready to tackle anything you throw at me today, because I have a secret weapon." He smiled conspiratorially at Jessie and turned to wink at Linda. Then, as he turned toward Jessie again, she noticed the small patch just behind his ear. She had seen them before on ferry passengers to Martha's Vineyard and on Whale Watch Cruises out of the New England Aquarium in Boston.

"What do you say we start with Bumper Cars, then work our way up to the two rides you most want to do Jessie?"

"That would be um . . . the Scrambler and the Vortex!"

Linda, who had an iron constitution from years of midways at fairs around the Boston area, appeared ready for anything. Hand in hand, with Jack on one side and Linda on the other, they headed for the Bumper Cars.

Chapter 90   The West Entry

"Oh my God! This is so good it should be illegal," Sasha said as she bit into the huge éclair Michelle had just passed to her. The group had entered through the West gate and were making their way - more accurately eating their way - over toward the midway where they planned to hook up with Linda.

Herbert, who was, according to him, more health conscious, was ordering a huge fried onion blossom at Chesley's Onion Blossom and French Fries stand.

Just across from them and Daniel was waiting for a big fresh lemonade. "Don't put the squeezed lemon in the cup," he said to the vendor. Knowing this was a trick they used to displace about one third of the lemonade, in hopes you would come back for more.

Just then Sasha gasped and moved behind Michelle. "Wha. . " said Michelle as Sasha whispered, "It's them! - - the guys who attacked me at Daniel's yurt. Do you think they followed us here?"

Michelle maneuvered her body to provide cover for Sasha as two thugs wandered by chatting nonchalantly, one of them using a crutch and limping on what appeared to be a knee injury.

 "I don't think so. I've gotten so paranoid lately that I am always checking my rear view mirror. I don't think anyone could have followed us without our noticing - - and I don't think they know you're here."

By the time Echo and Duggan were out of sight, Sasha was fuming. "Those bastards! I told them to drive west and not look back when I let them go. I should have let Cochise rip his throat out."

Daniel, noticing from across the way that something was amiss, hurried over to Michelle and Sasha.

"It's the guys who attacked Sasha at the yurt" she whispered.

"Maybe we should get out of here," Daniel said.

"Not on your life," replied Sasha. "I came here to enjoy the fair and that's exactly what I intend to do. I think Michelle is right, they aren't following us . . . but, are they here just to enjoy the fair or are they up to something?"

Chapter 91   Where the Twain Meet

Jack, Jessie and Linda climbed down from The Scrambler. "Let's do it again, Grandpa," she said.

"Whoa Jessie, go easy on your old Grandpa. I need to sit down for a minute." Jessie and Linda led him over to a picnic table and the three took seats.

"You know I was feeling fine all through that ride. The patch was actually working, but all of a sudden I'm feeling very weird."

"Are you gonna spew grandpa?" Jessie asked.

Linda asked, "Are you feeling nauseated Jack?"

"No, not nauseated. More like I'm hallucinating. As you were talking with me just then, your lips moved off your face and were talking to me from the air beside your head!"

At that moment Herbert and Michelle strolled up with Daniel and Sasha right behind, keeping an eye out for the devil's henchmen. They found Linda bending down over Jack Carrigain.

Coming up to her from behind, Herbert said, "Linda we've got a bit of a situation."

"Get in line, Jack here is acting like he just dropped acid. He's hallucinating. We just got down from a very wild ride but he should be puking not tripping."

Herbert came closer. "Hi Jack, I'm Herbert, I'm a friend of Linda's. Did you hit your head recently?" Now Jack was having trouble communicating but he shook his head. As he did, Herbert saw the patch behind his ear.

"Jack, what's in the patch behind your ear?"

"Anti-nausea, " Jack managed.

Herbert reached back and ripped the patch off. Almost immediately Jack began to feel the difference. His breathing normalized and he sat up from his slumped position.

"He's had an allergic reaction to the Scopolamine in the patch. I've seen it a hundred times when I was in the Coast Guard. It's one of the best anti-seasickness remedies there is, but one in a hundred people exhibit an allergic reaction and often the side effect is hallucinations. Scopolamine is derived from the nightshade family of plants and related to the hallucinogenic known as Belladonna."

"The good news is he will probably feel right as rain in about 45 minutes."

"Forty-five minutes!" Jessie groaned, a captive of youthful self-absorption. "Grandpa, I'll miss the milking contest."

Carrigain spoke weakly to his granddaughter. "I'm sorry Hon, maybe one of Linda's friends can take you over to the contest and I'll join you there as soon as I can."

Linda was sitting next to Jack, cradling his head and running her hands through his hair to comfort him.

"Jessie, I'll stay here and take care of your Grandpa. Michelle, would you mind taking Jessie over to the milking contest?"

"I've always wanted to see a milking contest," Michelle said.

"I'll go with you," Herbert said.

"No Herbert, you stay here with Daniel and Sasha to make sure they're safe . . . and let Linda know what's going on."

Michelle introduced herself to Jessie, "I don't know much about cows and milking Jessie, can you teach me?"

Jessie took her hand, "I'm in 4H at home - I have sheep, not cows - but I've learned a lot about cows from the other kids in the group. Come on, I'll help you."

After Jessie and Michelle had left, Herbert whispered to Linda, hoping Jack was too out of it to pay much attention, "Linda, I hate to interrupt things here but we just saw the pair who attacked Sasha at Daniel's yurt. I wanted to get out of here but Sasha insisted we not allow them to ruin our day at the fair. The fair is big but I'm not sure it's that big."

Linda thought for a minute and looked at Sasha. "They don't know anyone else but Sasha right? I think if you put a ball cap on her and keep her woven into the group, they won't be likely to recognize her."

As Herbert ran off in search of a ball cap Sasha sat down next to Jack while Linda and Daniel stood in front of her to block her from the view of by passers.

Chapter 92 The Oxen Barn

Michelle and Jessie were watching the clock in anticipation of the milking contest when they decided to stop in at the Oxen Barn to kill fifteen minutes before registration for the contest was scheduled to begin.

Michelle was not native to the area but she had been in New Hampshire for more than ten years and had been to the Sandwich Fair at least five times before, though she had never gone into the oxen barn or seen the oxen pull. Jessie, on the other hand, was at the fair for the first time, but as a 4 H member back home in Bridgton, Maine she knew a fair bit about livestock.

"These animals are monstrous! " Michelle gasped as they entered. "Are Oxen naturally bigger than cows?"

"No," replied Jessie. "Oxen tend to be males, because they're work animals and males tend to be larger. They're also usually castrated because that makes them gentler and easier to manage."

"Wonder if that would work with humans?" Michelle said with a wry smile.

"I suppose it would, but they would be less useful." Jessie responded.

Michelle, taken aback by the young girl's precocious remark, decided she would let that one go rather than exploring just what Jessie meant. "I'm not touching that one."

Jessie recited. " 'The cow is of the Bovine ilk . . . one end is moo, the other, milk.'" She laughed, "It's a two line poem by Ogden Nash. I learned it from my grandfather when I was just three and I've never forgotten it. Beside Shel Silverstein, I think he's my favorite."

"Oxen are big because they are allowed to live much longer than other members of the Bovine family which are raised for milk or meat and usually slaughtered before they get to be this big. If they were allowed to live longer they'd be nearly as big."

"What about the horns?" Michelle asked. "They all seem to have horns and the milk cows don't."

"Actually, almost all cows have horns, including dairy cows," said Jessie; "but horns can be a danger to both the cows and the farmer so dairy cows horns are removed when they are young. If you ever pet a dairy cow you can feel where the horns were removed right beside their ears at the top of their heads. The term they use for a cow whose horns are removed is 'polled', so for example you might see a program that says 'Polled Hereford'; that means it's a Hereford beef cow that has had its horns removed."

Jessie continued, quite enjoying the fact she was able to educate this adult on the finer points of the Bovine family. "Oxen though, need their horns for working. When they back up the horns keep their yoke from falling off. Sometimes they pull things by backing up if they can't be positioned to pull in the traditional way."

"Wow! There's a lot I didn't know about cows and oxen." Michelle said.

"Don't feel bad Michelle. Most people don't even know a cow has to have a calf in order to give milk. They just think you go out to the barn and milk every cow in it!"

"The largest Oxen on record," said Jessie, "were from Maine where I live. Their names were Granger and Katahdin, named for mountains in Maine, Together they weighed nearly ten thousand pounds!"

"Two and a half tons each?" Michelle said. "How does a little human-type-person control something so big?"

"How does an elephant trainer handle an elephant?" said Jessie. "Oxen, like elephants, are chosen for their disposition as much as their size. The funny thing is the people who I think are best at it, are the most gentle handlers."

"Really?"

"Yes."

"I was at the Fryeburg fair in Maine last year and watched this guy with a huge pair of oxen try to bully and whip his team into pulling this heavy load; Then up comes this little lady, not much bigger than me, with a team nearly as big as the bully. She petted and cooed and whispered and encouraged her team, calling them 'honey', and 'sweetie', and those two huge animals would have pulled for her till they dropped dead. She walked all over the tough guy's team."

"Afterward, I went to see her. She was feeding them sugar cubes and carrots. One of them actually had a thing for watermelon and she had some especially for him. I asked her about it. She told me that if people would treat animals the way we would want to be treated, the world would be a better place."

Michelle looked admiringly at the young girl.

"I was telling Grandpa about this on the way home that day and he said it was just like the Golden Rule. When Jesus said to 'do unto others as you would have them do unto you.' "

"You're Grandpa sounds like quite a guy." Michelle said.

As they talked they wandered down the aisle between the two rows of oxen toward the south end of the barn where the biggest ox in the barn stood crunching on a bale of hay. They reached the end and slowly made their way around the massive ox. The back doors of the big exhibit hall were open wide but only a truck with a horse trailer could be seen.

They stood looking up at him. "He's like a wall of animal." Jessie said. "Look I can't even see anyone else in the barn," she said pointing.

Then everything went black. Michelle felt Jessie's hand yanked from hers and she tried to fight back and cry out but the sack muffled the sound over her head.

"Throw them in the trailer and hide them under the hay." she heard a voice whisper to whoever was holding her hands securely behind her and binding them.

She tried to reach out but her arms were pinned by her side.

James Enright slapped a letter addressed to Jack Carrigain on a nail sticking out of the barn where tack was normally hung to clean and dry. Then he leapt into the truck towing the horse trailer and headed for the West gate.

Noting nothing suspicious about the truck pulling a horse trailer, a police officer waved them through the gate. Enright rolled his window down and said, "see you next year." and then they vanished in a cloud of dust.

Chapter 93   Spilled Milk

Jack was feeling much better when he, Sasha, Daniel and Herbert made their way to the milking contest.

"Jessie was saying that she is in 4H at home, Jack. Does she raise cows?" Linda asked.

"No, she and her folks live on a five acre tract that really doesn't have room for cows, so she has a sheep. She's always had this fondness for cows and oxen though. I don't think she was much older than four when she first asked my neighbor Hiram Ingram to show her how to milk a cow. He started by teaching her how to hook up a milking machine to a cow but she insisted she wanted to learn "the old fashioned way". Hiram was thrilled. He taught her how to move her fingers so she exerted pressure one finger at a time as she pulled on the cow's teat. Then he taught her how to squirt milk across the barn into the mouth of a waiting kitten. After that, I swear every kitten on the farm headed for the barn when Jessie showed up."

When they arrived at the ring where the competition would take place they looked around for Jessie and Michelle but could not see them anywhere.

"Maybe they got waylaid," Jack said. "I know that Jessie wanted to make a trip to the Oxen barn and she loves to go through the other livestock pavilions too."

Just then the announcer barked "last call to sign up for the Milking competition."

"I'm going to walk over and ask at the registration table if she signed up yet."

"I'll go with you Jack," said Linda.

"I'll join you," said Herbert and the three headed off to ask.

"I'm beginning to get a very bad feeling about this, " said Sasha.

"Let's not jump the gun Sasha." Daniel said, but he was beginning to get an uneasy feeling as well. "But what interest would they have in Jessie?"

Herbert hastened back to them alone. "She never showed up, Jack and Linda have gone over to the Livestock Pavilions, we're supposed to go and have them make a general announcement for Michelle and Jessie to come to the administration building."

Herbert looked concerned. "They know who she is," he said to Daniel and Sasha. "If they were willing to try and kidnap you Sasha, why wouldn't they try with her? Maybe Jessie was just in the wrong place at the wrong time."

Sasha pushed her own concern down and soothed Herbert. "Jack and Linda will probably find them at the Livestock Pavilions, Herbert. You know how kids are once they get in the presence of animals. I don't know Michelle well but I get the feeling she might be the same way."

Chapter 94 The Letter

Jack and Linda split up at the Livestock Pavilion with a plan to begin on the ends and meet in the middle in 5 minutes after they had gone through the pavilion in search of Michelle and Jessie.

Linda was first to arrive in the center row and Jack soon followed.

"No sign of them" said Jack, a look of concern furrowing his brow.

"I didn't see them either," said Linda. "We should try the Oxen barn. Jessie told me she wanted to see the oxen."

As the two hurried toward the oxen barn, the general announcement for Michelle and Jessie to report to the administration building blared out across the fairgrounds.

"I hope we don't miss them when they hear the announcement." Jack said.

At the door to the barn a docent was chatting amiably with a fairgoer. Linda politely waited a moment and then broke into the conversation.

"I'm so sorry to interrupt but we have a bit of an emergency. Did you see a woman and a young girl come through recently?"

"I'm afraid that describes about half the folks who've been through here today." The docent said.

"Wait! Jack said reaching for his wallet. I have a picture of Jessie in my wallet. Maybe this will help."

He showed the docent a photograph from Jessie's seventh grade photos.

The docent looked carefully. "You know, I did see them . . . Just a few minutes ago. This little one was giving the lady a real education as they walked through so she caught my attention." He paused, then added "funny though, I don't seem to remember them coming back out this way. They must have gone out the back, but that's a bit unusual since there's nothing back there but horse and cattle trailers from exhibitors."

Jack didn't wait for the docent to say another word as he dashed toward the back exit. Linda took the time to thank the docent and then hurried after Jack. She arrived at the back door just in time to see Jack removing an envelope from a nail sticking out of the wall. The envelope had nothing on it but the word 'Carrigain', scrawled in marker.

Jack, hands shaking visibly, opened the envelope. Linda held his arm and watched as he opened the single page.

"We have the kid and the woman.
Keep your mouth shut, go home and wait for our call.
NO COPS."

"Oh God, what have I done? If anything happens to that little girl I don't know what I'll do."

Linda put her arms around Jack. "We'll get her back Jack. We'll get her back."

Jack gave in to his horror and fear and the great, fearless icon of the North Country sobbed into Linda's shoulder. "I'm so sorry about your friend, but Jessie, she's just a little girl who didn't do anything. What am I going to tell her mother? Oh God, oh God, oh God."

Linda said, "Listen Jack, we've got to get back to your place and we should bring the others with us because they have Michelle too. If this is about Granite Skyway we're going to have to put all our cards on the table."

Chapter 95 Carrigain Farm

Jack Carrigain sat at the kitchen table in his house with his head in his hands. "Her parents are on their way over. It will take them a couple of hours to get here."

"Then while we wait for the call,Jack, we also have to bring everyone up to speed. The other members of The Trust, including Thomas were gathered around. As soon as he had heard about what happened Thomas had hustled down to Jack's home and was there with Metallak when the team and Jack Carrigain arrived."

Jack looked at Metallak and then at Thomas and said, "if anything were right in my world right now I'd be filled with wonder and surprise and a whole lot of questions, but right now I can't think of anything but little Jessie."

Linda called everyone around the table. "There's a few pieces to this puzzle I need to fill you all in on, so gather round folks. We need to come up with a plan once we get that phone call."

"Jack is the person who put together the Gazetteers. He and a group of his friends have been issuing essays opposed to Granite Skyway ever since the Androscoggin Stampede. I know you want to thank him for everything he has done to support your efforts, and I've already let him know that, but he's not going to be ready to hear those thanks, not with his little granddaughter's life hanging in the balance. And our concern about both Jessie and Michelle is our primary focus."

Just then Linda's smart phone sounded an alarm. She took it out and read it.

"The police are looking for Sasha and Daniel. They are calling them persons of interest in the bombing."

"Did we make a mistake coming out?" Sasha asked.

"No they already knew who you were," Linda said. They just hadn't turned your identity over to the police yet and Daniel was just a step ahead once they had you. These bastards have just turned up the heat."

"Sasha, maybe you should reconsider having Thomas get you back to Canada."

"I'm not going anywhere without Cochise, and my stuff is still at your yurt Daniel."

"Then let's go get him right now."

"Take my Land Rover," said Stonebridge. "The police are going to be looking for your Prius Daniel."

Sasha held up her hands. "Wait just a minute. I want to be clear that just because I go with Daniel to get Cochise doesn't mean I am going along with this plan to smuggle me back into Canada. I just don't want to leave Cochise alone and we may need him. I intend to stay here and clear my name . . . and Daniel's."

Daniel and Stonebridge swapped keys and he and Sasha headed for the door. "We'll stay in touch," he said as they left, "and keep us in the loop."

Chapter 96   A Song Softly Sung

Daniel and Sasha pulled off Interstate 93 with Cannon Mountain looming to his right and the towering cliffs of Eagle Crag and the Franconia Ridge to his left. The two were crossing the state to get to Daniel's yurt in the Baker River Valley.

"I know another way to go from here," he said. "It's a bit longer than just going straight down the Interstate, but there's something I've been wanting to show you."

He passed over Main Street in Franconia and onto Easton Road, a back road through a handful of small towns that would eventually land them in Rumney where they would pick up Cochise and then head back north.

It had gotten cold and was snowing lightly. The brilliant hues of fall were gone. Despite the fact that they were now in the White Mountains region and the boreal forest of the Great North Woods had subtly blended into the hardwood forests of the temperate zone, the road on both sides of this route seemed as if the Boreal zone had waged a war for ground here, holding the lowlands, tenaciously competing for position with the maples and oaks of the lower forests.

It was moose country. Spruce and fir dominated the landscape with occasional splashes of red from Mountain Holly and Mountain Cranberry dotting the bogs along the road.

"This was where Robert Frost walked." Daniel said.

"When I drive along this road I imagine him - the tapestry of a poem weaving around in his head - walking along this road alone; calling out to a neighbor splitting wood near the barn or hanging laundry on the line. They stop to greet him, share a few words and then return to their daily tasks."

"Let me show you something."

He took a sharp right and drove a hundred yards on a gravel road, then stopped. In front of them was an old rusty mailbox with the word FROST scrawled along its side in white paint, faded to ochre by the years.

Sasha jumped from the car and walked to the box, tentatively reaching out to touch its rough, rusty surface, running her hands along it, as if to conjure up the poet.

"If a box could talk . . ." she whispered.

In the background, up a dirt drive, stood the modest home where Frost had spent some of his summers, sometime between being fired as a professor at Plymouth State College and selected to read a poem at President Kennedy's inauguration.

Few words were shared between the two. They walked quietly up the drive and around the house to the barn. The modest museum, created here, was closed for the season but the quiet ambiance felt closer to his spirit than any tour could have provided them.

When they were back in the car headed west again, Sasha spoke.

"Thank you", she said thoughtfully. "It's easy to imagine why Frost was able to so beautifully reflect the spirit of the people and this place in his words . . . why he chose poetry as his vehicle . . . "

Daniel replied: "it's prose boiled down like sap, leaving only the essential elements."

Like a Frost poem, the road was winding, beautiful, well maintained.

They rounded a bend and before them lay a Tamarack bog, ablaze in gold.

Daniel stopped the car and they got out and sat on a boulder overlooking the scene.

The Tamarack gleamed, radiant yellow as they prepared to drop their needles in the final act of autumn's dance, highlighted by a light layer of snow dusting the brown grasses and the blues and greens of the spruce and fir and the brown and ochre blend of the cattails, stubbornly clinging to their summer form.

"It's a song sung softly after the audience has gone home." Daniel said quietly.

Tears spilling down her cheeks Sasha whispered "is our song almost over Daniel?"

Chapter 97 The Call

The telephone in Jack Carrigain's house blared out - - he had turned it up to be sure he did not miss the call.

"Hello?"

"Carrigain, we have your granddaughter here. We know you've been writing those damned essays against Granite Skyway. If you want to get her back, there will be an editorial written under your own byline supporting Granite Skyway in tomorrow's paper."

"Please, it's too late in the day to get into any of tomorrow's papers," Jack said, "I need another day. You have my word I'll do what you want if you release her now."

"Not a chance hotshot." came the reply.

"What about the other lady. Michelle?" Jack managed to ask.

"Don't you worry about her. We have other plans for her. We'll let her go when she implicates the rest of her group in the bombing. She's being difficult right now but I expect to turn her around soon enough."

"Be by the phone at noon tomorrow. I expect you to read me the editorial then." Then Enright abruptly terminated the call.

Chapter 98   The Yurt

Daniel drove the Land Rover up the Stinson Lake Road. "Get down," he said to Sasha, "just in case there's anyone looking for you." He pulled a ball cap over his own head and put on sunglasses.

He knew immediately something was wrong as soon as he drew near to the yurt's drive. Sure enough, State Police vehicles were parked in the drive. He drove on past, continuing another mile up the road to where he pulled off into the driveway of a friend who taught at the University and was on sabbatical. Daniel was pretty sure he was in England, but even if he showed up Sasha, would be able to explain the car.

Daniel got out, grabbed a strong piece of driftwood from beside the fast flowing waters of Stinson Brook to use as a walking stick and began to make his way down the brook. In twenty minutes he was within a few hundred yards of the yurt. He couldn't be sure whether the police had broken into it; but Linda had said no warrant had yet been issued for his yurt so he crept quietly toward the door.

He could see the officers gathered around their cars at the top of the drive. He entered the yurt and signaled with his hand for Cochise to lie down silently. He grabbed Sasha's backpack and then the two of them slipped quietly into the woods.

Thirty minutes later the passenger door of the Land Rover opened and Cochise jumped onto Sasha's lap.

"Ok, now we have to figure out how to get out of here without them spotting us." Daniel said.

"Can't we just keep driving here?" Sasha said pointing north.

"This is a three season road beyond the town line. The snow is going to make the road over Ellsworth Hill very slick," Daniel said "But with the Rover, we might be able to do it."

Then he heard the sound of sirens. "They must have figured out I was there," he said. "Looks like the decision has been made for us."

Daniel swung the Rover onto Stinson Lake Road headed for the town of Ellsworth. In 5 miles they arrived at the point where the pavement ended. They could still hear the sound of sirens behind them so the police had figured out what direction they were traveling.

"Hang on Sash, this could get a bit dicey."

Sasha called Cochise up front to sit on her lap. He was bigger than she was but he settled halfway onto her lap and the seat so she managed to get the seat belt around both of them, despite some yelping and grumbling from her friend.

As the road began to climb toward the height of land where the town of Ellsworth was located Daniel looked in his rearview mirror and saw the flash of blue lights behind them.

"Trouble" he said, just as the Rover slid sideways on a patch of ice. Daniel turned the steering wheel hard and gave the Rover gas - - managing to stop the slide and avoiding the ditch by a wolf's hair.

"The good news is if the Rover is having this kind of trouble here those cruisers are in for a world of hurt," Daniel said. Sasha couldn't turn in her seat because of Cochise, but as she looked in the side view mirror she saw the first cruiser go into a slide and the second cruiser, too close behind to stop, plowed right into him driving both cars into the icy muck of the roadside ditch.

"I think we lost them," Sasha said as they approached the height of land and crested it, looking down at a steep descent to a rapid upturn and an equally rapid ascent.

"Oh shit, they'll be sending cruisers up from the other side for sure." Daniel said.

"OK, this is going to be risky but better than heading into a bees' nest of cops at the head of the Ellsworth Hill road. Hold on tight."

Daniel took a sharp left and swung between a tiny chapel, St John's of the Mountains, and an equally small Town Hall. A sign that read "Dead End" greeted them as they passed the buildings.

"I suppose you know this is a dead end Daniel." Sasha said as the Rover bumped over the uneven road.

"Last winter I took Zach and some friends on a cross country ski trip up here. We skied from here all the way down to Rte 3, almost all of it downhill. I think that trail will be wide enough for us to pass in the Rover. I'm counting on it anyway."

The dirt road into the residential part of Ellsworth, all five or six houses, took a sharp turn to the left where a bank of gravel had been placed along the curve to keep vehicles off the trail leading into the woods.

"OK Sasha, we're going to be air-bound for a second." He hit the bank and the Rover traveled up it and for a brief moment hung in the air as the gravel ran out, and they were headed down on the trail.

Daniel slowed the Rover down, "there's no way they could follow us here", he said, "the only issue is making it down to the highway before they figure out what we've done, so I've got to keep moving as fast as the terrain will allow."

Chapter 99   The List

Jack hung up the phone. "They are going to make me come out in favor of the Granite Skyway Project if I want her back."

"What about Michelle?" Herbert asked anxiously.

"They're going to force her to accept responsibility for the bombing and Implicate the entire Trust."

"We have to stop them," said Herbert.

Linda pulled the list out of her back pocket. "Maybe this list will help. Look it over, see if you know anyone on the list, or if any of the names are familiar."

The list was short and spare - A name, a number and a few clipped notes - to remind Conrad Fleming of some important detail.

Everyone knew the name 'James Enright' already, but no one knew any more about him than they did before, which was nothing. He was a ghost.

The second name on the list was Kyla MacIntire, beside her name it said Lobbyist, VT.

The last three names were Will Duggan, Susan Wilson and Lawrence Echo.

The entire team surveyed the list. They were all drawing blanks. Then Herbert let out a whoop!

He pointed at the list. Kyla MacIntire . . . Mac! It had to be her. He reached into his back pocket and retrieved his wallet. "I think I put her card in here," he said. Pulling it out a moment later he held it up next to the list. The card said Kyla "Mac" MacIntire.

"Sonofabitch! She was dogging us all along. This is the woman who took Michelle and I to see Rifkin speak over in Vermont."

"So do I call her?"

"Let's think it through a bit," Hank suggested. "We need to move fast but we need to move carefully."

Jack listened as the group brainstormed a strategy for rescuing their friends. "You have to leave now. My daughter and her husband will be here soon. I think it's better if I face them alone."

"We can go up to my longhouse," said Thomas.

"No Thomas you don't have Wifi there," said Hank. "We may need to use the Web."

"Then let's go to my cabin." said Herbert. "I have Wifi and it's closer to where Michelle met Mac."

"Wait." said Linda. "At this point they know where every single one of you lives, the police anyway. We need to come up with somewhere else."

Jack said, "I have a cabin over on Burns Lake in Whitefield. There's WiFi there and no one is going to be looking for you over there." He reached into his pocket and pulled out his keyring, removing a key he handed it to Linda. "The alarm code is "Jessie". Once you enter the cabin it's on the wall to the left. You have 30 seconds to key it in."

Saying muted goodbyes to Jack the group headed out the door. On the porch Linda said to them. "I really think I should stay here and support Jack. I can be available by phone at any point if you need my input, even if you want to conference me into group discussions. I have my tablet as well in the car; I'll get it so we can use Facetime or Skype if necessary. Hank, do you have your iPad?"

"Never without it." Hank said.

"Thomas, do you want to put Metallak in the barn here while you go over to Burns Lake?"

Thomas nodded and led Metallak toward the barn.

"I think you need to go on the presumption the Police have make, model and license numbers on all your vehicles." Linda said. "Take back roads where ever you can, GPS should be able to help you."

"Hell there's not much but back roads from here." Hank said. "I'll take the lead folks, follow me."

Linda turned and went back into the house and the group piled into the two remaining vehicles.

Jack looked up from where he was putting wood into the wood stove. "I couldn't leave you to face them alone Jack."

"Thank you, Thank you so much Linda." Jack said quietly. He reached for Linda and she went to him. They held one another in silence for a long moment. Then Linda said, "why don't I make us some coffee and we can sit here by the stove and wait for them."

Chapter 100 Burns Lake

Hank Algren was first through the door at Jack's cabin on Burn's Lake. He keyed in the alarm code and headed straight to the woodstove and stooped to make a fire. "Shouldn't take long to warm things up in here," he said.

"I'll look around and see if I can find some more wood outside," said Zach.

"And I'll put a pot on the stove for the tea drinkers and make some coffee for the rest of us." said Herbert.

In less than fifteen minutes the group was gathered around the dining table in Jack's great room. Hank had set up his iPad and logged into the WiFi, which was not password protected.

"I've done a search on all these names," Hank said when everyone was seated with their steaming mugs. "There's not much information, except on Echo who has a fairly lengthy record including a series of offenses he committed after the good people of Thornton made the mistake of electing him to represent them in the legislature."

"Is he still a Rep?" Stonebridge asked.

"No, they shamed him into resigning. There's no way to constitutionally remove someone in New Hampshire."

"Does anyone have a better idea other than calling Mac directly?" Herbert asked. "We only spent the one evening together, but I didn't get the impression she was the kidnapping type." he said.

"I don't see any other option," said Stonebridge. "Anyone else?"

No one replied.

"Ok, here goes." said Herbert. He pressed send and Mac's cell number flashed on the screen as Herbert tapped the speaker button.

"Hi, you've almost reached Mac; You know what to do."

Herbert waited for the beep, "Mac this is Herbert, I was Michelle's plus one at the Rifkin event. She was kidnapped today at the Sandwich Fair, along with a young girl named Jessie. I'm guessing you didn't know this . . . well, I'm hoping. We need to find them Mac. Your friends are not good people. Call me, as soon as you get this. Call me NOW!" He left a number before hitting "end" on the phone.

Herbert sat back and ran his fingers through his short-cropped hair . . . "what the hell do we do now?"

He had barely spoken when an alert beep sounded from his phone. "Text" he said as he pulled the phone up and tapped the text icon and read.

"WAIT!" was all the text said.

The members of The Trust sat staring at the iPhone. After 5 minutes, the alert sounded again.

This time the message said, "Ruggles Mine".

Hank was on the hunt before Herbert put the phone down, his fingers flying on the keypad.

Then the phone chimed again. "Be Careful!" was the message.

Chapter 101 The Ski Trail

Daniel navigated his way down the trail that seemed to be part trail and part logging road. If they had been on a leisurely trip there would have been a lot of very scenic views to take in, but they had no choice, they had to keep moving.

After only a few more minutes the trail opened into a clearing that was obviously a landing area for a logging operation. Hundreds of trees had been cut and were stacked and awaiting transport to a mill.

"Should be smooth sailing from here", Daniel said. "As long as they haven't figured out where we are yet."

Then the junction to Rte 3 was in their sights. Daniel hit the pavement, turned left and headed north.

"Give Zach a call" Daniel said to Sasha. "Let him know we are on our way and we may be coming in hot!"

"What the hell does that mean?" Sasha said.

"No idea" replied Daniel, "I've just heard it in action movies so I thought I'd say it."

Sasha got Zach on the line and he said "Hold on, we're pretty sure we've located the kidnappers and they are down your way. We'll be out the door in a few minutes but we'll need an operational base when we get there. We suspect our homes are compromised.

"You can say that again Cuz," Daniel yelled from the driver's seat. "We already had a wild ride down from Ellsworth on that ski trail I took you on last winter, in order to avoid a dozen cruisers chasing us."

Daniel thought for a moment. "We aren't far from Dede and Mark Lugar's place up in the Mill Valley part of Thornton. Let me see if we can rendezvous there until we start the rescue. I assume that's what we have in mind."

"Right as rain Cuz"

As Daniel drove Sasha hit the speaker button and called Dede, who enthusiastically agreed to host the group.

"Oh my goodness, how exciting!" She said, "I've been following The Trust on Facebook and Twitter. It will be so much fun to join the fight to stop those damned towers! I have to protect all my babies you know."

Dede didn't have babies per se but her home had the feel of a modern day Eden with bird houses, hummingbird feeders, and a butterfly garden of sweet flowers providing nectar for winged creatures of every type, all of which somehow made it an attraction for deer and bear, chipmunks, foxes and turkeys as well. The deer herd that wintered in the conifers of the mountain behind her house made two trips, like clockwork, through her yard daily on their way to water. She had names for all of them, except the turkeys, and she watched over them from year to year giving Daniel and his parents regular reports on pregnant mamas, new babies and changes in the pecking order within the herd.

Daniel hit the brakes and veered right onto a bridge crossing the Pemigewasset and taking them over to NH Rte 175. He was ten minutes from Mark and Dede's and he could really use a hot shower. He needed to get out of his sweaty clothes . . . and if he had to admit it, probably needed to change his underwear after that ride.

"With entertainment like this," Sasha said sarcastically, "you couldn't drag me away from the fun, so you can forget trying to convince me to go back to Canada."

Daniel smiled broadly. "Music to my ears my Iroquois lady."

Chapter 102   Mill Valley

At the cabin on Burns Lake, Hank was doing some rapid research on Ruggles Mine in Grafton, just outside the towns of Canaan and Danbury. "Ruggles mine is the largest open pit mine in the state," Hank read. "Closed in 1960 as a mine and opened as a tourist attraction in 1963. The mine is currently closed as the owners seek a buyer for the property."

He continued to read silently, speaking aloud when he found something of value. Then he emitted a long and low whistle, "no wonder they're selling the place, they were charging $25.00 for adults to come in and walk around a used up old mine. I know I'm as tight as bark on a tree, but with prices like that, word must have gotten around pretty fast this was one tourist trap folks should avoid."

"It appears there's only one entrance so you have to drive three miles along an access road to get to the place."

"Sounds like an ideal spot for them to take Michelle and Jessie. Off the grid and well protected." said Herbert.

"How in the hell are we going to rescue Michelle and Jessie from a place so well protected?"

Thomas spoke up. "I think I could do some reconnaissance if we could get Metallak down there with us."

I noticed a horse trailer at Jack's farm," Herbert said. "I have a hitch on the back of my truck, we could trailer him down to Grafton. Let me call Linda and see if it's ok."

Linda answered her cell on the second ring. "It's pretty tense around here, I don't think it would help if all of you showed up. Let me see if I can figure a way to get them out of the house for an hour or so. I'll call you back as soon as I can."

In thirty minutes she called back. "Jack and I are going to take his daughter and son-in-law out for dinner since there's no food in the house. We'll be leaving here in about forty minutes and I figure you'll have no more than an hour to get in here and get out without them seeing you. The trailer is registered so it should serve as a way to make it difficult for someone to read your truck's plates from the back anyway."

"Herbert." Linda said.

"Yes?"

"I suspect you're only going to have one shot at this and the cops are looking for all of you. Make it count."

"Copy that" Herbert said.

The team managed to pick up Metallak and evacuate before Linda and Jack returned with Jessie's parents. This, despite the fact they had to make some adjustments to the internal setup of the horse trailer to accommodate Metallak's girth and antlers.

"I think I better ride in the trailer with him," Thomas said. "It's a pretty tight fit and I don't want my pal to freak out on us."

Herbert went back into the barn and returned hauling three bales of hay. "This should help keep you both comfortable and give ol' Metallak something to munch on," he said.

Part 8   Coming in Hot

Chapter 103   Rendezvous Point

"Look Conrad, you hired us so you wouldn't get your hands dirty." JEn was on a heated call with his boss and things were not going well. "The Trust is on the run with cops all over the state looking for them. They're prime suspects in the bombing up in Pittsburg and Jack Carrigain is about to come out for the Granite Skyway in an Op-Ed we'll be sure gets into every daily and weekly paper in New Hampshire, Maine and Vermont. You should be on your knees thanking me, not screaming at me over the phone."

Enright held the phone away from his ear, at arm's length and Duggan, Wilson and Echo could hear Conrad's rant from their positions at the entryway of the mine. Enright hit the end button. They were in for a penny in for a pound at this point. He'd have to deal with Conrad later.

An alarm sounded and Echo went over to the laptop to check on the motion cams they had hastily set up the day before to warn them if someone was approaching. Echo looked at the various screen captures. "Just a moose wandering through" he said.

At a pull off along the road into the mine, the group had discovered an old barn hidden in the trees. They chose this as their rendezvous point and pulled their vehicles and the horse trailer into it to prevent giving themselves away just in case anyone drove in after them.

Thomas helped Metallak out of the trailer and saddled him quickly. The two then headed out, bound for the mine rim.

At the time Echo had seen the moose, Thomas had spotted the cam from the LED light underneath it beaming through the darkening forest. He had pulled the deerskin over himself as he hugged Metallak's neck.

He didn't have a lot of time before darkness descended so as soon as he was past the camera, he urged the moose to a faster trot. He'd deal with the cam later.

They arrived at the rim of the mine with just enough light for him to see and Thomas crawled to the edge. Peering down with his binoculars, he saw activity in the office and store area where the entrance was. It looked like two people. If Mac was elsewhere because she was left out of the kidnapping, there should be four of them. He scanned the rest of the open pit and in a moment he saw Echo and Susan Wilson emerging from a cavern at the far end of the pit. Both were carrying trays with empty dishes which they balanced carefully as they walked over the uneven ground. Thomas raised the glasses and noticed there was a canvas tarp over the entrance to the cavern. This was either to provide some cover from the cold or to deny them light.

He continued to watch the cavern. He needed to know if someone was stationed there or if these people were so cocky they were just leaving their hostages by themselves. After fifteen minutes he felt confident there was no one else guarding Michelle and Jessie.

Wait, he thought, he had not looked to see if there was another cavern similarly covered. *Maybe the two were separated*. He double-checked. *No sign*. He crawled back and in a few moments he and Metallak were making their way through the woods back toward the rendezvous point with the team.

He paused at the webcam and reaching from behind the cam he flipped the switch - turning it off. This would either draw someone out to repair the cam or allow team two to slip unnoticed through the ring of Webcams he assumed they had set up around the mine.

Thomas sat beside a tree out of sight of the cam and waited to see if someone came to repair the cam. An hour later he mounted Metallak and slipped back to the rendezvous point.

"Michelle and Jessie are being held in a cavern on the far end of the mine. I think the two I saw coming back from bringing them food were Susan Wilson and Echo. They weren't armed but I can't be sure the other two aren't armed or if they hadn't just left their weapons in the office when they took them their food."

"I disabled one webcam which probably means they have a series of them, disabling the one should allow us to slip the second team past the monitors along the rim. "

"Shit!" Herbert said, "there's a lot of questions unanswered here. We have no idea if they're armed. Are these people crazy enough to kill people?"

"Does it matter?" said Hank, "We're not armed."

"Speak for yourself," said Thomas, pulling out a Buck knife.

"Remind me what they say about bringing a knife to a gunfight." said Daniel.

"A knife in the hands of a Ranger is as good as a gun in most hands," Thomas said.

"Remember what Michelle said about hurting anyone," Herbert said. "Defensive actions only."

Herbert looked around the group. "I have an idea. It may be crazy, but . . .."

"Crazy is about all we've got to go on Herbert. Let's hear it," said Hank

"Mac told us where to find these guys. She didn't have to but she did. I'm betting she's having second thoughts about all this and cares enough about Michelle she won't want anything to happen to her. Let me text her and ask her if they're likely to be armed. We may not like the answer, but at least we'll have one."

The members of The Trust stood silently. It was a risk but somehow each of them knew they needed the answer.

"Go for it." Sasha said and the others nodded in unison.

Herbert texted "Ready for rescue. Are they armed?"

The text response came back within moments: "Yes!"

As Mac was closing her phone it buzzed and the screen read "JEn". She paused for a moment and then hit the button that read, "send to messages".

Chapter 104 Assault on Ruggles Mine

At two am Thomas and Metallak led the group designated as "Team Two" through the moonlit woods and past the webcam he had disabled. "Stay close to Metallak," he said, " he can see better in the dark than we can, so he'll help get us to the rim without falling off it. If they see Cochise they'll just think he's a coyote. But just be aware, it's possible we may run into another one of those webcams that's working, if you're hugging Metallak there's a good chance you'll just blend in."

They arrived at the rim and one by one Thomas stationed Daniel, then Zach and finally Sasha at the points triangulated around the cavern where Michelle and Jessie were held. Then he headed back toward the rendezvous point but stopped when he came upon another webcam he spotted in the darkness. He disabled the cam and again waited on the back side of the tree where the cam was placed.

They ignored one bad webcam, he thought to himself, *maybe two will be the magic number.*

Fifteen minutes later he heard the sound of someone coming through the woods and saw the bobbing light of a flashlight. Will Duggan bent over the webcam and was just about to hit the reset button when he felt a cold steel blade against his throat and heard Thomas say, "I promised the group I wouldn't kill anyone tonight, but I didn't say anything about cutting them a bit. Maybe from ear to ear even, if I don't go too deep. Take your hands away from the cam and put them behind your back."

"How many more are there with you?"

"Three." Duggan replied.

"What do they have for weapons?"

"No weapons", Duggan lied.

Thomas cinched the zip tie he had placed on Duggan's wrists tight enough to turn his fingers purple.

"Ok, I'm going to ask you one more time. If you lie to me again I'm coming back for you later and we'll settle accounts then.

"One semi-auto rifle and one 357 Magnum." Duggan said.

Thomas retrieved Metallak who was tethered a few hundred feet away and walked back to Duggan.

"Sonofabitch, that moose . . . it was you?"

"Ahhh, you must be the brains of the bunch eh?"

Thomas removed Duggan's shoes and socks.

He sniffed the socks and screwed up his nose, "Jesus, when was the last time you changed these?"

"Probably about the same time you did," he said, giving Thomas a once over.

"Good point." said Thomas and he removed his own shoes and socks and stuffed both pairs of socks into Duggan's mouth. Placing Duggan's shoes on his own feet, he headed off with Metallak in tow.

An hour later at the office of the mine where the members of the Cabal were waiting out the hours before their noon call with Jack Carrigain, another alarm sounded on the laptop and Echo said," He's suppose to be fixing the webcam not setting off a new alarm." When he went over to check it he saw the alarm was for the cam just outside the door of the entrance. He looked at the cam screen and exclaimed, "it's that damned moose again. I'm gonna to get rid of it once an' for all." He grabbed the AR 70 and headed out the door. Once outside he aimed the rifle at Metallak and just as he was about to pull the trigger, Thomas knocked the barrel of the rifle into the air where it discharged harmlessly but shattered the quiet of the night. The roar echoed through the canyon of the mine and down the valley to town.

Enright came roaring out of the office.

"You idiot, you'll wake up the whole goddamn town!"

By the time Enright looked up at Thomas who had the rifle trained on him, Herbert hit him in the jaw with a left hook that dropped him in his tracks.

At the south end of the mine, Daniel, Zach and Sasha heard the rifle discharge. They were waiting for dawn but each decided simultaneously a rifle shot was a call to action. Headlamps flickered on and in the growing light of dawn they each began their descent down the mine walls, rappelling as quickly as they could, leaving Cochise at the rim.

Outside the office Herbert and Stonebridge were tying up Echo and Enright. Hank and Thomas steeled themselves for a final assault on the office.

Hank looked at Thomas who still had the rifle, but had put the safety on. "Just like old times eh?" He said.

"Yes indeedy, Kemo Sabee, allow me to go first."

The two former Rangers burst through the door into the office.

The room was empty. Susan Wilson was not there.

Chapter 105 The Cavern

Daniel was first to reach the ground followed by Sasha; they unclipped and headed for the cavern with the canvas cover. Zach was close on their heels. They entered the cavern and found Wilson with the muzzle of a pistol pointed at Michelle's head.

"Surprise." she said. "Put your hands on your heads and sit your asses down if you want your friend to keep her head."

All three friends complied.

"Now Michelle and Jessie and I are going to walk out of here and you three are going to stay put for 30 minutes or I'm going to give Michelle here a permanent *Permanent.*"

"Get up Jessie, let's go."

Wilson gave a yank on the canvas cover and pulled it down from the top of the cavern entrance, then she backed slowly out of the cavern with Michelle and Jessie following, their hands tied behind them.

She was three steps outside of the opening when Thomas came flying out of nowhere like a linebacker, hitting her hard and driving her away from Michelle and Jessie. The handgun's discharge was nearly deafening inside the cavern but Zach, Daniel and Sasha were already heading for Michelle and Jessie determined to be sure they were out of harm's way.

Hank was tying up Wilson when they heard the sound of sirens. Stonebridge and Herbert arrived breathlessly only moments later.

"Someone must have called the police when they heard the rifle go off." said Stonebridge. "We locked the front gate but it won't take them long to find the real estate agent that has the key and then they'll be in - or they'll just break the door down."

Suddenly overhead came a thrumming of rotors as a large helicopter came into view above them and began a descent toward the flat ground at the center of the mine pit.

"Damn," Hank said dejected. "Those cops must have had a chopper nearby. Looks like there's no good exit strategy for us."

The chopper settled and the door to the chopper opened and the pilot hopped out, lifted his hat to reveal a mop of bright red hair and bowing to the group said - "Did someone call for an Uber?"

Chet Wincowski smiled as Donna Barza and a grinning Linda Levy jumped out.

"Let's get out of here before the Welcome Wagon arrives," said Linda. "We can negotiate your surrender later - on our own terms."

As they walked to the Chopper, Herbert said to Donna Barza "guess you aren't going back to your old job huh?"

"It sucked anyway," said Barza as they climbed in. "Besides, I've already been offered a much better one."

"What's that?"

"She's going to be working for me," said Mac, turning around from the copilots seat. We're going to be managing Green State Power's "Greenway SmartGrid" proposal that we expect will replace Granite Skyway when all this becomes public."

"That is if you all forgive my trespasses and help me stay out of jail."

The members of The Trust piled into the chopper and it began to lift off. As it cleared the Rim, Chet slowed his ascent and Linda opened the cargo door as Sasha whistled once. Cochise flew through the air and into the cargo area in a single graceful bound and then they were off.

Sasha was grateful to be united with Cochise and she turned to say "What should we do about Metallak Thom . . ." Her voice trailed off as she looked at Thomas slumped over on his seat.

"Hank! She said urgently, "Thomas!"

Hank crab walked to his friend. He pulled aside Thomas' jacket to find his shirt soaked with blood. He felt for a pulse. Turning toward the others, he shook his head.

Then Hank Algren sat down on the floor at the feet of his fallen brother and sobbed uncontrollably and without shame.

Chapter 106 Choices

Choices
By James Kitchen

With the surrender of the group calling itself "The Trust" this week, a skirmish, albeit an important one, in the ongoing battle to determine our energy future has come to an end.

But the battle itself continues.

As the dust clears, however, we find ourselves with a new set of choices. Choices that will allow the people and the agencies involved to decide between two very different competing visions of our energy future.

With the resignation of Polaris Electric's CEO, Conrad Fleming, and the arrest of the members of its "Shadow Cabal", Granite Skyway has announced they, nevertheless, plan to continue to seek approval for the project.

However, the emergence of a competing proposal, Green State Energy's "Greenway SmartGrid", has changed the landscape of the debate. Their proposal embraces local renewable sources of energy as a critical component in a more decentralized approach; maintains the use of existing structures and rights of way without the need for new scars upon the land or mega-towers that mar the viewscape and threaten the tourist industry. Their proposal offers a clear alternative pathway forward.

An announcement from the head of Hydro-Quebec that a new approach to the creation of hydro facilities will be adopted, substantially reducing the environmental impact and the impact on First Nations peoples.

This has all boiled down to choices reflecting those we have presented in this series of articles.

Just what role "The Trust" played in this we will never know for certain, but we can say their efforts, along with those who called themselves "The Gazetteers", have moved the center of gravity on the debate and helped make the public more aware and more involved in the process.

Ironically, if Granite Skyway is approved, little will have changed in terms of the existing energy regime. Yet everything will have changed for the people of the State. A new transmission line, used for only the delivery of hydroelectric power from Quebec will be constructed and the economic and environmental impacts predicted and unpredicted alike, will harden into place.

If the Greenway SmartGrid is approved, great changes will occur in the energy regime but the lives of the people will continue much as they are today, with the notable exception of the improved job opportunities and stronger economy inherent in this new energy regime.

Even without considering the serious crimes committed on behalf of Granite Skyway recently, we think the choice is clear.

That is why both the Business Digest and the NH Guardian newspapers have joined together, in this our final article of the series, to give our endorsement to the Greenway SmartGrid proposal.

Chapter 107   The Deer Farm

Linda Levy climbed out of her car and walked into the office of the Algren Deer Farm, as Max lounged in the back window of her mustang. Nearly seven months had passed since the events of the evening at Ruggles Mine. She was here to make sure Hank was not going to miss the final phase of Osita Aniemeka's performance art "Hope in a Washline".

Lucy was at the desk preparing a shipment of deer antler for China.

"Hank around?" Linda said.

"He's out in the pasture. You can go ahead out Linda, just be sure to secure the gate behind you."

Linda walked out into the pasture.

Hank stood, head down, speaking softly to Metallak as he scratched the old Moose behind the ears and the stumpy new set of antlers just coming in. Metallak grunted and cooed his appreciation, especially when Hank moved his hands up to scratch the area around the emerging antlers.

Without lifting his head he said," They itch something awful when they're first coming in."

"He seems content," said Linda. "Thomas would be happy to know that."

"He has days. . ." said Hank wistfully. "Then there are the moments when you just see in his eyes he's thinking about cruising the forest with Thomas. Especially when those damn dogs get to baying".

"You ready?" Linda asked.

"Yeah. I was up at the longhouse a few days ago. I picked up a few things. Lucy has chosen some really great old clothes representative of our own story, along with a set of antlers. That's five thousand that I won't see, but what the hell. "

The two walked slowly toward Linda's car.

"Granite Skyway is no more, Hank. As of yesterday all charges against all of you have been dropped. I'm going to pursue the copyright on Osita's art just to be sure we have some control of this right-of-way if we can, and if needed. "

Hank just nodded his head.

Linda got into her car and Hank and Lucy followed in the farm's truck.

Chapter 108   Waiting So Long

Just up the road they pulled into a temporary parking area where Dr. Osita Aniemeka was joyfully directing traffic - hundreds of people carrying brightly colored clothing, some adorned with the names of loved ones, some with carefully waterproofed packages bearing a more lengthy story they yearned to tell.

John and Kathy Rocker carried the scrubs that saved a mama llama.

Sandra and Peter along with Robbin and Tim, carried a colorful flag that simply had the word "Asquamchumaukee" emblazoned upon it.

Linda spotted Jack and Jessie and they came over. Jack embraced her warmly and kissed her. "Well here we are," he said. "A bittersweet moment, filled with new hope."

A white wolf, his ears flat against his head came whining and yipping excitedly, not sure who he should greet first, but excited to be reunited with all his old friends. Right behind Cochise, Sasha, Daniel and Zach approached with Stonebridge looming over all four of them.

Michelle and Herbert walked up with Mac.

As if to affirm their journey together, The members of The Trust joined hands and walked to their designated spot on the curving, massive wash line, joining with hundreds of others each eager to share their own song.

At the designated moment, each member placed his or her contribution on the line as the colorful ribbon took shape.

Then they paused for a moment at the sound of a chopper, piloted by a man with an unmistakable mop of red hair, Chet Wincowski and a smiling Donna Barza in the copilot seat looked down on the crowd.

Looking up to a height of land that descended to a spot where the washline curved beside the river, the members of The Trust watched as the chopper lowered a bronze figure of a man, his arms outstretched in celebration, one arm in the air, the other resting on the neck of a massive moose. The sculpture was a last minute addition, a gift of Mac and renowned New Hampshire sculptor Emile Birch.

Hank watched as the sculpture was secured at the height of land. Then he turned, took Lucy's hand and walked away.

Those close enough to where he walked heard him . . . he was singing, sort of . . .it sounded like he was singing "Sunshine of Your Love."

He paused and turned one last time toward the rise. Striking a rocker's pose, left hand on an imaginary guitar neck, his right hand high in the air, he struck his air guitar one last time.

Then he turned and headed for home.

Afterword

No literary work exists in a vacuum. Every author draws upon his or her experiences, friendships, recollections; and, of course, imagination, to create the characters and scenes within the work. In the case of this book I have drawn on stories told to me by old friends like the late Senator Ed Bennett who told me the story of the fictional politician "Frost Heaves" who he made up from whole cloth and conned a journalist into believing.

The courtroom scene with Linda Levy actually took place but the characters involved were different.

The hair raising story of the "Wrong Way Senators" was told to me by one of the participants, though I would not dare to guess how much it was embellished, nor will I divulge the name of the storyteller.

New Hampshire's Secretary of State is indeed William Gardner, the longest serving Secretary of State in our history and one of the smartest politicians I've ever known, though the story of his news conference in this book is completely fictional.

The photographer Clyde "Micky" Smith Jr., who passed away in 2008, was, indeed, one of the finest wildlife photographers of his era and the story of his near encounter with a black bear, as a child, was told to me by his father Clyde Sr. the actual fire warden in the tower atop Mt Cardigan for many years. I have taken some lovingly crafted liberties with his back-story - particularly as it related to his life in Vermont and his relationship to the main characters of the book but otherwise he was the real deal. Yes, he really did hike down the mountain to school every day and back up after.

The Republic of Indian Stream existed for a brief moment in time, as did Metallak - the Lone Indian of the Magalloway and Moll Ockett, though to the best of my knowledge they never begat any progeny. Metallak was said to ride a moose, though no documentary evidence exists of this.

Camp Mowglis 'The School of the Open" does exist and manages, despite all the odds, to provide young boys 6-16 with a summer that is 'unplugged" and awesome. Alcott Farrar Elwell was Director there for many years and to the best of my knowledge the stories about him in this novel are accurate, as are the stories of

Wah-Pah-Nah-Yah, whom I had the good fortune to meet in 1976 when he returned to visit the boys and to make some needed repairs to his amazing murals.

I grew up listening to stories of "The Colonel" and Wah-Pah-Nah-Yah told around the campfire by Mowglis' Director William Baird Hart Sr.. Of all the touchstones in my own life, Mowglis had the greatest impact on me.

The new Director Nick Robbins has renewed the spirit and rigor of the program and the camp now has a waiting list. I suspect the day will come when a new father will call his parents first to inform them of the birth of a son and the second call he'll make will be to Mowglis to secure a spot on the waiting list.

There is no Firearms Owners of NH or Alphonse Ruger though other similar organizations and people exist.

The historical information about both Jimmy Carter and John Durkin are true. Sadly, John never really got the credit he deserved for this landmark legislation.

Believe it or not, the core story of the Mama Llama's surgery is true as told to me by a dear friend and later affirmed by the surgeon and his assistant.

Ruggles Mine exists and, as of this writing, is closed and for sale.

ABOUT THE AUTHOR

Writer, artist, businessman, outdoorsman, activist and recovering politician; Wayne King put himself through college as a guide in the White Mountains. In 1983 he was elected to the NH House of Representatives and served for three terms before being elected to the State Senate, the youngest State Senator in NH history, where he served for another three terms. In 1994 he was the Democratic nominee for Governor. He is also the founder of The Electronic Community a group of social entrepreneurs working on social and development issues in West Africa on behalf of the Ford Foundation, The World Bank and other philanthropic sponsors. He has also been Publisher of Heart of NH Magazine, and, most recently, CEO and President of MOP Environmental Solutions, Inc.

Prior to writing "Sacred Trust", King published four other books: *Washday* (2009) – a photographic homage to the washline; "*Asquamchumaukee - Place of Mountain Waters (2015)*, a Photographic Ramble Through the Baker River Valley of New Hampshire; *A Spot on the Porch (2017)*, a celebration of his hometown on the 250th anniversary of its founding; and, "Creating *Electronic Communities* (1998), A Guide to Accessing and Utilizing the Internet" Authors: Wayne D. King, Chidi Nwachukwu and Philip "Kip" Bates III.

He lives in Rumney, New Hampshire with his wife Alice and from time to time their son Zachary.

Made in the USA
San Bernardino, CA
13 August 2019